Copyright © 2023 Brian Jay Nelson

Digital Book ISBN: 978-1-64873-390-1
Paperback ISBN: ISBN: 978-1-64873-389-5

Printed in the United States of America

Published by:
Writer's Publishing House
Prescott, Az 86301

Cover and Interior Design by Creative Artistic Excellence Marketing
Project Management and Book Launch by Creative Artistic Excellence Marketing
creativeartisticexcellence.com

Acknowledgments

Dedicated to Our Military Veterans who Patriotically served, and especially those who lost their lives and became disabled through their efforts to preserve our precious freedoms…

Branchview – The Fall of the Secret Society

By Brian Jay Nelson

For our struggle is not against flesh and blood,
but against the rulers, against the authorities,
against the powers of this dark world, and against
the spiritual forces of evil in the heavenly realms.

Therefore, put on the full armor of God, so that
when the day of evil comes, you may be able to
stand your ground. Ephesians 6:12-13

Contents

Chapter One:
The Homecoming

As the morning sun graced its' presence on the Connecticut coastline, the dew glistened on the beautiful cherry blossom trees in the Branchview Gardens. The sweet fragrance of the blooms wafted through the open French doors of the verandah, and the windows of the kitchen, where the housekeeping staff busied themselves preparing breakfast for the household. Spring had finally arrived after a cold, dark winter in which the country had been immobilized by a worldwide pandemic, and survived the first wave of a civil war. Steven, Loraine, and the others who had been held in check at their Florida residence, were finally able to travel, and had returned to the Great House for the summer season. Unbeknownst to the sleeping household, they had all checked in late the previous night, and were about to make a surprise appearance.

Mrs. Porter breezed into the kitchen as though she had never been gone, and Andrea Freeman tagged along behind, trying to keep up.

"Good morning, everyone." She announced.

Sharie and Mary Wallace led the procession of joyous fellow workers who rushed to greet the women.

"Goodness!" Sharie exclaimed as she hugged each woman. "When on earth did you two get back."

"2:35 this morning." Mrs. Porter sighed. "Steven insisted on driving through the night."

"Now, Mrs. Porter!" Andrea grinned. "You were just as anxious as the rest of us to get here."

She waved off the comment with a chuckle. "I have a feeling my back will never be the same after that trip." She grimaced as she lightly stretched.

"You two ladies should take the day, and rest." Mary suggested.

"Mary's right!" Sharie added. "We have everything covered today."

"Heavens no!" Mrs. Porter complained. "I have to get Steven's coffee ready, and brew a pot of tea for Loraine." She nervously twittered about. "I hope you stocked up on Chock Full O' Nuts. Mr. Spencer won't settle for anything less."

"I got it covered, honey!" Mary chuckled. "I bought four large containers from the Stop N' Shop yesterday"

"I better get right on it then. They should be coming over from the South Wing any time now."

"It's good to have you all back with us." Sharie cheerfully stated, as her and Mary turned their attention to Andrea.

"Where's your handsome husband, and that beautiful baby?" Mary inquired with hands on her hips.

"They'll come over from the house a little later." Andrea replied. "They're having breakfast with Tina and Philip."

"Oh! I bet that little man's getting big."

"You wouldn't know him." She smiled. "He's already talking, and chatting up a storm."

Sharie took an apron from the pantry, and tossed it to Andrea. "You may as well put that on, and jump in, baby. We have hungry people to feed."

In the Dining Room, Gerard sipped on his glass of orange juice as he read the Wall Street Journal. He glanced up just as Steven and Loraine strolled into the room.

"Surprise! Surprise!" Loraine cheerfully chanted.

With a smile on his face, Gerard stood to greet them both. He shared a hearty, brotherly hug with Steven, and an amicable embrace, and peck on the cheek with Loraine. "It's good to see you two live, instead of on a zoom call."

"Indeed!" Steven replied with an agreeing nod, as he glanced around the room. "It seems like an eternity since we last sat at this table together."

"Speaking of that…" Gerard motioned for them to sit down. "I hadn't expected all of you until later today."

"Steven and Tony both decided to drive straight through."

"You all took quite a chance driving that late at night. There's still quite a few rebels patrolling the roadways."

"We figured that our combined super powers would suffice if we encountered any problems." Steven chuckled. "Besides, we had Millie with us. She's a one woman wrecking crew."

"I agree on that point." Gerard laughed. "Where is Millie?"

"She insisted on taking care of the twins while Steven and I had our breakfast. I'm sure she'll eventually make her way around to see everyone."

The swinging door to the kitchen flung open, and Sharie cheerfully sauntered in.

"I thought I heard familiar voices in here.

She wasted no time in greeting the couple with a warm embrace.

"Mrs. Porter is preparing your coffee and tea, and we'll start bringing out the food shortly."

"Surely, you'll join us." Loraine stated. "We've so much to talk about."

"You bet! I'll be back in shortly."

Once Sharie departed again, Gerard took on a more serious tone as he addressed Steven.

"I'd like to get together with you later this afternoon to get you caught up on the happenings around here." He sighed. "Ezekiel should be here by then, and we can meet with him and Philip."

"Everything is okay, I hope."

"Due to our seemingly endless conflict with the Secret Society, we've decided to take Branch Consolidated in a more radical direction."

He glanced across the table with raised eyebrow. "It's quite a gamble, but we all agree it could work quite well in the favor of the Patriots."

Steven answered with an assured wink. "I can't wait to hear about it."

"Since you gentleman will be busying yourselves this afternoon, I do believe I'll gather up the ladies to go antiquing." Loraine declared.

"Oh boy! There goes a big chunk of our budget right there." Steven jokingly quipped.

After breakfast, Steven wandered into the massive Grand Corridor. He walked across the ornate marble flooring to the Steinway Grand Piano in the center of the room. He took a seat on the bench, and hit a few notes to see if it was tuned properly. He proceeded to play an eloquent tune, flawlessly. Millie also entered, but he was too enraptured in the music to notice. She stood silently in the shadows, thoroughly enjoying the performance of a tune she was very familiar with. As Steven hit the last subtle note, she made her presence known with enthusiastic applause.

"You certainly know how to make the keys sing on that Steinway." She said as she paced toward him.

Steven smiled, and scooted over to make room for her to sit next to him.

"The intro to Firth of Fifth. Where in the world did you ever learn to play that?" Millie inquired.

"I heard it on one of the cassettes in my father's old music collection."

"It's quite a complex piece of music. Did you learn it by ear?"

"I had it down after the second listen." He winked, while Millie shook her head with amazement, and looked off with a reminiscent smile.

"I remember going to see Genesis at the Rainbow in London with my parents when I was just a young girl. We sat in the front row, and Peter Gabriel was dressed in some sort of ridiculous tulip outfit." She laughed. "He was quite a scary character back in those days."

"Wow! How did you ever score front row seats for that?"

"Oh! My parents were well connected with all the British acts back then. Jeff Beck, Rod Stewart, and Mick Jagger were all frequent visitors to our household."

Steven's jaw dropped with awe. "Millie, your stories never cease to amaze me." He chuckled as he shook his head. "You are definitely one of a kind."

She kiddingly elbowed him in the rib. "I most certainly am, and don't you ever forget it, Steven Spencer."

Steven shared a pleasant laugh, then paused in thought. "Any word on when they'll let you return to London?"

"Who knows?" She grunted. "The military had no problem flying me here, but now the bastards in government won't allow them to fly me back." She let out with another grunt of disgust. "Unlike here, they still have everything shut down due to the virus."

"That must be tough for Bill, being by himself in a strange country."

"He isolates, and keeps busy with his art." She paused. "I imagine we'll have to hold quite a liquidation sale before we can finally return to the States for good."

"MI6 hasn't kept in contact?"

"They've been unusually silent. I do believe there might be something brewing behind the scenes."

Steven gave a thoughtful nod. "I guess all we can do is wait and hope."

Loraine wasted no time in gathering together Tina, Sharie, and Sandy Benson for a short road trip to New Haven. The sharp dressed ladies strolled down the sidewalk in front of several varied shops, and boutiques in the city's historic district. They sadly took notice of the many businesses that had not survived the financial crisis spurned from the virus, and the civil war.

"It looks as if things are finally starting to spring back to life here." Sandy commented.

"I'm surprised at the number of shops that were able to stay in business." Tina added.

"Is this the first time any of you have been out and about since I was last here?" Loraine asked.

"Oh, mercy, yes!" Sharie exclaimed. "We've all been held prisoners in our own homes."

"The state of Connecticut was obviously a lot stricter with their regulations than Florida." Tina stated.

"We were rather lucky with that." Loraine replied.

An antique store with a rustic sign, and a clutter of items sitting outside caught Loraine's eye.

"For some reason, I'm feeling very drawn to that store." She announced with determined eyes. "Let's go check it out, ladies."

The four women entered, and an older woman with a bold expression peeked up from her romance novel to acknowledge them as they sauntered by the weathered front counter. The store had the stale smell of dust that most shops like it often had. While the rest of the women took interest with the estate jewelry in the display case, Loraine's eye caught a life size statue pushed off in a far corner that seemed forgotten among the mish mosh of furniture. She immediately hurried to check it out, and the older woman rose from her perch, and followed with an unsteady gait.

Loraine stood in awe at the intricate beauty of the nude carving.

"That's one of my finest pieces in the store." The old woman stated.

"That's quite obvious." She gasped. "It's absolutely gorgeous."

The other women had now noticed it as well, and wandered over for a look.

Tina surveyed it with wonder. "The artist definitely succeeded in creating the perfect woman."

"You'd certainly know all about that." Loraine slyly winked, and smiled in response.

"I've had quite a few looky lou's on that piece over the years. Especially horny old men. But there never has been any takers." The old woman further commented. "I think she's a bit pricy for most of my customers."

By this time, all the women had gathered, and were gazing with open mouths at the flawless statue. Loraine ran her hands across the surface of the smooth marble, and inspected it closely with admiration.

"What I'd do to have a body like that statue." Sharie quipped, while Sandy gave an agreeing nod.

"How did you ever come about obtaining this piece?" Loraine inquired further.

"I found her at an estate auction over in Cambridge a few years back. There was an accompanying male statue as well, that was just as anatomically correct." She sighed. "But unfortunately, someone outbid me for it."

"How sad." Tina remarked with a frown. "He was obviously her mate."

The old woman only answered with a stern, awkward expression toward the doe eyed Tina, as Loraine continued to look the piece over.

She looked up at the woman with desperately inquiring eyes "How much are you asking?"

She gave a hopeless sigh, and shook her head with unwavering doubt. "I'd have to get at least $3100 for that, honey."

"Oh dear!" She pondered. "Steven is going to kill me, but I must have it." She pondered further. "If I paid you cash today, would you take $2700 for it? I believe that's all I have left in my purse"

All the woman looked toward Loraine with wide eyed surprise, and the old woman gulped, and nearly swallowed her dentures, as she replied. "Sold! She's all yours, sweetie!"

Sharie turned to Sandy, rolling her eyes, and mumbled under her breath. "I do not want to be around when she tells Steven."

While Loraine closed the deal with the woman, Tina glanced back at the statue, and it seemed that for a moment its' eyes had lit up with life and excitement. She gasped, reacting with startled shock, and shook her head in disbelief. Sandy stood close by, and took notice of her strange reaction.

"What's wrong Tina? You look as though you've seen a spirit."

"I think that cocktail I had for lunch must've hit me a little harder than I expected."

Sandy responded with an inquisitive expression, as she quickly glanced at the statue, then back. "Did you see something?"

Tina moved in closer, and whispered discreetly. "I could swear that statue's eyes came to life. It even creeped me out."

"If I hadn't witnessed half the things I've seen since coming to Branchview, I'd have to say you were crazy." She chuckled. "We shouldn't mention it though." She paused. "Come on! Maybe we should just wait outside."

The old woman anxiously counted out the large stack of bills on the top of the counter. "I honestly thought that statue would be with me until the day I died."

"I promise she'll have a good home." Loraine smiled. "Just write me up a receipt, and I'll have someone pick her up first thing tomorrow morning."

"Yes ma'am!"

Chapter Two:
David Vs. Goliath

While Loraine and the ladies had their special day out and about, the four key members of the board for Branch Consolidated met in the company conference room. Philip and Ezekiel were already there when Steven and Gerard arrived. They were also surprised to see a few unexpected guests. Joining them at the conference table were Agent Guitierez, his partner Agent Devika Banerjee, Joey Arcovio, and last, but certainly not least, Millie, who leaned back in her chair with a sly grin.

"You're certainly full of surprises, Millie." Steven sighed, as he and Gerard took their seats. "Why didn't you tell me earlier today?"

"Oh Steven!" Millie chuckled. "You should know by now that I just can't resist the element of surprise."

He shared an expression of amusement with her, before moving on to the others. He first, looked toward Philip and Ezekiel. It was unusual to see them dressed in business suits, with their long hair tied back in pony tails. Steven's own hair had grown past the acceptable length of a businessman. It rested comfortably on his broad shoulders, but complimented him well. He still opted for the more casual look of an open collared shirt, and sport jacket.

"Gentlemen! It's good to be in the same room with you once again." He smiled.

"I've missed my coffee buddy." Philip quipped with a welcoming grin.

"It's good to see you as well, Steven." Ezekiel declared. "I regret that this particular visit will be rather short term. I had to leave Meryl in charge of our interests." He glanced around the table. "As most of you know, Greece is embroiled in their own struggles with the Turks. They're determined to seize the Aegean Islands, where we happen to reside."

"I'm sorry that's happening, Ezekiel. I know how much you and Meryl love it there." Steven replied with sympathy, as his eyes wandered to Agent Guitierez. "Agent G! It's good to see you as well." He veered a wary eye toward Banerjee. "Are you sure she can be trusted?"

"I assure you, Steven…" She squeezed the agent's hand under the table, and boldly interrupted.

"I am fully aligned with the Patriot cause, Mr. Spencer." She paused. "I despise the Secret Society, and what they are trying to do to this country, and the world." She emotionally sighed. "My parents immigrated here legally, and became citizens the hard way." She emotionally choked for a moment. "I served proudly in our military, and I am ready to help you defeat our evil enemy in any way that I can."

Guitierez flashed an assuring grin toward Steven, who gave an approving nod. "Very well! Welcome to the team, Agent Banerjee." His eyes danced between the two anxiously. "I assume you both turned off the GPS on your cell phones."

"Of course!" Guitierez exclaimed, as he glanced with assurance toward Banerjee. "There are very few within the agency that we can fully trust."

Steven finally turned his attention to Agent Joey Arcovio. "This is one that we can surely trust." Steven smiled. "We've been through a lot together already."

"I'm also ready to fight these bastards in any way I can, Mr. Spencer."

Everyone at the table showed amusement at the young girls' enthusiasm and vigor.

"I'll have to arrange a meeting with you and Mrs. Porter." He chuckled. "I'll never hear the end of it, if I don't."

"I look forward to seeing her, and the others as well." She anxiously replied. "You're all like the family I never had."

Philip intervened. "Since we've all exchanged pleasantries, I suggest we get on to business matters, and let Steven know the direction we all plan to move in." He gestured to Gerard. "That is, unless Mr. LeRoux here has something he'd like to say first.

Gerard shook his head, and gave a yielding wink for him to continue.

"As we all know too well, something needs to be done to bring down the Secret Society, and especially the Conglomerate International Bank."

"I can say first hand that the task is equivalent to David challenging Goliath." Millie commented with a sigh.

"I agree, Millie." Philip answered. "But if you recall, David emerged the winner in that confrontation." He grinned.

"What other drastic measures can we take?" Steven inquired. "We've already shed the international companies that were affiliated with the mission of the Secret Society. If we leave ourselves any more vulnerable, they'll begin to buy up our affiliates, and eventually destroy us."

"Steven's right." Guitierez remarked. "Between the Society and the bank, they control everything, and can break laws without any repercussions from the corrupt justice system."

Philip paced in front of the gathering with his hands clasped in front of him. "That's precisely why we need to totally separate ourselves from their entire system."

Everyone sat forward in their chair with a puzzled expression, while Philip exchanged a confident grin with his brother, and Gerard.

"We've decided to leave the stock exchange, go independent, and totally abandon the fiat system altogether."

"That sounds like pure insanity!" Banerjee exclaimed.

Philip raised a calming hand. "Let me explain things further." He paused. "The Conglomerate Bank is lending money to country's all over the world faster than they can print it." He motioned for Gerard to take the floor. "I'll let our business guru take it from here."

Gerard stood up, and took command of the conversation. "Everything Philip just mentioned will lead to inflation, which will devalue the dollar, and cause a worldwide recession." He paused. "That will open the door for their alliance to create a great reset that will affect the entire world. The United States, as well as the majority of the world will become a third world wasteland." Everyone gave an anxious sigh, as he continued. "There will only be the ruling class, and the peasants. Just as they've always wanted."

"I still don't see how we can stop this." Steven anxiously stated.

"We don't stop it." Gerard remarked with a grin, and motioned again for Philip to explain.

"As a few of you know, my brother and I, along with our trusted allies, hold access to a majority of the world's gold, silver, and precious metals." He glanced to every face before him. "These are stores that the majority of the world don't even know exist." He paused to stress his point. "Along with our allied companies, we'll start our own stock exchange with crypto currency as our base." He chuckled. "We'll bankrupt and destroy their fiat system of currency before they even realize what's taking place."

"If that were to be the case, I'd venture to say that anyone who was invested in this new system ahead of time would benefit the most" Millie theorized.

"And you'd be precisely right, Millie!" He replied with exuberance. "The balance of wealth will shift from them, and go to the people they have used their power to hold in check for centuries."

"But these people are not stupid, Philip." Steven remarked. "Won't they shift their wealth into the new system before theirs crashes?'

"That's where our allies in the justice system come in." He motioned to Guitierez, who promptly joined in the conversation.

"Our covert team of cyber experts, including Agent Arcovio here, have succeeded in hacking into our own system to confiscate covered up evidence. They also have the ability to hack into the networks of our known enemies to prevent them from transferring monies into the new system." He paused with a thought filled sigh. "While I'm on that subject, I'll have you all know that our allies at the NSA have also gathered sufficient evidence that proves this past election was a fraud." He paused with a smile. "President Chamberlain actually won by a landslide. We have all the incriminating info, and they have no idea we possess it."

Steven sat forward with astonishment. "If they ever start arresting these people, there won't be enough prison cells in the world to hold all of them."

"Then we'll just have to keep the miserable bastards in tents." Joey enthusiastically replied. Her comment brought a round of amused snickers from those in attendance.

Philip gestured toward Millie. "Ms. Sandstrom will also be a valuable part of our team." He nodded with a smile. "Since London is the home base of the Conglomerate Bank, and is also believed to be the place where Kenneth Laszlo is taking refuge since fleeing the U.S., she'll be working as a vital link between us and the trusted agents of MI6."

"…And, I'm as determined as anyone in this room to defeat these scoundrels, so I can finally retire, and get on with my life." Millie quipped.

"We'll win, Millie!" Philip gave her an assured wink. "We all must be patient, vigilant, and have faith."

All, including Agent Banerjee sat in a quiet moment of pondering thought.

"We know we can trust Ms. Sandstrom, but how do we know we can trust the other MI6 agents?" She asked.

"Trust me on this!" Philip answered with a confident grin. "My brother and I screened, and handpicked our worldwide team. We already know who all the good and bad players are. Some that are on our team may even surprise you."

Guitierez gave him a quick wink, and an all knowing nod of confidence. Steven, however, was still a bit skeptical.

"How do we know our affiliated companies will follow us when we leave the market?" He asked.

"We're working diligently to communicate our mission with them, Steven." Gerard replied. "In fact, we're screening several other worldwide companies who are hoping to join our consolidated network. We'll only accept those who share our vision."

"Any company that stays within the present fiat system will also die with that system." Ezekiel added.

"When the time presents itself, we'll publicly announce the split from the stock exchange." Philip further added.

Steven shook his head with amazement. "I must say that this all took me quite by surprise." He pondered for a moment before glancing around the table. "I'm all in."

"Let's do this then!" Joey exclaimed.

"Very well! In conclusion…" Philip paused with emphasis. "I needn't remind you that we are all entering the greatest battle of our lives. These people are powerful, and will not go down without a valiant fight." He emotionally looked to each person in attendance. "This battle will not be as much a physical fight, but rather a strategic mental conflict. We have to make all the right moves, but I have faith that good will triumph over evil." He glanced toward Millie with a smile. "Ms. Sandstrom made a statement earlier that got me thinking." He paused. "I think the official name of our mission should be operation David vs. Goliath."

His suggestion was met with shouts of approval, and a standing ovation by all in attendance.

Chapter Three:
Hope Springs Eternal

In the woods on the Branchview Estate, Spring was finally arriving again. The canopy of tree branches were still quite bare, but were showing signs of returning to their full summer foliage. There was still a damp chill in the air, but the fragrant smell of the new season was pleasant, and fostered new hope in all who took the time to take it in. In the deep underbrush, the creatures of the woods stirred in anticipation. Some just waking from a long seasons' slumber. In the center of the clearing, the two immortal sisters, Nebriana and Claudiana strolled toward a traditional reunion, and met with a warm embrace.

"It's been such a long, lonely winter." Claudiana stated. "I can't tell you how good it is to see you again, sister."

"I've missed you as well. Nebriana replied. "I certainly hope you can stay, and visit for a while, before you go back to the north land."

"I most certainly will." She smiled. "Of course, I'll have to protect my fair skin from the growing intensity of the sun."

"We'll spend the heat of the day sipping cold chamomile tea in my lair." Nebriana assured.

"And of course, Green Man and the Woods people would be very grumpy if I left without seeing them as well."

"You'd break the big guy's heart." Nebriana joked, and they both giggled. "Has anything earth shattering took place while I've been gone?"

Claudiana sighed. "Maybe we should go sit under that old oak and chat." She pointed in that direction, and they both strolled that way as she conversed. "Stargazer somehow returned through the portal last summer, just prior to Zeus and Charlotte permanently sealing it."

"Why didn't he immediately make us aware of this?"

The two women settled themselves comfortably at the base of the tree.

"You should know Stargazer." She grunted. "He's a free wheeling spirit that is totally unpredictable."

"Now I know why he's been on my mind lately. Is he still here?" Nebriana asked with excitement in her voice. "I'd love to see him."

Claudiana sighed once more. "I'm afraid he's permanently trapped here now." She paused. "Shortly after you left last fall, he returned from visiting Deer Island, and set up camp on the western side of the woods." She shrugged. "We've only spoken on a few occasions."

"I must alert Steven Spencer, and let him know he's there."

"Oh!" She rolled her eyes with a grin. "Has that handsome hunk of a man returned as well?"

"My senses picked up on his presence when I arrived." She nodded. "I'll have to telepathically summon him to the woods."

"I do wish I was graced with your abilities, Nebriana." She giggled. "If I were able to summon a man at will, my winters surely wouldn't be as lonely."

"Nor as cold either." Nebriana humorously replied.

Steven returned to Branchview from his meeting, and was joyfully greeted in the foyer by young Tricia Benson. He went to one knee as the little girl ran to embrace him.

"Uncle Steven!" She exclaimed. "I missed you so much."

"I missed you as well, Tricia." He announced. "I heard you took very good care of Midnight while I was gone."

She nodded. "I was here every day after school."

"Thank you so much." He winked. "I knew I chose the right person to do the job."

She answered him with a pleasing smile. "Speaking of school. How's everything going with that."

"Fine!" she answered with a distressful sigh.

"That's doesn't sound too convincing."

"Do we live in a racist country, uncle Steven?"

Steven signaled a definite no. "Racist do exist, unfortunately. But on a large scale, our country is not racist."

"I thought everyone got along just like we do with the LeRoux's."

"For the most part, they do." He sighed. "Who told you this country was racist?"

"My teacher at school." She replied. "She told me that the Branch's were racist because they used to have servants."

"Did she now?" Steven asked with rising anger.

Mary had entered the foyer without anyone noticing, and immediately inserted herself in the conversation.

"That's an outright lie!" She exclaimed. "Most of the Branch family took in freed slaves after the first civil war. They gave us all a home, employment, and treated us with decency." She trembled with frustration. "That teacher must be one of them far Left Liberals that want to separate us all, and spread hate."

Tricia looked at Mary in a very perplexed way. "What's a far Left Liberal, Ms. Mary?"

Steven and Mary exchanged a wide-eyed glance, and he cleared his throat before speaking.

"What else did this teacher tell you and the other students, Tricia?"

"She said that there's no difference between a boy and a girl, and that we can change our sex any time we want."

"Lord have mercy!" Mary exclaimed, distressfully placing her hand to her head.

Steven placed his hands lightly on the girl's shoulders, and looked her straight in the eyes.

"How old are you now, Tricia?"

"I just turned eight 3 months ago."

"How would you like to leave that public school, and receive your education right here at Branchview?"

"Really! I'd like that a lot."

He glanced back at Mary, while still addressing the girl as well. "I happen to know someone right here in the family that just graduated with a degree in education."

"You talking about our Deanna?" Mary inquired with a sly grin.

"None other." He smiled. "I understand she hasn't been able to get a job."

"She's been on that computer machine every day, trying to find something." Mary stated with her hands on her hips.

Little Tricia quietly followed the conversation between the two adults. Suddenly, Steven looked upward as if listening to something, and Mary took alert notice.

"Is everything alright, Mr. Spencer?"

Steven snapped back to his senses, and answered. "I think someone just summoned me, Mary."

"One of the ghosts?" Tricia asked, prompting both adults to struggle at keeping a straight face.

"Kind of like that, Tricia." He paused, quickly changing the subject. "Why don't you go finish your homework, and when your parents get home from work, I'll go over to the Carriage House, and talk to them."

"Okay, uncle Steven." She answered before hurrying away from the room.

Mary rested her hand on Steven's arm, and whispered. "Bless you, Steven."

Steven drew a deep sigh, as Mary swiftly went on her way. He turned to leave once again, just as Loraine and Sharie entered the house. Sharie greeted him with a quick wave, and continued up the stairs without a word, leaving Steven rather puzzled.

"Hello, darling!" Loraine cheerfully announced, before kissing him on the cheek.

"What's with Sharie? She seemed in a bit of a hurry to flee the room."

"Who knows?" She shrugged. "Perhaps she had personal business to tend to. We didn't bother stopping on the way back from New Haven."

"So, how was your day?"

"Absolutely wonderful!" She exclaimed. "It was so good to get out with the ladies again."

"Who all went?"

"Tina of course, and Sandy was lucky enough to get a day away from the salon."

Steven noticed that she only carried her purse, with no bags, and was rather perplexed.

"Don't tell me you didn't buy anything?"

"I'm afraid I did." She sighed, and winced her face. "They're delivering it here in the morning."

Steven looked upward with dread. "I thought we agreed not to make any large purchases until the economy stabilizes."

"I know." Loraine shook her head. "But I just couldn't resist, and I know that you're absolutely going to love it."

He rolled his eyes. "What is it, Lori?"

"I'm not going to tell you." She answered with a sly grin. "You'll just have to wait, and be surprised." She hurried to her next question before Steven could say another word. "Where are you off to now?"

"I was just summoned by Nebriana a short time ago, and I was going to meet up with her."

"Oh! Would you mind if I tagged along?"

"I think she specifically wanted to talk to me."

Loraine was visibly miffed by his response. "Very well then. You just go on ahead, and meet with your beautiful faire goddess." She swiftly exited to the South Wing without further word, leaving Steven quite flabbergasted.

A short time later, Steven donned a stylish spring jacket, and treaded briskly along the Branchview pathway. The late day sun filtered through the trees of the surrounding woods, but a persistent chilly wind off the Atlantic reminded him that summer had not yet arrived. He had missed these daily walks toward Lighthouse Point. They always gave him time to unwind, and fuel his creativity for his writing sessions. He reached the midway point of the pathway where a dirt walking path branched off into the deep woods. He could sense the eyes watching him, and paused to look around, but saw nothing. When he started to progress forward once again, there she stood in the middle of the pathway, along with another radiant beauty that Steven had never met.

"Well! You do enjoy the element of surprise. Don't you?" Steven announced with a sly grin.

"I savor it." Nebriana cleverly quipped, while her fair skinned sister lightly elbowed her. "This is my sister, Claudiana. As you can see by her appearance, she's better known as the Frost Queen."

"With a warm heart to match her beauty, I'm quite sure." He cordially nodded.

Claudiana breathlessly sighed. "He's even more charming in person."

"Cool your engines sister. Steven is a one woman man."

"Such a pity for me." She playfully frowned.

Steven chuckled with amusement, and quickly moved to get to the point.

"What type of issue made you summon me here, Nebriana?"

"I wanted to make you aware that someone else escaped into our world before Zeus sealed the portal."

Steven looked upward with a sigh. "I've only been back a day, and already the difficult incidents are beginning to present themselves." He paused. "Who is this person, and where are they?"

"It's Stargazer."

Steven reacted with startled surprise as Claudiana chimed in.

"He set up camp on the northwest side of the woods."

"He spent the winter out there?" He asked with disbelief. "It's a wonder he didn't freeze to death."

"He is quite a survivor, Steven." She continued. "Besides, I checked on him occasionally, and shared my stash of the forest nectar with him."

Steven reacted with an amused eye roll. "That would definitely work well at numbing someone from the cold." He paused to ponder. "Has Poseidon been made aware of this?"

"Not yet." Nebriana stated. "I only found out earlier today, when I returned."

Steven looked upward at the sky, and then checked his wrist watch.

"It's getting a bit late in the day to go that deep into the woods. I'll meet with Poseidon this evening, and we'll ride the horses out there sometime in the morning."

"What do you plan to do?" Nebriana asked. "There's no way he can return to his own time, or anywhere else for that matter."

"I'll think of something." He answered, before gesturing to both women. "It's good to see you again, Nebriana." He turned to Claudiana, who observed him with flirty eyes. "And it was a pleasure to meet you, Claudiana."

"It was definitely my pleasure to finally meet you." She replied with a seductive wink. "Perhaps you'd like a companion on your evening stroll."

"I'll have to take a rain check on that, Claudiana." He grinned. "I have to pay a visit to the Benson's. Little Tricia confronted me today about a problem she's having at school."

"She's such a cute little girl." She replied. "I often see them when they're walking the path."

"It's nice to know we have such lovely guardian angels watching over us."

Claudiana responded with an audible sigh, and google eyes.

On the northwest side of the property that bordered the main road, a black SUV pulled off to the berm, and two men emerged, dressed casually for hiking. The one man popped the back lid, and took out a pair of lock cutters. Alertly scanning their surroundings first, they then proceeded over to the cyclone fence that lined the property, and began cutting away an access. They bended back the cut portion, and carefully squeezed through.

"That was easy enough." The square jawed, broad built balding guy with a rough Boston accent stated.

The dark haired man, who was clearly the more intelligent of the two, set the cutters against the fence, and glanced around at the trees that surrounded them.

"The timber on this property is worth a fortune in itself." He arrogantly grinned. "We could sell it for top dollar to the Chinese."

"Imagine all the housing units they'll be able to place in here, once this land is cleared." The bald guy added with wide eyes.

"Let's walk in just a bit further. I don't want to be in here after sunset."

The sound of a guitar strumming caught both men's attention, and the dark haired man turned to the bald guy.

"Do you hear that, Leo?"

"I sure do, Mr. Irving. We're not alone out here."

Irving listened a bit more, and then pointed. "I think it's coming from that direction." He stated, motioning for him to follow.

The men ventured a bit deeper into the woods, and they heard whispers around them.

"What the hell was that?" Leo asked with alarm.

Irving halted, and glanced around anxiously, before motioning for Leo to continue on. A short distance further, they came across Stargazer's camp. It was a simple lean to shelter, built from plywood, with large tree branches for the frame. Stargazer was sitting near an open fire pit playing a visibly worn acoustic guitar. The smell of a stew wafted from the kettle that rested over the fire.

"Looks like we have a squatter here, Leo." Irving arrogantly stated, while continuing on toward the old Indian.

"Excuse me old man." He strolled confidently closer. "You'll have to vacate these premises. This is private property."

Stargazer paused his playing, and carefully set the guitar aside. "I'm a friend of Steven Spencer. Do you work for him?"

Irving glanced at Leo, and chuckled. "I'm afraid you're mistaken, Tonto. This property is now owned by Midland Enterprises."

Stargazer stood, and glanced around up toward the tree tops, which amused the two men. He then looked directly at them, and defiantly shook his head.

"You lie!" He charged. "The forest whispered that to me."

The response caused both men to laugh out loud, and Leo strolled over, and promptly grabbed the guitar, and smashed it to pieces. Irving then glanced at the old man.

"I'd take that as a warning, chief." Irving said with a confident chuckle. "We certainly wouldn't want to hurt an old Indian. That just wouldn't be politically correct."

Leo kicked the pot of stew over into the fire, and laughed. Stargazer calmly observed, before boldly turning to Irving.

"This is my home. I'm not going anywhere."

"Suit yourself." Irving answered, as he gestured to Leo.

Leo pulled out a pistol, but Stargazer was no longer there.

"Where in the hell did he go?"

Just then, a threatening growl erupted from behind then, and they turned quickly to see a wolf angrily stalking.

"Shoot the damn thing!" Irving ordered.

The wolf leaped through the air toward Leo, and he shot the gun wildly at the canine, who disappeared in midair.

On the other side of the deep woods, Nebriana and Claudiana heard the gunshot, and reacted with alarm, as they returned from their meeting with Steven.

"That came from the direction of Stargazer's camp." Claudiana stated with much concern.

"I sensed there was an enemy energy nearby." Nebriana answered. "We must hurry, and check this out."

Leo and Irving looked around with heightened anxiety, but the wolf was nowhere in sight. All they could hear was the much louder whispering in the trees around them. Leo suddenly turned when he heard a branch snap, and found himself face to face with Green Man. The towering god angrily picked the terrified man up by his throat with one hand, and pitched him hard against a tree. The impact instantly snapped his neck and spine. Irving watched in horror, and turned to run. His foot snagged on a root, and he fell forward onto the ground. Before he could pick himself up, a tangle of roots enveloped his legs, and continued crawling up to his torso. He struggled, but couldn't escape. His terror filled screams echoed throughout the woods, until the roots finally smothered them out. In a matter of seconds, the roots totally enveloped his body, and pulled him beneath the ground.

The roots followed suit with Leo's lifeless body. Stargazer reappeared and stood with Green Man, as the roots pulled him to the depths, and digested him within the earth as well.

"Thanks for the help." Stargazer commented while laying his hand against the immortal's large branch like arm.

"I believe those might be the men you warned us about." Green Man stated.

"I do believe so, my friend." He sighed. "More will come in their wake."

The grandfather clock in the Branchview Foyer chimed at midnight, and echoed throughout the sleeping household. The spirit of Daphne Branch stood before it, and listened with pleasure as it rang out 12 times, and its' pendulum clicked like a beating heart afterward. Maggie's spirit appeared as well, and stood beside her.

"I just love the sound of that old clock, Maggie."

"I know. It never gets old." She paused. "I'm getting ready to go back to the light." The little girl stated with sober eyes.

"Have you checked on the children?"

"They're sleeping really good."

"As are the others." Daphne smiled. "It's so good to have Steven and Loraine back with us."

"Can we talk to them tomorrow?"

"I think we should let them get settled in a bit." She sighed. "I'm afraid there will be some desperate days ahead here at this old estate, and they'll definitely need our support."

"They can count on us." Maggie responded with a sweet smile. "Do you want to walk me back to the light?"

"Of course, dear." She answered as they began to stroll away.

Daphne paused her progress to ponder in thought.

"Maggie…., do you enjoy it in the light?"

The little girl paused as well, and nodded. "It's beautiful there."

"Do you ever see Darren?"

Maggie nodded again. "He's always asking about you." She looked up at her. "I wish you'd join us there."

"Perhaps I will someday." Daphne emotionally sighed. "I must prepare myself mentally first." She looked down at the little girl, and took her hand. "For now, let's just get you back for the night."

Chapter Four:
She's Alive and She's Naked

In the early morning hours, Steven and Philip set about on horses to venture into the deep woods on the Branchview estate. Steven rode on his black Morgan, while Philip rode atop Loraine's chestnut Haflinger mare. The fog had settled heavy over the woods from the still cold waters of the Atlantic. It had also rained sometime during the night, and the leafy underbrush, and moss were still quite wet. The fresh smell of a crisp morning lingered in the air as they sauntered along. Evading their eyesight, a lone wolf shadowed them, and observed their progress from a distance.

"It was fine for Lori to allow me the use of her horse." Philip stated. "I really should get a mortal one. Pegasus is quite the free spirit."

"There's room for three more in the new stable I had built." Steven smiled. "Riding a horse can be quite habit forming."

"I agree. There's nothing quite like an early morning ride."

The horses spooked a bit, and the men moved quick to calm them. Stargazer emerged from virtually out of nowhere, without rustling a sound from the loose underbrush. He held his hands up as well, and calmly placed them on the snouts of the equines.

"What beautiful horses." Stargazer commented. "I greatly miss the one I left behind in 1697."

The two men dismounted, and shook hands with the old man.

"I still see that you prefer the element of surprise." Steven laughed.

"I've been tracking you two for at least fifteen minutes."

"Nevertheless, it's good to see you again, Stargazer." He gestured toward Philip. "This is my good friend, Philip Seagraves."

"No introductions needed." He nodded with a sly grin. "I know who you really are."

Steven and Philip exchanged a quick, concerning glance.

"I suppose you learned that from either Claudiana or Nebriana while they were under the influence of the forest nectar." Philip sternly stated.

Stargazer shook his head, and chuckled. "My people were well acquainted with the gods. Your secret was always safe with us. We came here from another world as well."

"I'm sorry. I don't quite remember ever meeting you."

"You knew my father quite well." He grinned. "The gods called him Giant Eagle."

Philip reacted with an enlightened expression. "I remember him and the Wangunks. That had to have been in the late 16th century."

"And of course, you and your brother met Stargazer at the same time I did in 1697." Steven joined in.

"I apologize, but that part of my memory was erased."

Steven quickly spoke up to move the conversation along.

"So, I understand your stranded here in our time." He stated. "What in the world made you come here?"

"I, like my ancestors have time traveled through that portal several times." He explained. "I came here to make sure you and Charlotte had made it back safely."

"I hope you understand that we had no other choice than to permanently seal it." Philip reasoned.

"Too many innocent people had wandered into that portal over the years, and were never seen or heard from again." Steven added, and quickly moved to something else. "I also understand you've set up residence here in the woods. Surely, we can find you more appropriate accommodations."

"I feel much more at home, here in nature." He smiled, as he gestured all around them. "My camp is just a short distance ahead. We can go there and talk."

The men chose to walk with Stargazer, while leading the horses the short distance.

"I had two visitors here last evening." Stargazer announced. "Their intent for being here was not good."

Steven and Philip exchanged a puzzled, and concerned expression.

"What did these men want?" Philip asked.

"They wanted me to leave." He shrugged. "Said I was trespassing on their property."

"Their property?" Steven questioned. "This property has been in my family since colonial days."

"And before that it was my ancestor's land" Stargazer grinned.

"Did these men say who they were?" Philip further inquired.

"Didn't get their names. But they did claim that the property was now owned by a company called Midland Enterprises."

Steven was further perplexed. "I never heard of such a company." He paused to ponder. "I'll check with Gerard about that."

"Those two fellas tried to rough me up. They broke my damn guitar, and ruined my stew." He shook his head. "But Green Man and the root systems of the great trees stepped in to take care of those scoundrels."

Steven and Philip abruptly halted, and reacted with alarm.

"Green Man was there?" Philip questioned with much concern.

"If they saw him, and escaped, all the secrets of this woods could be compromised." Steven added.

"They didn't escape." Stargazer nonchalantly chuckled, while Philip and Steven reacted in a panic.

"Where are these men now?" Philip demanded to know.

Stargazer gestured towards the woods floor.

"You buried them?" Steven asked with urgency.

Stargazer shook his head with little concern. "The roots digested them into the earth."

Philip and Steven were speechless, and gazed at each other with horror filled thoughts.

At the same time as the meeting in the woods, a sheriff's department cruiser pulled up behind the abandoned SUV on the main road, outside the estate. Young officer Petty casually got out, and checked around the vehicle thoroughly. He looked toward the fence that separated the woods from the right of way, and noticed where it had been cut.

"Dispatch!" He talked into the mic of his radio. "This is Officer Petty." He waited for an answer to go ahead. "I'm out here on Indian Hill Road, on the northwest side of the Branch Estate." He paused to look at the license on the abandoned car. "I have an abandoned car on the side of the road. It's a blue Nissan Rogue, Massachusetts license plate KB32LX. Can I get a check on that?"

"Copy!"

"You also might want to notify someone at the Branch Estate as well. Their security fence has been breached."

It was late morning when Steven made his way back to the Branchview mansion. He opened the front door, and scanned the foyer before ringing the spirit bell.

Mrs. Porter was in the kitchen preparing lunch when she heard the bell. She looked over at little Tricia who was curiously watching from her perch at the kitchen table.

"I'd love to disable that blasted bell. Everyone who enters the house seems to think they have to ring it."

"I could go see who it is, Mrs. Porter."

Loraine also looked up from her computer, as she typed away within the confines of her spacious office in the South Wing. She looked toward her children who were playing with toys on the floor near her desk.

"That must be your dada. I can't wait to show him what they delivered this morning."

She glanced admirably at the statue which now stood in a prominent space within the office. She drew a deep breath as she stood up, and turned toward Millie whose attention was deeply engrossed in a paperback spy novel.

"Mother! Please watch the children. I'll be back in a jiff."

Millie waved one hand at her, but her attention never left the book in front of her.

After Loraine hurried from the room, Olivia curiously wandered over to the statue, and looked up at it.

"You're very pretty." She stated.

Millie glanced up, and smiled at the thought of her granddaughter conversing with the statue. London also joined his sister, and looked up with wonder at the curvaceous work of art.

Olivia reached up, and embraced the open palm of the statue with her tiny little hand. Almost immediately, the statue came to life in the form of a beautiful woman with long golden blonde hair. She looked around the room with surprise, while the children silently watched, and an oblivious Millie remained occupied with her novel. She surveyed her body with an expression of enthusiasm, and quickly departed the room. Olivia calmly walked over to Millie, and tugged on her sleeve.

"Grandmama!" Millie glanced up with a smile toward the child. "The naked lady! She's alive!"

Millie immediately looked toward where the statue was, and saw that she was now gone.

"Oh dear, Olivia! What have you children done?"

In the Foyer, Loraine greeted Steven with a kiss.

"I am so glad you're home darling. I have something I'm dying to show you."

"First, we need to go into the Sitting Room. I have something to tell you, and it can't wait." Steven countered.

Just as they entered the Sitting Room, and closed the double doors, Tricia entered the Foyer, and looked around to find no one was there. First, she turned to the stairway, and then to the door to the South Wing, that Loraine had left wide open. She then proceeded through it.

The naked woman wandered through the Grand Corridor Ballroom, looking upward at the vaulted ceiling in total awe. Little Tricia also entered, searching out whomever it was that may have rung the bell. When she saw the naked beauty, her eyes grew wide, and she gasped before turning to run from the room. She ran back into the kitchen in a panic.

"Mrs. Porter! Mrs. Porter!" She cried. "There's a naked lady in the Ballroom!"

"Oh heavens! Don't tell me another wandering ghost has entered the premises." She turned the burners off on the stove, and walked around the counter. "Come on, little one! Let's go have ourselves a look."

Just as they entered the Foyer, the naked woman nonchalantly made her entrance from the South Wing.

"See, Mrs. Porter!" Tricia pointed with excitement. "I told you she was naked!"

"Oh my!" Mrs. Porter replied, while shielding the young girl's eyes from the view. "I demand that you tell me who you are young lady, and what you're doing naked in this house."

Before the woman could attempt to speak, Millie hurried in from the South Wing with the children in tow. She screeched to a halt, and gazed slack jawed at the beautiful woman who seemed to be totally unconcerned with her nudity.

"Oh my God! It's true!

Just then, the doors to the Sitting Room swung open, and Steven and Loraine entered the foyer.

"What in the world is going on out here?" Steven blurted out, before noticing the woman.

Simultaneously, Mary entered from another portion of the house, and halted, wide eyed as well.

"Lord have mercy!" Mary cried out.

Olivia hurried to her mother's side with excitement.

"Mommy! Mommy! The pretty statue came to life!"

"So, this was your surprise Lori, and quite a surprise it is." Steven commented sarcastically.

Loraine was in shock at the incident, while little London found amusement, and ecstatically giggled.

"Oh, dear Lord! This can't be real." She turned to Steven who was gazing admirably at the beautiful woman.

"Oh, Steven! Could you put your eyeballs back in the sockets, and please cover this woman's private parts with your jacket?"

"Oh! Uhh! Err! Yeah! Right away, dear!"

Steven hurried, and gently wrapped his spring jacket around the woman, and she gave him a pleasing smile in return. The jacket just barely covered her shapely bottom.

"I'll run, and get her some clothes." Mrs. Porter said as she hurried up the stairs.

Mary walked up beside Loraine, and folded her arms in front of her.

"Mrs. Spencer! I do declare! That young woman is an absolute goddess."

"We'll just have to find out who this goddess is." Loraine replied sternly.

"I'll take the children in the other room." Millie offered.

"I'll go along and help Ms. Sandstrom." Mary added

While Mary and Millie led the children from the room, Loraine approached the young woman.

"You need to tell us who you are, if you can."

The woman timidly placed her hand to her mouth, and shook her head.

"I don't think she can speak, Lori." Steven stated in a serious tone.

Loraine tried sign language, but she only shrugged shyly in response.

"I suppose I'll have to work my magic to make her talk." Loraine sighed. "I'll take her in the Sitting Room while you go speak to the children, and my mother. Perhaps they can shed some light on what may have brought her to life."

Steven rolled his eyes as he walked past his wife.

"We should've stayed in Florida."

After everyone left the Foyer, there was a knock on the door, and Mary hurried in from another room to answer it.

"Lord have mercy! What now?"

She swung the door open to find Sheriff Albertson standing there.

"Sheriff! I certainly didn't expect you."

"Mary." He politely tipped his hat, and nodded to her. "I would've called ahead of time, but I felt this was important enough to pay a visit in person. Is Mr. Spencer around?"

"He's in the other room with the children. Stay right here, and I'll go fetch him."

Behind the closed doors of the sitting room, Loraine sat with the woman who now wore a robe. The woman remained politely silent, and calm.

"We're going to need you to talk, sweetheart." She sighed. "I certainly hope this works. I've never tried it before."

Loraine placed her hand lightly on the top of the woman's head. "I call upon the divine power of the universe to enter my being, and transfer your power to this woman, that she may speak, and understand the English language."

Nothing happened immediately, but Loraine was persistent, and mouthed the words silently once again. A surge of electricity suddenly filled the room with a flash, and jolted both the women with tremors.

Steven was just entering the Foyer when the loud bang was heard, and a flash of light entered the area from beneath the closed Sitting Room doors. The two women shrieked loudly from within the room.

"What in the blazes was that?" The sheriff asked. "It sounded like someone got hit by lightning."

The two men hurried, and opened the door to see the two women sitting rather frazzled, and disoriented on the couch.

"Lori! Are you both okay?" Steven cried out with concern.

"Oh yes! That was quite a lightning bolt that struck outside." Loraine quickly replied, while the other woman eyed Steven with flirting eyes.

The sheriff was totally confused by the state of affairs, and spoke up as he glanced out the large picture window. "That's impossible! The sun is shining, and there's not a cloud in the sky, Mrs. Spencer."

"Oh well! You know lightning can be very unexpected, Sheriff."

"Who's the handsome one that gave me his jacket in the Foyer?" The woman interrupted in perfect English, and Loraine quickly answered in a stern fashion.

"That is my husband."

"And, who is this young lady?" The sheriff probed, causing Loraine to stammer for an answer.

"My name is Angelique. Angelique Devine." The woman answered for herself, leaving both Loraine and Steven rather flabbergasted.

The sheriff removed his hat out of respect. "Well! The name certainly suits you, ma'am. You're a very beautiful woman."

"Thank you…" She waited for him to introduce himself as he nervously stammered.

"I'm Sheriff Albertson."

Angelique nodded, and Steven quickly intervened.

"Ms. Devine is a houseguest that I have not formally met until now. It appears she obviously slept in late this morning." His eyes darted to Loraine with urgency. "Isn't that right, sweetheart?"

"Oh yes! She's visiting here from New York City." Loraine stated.

"I certainly hope you enjoy your stay here at Branchview, Ms. Devine."

"I'm sure I will. Thank you, Sheriff."

"I believe there was something you wanted to discuss with me, Sheriff Albertson?" Steven inquired, while staring nervously at the two women.

"Oh! Right! Yes!" The sheriff stammered. "Is there a place we can speak in private?"

"We can talk in my office." Steven answered as he herded the sheriff from the room, then turned for a final glance at the two women before shutting the doors behind them.

Loraine waited until she no longer heard the men's voices in the outer Foyer, before speaking in a low tone.

"Angelique Devine? How in the world did you come up with that name?"

"My creator gave me the name Angelique, and I heard you mention something about the divine power of the universe when you activated my brain. I thought it sounded like a perfect last name."

Loraine paced closer with curiosity. "You mentioned that your creator gave you the name Angelique. Who exactly was that?"

"It was my beloved Mario. His hands created me to be the perfect woman."

"I'd have to admit that he was quite a talented artist." Loraine commented with a sigh.

"He was also a beautiful man. The love within his heart brought me to life with a single kiss."

"I'm taking a wild guess in saying that Mario was the other statue." Loraine stated as she sat back down next to her.

"Yes!" Angelique perked up with excitement. "Do you know where he is now?"

"I know he was purchased by someone else at the auction where you were sold. That's all I know."

Angelique's eyes narrowed with anger.

"Oh! That despicable woman! She took him away from me.

"So, it was a woman who purchased Mario?" Loraine sat forward with active thought. "Now that I know that much, you need to tell me what happened that caused the two of you to become statues in the first place."

"It was that witch!" Angelique trembled with anger.

"The woman who purchased Mario?" Loraine inquired.

"No! This woman's name was Liddy McPherson."

Loraine put her hands distressfully to her head.

"Why am I not surprised? Will I ever cease to hear that dreadful woman's name mentioned within this household?"

"You know this woman?" Angelique anxiously asked.

"Fortunately, I've never met her personally. But I do know of her handiwork." Loraine replied. "I've made a career out of righting all the wrongs that she created during her miserable existence." She sighed bcfore continuing. "May I ask what year this incident occurred?"

"I believe the year was 1899."

"You mean to tell me that you and Mario have existed like this for over 120 years?"

Angelique sadly nodded in response.

"Oh my!" She distressfully exclaimed.

Angelique emotionally took hold of Loraine's hands, and gazed at her with pleading eyes.

"Can you please reunite me with my Mario, and give him life once again, as you did for me?"

"It may take us awhile to sort this whole thing out. But I promise you that I will try my best."

Angelique took a deep breath, and rubbed her belly with her hand.

"I'm very hungry. Could you possibly get me something to eat? I haven't eaten in over 100 years."

Loraine glanced at the mantle clock before answering.

"It is lunch time." She sighed. "Perhaps this is as good a time as any to formally introduce you to the others in the household. You've already created quite an impression"

Both women stood, and Loraine surveyed Angelique in thoughtful ponderance.

"First, we must get you dressed in proper clothes. You're a tad bit taller than me, but I do believe you may be able to fit into one of my dresses."

"I like the one you're wearing."

"I refuse to shed this dress here in the Sitting Room. We'll simply have to choose one from my closet."

In the study, Sheriff Albertson was bringing Steven up to speed on a story he was already quite aware of.

"So, basically you're telling me that these two men from Boston are missing somewhere in our woods?" Steven innocently inquired.

"Presumably. They haven't checked in with their employer or their families in over 24 hours, and by all indications, they entered your property illegally at the spot that their car was abandoned."

"And, somehow you believe they may still be out there?"

"We don't know for sure." The sheriff answered. "Would you mind if me and my deputies searched the woods?"

"Not at all, sheriff. Just be careful in the underbrush. There may still be some old long forgotten traps out there."

"Hopefully, nothing else." He chuckled. "I've heard some wild stories about those woods over the years."

Steven only answered with an amused smile, while the sheriff stood, and prepared to leave.

"We did venture a short distance in this morning, and noticed an encampment."

"We're all aware of that. We had a squatter that Philip Seagraves escorted from the property last week."

"Last week? I suppose it wouldn't be fruitful to question that person then."

Steven shook his head in reply, and the sheriff slowly rose from his seat.

"I don't want to take up any more of your time, Mr. Spencer."

"No problem, sheriff. I'll escort you out."

Steven started to stand, but the sheriff waved him off.

"No need for that." The sheriff chuckled. "I'm beginning to know the way by heart."

Steven waited a few patient moments after the sheriff departed the room before dialing out on his cell phone.

"Philip! I just spoke with the sheriff. He and his men will be scouring the woods for those missing men this afternoon. Please make sure you alert Nebriana, and the others. Especially Green Man." He paused to listen. "Yes, I know. We have to make sure no one ever learns the secret of those woods."

A short time later, Loraine and Angelique, who was now fully dressed, entered the dining room for lunch. Olivia ran to her mother, and pointed toward Angelique with excitement.

"Mommy! Mommy! The pretty woman isn't naked anymore."

"That's right, sweetheart. We found the pretty woman some clothes." She turned to Mary, who was pouring drinks, and whispered sarcastically under her breath. "Not that it mattered. Most of the household has already seen her bare assets."

Angelique went down to one knee to address Olivia.

"You're the sweet little girl who brought me to life."

Little Olivia giggled, while Loraine looked to Angelique with a puzzled expression.

"What exactly do you mean by that, Angelique?"

"This little one simply touched me, and transformed me into a woman again. I'd have to say it was a miracle."

Loraine looked first to Olivia, then to Millie, who sat at the table rather sheepishly.

"Is that how it all happened, mother?"

"I suppose so, dear. When I looked up from my book, she had already transformed, and left the room."

Loraine was speechless with awe, and looked to Mary next, who only shrugged before walking back toward the kitchen.

"Stranger things have happened, Ms. Lori. I'd think you'd be used to it all by now."

Angelique caught eye of the loaf of bread sitting on the table. She grabbed the whole loaf, tearing a large bite from it with her teeth.

"I am so hungry." She slurred, while chewing with her mouth full.

Loraine sighed, and distressfully placed her hand to her head.

"Oh dear! One of the first things I'll need to do is teach that young lady proper etiquette."

Chapter Five:
Laszlo's Revenge

In an elaborate, and ornate meeting room in London, several well-dressed men and women sat around a long table for a business meeting. Sitting at the head of the table was Kenneth Laszlo, and to his right was Lucifer Morningstar. Laszlo rang a handbell to commence the meeting.

"Distinguished members of our Secret Society, I welcome you." He paused with a grin. "It's come to my attention that Branch Consolidated, and its' affiliated companies have decided to leave the New York Stock Exchange in order to start their own Exchange." He arrogantly chuckled before continuing. "Exactly what their reasoning is for this is not yet known."

"Perhaps self-destruction." An older man with a mustache quipped, igniting a chorus of laughter around the table.

"Whatever their reason might be, I'm sure they have some sort of agenda in mind. Gerard Le Roux and Steven Spencer are intelligent men, and I have reason to believe they may have some heavy hitters backing them up." Laszlo added.

"What can we do to counter it?" A staunch, middled aged woman inquired with concern.

"Mr. Morningstar and myself are working on that." He motioned with a nod for Morningstar to take the floor.

"As Mr. Laszlo stated, we're monitoring the situation quite closely. You must all remember that we're a global entity, and much larger than their little band of flag waving Patriots." He arrogantly smirked. "We will counter every move, and crush them without mercy."

"We were able to hack into the Lockeport recorder of deeds office, and change the deed for the Branchview Estate into the name of an associate of mine in Boston." Laszlo continued. "We've also convinced the publisher of both him and his wife's books to drop them from their catalogue. My personal ambition is to ruin and destroy Steven Spencer and his little empire." He exchanged a devious grin with Morningstar, and motioned to a well groomed man to his left. "I've enlisted our attorney, Barclay Rutherford to help me do just that." He paused to glance at those in attendance. "Upon discussion with Mr. Rutherford here, I've learned that ironically, he also has a personal issue with Mr. Spencer, that I will not discuss at this time."

Laszlo paced away from his place at the head of the table, and brandished a pistol from beneath his suit jacket, causing everyone at the table to gasp.

"Which leads me to our next subject." He began to pace slowly around the table. "It's also come to my attention from a reliable source that we have a mole within our fold." He chuckled. "It appears this person is really a part of the MI6, and is supplying data to none other than Mildred Sandstrom, who happens to be Steven Spencer's mother in law. "He paced a few more steps, then without warning, he shot a younger man point blank in the back of the head without even a blink of remorse. Blood spattered everywhere, and on everyone nearby. People reacted with repulse and shock as they viewed what was left of the man's head, plopped face down to the table."

Laszlo arrogantly glanced around the table. "That, my friends, is how we deal with traitors to the Secret Society." He gives a quick wink. "All of you should take special note of that."

He then turned back toward Barclay Rutherford, and gestured. "I'll be shipping you off to the United States as soon as possible. I'll send a driver to your house at six this evening."

"I can hardly wait." Barclay replied with a smirk.

Back at Branchview, Loraine was very befuddled as she sat at the desk in her office. She perked up when Steven and Philip entered the room.

"Oh darling!" She exclaimed. "I'm so glad you're back."

Steven strolled around the desk, and kissed her on the cheek. "Please tell me there's not another issue."

"Oh, I wish I could. They seem to be mounting by the moment."

"What now, Lori?" Steven asked as he distressfully placed his hand to his forehead.

"Our agent hasn't been returning my calls, so I demanded that his secretary tell me why." She sighed, while Steven simply gestured for more. "It appears as though he's dropped us from his client list, and all of our books have been cancelled by the publisher."

"Despite all of them being best sellers." Steven grunted. "I'd say were being censored."

"Sounds like the doings of Kenneth Laszlo to me." Philip firmly stated.

"Yes, it does." Steven remarked. "That man is getting to be quite a pain in the ass." He turned his attention back to Loraine, changing the subject.

"Where is our lovely visitor?"

"She's resting in her room. Tina and I are taking her shopping for clothes this afternoon."

"Certainly, you have enough clothes to share with her. You have a whole walk-in closet to yourself." Steven remarked with a tinge of sarcasm.

"I'm afraid with those perfectly sculpted breasts of hers, she'll need at least a size larger than what I wear."

"Can someone please tell me what you're talking about?" Philip inquired.

"I'll have to fill you in later. You and Tina could definitely relate to this story." Steven answered.

Just then, Millie hurried into the room with urgency, appearing to be quite frazzled.

"Oh! Thank heavens you two gentlemen are here. I desperately need to speak with you both."

Philip and Steven exchanged an eye roll as they turned their full attention to Millie, who took a deep breath.

"My MI6 informant who had infiltrated the Secret Society has been compromised. They discovered his body floating in the Thames this afternoon."

Loraine stood, and walked around the desk to join the two men as they all continued listening.

"It's obvious someone within MI6 tipped them off, and if that's the case, they know about me as well."

"You're well protected here at Branchview, Millie." Steven stated.

"It's not me that I'm worried about." Millie replied, while bursting into tears. "I'm afraid those bastards will harm Bill."

Philip firmly took hold of Millie's shoulders to calm her, and addressed her with concern.

"Listen to me, Millie. I'll handle this personally." He assured. "I'll summon Pegasus, and leave for London immediately." He wiped away a tear from her face. "London is five hours ahead of us on the clock. If we leave now, we should get there before midnight. We'll bring Bill back safely. This I promise."

"Thank you, Philip." She replied with much relief.

He turned to Steven with a serious expression that also brimmed with anger beneath the surface.

"I'll have one of my contacts in London retrieve, and hold him in a safe place." He took a moment to catch his breath. "Please take care of Tina and the baby while I'm gone."

"I promise they'll be safe as always." Steven assured.

"As far as I'm concerned, this war between us and the Secret Society has officially escalated." Philip sneered before storming out of the room.

Meanwhile in London, Kenneth Laszlo sat back in an easy chair, cradling a glass of wine, reflecting fondly on the days' events. Mr. Morningstar strolled from the shadows and settled into an adjacent chair.

"Well, Mr. Morningstar. I would say that we've had ourselves quite an accomplished day." He saluted him with his wine glass.

"They fished our poor, misfortunate MI6 operative from the Thames shortly after we dumped him there."

"Just as I'd hoped." Laszlo chuckled. "That'll send them a message of who really has the upper hand."

Laszlo stood up, and poured another glass of wine for himself, and one for Morningstar.

"Next, I'll strike at the heart of Mildred Sandstrom." He handed the glass of wine to Morningstar.

"What's your plan, Kenneth?" He asked, as Laszlo settled back in his seat.

"I learned that her husband, Bill Crawford is staying in a rented farm house near Hergest Ridge." He grunted, and wickedly smiled. "I've sent a team to assassinate him."

"How sinister of you." He raised his glass to salute him. "Your father would be very proud of you."

Laszlo responded with a pleased expression.

"I take that our Mr. Rutherford embarked without a hitch?" Morningstar continued.

"He's on my private jet as we speak." Laszlo grinned. "He should be resting comfortably at my sisters' house in the States by this time tomorrow."

"And then, the destruction of Steven Spencer, and the Branch Estate will commence." Morningstar added, prompting a sinister laugh from both men.

The thunder rumbled loudly, and lightning flashed outside as Steven held a late day meeting with Ezekiel, and Gerard in the Branchview Study.

"The stage is set, and everything is ready for the exit from the Stock Exchange, and launch of our new platform." Gerard began. "The Secret Society will never see it coming this soon."

"We've decided to call it Black Friday, the sequel." Ezekiel mused.

"I take that Agent Guitierez team is all set, and ready to go?" Steven probed.

"They've set up shop in the basement of Corporate Headquarters." Gerard answered. "They are working under the tightest of security, and the new internet service should come on line overnight. It should all go off without a hitch."

"The bastards will never know what hit them." Ezekiel chuckled.

"After the day I've had, please excuse me if I'm a bit skeptical." Steven stated. "The sheriff and his men recovered one of the intruder's guns in the woods, but luckily failed to find anything else." He sighed. "I'm sure they won't give up, and I have a strange feeling we haven't heard the last from Midland Enterprises either." He turned to Gerard. "Were you able to find any info on them?"

"It appears that they're headquartered in Boston, and have alleged ties to organized crime." He answered.

"I'm certainly not surprised about that." Steven quipped. "I have no doubt that they're also tied in some way to the Secret Society."

"Nebriana and the others have the situation in the woods well under control. I'm sure that the deputies won't find anything else." Ezekiel assured.

A loud boom shook the house, rain slapped against the window, and lightning flashed, causing all three men to flinch.

"That's quite a storm that blew in from the Atlantic." Ezekiel commented.

"I only hope that Philip and Pegasus were able to reach Bill before Laszlo and his henchmen." Steven stated with concern.

"We can only hope." Ezekiel replied.

"Where's Millie?" Gerard inquired. "I thought for sure she'd be sitting in on this."

"She was quite shaken by the day's events. Lori gave her an herbal sedative to calm her down."

All the men glanced anxiously at each other, as the clock chimed at 4PM. Steven listened, then turned to Gerard.

"Remember, we have a school board meeting to attend at seven tomorrow night." He then glanced at Ezekiel with amusement. "Would you care to tag along?"

"I'll have to pass on that one." He answered. "I've a feeling that storm is going to be more violent than the one outside."

Inside a darkened farmhouse in England, the silence of the night is shattered when the door is kicked in. Three hooded thugs entered carrying semi automatic rifles. Suddenly, the light flicked on in the room, and Philip, appearing in the guise of Poseidon strolled up to the surprised men, tapping his staff on the floor in front of him.

"Are you gentlemen looking for anyone in particular?"

"We're looking for the old man." Said the lead man in a heavy cockney brogue.

"The old man's out for the night." Philip stated with a smirk.

"So, who the hell are you?" He laughed. "Some kind of Comicon character?"

"I am your worst possible nightmare."

The lead man motioned to the others, who then raised their weapons.

"Kill the bloody bastard."

The quiet, peaceful darkness outside of the farm house was disrupted by the sound of rapid fire gun shots coming from within the dwelling. Seconds after it seized, the sound of a violent struggle and screams ensued that was quite brief in duration. Inside, in the aftermath, the walls were splattered with blood, and the dead bodies of the three assassins were strewn about the room. Philip walked over to the lead man, whose now vacant stare looked upward toward him. He grunted with disgust as he laid a blood stained calling card of a three pronged staff on his dead body.

"That should send a message to your superiors." He looked away in seething anger. "No one messes with my family."

With one final glance around the room, he stomped out the door, and into the darkness.

As the evening hours winded down at Branchview, Loraine relaxed on the couch, watching TV in the Great Room of the South Wing. Steven wandered in from an adjacent room, and settled next to her, wrapping his arm around her, and snuggling close.

"I finally got the children to sleep." He sighed. "Now you and I can finally have some cuddle time."

Loraine smiled, and contently rested her head on his chest.

"We bought Angelique some nice clothes today. I only hope she doesn't grow out of them."

"What do you mean by that?" He mumbled with a perplexed expression.

"That woman eats like a horse. I've never seen anyone with such an appetite."

"Maybe you can persuade her to go to the gym with you, Tina, and your mother."

"I suppose so." She grunted. "Her and Tina have seemed to bond quite quickly."

"It isn't like they don't have anything in common. They do share similar origins." They both laughed, and snuggled ever closer.

Steven leaned back, exhaled a deep breath and closed his eyes.

"It's been an exhausting day. I only hope that everything goes smoothly tomorrow."

Loraine grabbed the remote, and began to channel surf.

"There doesn't seem to be anything good on TV anymore." She complained. "Is there anything in particular you'd like to watch, darling?"

She looked up at him when he didn't answer, and saw that he was fast asleep. She carefully, and quietly scooted away from him, grabbed a crocheted blanket from the back of the couch, and covered him. She stood back with a sigh, and watched him sleeping.

"So much for a romantic evening."

Back in England, in an upscale mansion outside of London, two men watched over Bill Crawford in the ornate Sitting Room. Bill became rather perturbed, and verbally lashed out.

"I demand that someone please tell me what I'm doing here." He shook his head with frustration. "First, you snatch me from my house in the middle of the night, and bring me here. Then, you watch over me like I'm some kind of a criminal."

An older gentleman with a kind face sauntered into the room in the middle of the rant.

"We brought you here to protect you, Mr. Crawford. Some very bad men are trying to kill you."

"Who in the world would want to kill me?" Bill asked.

"Kenneth Laszlo, and members of the Secret Society. They know of your connection to Branchview."

Bill took a deep breath, and settled a bit.

"My apologies for not introducing myself, Mr. Crawford. I'm Victor Blaney. I'm an associate of Philip Seagraves, and Ezekiel Sphere." He firmly shook Bill's hand. "Philip will be along shortly to return you to the States."

"Quicker than you think, Victor." Philip announced, as he marched into the room.

"Philip!" Bill exclaimed. "I can't tell you how glad I am to see you."

Philip smiled, then turned to Victor. "Thank you for your help, old friend."

"Anytime, Philip."

"We need to leave right away, Bill."

"What about all of my art work? It's all back at the farm house."

"We can't go back." Philip replied. "I promise I'll explain everything to you later."

"Your ride is waiting patiently out in the back." Victor stated while motioning toward the window in the room.

Bill wandered over to the window, and glanced out to see the fabulous white winged horse. He then glanced back toward Philip with disbelief.

"Yes! It's exactly what you think it is." Philip said with a grin.

Bill gave a slow, accepting nod in return. "I've never even ridden a horse before."

"He's quite gentle." Philip assured. "Victor's men will help you mount, and all you have to do is lean forward, and carefully caress his neck. Pegasus will do the rest."

"You're not going with us?" Bill asked.

Philip subtly shook his head. "I'll be following along shortly. I need to make a long overdue visit to Mr. Laszlo." Philip smiled. "I've arranged for the Nereids to escort you back to the beach at Lighthouse Point. You should be there by dawn, and I'm certain Millie will be waiting patiently."

Bill firmly shook Philip's hand. "Thank you, Philip."

In the elaborate bedroom of his London mansion, Kenneth Laszlo entertained a young call girl who barely looked of legal age. He dallied his fingers through her hair, as she shyly sat at the edge of the bed in a revealing negligee.

"They've certainly channeled some very beautiful girls in from the Ukraine. I'm guessing that you must've fetched quite a high price, sweetheart."

His cell phone rang, and he reached down on the side table to answer it. "Speak to me!" He arrogantly announced before listening.

"What do you mean they're all dead?" He listened.

"I'm certain that man hasn't left the country yet. I want him found, and killed!" He commanded, before ending the call, and angrily slamming his cell phone down onto the table.

"That's not going to happen." Philip announced, as he boldly strolled into the room. "Mr. Crawford is in flight to the United States as we speak, and might I add that he's very ably protected."

"Who are you, and how did you get past my security?"

"Who I am is none of your concern, Mr. Laszlo. And yes, I am quite skilled at evading security systems."

"Try evading this." Laszlo quipped as he brandished a pistol, and began firing at him.

The young girl covered her ears, and curled up at the headboard of the bed.

After emptying an entire clip, he dropped the gun in stunned amazement that Philip was still standing.

"Funny! Your father had that same look on his face when he tried to shoot me with his revolver."

"What in the hell are you talking about?"

Philip chuckled as he strolled closer. He paused to offer his hand to the young woman, who fearfully accepted it. He gently pulled her to her feet, and spoke a few words in Russian to her. She nodded, put on her coat, and took a secure stance behind his muscular body.

"To answer your earlier question, Mr. Laszlo. I am the man who killed your father."

"That's a lie! It was Steven Spencer!"

"And who told you that?"

"Lucifer Morningstar."

Philip laughed heartily at his answer. "The father of lies, himself. Anyone who believes him is a fool."

Philip grabbed a pad and pen that was on a side table, scribbled something, then handed it to the young girl with one of his calling cards.

"Hail a taxi, go to this address, and show them my card. The people there will pay your fare, and help you. Do you understand?"

The young girl nodded rapidly, and quickly departed the room.

"Did you really kill my father?" Laszlo nervously asked.

"Yes, I did. And I assure you, Steven Spencer had nothing to do with it."

Without warning, Philip grabbed Laszlo by the collar of his robe, and slammed him hard against the wall like a discarded rag doll. He cowered on the floor as Philip took a stance over him.

"Are you going to kill me too?"

"No, Mr. Laszlo. I'll save that honor and pleasure for someone who will savor the opportunity much more than myself."

Philip pulled out another of his calling cards, and handed it to Laszlo, who examined it before looking back up.

"This was the same card that was found on my fathers' body."

"Precisely! You need to show that card to your good friend, Mr. Morningstar." Philip grinned. "Tell him I sent my regards."

Without another word, Philip calmly strolled from the room, and disappeared into the shadows of the dark house. After he was gone, Laszlo looked at the card with deep thought. He then grabbed his cell phone, and dialed a number.

"Yeah! It's time to make a statement." He nodded with a tinge of anger. "Whatever it takes. I want Steven Spencer dead, and have Morningstar come to my house immediately. I need to know who this invincible bastard is with the trident calling card."

Chapter Six:
An Unwelcome Visitor from The Past

Loraine sat silently on the piano bench in the darkness of the Grand Corridor Ballroom. Her deep thoughts were interrupted by the sound of heels slowly clicking across the tile flooring. She subtly turned to see the spirit of Daphne Branch approaching. She leaned against the back side of the piano momentarily.

"If you're going to sit there, you should play something."

"I so wish I could." Loraine chuckled. "I'm afraid musical talent is quite absent in my genetics."

Daphne strolled around, and took a seat on the bench beside her. She gracefully began to play a familiar tune, and sang a bit of the chorus.

"It's a great day to be alive…" She smiled.

"You've been listening in on me, haven't you?" Loraine cleverly quipped.

"Always, my dear!" She laughed. "I heard you singing that song to the children. It's quite a catchy tune."

"Speaking of the children." Loraine anxiously sighed. "It appears that they've somehow acquired supernatural powers. Little Olivia turned my statue into a living woman."

"Oh yes! The beautiful naked woman." Daphne laughed with great amusement.

"I'd laugh with you, but I fear what future atrocities those children might innocently cause with those powers."

"I suppose you should start tutoring them on when it's appropriate to use those powers, and when it's not." Daphne suggested.

"But I never taught them magic in the first place. How in the world did they acquire it?"

"You are aware of the magic within the summer Gemini moon?" Daphne countered her question.

"All too well." Loraine chuckled. "It's very powerful in both positive and negative ways."

Daphne closed her eyes for a moment, then opened them again before speaking.

"In every generation of this family, a set of twins are born within that summer moon cycle." Loraine listened with great interest as the spirit continued on. "At least one of those twins is always gifted with the powers of magic. The other is usually very gifted in a variety of other ways."

"I nearly forgot." Loraine thoughtfully stated. "Charlotte and Penelope were also twin sisters of the summer moon."

"As were you, my dear."

"What on earth do you mean, Daphne? I'm an only child."

Daphne paused with a sigh. "You had a twin brother that you never knew, who died at birth. He's watched over you as a guardian angel throughout your entire life."

Loraine was totally flabbergasted by the revelation.

"Why didn't my mother ever tell me this?"

"Oh sweetheart! She was so heartbroken over losing a child that she could never bring herself to speak of it." She paused in thought. "Like the children, you have a birthday coming up in June. Perhaps it's a good time for you and your mother to discuss this issue." She flashed a compassionate smile. "This has haunted her throughout her life. I think it's time to help her find closure."

Loraine thoughtfully nodded in agreement, before glancing around the room. "Where's Maggie tonight? She's usually right here with you."

"She returned to the light a bit earlier."

"Why don't you go with her, Daphne? I'm sure Darren would love to see you."

"I wish it was as easy as that." She sadly stated.

"You do love him, don't you?"

"With all my heart." Daphne sighed.

"Then what in the world is holding you back, sweetheart?"

Daphne began to weep. "I blame myself for his death. He was such a wonderful man, and had so much to live for. He gave it all up for me."

Loraine looked upward, and rolled her eyes.

"You have to let go of that guilt. It doesn't matter anymore." She reasoned. "I think it's about time you two discussed this as well." She paused with a sigh. "You need to go join him in the light."

Daphne looked at her with melancholy eyes, and forced a smile.

"Perhaps I will." She gratefully nodded.

As she stood, she gently, and briefly laid her hand lovingly on Loraine's shoulder. She then began to slowly stroll away.

"Sleep well, Lori. I'll see you again tomorrow."

Loraine emotionally smiled as she listened to the sound of her high heels click away, and watched as the spirit of the elegant woman gracefully disappeared into the shadows.

"Goodnight, Daphne!"

As dawn approached onto the world of Branchview, a sliver of light appeared on the horizon over the mighty Atlantic. A chorus of Nereid Mermaids heralded the new day, and announced their approach, as they guided the winged horse Pegasus, and its' very special passenger.

By the time Bill Crawford had made his way to the Great House from his landing at the beach of Lighthouse Point, the morning sun was just beginning to filter through the semi circled window above the front door, and shined across the tile flooring of the Foyer. Bill entered the house quietly, but he was so excited to finally be there that he couldn't resist giving the spirit bell a quick ring to announce his arrival.

Mrs. Porter had just begun preparations for the morning breakfast when she heard the bell ring.

"Good grief!" She fussed. "Whoever that is, they're going to wake the whole household."

She ambled away as quick as she could to see who it was.

Bill stood, bathing himself in the rays of the morning light, when Millie emerged from the Sitting Room. She had stayed up the entire night, awaiting his return. She stood for a moment, suspended in emotional surprise before they hurried into a loving embrace.

"Oh Bill! I thought for sure I'd lost you."

Mrs. Porter stormed into the Foyer, ready to unleash holy hell on the person who had rang the bell. She came to a sudden halt when she saw the couple in their emotional embrace. She backed off, and gave an approving smile before retreating back to the kitchen.

Bill appeared quite star struck, and rather dazed. "Are you alright, dear?" Millie asked. "You appear as though you're in a trance."

"I just had the most amazing experience of my life." Bill marveled. "I flew all the way across the ocean from England on the back of a winged Pegasus horse."

Millie stood back, and eyed him awkwardly.

"Bill Crawford! Have you been smoking the marijuana leaf while we've been separated?"

"No Millie! It's the truth." Bill stated in all seriousness. "We flew just above the rains most of the way, and we were guided by a school of Nereid Mermaid warriors."

"Good heavens!" Millie looked away in utter disbelief. "I swear, our experiences here at Branchview become more bizarre by the day." She took hold of his hand. "You mustn't tell anyone else what you just told me."

"You're the only one, sweetheart. I swore secrecy to Philip, and we both know who he really is."

"Where is Philip? I assumed he'd be with you."

"I'm certain he isn't far behind." Bill assured. "He had some business to tend to in London. And between us, I wouldn't have wanted to be on the receiving end of that business."

"We need to get some coffee and breakfast in you, my dear." Millie fussed, straightening the collar of his shirt. "Come along! I want to hear every detail of your experience."

Bill grinned pleasingly as she led him along by the arm. "Yes dear!"

As the morning sun progressed to warm the world surrounding Lighthouse Point, Steven sat on one of the rocks staring dreamingly out over the Atlantic. He could hear the sound of Mermaid chatter echo in on the breeze, and he closed his eyes, and smiled. When he opened them again, he could see an imposing figure emerge from the depths, and progress slowly to shore. As Poseidon trudged inward in his godly form, he waved to Steven. When he reached shore, he transformed to the familiar presence of Philip Seagraves. Complete with his dry land clothes, and flowing black hair. It was as though he'd never been in the water. He marched in, and took a perch on a rock close to Steven.

"What a splendid morning." He proclaimed, taking time to breathe in the salt air. "I just love the smell of the seashore after a rain."

"I'll second that." Steven stated with a nod, as he continued to gaze outward over the water. "Thank you for saving Bill."

"We got to him in just the nick of time." He sighed. "I trust that he's resting well at the house."

"He and Millie are sharing some much deserved quality time together."

Philip looked outward as well, and smiled as the subject shifted. "Does she ever talk to you?"

Steven also smiled fondly at the question, knowing quite well who he was talking about. "All the time. Telepathically, of course."

Philip took a deep sigh, and continued the conversation. "I really did love her, you know? I still do."

"As a happily married man with children, I'm embarrassed to say I love her too."

"You should never be embarrassed of love, Steven. It's a wondrous thing." He paused in thought. "Besides, I feel very strongly that you two are together in the parallel world."

"Alfheim?" Steven questioned.

Philip shook his head. "Those are the hidden worlds. The parallel world is an identical place to earth within another dimension. Our identical selves, or twin flames dwell there, and carry on with life just as we do here."

"Are you there as well?"

Philip shook his head again, and laughed. "None of the gods dwell there, because we have immortality here."

Steven pondered his statement with perplexed thought. "How is it that Amphitrite can dwell there? She's a goddess."

"Because I granted her immortality in this life." He leaned forward to explain further. "You see, other than the gods, all people have a twin soul. Because Amphitrite was not born to be an immortal, her twin soul has dwelled, and evolved in the parallel world." He sighed. "I believe the immense love that she felt for you, stemmed from your souls being intertwined over several lifetimes there."

"What about Loraine?"

"Perhaps she's with someone else there." He shrugged. "Twin flames often make alternative choices that change the course of how we live our lives both here and there."

Steven was totally blown away by the revelation. "Why are you telling me this? Surely it's highly confidential information."

"Because I trust you like a brother, Steven." He paused a moment in thought. "I have learned more from you than I have from any other man in my entire existence. I credit you in enlightening me, and reminding me of my true mission here on earth."

"I'm truly humbled and flattered by that, Philip."

The two men firmly shook hands, and Philip became uncharacteristically emotional.

"In my short time here at Branchview, I've learned to humble myself before my God, and seek forgiveness and salvation from my terrible past transgressions."

"Just as Charlotte did?"

"Exactly! If Charlotte was able to gain redemption, then surely an old sinner such as myself has a fighting chance." Philip chuckled.

"I believe you will." Steven tapped his muscular shoulder in a show of confidence as he stood up. "Right now, I think we should go and embrace and kiss our wives and children. Then we'll go forward, and make this a productive day."

"Yes, we will." Philip answered with a nod of agreement.

At the Seagrave's House, Tina and Angelique shared conversation at the dining room table. Young Charles sat in his booster seat, and fiddled with the Cheerio's in his cereal bowl. Angelique watched curiously as Tina poured cream into her coffee, and spooned in two scoops of stevia as well. She followed suit with her own cup that Tina had poured for her.

"What is this drink?" She asked.

"It's called coffee. It's a favorite beverage for many people in this world." Tina smiled. "Personally, I prefer to drink it only in the morning,"

Angelique gripped her cup with both hands, and chugged down the whole contents in one gulp, causing Tina to react with a raised eyebrow of disbelief.

"That was quite hot going down, but it was very yummy" She remarked. "Could I please have another?"

"Of course!" Tina answered as she poured another from the carafe into her cup. "But first, I need to show you the proper way of drinking it."

She demonstrated with her own cup, while Angelique watched closely.

"You see this little loop on the side of the cup? You grip that with your fingers like this." She followed her example. "Then you casually lift the cup to your lips, and sip it like this." Angelique did the same.

"Did I get it right?"

"That's more like it, dear. Coffee is a drink to be savored, and not chugged."

Angelique took a sip, and responded with a pleased smile.

"We must get you refined to acceptable behavior. Otherwise, you'll be looked down upon by other humans."

"It certainly isn't easy." She sighed. "How long did it take for you when you transitioned to a woman?"

"It took a while." She chuckled. "I was a bit of a wild child."

"That's an understatement." Philip commented as he entered the room, and embraced Tina from behind.

Angelique eyed him up and down. "Who's this guy? He's a real hunk."

"Angelique, this is my husband, Philip."

"Lucky you!"

"I've heard a lot about you from Steven, young lady." Philip nodded. "You're just as lovely as he mentioned."

Philip jokingly messed his son's hair as he took a seat at the table. "What marvelous plans do you ladies have for the day?"

"We're going with Loraine over to Cambridge today." Tina answered.

"We're hoping to find out who purchased my beloved Mario." Angelique added.

"Be sure to keep an eye on our newcomer here." Philip stated with concern to his wife. "She's not yet aware of the dangers of this world."

"Trust me! We'll have her on a short leash." Tina replied with amusement.

"And, be very careful." He warned. "Somehow, I'm sensing a bit of uneasiness over all of this."

Over at the Branchview House, Steven was just returning from his morning walk, and was cheerfully greeted by Loraine, who hurried in from the Sitting Room. She was wearing a stylish summer dress, laced sandals, and it was quite obvious that she took extra time to style her hair, and apply make-up that accented her pretty features. Steven eyed his wife admirably as she strolled toward him.

"I'm glad you got back before I left, sweetheart." They exchanged kisses. "The ladies and I are going over to Cambridge. The woman at the antique store gave me the name of the auction house where the statues were sold. Perhaps we can locate the other woman who purchased Mario."

"Sounds like a full day's adventure. Who's watching over the children while you're gone?"

"Bill and Mum said they would gladly watch them. And, of course we always have Gramma Daphne and little Maggie." She grinned. "Those two are always watching from the shadows."

Steven glanced around the perimeter of the Foyer with a sigh.

"I know that quite well." He took hold of Loraine's hand. "We have to take pre-cautious measures to harness Olivia's powers until she learns how to control them."

"I so agree with that." Loraine sighed. "We need to keep an eye on baby London as well. You know what they say. Still waters do run deep."

Mary entered the Foyer with an announcement.

"Mr. Spencer, there's a gentleman at the front gate who requested to see you. He said it's very important business."

"I wasn't expecting anyone, Mary. Does this man have a name?"

"He refused to give me a name, but said it was vital that he speak to you. Should I turn him away?"

"This is against my better judgement." He stated with a thought filled sigh. "But, go ahead, and let him in."

"Whatever you say." Mary reluctantly stated as she pressed the access button near the front door, before swiftly exiting the room.

"Perhaps I should leave you alone with your business." Loraine smiled. "I'll be in the Sitting Room reading a book. Tina and Angelique should be along shortly."

"Oh, and Darling!" Steven announced, causing Loraine to turn and pause in the doorway. "You look absolutely stunning today."

"Oh, Steven! You do have quite the way of making a woman swoon." She kiddingly shook her head. "Even your own wife."

Steven nodded to her with a sly grin, as she pulled the doors closed behind her.

He then paced about the Foyer in anticipation, until finally there was a knock at the door. He casually strolled over, and placed his hand on the door knob, pausing before slowly opening it. On the other side, stood a well groomed man around his age, wearing an expensive suit, and carrying an equally impressive looking custom leather briefcase.

"Good morning! Mr. Spencer, I assume?" He inquired in a distinct British accent.

"That's me! How can I help you Mr….?"

"Rutherford! Barclay Rutherford." The man confidently answered, while offering a handshake that Steven reluctantly accepted. "May I come in?" Steven stepped aside, and ushered him in.

He continued talking as he entered, taking in all the sights around him.

"What a marvelous relic of a house, Mr. Spencer. Such a pity it will have to be razed."

"Excuse me!" Steven exclaimed with disbelief. "Over my dead body."

"That would be a drastic measure." Barclay arrogantly quipped. "I'm the attorney representing the rightful owners of the Branchview Estate."

"I don't recall ever requesting your services, Mr. Rutherford." Steven countered. "I am the only rightful owner of this property."

"Not according to the title which list my client, Midland Enterprises as the owner."

"I can't wait to see what type of scam this is." Steven sarcastically responded.

Rutherford laid his briefcase down on the Foyer table, and popped it open, producing a copy of the title, and other paperwork.

"I'm afraid you're quite mistaken about that. Daniel Branch III sold the property to my client prior to his passing. It's stated in this paperwork that the property would officially change hands exactly three years after the signing."

Steven impatiently grabbed the paperwork, and surveyed it.

"This has to be a forgery. My brother would never sell this property without discussing it with the rest of the family."

Rutherford tgook the paperwork from his hand. "Mr. Spencer! It is common knowledge that your brother was a notorious drunk, and often made brash decisions." He replied with a smirk.

Just then, the doors to the Sitting Room opened, and Loraine marched into the Foyer, unaware that the two men were still there. She quickly halted with a shocked expression that quickly turned to boiling anger.

"What in the bloody hell are you doing here, Clay?"

"Loraine!" He exclaimed with the same arrogant smirk. "Is that any way to greet a dear old friend?"

"I'd rather welcome a venomous serpent into my house before I would you." She fumed.

"My feelings are so hurt, sweetheart." Clay mocked. "Especially after all those intimate moments we spent together."

"I loathe the idea that I ever had feelings for a low life scoundrel like you."

Steven displayed puzzlement, as he observed the bickering between the two. Impatient, and unable to listen any further, he intervened.

"Mr. Rutherford! I think it's time you left, before I have you physically removed from the property."

"If Steven doesn't perform that task, I certainly will." Loraine further added with raging anger.

Rutherford remained calm as he pulled another set of papers from his case, and handed them over to Steven.

"Very well then! Consider this as you being served notice, Mr. Spencer." He said with a smug grin. "You're to report to district court on the date listed. Failure to show will result in your arrest, and we will be forced to physically remove everyone from these premises."

Steven shockingly looked over the first few pages, as Rutherford sarcastically chuckled, and headed for the door. He paused before leaving, not being able to resist throwing one more jab.

"It was a pleasure seeing you again, Loraine."

"Get out of my house, you slithering snake!" She growled as he confidently departed.

Once he was gone, Steven looked to his wife with disbelief.

"Would you mind telling me what in the hell that was all about?"

"Oh! Clay and I were engaged in England prior to you and I meeting here in the States."

"And, you never considered telling me about this?"

"I didn't feel it was important enough to mention" She sighed with frustration. "I never really loved him. I was just young and naïve, but fortunately, I realized what an irreputable asshole he was before it was too late."

Before another word could be said, Tina and Angelique waltzed through the front door, and into the awkward fray.

"We're ready to go, Lori." Tina announced cheerfully as she gently bounced baby Dimitri in her arms.

Angelique quickly sensed the tension in the room, and reacted.

"I think we may have walked in at a bad time."

"I apologize!" Tina quickly remarked. "We'll take Dimitri to the Nursey while you two finish your conversation."

"That's quite alright, Tina. We're finished here." Steven sternly answered, as he motioned for her to hand the baby off to him. "I'll take Dimitri, and you ladies can be on your merry way."

Loraine spoke under her breath as she breezed by him, marching toward the door.

"We'll discuss this later."

"Yes, we will." Steven answered as his wife stormed ahead of the other two women, who exchanged a quick eye roll before parting.

When the ladies were gone, Steven kissed the baby on the forehead, and headed toward the South Wing, conversing with the wide eyed toddler as he strolled through the doorway.

"Well, young man! Women and life! See what you have to look forward to?"

Chapter Seven:
The Resistance Takes Shape

In a basement communications center of Branch Consolidated Industries, Special Agent Joey Arcovio and her computer intelligence team are poised for the great transition that will separate Branch Consolidated and its' affiliated companies from the system now dominated by the forces of the Secret Society and the Conglomerate International Bank. They christened the new stock option system as the BCI Exchange which would only operate within the new gold and silver based BranchCoin cybercurrency that they originated.

Agent's Guitierez and Banerjee, along with other FBI agents loyal to the cause, supervised the operation, while Gerard, Philip, and Ezekiel all observed.

"Okay, people!" Guitierez announced. "The mission will commence in exactly 30 minutes." He paced the room. "The enemy will attempt to buy up all of our stock at the opening bell, but they won't have the capability of accessing the new internet we brought online last night. At least without hacking into it. It is imperative that we shut down all unauthorized IP addresses that are not a part of our new internet operation. We must accept only those pre-approved investors, and only those who have transitioned currency into the BranchCoin system." He chuckled. "In reality, it's illegal as hell. But in war, all options are on the table." He paused to glance at the clock. "You people are the best of the best. Let's win this round."

"Yeah! Let's cook these bastards." Joey enthusiastically added.

"Imagine the surprise, when our enemy realizes that we are operating on an alternative internet." Gerard mused.

"I'd give anything to see the expression on Laszlo's face when he realizes we beat him at his own game." Ezekiel added with a confident grin.

Meanwhile, in an undisclosed location in London, a similar operation was taking place, under the supervision of Kenneth Laszlo, Morningstar, and high ranking leaders of the Secret Society, and the Conglomerate International Bank. Laszlo confidently paced in front of the group, and began to briefly outline their goals for the day.

"Ladies and gentlemen. This is our day to claim victory over the resistance." He mustered a sly grin. "Our enemies at Branch Consolidated will fail before they ever get any footing." He laughed. "The fools actually think they can fight us."

Laszlo flipped to a blank page of a large note pad on an easel, and began to scribble his plan on it.

"The first step we all took was to sell off all of our gold and silver assets, and we converted it into fiat cash. That was done before the close of yesterday's market." He sketched further on the pad, and spoke while doing it. "That caused the gold and silver market to lose close to 50% of its' value." He turned to face the assembly once again. "This morning we will utilize our cyber army all over the world to use all of our assets to buy up the majority of BCI stock, therefore becoming majority holders, and virtual owners of the exchange." He chuckled arrogantly. "Their gold and silver base currency that they plan to convert into their own form of cybercurrency, will fail miserably, and become worthless. Our own cybercurrency, which will be serviced by our old friends at the Conglomerate International Bank, will become the new world currency." He flipped a page, and sketched further as he talked. "That, my friends, will explode our wealth and power, while the undesirables of this world will be propelled into poverty, and lose their freedoms. Small businesses, and corporations who fled to the new platform will all go under, and our large conglomerates will grow, and become even richer." He chuckled once again. "The entire world will be at our mercy."

The room erupted in applause and cheers, and a confident Laszlo turned his attention to Morningstar who sat observing with a critical eye, with his arms folded firmly in front of him. Laszlo motioned to draw everyone else's attention toward him as well.

"I have to ask our trusted advisor, Mr. Morningstar, what his thoughts are on our glorious plan."

"You're The financial expert, Mr. Laszlo. I most certainly trust that your plan will work." He stood and faced the others in the room. "I only request that I be the first to dance on the rubble of the Branch empire, and the graves of Steven Spencer and Gerard LeRoux."

The room erupted once again with boisterous laughter, while Laszlo and Morningstar exchanged assured glances. Laszlo hit the buttons on the remote to light up a bank of televisions lined along the wall.

"Let the show begin."

Within a few short minutes of the opening bell, it became obvious that something was wrong. The entry level stock values on the BCI exchange were remaining stationary. Laszlo immediately sensed that something was awry.

"What in the hell is going on? We were supposed to have already purchased the bulk of the stock."

His cell phone rang, and he answered with angry impatience.

"Talk to me." He waited. "What do you mean, we're being blocked from purchasing stock?" He listened further. "Impossible! Another internet platform could not exist without our knowledge." He sneered as he listened further. "Earn your damn money, and hack into that platform ASAP." He hung up, cutting the conversation short.

Morningstar glanced over to him with a concerned look.

"What's going on?"

"Those bastards are operating on an alternative internet. We're blocked out."

"Do something! Dammit!" Morningstar demanded.

Moans and rumbles rose from the assemblage in the room as they watched the screen.

"Look at the gold and silver prices." A man in the room yelled out. "They're going through the ceiling."

Laszlo took a place in front of the screens, and observed with disbelief.

"They bought up all the gold and silver we dumped" He dialed out on his phone, and spoke into it with urgency. "Start buying as much gold and silver as you can before it reaches any higher." He demanded. He stayed on the line as another person in the crowd called out.

"Look at BranchCoin!" Another person in the crowd called out. "Its' value is ticking higher by the second."

"You mean to tell me we're being blocked from making any trades at all." Laszlo listened for another moment. "We're supposed to have the most hack resistance system in the world, and now you're telling me that they've seized our computers." He paused, waiting for an answer on the other end. "Fix it! Now!" He angrily ended the call.

"The New York Stock Exchange has already lost over a quarter of its' value." A woman from the Conglomerate bank cried out with panic in her voice. "The fiat dollar is dropping fast as well. We'll lose everything!"

"We have to shut the Exchange down, or the market will crash." Another man suggested with panic in his voice.

"You blithering moron! Do something!" Morningstar demanded.

Laszlo turned to another man in the room with urgency. "Arthur! Make the call to New York! Shut the damn thing down!"

"How in the blazes could our plan fail so miserably?" Morningstar growled.

"I don't know. I thought surely we had this." Laszlo replied with frustration. "They must have had some sort of outside help. There's no other way they could have countered our strategy by themselves."

Morningstar let out a guttural rumble, and his eyes glowed red as he turned away with anger.

"Poseidon and Zeus!" He angrily seethed.

"What did you just say?" Laszlo asked, startled by his ungodly demeanor.

"Nothing, you fool." He roared, slamming his fist on the thick walnut table, and splitting it down the middle. Everyone in the room reacted with shocked silence as Morningstar let loose with his wrath.

"I'm taking control of this operation from this moment on, since no one else in this room has the capability, or intelligence to do so." He declared while pacing like a caged animal, eyeing everyone with an intimidating glare. "I refuse to let a small minority of bloody Patriots defeat our cause." He paced some more, and began to settle a bit. "We will plan a string of disastrous events that will take place around the world simultaneously. Explosions! Mass killings! Whatever it takes to bring the common individual to their knees, begging for mercy." He paused to concentrate for a moment, then turned with a sinister grin. "I intend to deploy every effort possible to destroy Branch Consolidated, and I further demand that someone kill that bastard, Steven Spencer."

Laszlo apprehensively approached him, and displayed the Trident business card that Philip had left with him.

"You muttered the name Poseidon." He cautiously stated. "Would that have anything to do with this business card that my overbearing visitor left?"

Morningstar snatched the card from his hand, and crumpled it.

"That's no concern of yours." He roared. "You need to put your energies into repairing this disaster that just took place."

Morningstar stormed out of the room, leaving Laszlo in pensive thought.

Back at BCI headquarters, a more celebratory reaction came from those watching the screen.

"They just closed down the New York Stock Exchange." Joey stated as she continued to work diligently. "We were successful in seizing and blocking all of their servers.

Agent Guitierez watched the screen over her shoulder as she worked at a lightning speed pace.

"Things have definitely shifted to our favor for the time being. In less than an hours time, many average people have become millionaires." He replied enthusiastically.

"I can't believe we actually pulled it off." Banerjee joyfully proclaimed.

"We may have won this round, but they'll definitely regroup, and come after us again." Guitierez warned.

"You're right about that." Gerard added. "We have to predict their next move, and counter it."

"I'll meet with Philip and Steven later today to discuss the issue." Ezekiel suggested.

"Good." Guitierez nodded with determination. "Thankfully, tomorrow's Saturday. So, let's finish up the day, catch our breath, and plan on meeting back here tomorrow to go over that new strategy."

It was late in the afternoon when Loraine and the other women pulled up in front of the grand entrance of a large estate with beautiful landscaping in Cambridge. Loraine peered out the open window of her SUV, and looked up at the marquee above the opened gate that read "Sharondale", and then glanced ahead at the sprawling mansion.

"I don't see an address, but this has to be the place that the woman at the auction house told us about." She stated.

"It's every bit as grand as our own Branchview." Tina added.

"I can't wait to lay eyes on my Mario once again." Angelique sighed.

"Just be careful of what you say, Angelique." Loraine warned. "Let me do all of the talking."

Loraine slowly proceeded through the gate, and up the short drive to the loop around that housed an enormous, ornate fountain in the middle. All the women marveled at the intricate detail in its' design. She parked within the circle, and they all proceeded to the large entryway of the grand house. Before they could even knock, an attractively dressed woman in her mid 40's opened the door to greet them.

"I certainly don't recall putting out a casting call for my new movie." She quipped. "Why else would I be graced with the presence of such beautiful women?"

"Oh! We're not here for that." Loraine chided with amusement. "The Cambridge Auction House sent us here to view a statue that you purchased a few years back."

"And which one would you like to see, Mrs. Spencer?" She asked with a smirk.

"How do you know my name, and may I request a formal introduction?" Loraine asked.

"Pardon my rudeness, Mrs. Spencer. My name is Sharona Van Arsdale. Please come in."

"So, that's why this place is called Sharondale." Angelique commented.

Sharona only answered with a fake smile, and ushered the women into the Foyer.

These two women are my friends, Tina Seagraves and Angelique Devine.

Sharona only acknowledged them with a half-hearted nod, and continued conversing with Loraine.

"I'm a longtime fan of your books, but I recognize you more as the wife of the great Steven Spencer." She noticeably sneered at the mention of Steven's name.

"Do you know my husband?"

"Of course." She quipped. "Why wouldn't I be fully aware of the man who killed my father?"

"Ms. Van Arsdale, I can assure you that my husband did no such thing. Steven is a kind, and gentle man who would never hurt anyone." Loraine shot back in defense. "I don't even have any clue who your father is."

"Perhaps the name Charles Laszlo will ring a bell?"

In a quick moment of shock, Loraine and Tina exchanged a fleeting glance at each other.

"I believe you know my brother Kenneth as well. He's certainly not a fan of Branch Consolidated Industries." She sensed the quiet uneasiness in the women, and changed the subject promptly.

"Nevertheless, I still welcome lovers of the arts, regardless of our differences." She motioned to a room beyond two large cathedral style doors. "Shall we have a look at that statue, ladies?"

The women proceeded into the room which rivaled the Grand Corridor and Ballroom at Branchview in both size and grandeur. Lining the sides of room, as well as the far end, were countless life sized statues of only men. The majority of them were posed in a defensive nature, some clothed, some not. But they all had terrified expressions on their faces which lent a sense of horror to the dimly lit hall. In the center of the room was a circular fire pit that housed an eternal flame. Though quite ornate, it had as much charm as a medieval torture chamber.

"Welcome to my hall of statues." Sharona proudly proclaimed.

"They're all men!" Angelique remarked.

"Of course, they are, Ms. Devine. No one can ever accuse me of being a lesbian."

"How are you able to keep that flame constantly lit?" Tina inquired as she curiously examined it. "It seems to be coming from the center of the concrete."

"I assure you. There is a pipe there. We have our own natural gas well on the property. The only way it can be shut off is by that valve on the side of the pit." Sharona answered in a snooty tone. "I like to call that my eternal flame."

At the far end of the room, the naked statue of Mario stood gazing forlornly into space. Angelique ignited with excitement when she saw him.

"There he is!" She yelled, running over, and throwing her arms around it.

Loraine and Tina couldn't help but notice the eyes of the statue come alive with joy.

"It seems that your beautiful friend has the same passion for that statue as I do." Sharona remarked.

The women strolled over, and watched as Angelique lovingly stroked the sides of his face with her hands, and kissed him.

"Oh my!" Sharona exclaimed. "I'm getting quite heated up just watching this. I certainly hope my handsome statue doesn't respond in a stimulating way."

"Whew!" Tina quipped. "They certainly weren't lying when they said he was well endowed."

"I'd like to buy him." Loraine stated firmly. "How much would you be asking?"

"I'm sorry, Mrs. Spencer." Sharona boldly answered. "He's not for sale."

"Oh! Come now, Ms. Van Arsdale." Loraine pleaded. "Everything has a price."

"I have all the money I need, Mrs. Spencer. The statue stays."

Both Loraine and Tina reacted with disappointed sighs.

"Now, if you'd please pry your horny friend from my statue before she sheds her clothes as well, I'd greatly appreciate it. I have many obligations I need to tend to, and very little time."

Both Loraine and Tina approached Angelique, to pull her away from Mario.

"Come along, sweetheart." Tina sadly lamented. "It appears we've worn out our welcome."

Angelique resisted, and wept sadly as the women tried to lead her from her long lost sweetheart. Tears rolled down Loraine's face as well as she tried to console her.

"It'll be alright, sweetheart." She whispered. "I promise we won't give up on you."

Loraine glanced back at the statue, whose eyes were also now filled with deep sorrow.

"We'll be back for you, Mario." She whispered. "I promise you that."

As the women were led from the dark, cavernous hall, Loraine felt the desperate eyes of the other statues pleading for her help. It was almost too much to bear. She could tell that it greatly affected Tina as well, who busied herself consoling a heart broken Angelique.

As they all exited once again into the Foyer, Loraine heard an all too familiar voice come from the top landing of the stairs.

"Darling! Have you given any thought as to where we can dine tonight?"

Loraine's eyes filled with anger as Barclay Rutherford revealed himself when he reached the second landing. He paused with his usual arrogant smirk when he saw her.

"How graced can I be to encounter my former sweetheart twice in one day?" He sprinted down the last few steps, and placed his arm around Sharona. "Perhaps, you decided to follow me."

"Don't flatter yourself."

"And you brought two very lovely friends as well." He quipped with wide eyed stares toward the women.

"Neither of which would ever have any interest in a scoundrel like you." Loraine seethed.

"I see you and Mrs. Spencer are somewhat intimately acquainted." Sharona stated with obvious disdain. "Was she one of your little brief affairs?"

"Hardly." He laughed. "Loraine and I were once very close when we were both still in England."

"A fact that I'll forever regret." Loraine replied.

While Barclay and Loraine were bickering, the curious eyes of Angelique surveyed the pictures on the surrounding walls. One portrait in particular caught her attention.

"That's her!" She announced, pointing as she marched toward the painting.

All conversation stopped, and everyone focused on Angelique, who had become emotionally overcome with anger.

"That's that bitch, Liddy McPherson." She proclaimed. "She's the one who did this to me and my Mario.

Loraine and Tina exchanged quick, panicked looks, while Sharona adopted a more enlightened expression.

"So, you're somehow acquainted with my grandmother." Sharona stated as she strolled closer with her arms firmly crossed in front of her. "How could that possibly be? She's been dead for many, many years." She swung around and peered at Loraine with intimidating eyes. "How coincidental that she was killed by a Branch as well."

Sharona sauntered uncomfortably close to Angelique as the young woman trembled.

"Now I see the resemblance, my dear." She nodded. "You were the other statue at the auction. And, how on earth is it that you now live and breathe?" She turned to address Loraine and Tina in a hushed voice. "Could it be by some supernatural magic?"

"You had no right to take him away from me." Angelique retorted. "He created me with his own hands, and I loved him."

"I had every right to take him away." Sharona countered defiantly. "He was the final piece of my grandmother's collection."

"All of which were once alive, I'd venture to say." Loraine boldly remarked.

Sharona only answered her statement with an arrogant grin, and sauntered closer to her and Tina.

"Need I warn all of you that I possess enough wealth and power that I could devastate your lives with a simple wave of my pinky finger."

"Oh! Let me warn you, sister!" Loraine fumed. "You wouldn't want to know the power that I possess in my little finger."

The comment prompted an amused grin from Tina, and struck a raw nerve with Sharona.

"I do believe it's time for you ladies to leave." Sharona stated with a snap of her finger.

A large framed, young body guard who had unnoticeably been sitting in a corner chair, came to her beckoned call.

"Bruno! Would you kindly escort these ladies out of my house."

As the women were herded toward the door by the big brute, Loraine's eyes glanced toward Barclay with a hardened glare.

"We'll see you soon, Lori." He remarked in a taunting fashion.

"For your sake, I certainly hope not." She replied.

After they departed, and the door shut, Barclay turned to Sharona.

"What should we do about them?" Barclay asked. "I know Lori well enough to know that she's not one who easily gives up."

"And neither do I." She answered with pondering thought. "I need to find out what sort of strange, enchanted magic brought our beautiful stone princess back to life."

"I sense an evil plot brewing in that wicked little mind of yours."

She simply chuckled with a sinister laugh, and pulled him in close for a passionate kiss.

At Branchview, Steven, Philip, and Ezekiel were gathered around a computer screen in the study, summarizing the successes of the day's events.

"I'd have to say, with all things considered, the BCI index had quite a successful launch." Ezekiel declared.

"Indeed! BranchCoin rose in value over 50%, and we now own at least 70% of the known gold and silver in the world." Steven added before taking a quick sip of coffee. "I also think it was a very wise decision to keep it a private exchange, specifically for our partners, and preapproved investors." Steven added. "Being on a separate internet, will make it difficult for them to hack into our system as well."

"I think in the long haul, it will smother out the Secret Society and the Conglomerate Bank's influence, and give the power and wealth back to the ordinary people that deserve it." Ezekiel stated with enthusiasm.

Steven raised his coffee cup in a cheer. "Here! Here! We've only just begun."

Philip leaned back in his seat in pensive thought. "We certainly can't rest on our laurels." He warned. "We caught them off guard, but I'm sure they're working overtime to counter us." He leaned forward, cupping his hands. "We have to stay ahead in the game. Their fiat dollar will be destroyed, but we have to be sure that their rival cyber currency fails as well."

"I agree, Philip." Steven replied. "We have to convince our partners to have their merchants convert to our currency before they beat us to the mark. All of our merchant's in Lockeport already accept the BranchCoin."

Steven's cell phone that was resting on top of his desk rang, and he glances down at it.

"That's Lori! I'll put it on speaker so we can see what those ladies are up to." He chuckled, before answering. "Hello there, sweetheart."

"Steven!" Loraine's voice spoke with urgency. "We found out where Mario is. But do you know anything about a woman named Sharona Van Arsdale?"

"I know she was the much younger wife of film mogul, Devon Van Arsdale. When he died rather mysteriously, she inherited everything, and became one of the richest women in the world."

"I wouldn't be surprised if she had something to do with that mysterious death." She quipped.

"I'm assuming that she's also the one who now possesses Mario."

"And, that's not all." She sighed. "Were you aware that she is the daughter of Charles Laszlo, the sister of Kenneth Laszlo, and the granddaughter of Liddy McPherson?"

Steven sat back in his chair, totally blown away by the revelation, while Philip and Ezekiel listened with full interest. "That's one evil upbringing." He replied.

"There's one more thing you should know." She continued. "That scoundrel, Clay Rutherford was there with her as well. I assume they must be an item."

"Where are you now, Lori?" Steven asked with deep concern.

"We stopped for a bite to eat just outside of Cambridge."

"Lori! You and the ladies need to get out of there, right away." Philip spoke up, and warned with urgency. "You walked directly into the devil's den."

"But we just can't keep poor Mario with that horrible woman."
Philip and Steven exchanged frustrated eye rolls.

"You need to listen to me and Philip. Get out of that town, and head back to Branchview right now." Steven drew an anxious breath before continuing. "I promise, Philip and I will find a way to get Mario back."

"Philip, darling!" Tina's voice chimed into the conversation. "If you could have only seen how much love Angelique has for him. It reminded me of you and I."

"Tina! Now listen!" Philip ordered with restrained impatience. "Don't make me come up there, and get you." He warned. "These are very powerful and dangerous people. For once, please let your common sense overrule your emotions."

"Are you saying that I'm over emotional?" Tina defiantly asked in response, prompting Philip to growl, as he tried to restrain his anger. Ezekiel couldn't help but be amused as he silently listened.

"Lori! Please just come home like we say." Steven pleaded. "I promise you again, we'll come up with a failsafe plan."

"Oh! Very well!" She complained. "We'll be rather late, however."

"I love you, sweetheart!" Steven concluded with a forced smile.

"Oh yes! I know! Ta, ta, darling!" She ended the call in a huff.

"Women!" Philip vented. "You think they'll actually listen to us?"

"One can only hope for a miracle." Steven sarcastically answered as he glanced at the clock. "I have a school board meeting that I have to attend after dinner." He looked to Ezekiel. "I'll see you at BCI headquarters tomorrow." He looked back to Philip. "I'll see you when I get back. Hopefully by then, the ladies will have returned."

"If not, then we'll obviously have an unplanned road trip." Philip replied with worried frustration.

In a darkened Parlor of his London residence, Laszlo paced impatiently, while Morningstar relaxed in a high back chair, sipping pensively from his glass of wine.

"How could they have been a step ahead of us the whole time?" Laszlo ranted. "They countered our every move with mastery."

"I suppose you need to motivate your subordinates to find out." Morningstar quipped.

"You know something. Don't you?" Laszlo pointed with an accusing finger. "You better not be working against us."

Morningstar set his glass of wine down, calmly stood, and moved intimidatingly close to Laszlo.

"Do you have any idea who I am, Mr. Laszlo?"

"Of course." Laszlo turned away. "You are the worldwide leader of the Secret Society."

"Among many other things, I should say." Morningstar smugly replied. "Were you ever curious as to the origin of my name?"

Laszlo turned, and faced him once again, and mockingly began to laugh. "You do have quite an ego. Don't you, Morningstar?

Morningstar ignited with rage, gripping him by the throat with one hand, and holding him up, while his feet dangled two feet above the floor. Laszlo was unusually wide eyed with fear, and in awe of his immense strength.

"Let's get one thing perfectly clear." Morningstar sneered, while his eyes glowed bright red. "I don't work for you. You and your friends work for me." He paused with a deep growl that shook the room. "You all sold your souls, and I purchased them. I am your master, and you'll do as I say!" He roared, as he tossed Laszlo to the floor like a discarded toy.

Laszlo gazed up at Morningstar with terror in his eyes. "If you are indeed who you say you are, then who is the man with the trident business card?"

"I'm sure you've heard of the god, Poseidon." He answered in a gravel tinged voice.

"Only from mythology. Surely, he isn't real."

"Just like me. He indeed is very real!" Morningstar roared as he shapeshifted into his true form, causing Laszlo to recoil in further fear and shock.

Laszlo hyperventilated as he gazed at the grotesque figure before him. "Did he really kill my father?" He asked.

"Yes." Satan grumbled. "He's also been aiding the American Patriots in their struggle against us."

"Surely you have the power to destroy him." Laszlo timidly stated.

"That, I do." Satan sneered. "But I'm not permitted to do so by the decree of the Divine Creator."

"You mean to tell me that God actually exist as well?" Laszlo inquired with amazement.

"Oh! Most certainly!" He wheezed with anger. "In everything you see." He motioned all around them. "But this world belongs to me, and I will claim it once and for all when I defeat the Creator's Son, and kill the appointed gods in the great battle."

"If you're speaking of Armageddon, this is all a bit much for me to take in all at once. I am an atheist." Laszlo stated as he relaxed a bit. "The Christian Bible seems like a wild fairy tale."

"I assure you that it isn't, Mr. Laszlo. And you're a fool if you don't believe me."

Satan paced away from him for a moment, then shape shifted back to the likeness of Lucifer Morningstar, before offering his hand, and helping Laszlo back to his feet.

"Enough chatter for now." He paused with a smirk. "Beginning tonight, I want your people to create utter chaos throughout the world. We will strike fear into the hearts of the common population. They will comply, or they will die." He chuckled. "Can I count on you not to disappoint me again, Mr. Laszlo?"

Laszlo replied with a slight nod, and Morningstar responded with a grunt.

"Now, go about it, and make it happen." He ordered, as he turned to depart the room.

As he reached the door, he turned to address him once again.

"And, Kenneth…You are never to speak to anyone about what we discussed, or what you saw here tonight." He warned. "If you do anything to compromise my true identity, I will bring insufferable death to you, and all those close to you." He paused to drive home his point. "Am I clear on that?"

Laszlo swallowed the threat hard, nearly sucking his Adam's apple into his chest. "Loud and clear, sir."

Chapter Eight:
The Battle Intensifies

The town hall in Lockeport was brimming to capacity as citizens crammed in to protest the Progressive curriculum set down by the school board. Steven sat in the front row with the LeRoux's, their daughter Deanna, Mary Wallace, and Eddie and Sandy Benson. The school superintendent, Latasha Hampton sat in the center of a long table on the elevated stage, flanked by the other board members. She eyed the crowd with visible disdain, while maintaining what appeared to be a permanent stink face expression.

Mary and Sharie challenged her with a hardened glare of their own.

"Who does that uppity woman think she is anyway?" Mary quipped to Sharie.

"If that sister thinks she can intimidate me, she better think wiser of it." Sharie replied with indignance.

Latasha pounded a gavel on the table to silence the crowd.

"I'd like to open the meeting at this time." She rolled her eyes in an annoyed fashion before beginning. "It's come to my attention that many of you have shown displeasure with the enlightening curriculum that I have chosen."

"Enlightening!" A man near the back exclaimed. "You're teaching our children to hate their country."

She motioned to calm the upset crowd once again, and then set stern eyes on Steven.

"We have a respected pillar of the community among us tonight." She remarked with an arrogant smirk.

"Would you like to say a few words, Mr. Spencer?"

Steven shot up from his seat without hesitation. "It's come to my attention that what the young man in the back said is true." He challenged her with a stern glare. "I believe one of your teachers referred to the Constitution as an outdated relic, said there was no set gender, and stated that we are a racist country."

"Why do you find all that so hard to believe, Mr. Spencer?" She paused. "If you'd look back at the history of this country, you'd see that it was all true."

"If you were a legitimate educator, and truly knew your American history, Ms. Hampton, you'd know that was mostly false." Steven countered.

"He's right! We're not racist!" An angry woman complained, while Latasha kept focused on Steven, and grunted in a wise cracking way.

"Says the man with a family that was the biggest offender." She snidely replied.

"Some of the members of my family may not have been saints, but for the most part, many of them helped to further the cause of freedom, and they also generously contributed to charity." He fired back.

"Mr. Spencer's right." Mary stated. "They took me in as a member of the family, and treated me with respect." She nodded. "I'd still be living in a homeless camp if it wasn't for them."

"I can't tolerate you calling our country racist." Sharie added with anger. "If that was true, entitled underachievers like yourself would never occupy a position such as yours."

"You have no right to address me in that fashion, Mrs. LeRoux." Latasha complained with trembling anger.

"I beg to differ, Ms. Hampton." She defiantly replied. "I am a free woman, and can speak to you in any fashion I choose." She paused, standing firmly. "And, may I remind you that you are not the boss of me? You work for me, and the rest of the good people in this room."

"You tell her, sister!" A woman in the crowd yelled, as Gerard took the floor.

"My wife is right, and we have the power to fire you, or anyone else at that table."

"Fire the bitch!" A man yelled.

"Fire them all!" Someone else exclaimed

The room ignited with the repeated chants of "You're fired, you're fired!" While Deanna and Mary exchanged a fist bump, the rest of the Branchview family exchanged amused smirks.

Gerard silenced the crowd once again, then turned his attention back toward Latasha who held a stern stare on him.

"See!" Latasha pointed to the crowd. "I wouldn't be heckled in such a disrespectful way if I were a white woman."

"One shouldn't use the color of their skin as an excuse for not earning respect, Ms. Hampton."

"He's right!" A woman near the back stood up and exclaimed. "I'm Black, and proud of it. But I don't use my color as a crutch to get ahead of everyone else, and I teach my children not to do it either."

Latasha reacted with frustration, and focused on Gerard once again.

"Mr. LeRoux. I'm sure you've encountered prejudice many times in your climb to the top, and I'm sure that climb was tougher because you were Black."

"Perhaps you should know someone's history before you decide to put your foot in your mouth, Ms. Hampton." He paused with emphasis. "My ancestors were slaves who escaped to Canada via the underground railroad, and they were aided by good hearted White Americans that included members of the Branch and Locke family." He began to pace as he lectured. "I graduated at the top of my class at Guilford College, came to this country, and earned a position at Branch Consolidated. All these years later, without using my Blackness as a way to advance myself, I am now the President and CEO of that very same company." He stopped, and glared at Latasha, who was sinking in her seat. "That is what earning respect is all about, Ms. Hampton."

Latasha fumed, but dared not refute what Gerard had said. After a short pause in thought, he concluded.

"I follow the teachings of the great Martin Luther King, and I'd suggest that everyone else in this room do it as well. I look forward to a day when I am no longer identified as Black, or even African American." He glanced around the room. "Hell! I wasn't even born in Africa. I was born in Canada. I immigrated here, and I earned my citizenship to this country that I love dearly." He paused, and gestured to Steven, and the others. "I also look forward to a day when my good friends are not identified as White, and an enemy to my race. We're all Americans, dammit!" He vented, before pointing an accusing finger toward Latasha. "It's racist like you, Ms. Hampton who are continuing to divide us with your misleading rhetoric."

The crowd erupted in a standing ovation, and a frustrated Latasha slammed her notebook shut, stood, and angrily stormed from the room.

As Gerard humbly took his seat, he was greeted with a cordial, smiling nod from Steven, and the others. Sharie leaned in, kissed him, and whispered loudly in his ear.

"I am so proud of you, baby!" She proclaimed.

Gerard turned to scan the crowd, as the cheers, and claps persisted. Leaning against a back wall, the spirit of his great grandfather stood proudly watching with an exuberant smile on his face. Tears welled in Gerard's eyes, as he acknowledged his presence with a respectful nod. The spirit acknowledged him back, before turning, and disappearing as he strolled away.

In the outer portion of the meeting hall, Latasha pulled out her phone, speed dialed, and nervously waited for the other party to answer.

"Yeah, it's me!" She grumbled with indignance. "We have a huge problem here in Lockeport."

As the citizens filed out of the meeting hall, one of the board members, Pamela Priestly, waited patiently by the exit door. When she saw Steven and Gerard in the crowd, she waved her hands to get their attention.

"Mr. Le Roux! Mr. Spencer!" She called out, succeeding at getting them to look her way.

As both men strolled over toward her, she was eager to initiate a conversation.

"My name is Pamela Priestly. I'm one of the board members."

Both Gerard and Steven drew a sigh, anticipating a tongue lashing from the middle aged woman.

"First, I want to express my support for what you both said in there." She smiled. "I believe the children in our school system are being brain washed, and I was hoping you both might be of help."

"What more can we do, Mrs. Priestly." Gerard sincerely asked. "We've already publicly spoke our mind."

"I heard you were starting a private school called The Branchview Academy."

"That's correct." Steven answered. "But it's only for our own children, and those of our employees at Branch Consolidated."

"There's something you both should know." She nervously stated, as her eyes darted all around her. "Would you gentlemen take a walk with me outside? I wouldn't want the wrong people to hear our conversation."

The two men exchanged puzzled glances as she urged them on. Once a safe distance from the crowd, she began to speak once again.

"I'm not sure if either of you are aware, but I am the only board member that is actually from Lockeport." She stated as they strolled by the enormous fountain outside the hall. "All the others are from somewhere else, and were put into their positions by outside money."

"Where did this outside money come from?" Gerard inquired.

"I don't really know." She answered with visible frustration. "I do know that it is people with unlimited power and wealth." She continued with certainty. "They have threatened both me and my family for being at odds with the decisions of the other board members."

"I still don't understand what you want us to do, Mrs. Priestly." Steven stated. "We're only two men against what appears to be a very powerful influence."

"If you'd be willing to open your doors to other children of the community, I personally know many parents who would want to enroll their kids."

"That sounds like a wonderful thought." Steven sighed. "But it cost an enormous amount of money to educate children. We've had to split the costs with our employees to ensure that their kids are properly educated. We're just not fiscally prepared to educate the rest of the community as well."

"I know that many would be willing to pay." She replied. "Most of our high school aged children have already had their minds poisoned by the school system. It may be too late for them, but there's still hope for the younger children."

"I'm very sympathetic with your intentions, Mrs. Priestly. But as Steven said, we are in no position to be designated as an open enrollment Charter School."

"Gentlemen! I have 20 years of administrative experience, and I would be willing to resign my position in order to run your school at a meager salary. There are other frustrated, but dedicated teachers who would be on board with us as well." She stated in all sincerity. "I have faith that we can save the youth of this community."

Steven and Gerard exchanged anxious glances, as she hurried to conclude.

"Please sit down with me in the coming days." She pleaded. "I have so many ideas on how we could make this work."

Gerard and Steven exchanged a cautious nod.

"Very well, Mrs. Priestly." Gerard replied as he pulled a business card from his wallet. "Call me at my office Monday morning, and we'll discuss this further."

"Bless you both!" She exclaimed with much gratitude.

As the woman strolled away, Steven glanced at Gerard with a sigh. "Well! I'd be willing to bet that those outside sources have their roots in the Secret Society."

"I'd say that was an accurate assumption." Gerard wryly replied.

Among the other people leaving the meeting hall, Tre Russell strolled along the walkway with his mother, Priscilla.

"We need to somehow rid ourselves of these educators that want to divide this country, and send it back to the stone age." Priscilla commented with anger and frustration.

"I agree, mom." Tre answered. "I was lucky that you and dad took the time to preach truth, common sense, and good values to me."

Priscilla reacted only with a pleasing smile, as they continued on, enjoying the pleasant spring evening.

"I got to ask you this, mom. Who was that fine looking lady sitting with the LeRoux's?"

"Trevane Russell!" His mother came to a halt. "You know who that young lady is. She's their daughter, Deanna."

"That's Deanna LeRoux!" He exclaimed with much surprise. "The last time I saw her, she was a skinny little kid."

"Uh huh!" His mother answered with an all knowing smirk. "That child's done blossomed into a pretty young woman."

"She got a boyfriend?"

"Now how would I know that, son?" She quipped. "I'm supposing you just need to go ask her for yourself, before some other fella beats you to it."

"Yeah!" Tre answered with pondering thought. "I suppose you're right, mom."

"I know I'm right." She laughed.

At Sharondale, Sharona and Barclay relaxed in the Parlor, enjoying a nightcap. Sharona playfully rubbed her bare foot up and down his leg to pull his attention away from his laptop. He responded by setting it aside, and flashing a confident grin.

"Are you trying to seduce me, dear?"

"Is it that obvious?" She countered with a wicked grunt. "Actually, I want you to tell me all you know about Loraine Spencer."

"I could fill a whole evening with that." He laughed. "What do you want to know specifically?"

"Does she have some sort of magical powers?"

"When I knew her, she was a rather peculiar young lady." He looked off in thought as he recanted. "She studied science quite extensively, and was interested in all sorts of herbal, and natural remedies." He shrugged. "As far as I know, she didn't study any of the dark arts, or dabble in anything supernatural."

"Hardly seems like anyone you'd have interest in. How did you meet?"

"I was an acquaintance of her father, and met her when she was only 19." He paused in fond thought. "She was the sexiest little vixen I'd ever laid eyes on. I simply had to have her."

Sharona stiffened, and took on a stern demeanor. "So, obviously she must've been quite fascinated by a mature, dapper gentleman such as yourself."

"Oh yes!" We had quite an affair, and I had even asked for her hand in marriage."

"What happened?"

"One evening when her father and I were discussing business at a local pub, we came across a few charming ladies, and enjoyed a few too many drinks with them." He sighed.

"You naughty boy!" Sharona scolded.

"Needless to say, we carted these two women off to her father's residence where we engaged in some very steamy sex."

"Yum!" Sharona purred. "Do tell me more."

"In conclusion, Loraine happened to stop by to visit her father unexpectedly. She had a key, and she walked in on us."

"She must've been absolutely enraged." Sharona smirked.

"That's putting it mildly." He chuckled. "She left for the States a short time later, and I never saw her again until earlier today." He grew rather frustrated, and leaned into the conversation. "Why all this interest in Loraine Spencer?"

"It appears I've struck a nerve, darling." She smugly quipped. "Actually, I'm more interested on how she could've brought the beautiful Miss Devine to life." She stood, and began to pace in front of him. "If I could only learn her secret, perhaps I could bring my grandmother's statues to life as well."

"Have you lost your mind, woman?" Barclay sneered. "Whatever would be the reason for doing that?"

"Power, my dear Barclay! Power!" She exclaimed while lightly stroking the side of his face. "They would be my own personal slaves, and would obey my every command." She sat back down, and playfully ran her fingers through her hair. "I need you to do me a favor, and if you don't comply with my wishes, I will have my brother deal very harshly with you."

"What do you need?" He meekly sighed.

"I need you to arrange the kidnapping of Angelique Devine."

"For what purpose?"

"So that she can tell me everything she knows about bringing those statues back to life." She paused with emphasis. "Can I count on you to bring her here unharmed?"

"I can arrange it." He sighed. "What do you plan to do with her after she tells you everything you need to know."

"She's a very lovely girl." She giggled wickedly. "I'm sure she'll command a very high price to the elite clients within our human trafficking pipeline." She stood to conclude the conversation. "I'll be in bed waiting for you, darling."

"I'll be up shortly." He uttered in a low tone.

Sharona sashayed from the room, leaving Barclay to only ponder in anxious, and worried thought.

Back at Branchview, Steven returned from the meeting with the others. He was relieved to find Loraine, and the other women, keeping company with Philip, Ezekiel, and Meryl in the Sitting Room.

"Thank God you're back!" He exclaimed, as he rushed to kiss his wife.

"Oh Steven! Was there really ever any doubt?" She grunted. "Sometimes I think you totally discount my intelligence."

"Never your intelligence, my dear." He sighed. "It's more your perpetual stubbornness that worries me."

"Good grief!" Philip complained. "Could you two please save your marital bickering for a later time?" He scowled at both of them for a long moment, like a father scolding his children, before continuing. "Now, we need to come up with a plan to somehow rescue Mario from this horrible woman."

"I can't believe that Liddy McPherson was actually her grandmother." Loraine huffed.

"With that being the case, it appears Liddy either had affairs or was married to some of the richest men in New England." Steven commented.

"Somehow, something doesn't add up here." Ezekiel added. "If Liddy's son was the late Charles Laszlo, wouldn't he have been a warlock?"

"Who's to say he wasn't?" Meryl quipped. "We know he was a member of the Secret Society."

"Who cares about who was a witch, and who was a warlock?" Angelique complained. "That has nothing to do with rescuing my Mario."

"She's right!" Tina shot up from her seat. "It was little Olivia who broke the spell on Angelique. Perhaps she could do the same for Mario."

"Surely, you aren't suggesting that we take my child to that house of horrors?" Loraine countered.

"I absolutely forbid that from happening." Philip firmly interceded.

Steven drew a weary sigh, and stood to restore order to the room. "Please, everyone!" He reasoned. "It's been a very exhausting day for all of us. Give me a chance to research the Van Arsdale's a bit, and then we can devise a failsafe plan."

"Steven's right." Ezekiel stated. "We all need to rest our minds tonight, and work on this again tomorrow."

"I agree!" Angelique conceded. "I suppose my emotions are overriding my common sense. We need to know more about who we are dealing with here. Tina offered a sympathetic smile, and an assuring pat on her shoulder in response.

"With that said, I think that it's time for us all to retire." Philip said while he motioned Tina along. "Goodnight, everyone!"

The remaining attendees filed out of the Sitting Room as well, leaving only Steven and Loraine.

"I'm sorry I was short tempered with you." Steven apologetically stated. "I don't know what I'd do if I ever lost you."

"Oh, Steven! I'm sorry as well." Loraine sighed as the couple kissed.

"I suppose I should go to my office, and see what information I can pull up on the Van Arsdale's." Steven wearily commented. "Would you like to join me?"

"I would, but I need to text my mother, and have her meet me in the Grand Corridor. I have something very important to discuss with her."

Steven smiled, and gave an agreeing nod. "Will you wait up for me?"

"I'll keep the bed warm." She smirked.

A short time later, Loraine quietly paced into the enormous Grand Corridor. Only the dim accent lights along the walls and above the ballroom floor were illuminated. She settled onto her favorite bench, and searched the vastness of the room around her. In quiet, serene times like this she could almost feel the eyes of Branchview's past silently watching from the darkened shadows.

As she dreamily stared off in deep thought, she was initially interrupted by their cat, Midnight who had snuck onto the scene, and affectionately rubbed against her leg. Then the sound of heavy footsteps could suddenly be heard making their way with purpose across the tile floor. She fondly smiled to herself, and mumbled inaudibly. *"Mother.."*

Millie approached, wearing a short white silk robe, and black stiletto heeled shoes. Loraine couldn't help but be somewhat amused at her appearance.

"I certainly hope I didn't interrupt a romantic moment."

"Not quite." Millie chuckled. "Mr. Bill is already fast asleep." She sat down next to Loraine with a sigh. "I think I've worn the old boy out since he returned from England."

"That's far more information than I need to know." The two women shared a quick laugh.

"Now, what prompted you to summon your mum-mum at such a late hour?" Millie asked.

Loraine paused for a long moment, pondering what to say next. "Why didn't you ever tell me that I had a twin brother?"

Millie looked away, and sighed deeply. "How in the world did you find that out?"

"Let's just say that a very wise old spirit told me."

Millie responded with an understanding nod before continuing. "His name was Lawrence. He arrived 9 minutes before you." She emotionally struggled. "He was a stillborn."

"Yet, I lived? What on earth happened, mother?"

"Somehow, the umbilical cord got tangled around his neck in the womb, and he suffocated." She burst into tears. "I'd hoped I'd never have to speak of that tragic event ever again."

"Oh mum!" Loraine sympathetically embraced her. "I'm so sorry! But I still don't understand why you never told me."

Millie held her daughter at arms length, and stared intently into her eyes. "Because I never wanted you to think you were any less loved." She forced a painful smile. "When you came out next, my sorrow and pain quickly turned to joy when I saw that you were alive and perfect." She took a tearful pause. "Oh! What a beautiful baby girl you were."

"I can't imagine how hard all that must've been for you."

"It's not easy when a woman loses a child." Millie looked off into the darkness. "But I realize now, how blessed I was to have had such a beautiful daughter at the same time." She turned back toward Loraine, and gave an assured nod. "I am so proud of the woman you have become, and so thankful that you've given me two gorgeous grand babies."

"I have to ask you this, and then I promise I'll never speak of it again." Loraine stressed. "Was there a full moon that night?"

"Oh yes!" Millie exclaimed with a fond smile. "It was a beautiful summer moon. Of course, the emergency room was filled with crazies that night." She smirked. "There was some strange bloke in there that swore he was a werewolf. He put on quite a show, but thankfully never did transform." Both women laughed heartily for a moment. "Why do you ask?"

"You know that magical gift that Olivia possesses?" Loraine paused, as Millie intently listened. "As you know, I possess it as well."

"And, you're both twins of the Gemini moon." Millie concluded with an enlightened nod. "That makes you both all the more special."

"It should be interesting to see what sort of powers baby London possesses."

Millie looked thoughtfully into the darkness. "I can't help but wonder what baby Lawrence would have brought to this world, if only he had lived." She stated tearfully.

"I'm sure he would've been a very special person who would've been very protective of his little sister." Loraine paused, and smiled through sentimental tears. "I love you, mum!"

"I love you too, sweetie!" The two women embraced tightly.

From the dark shadows of the room, Daphne Branch observed the emotional scenario with a benevolent smile, and whispered softly to herself. "Well done, Lori."

Chapter Nine:
The Mysteries of The Atlantic

In the South Wing, a weary Steven departed the study, and he made his way to the Master Bedroom where he found Loraine had not yet returned. He put on some soothing music, and crawled beneath the covers. Bumpers followed, taking his spot at the foot of the bed, while Midnight also hurried into the room, where she snuggled in close to Steven.

As he settled in comfortably, he stared at the ceiling in deep thought. *"What a day."* He whispered with a sigh as the cat and dog appeared to be listening attentively. "Sometimes, I wish I could just escape all of this turmoil." He gently closed his eyes, and quickly drifted into a deep sleep.

In his dreams, his spirit left his body, while both cat and dog curiously and quietly observed. He drifted from the room, taking flight like a bird, flying high above the treetops of the vast estate. He breezed by the lighthouse, barely eluding the revolving beacon that split the darkness. He then landed gracefully on the beach near the water's edge. There, he paused looking outward to the ocean with a longing, and listened to the haunting Mermaid chants that carried on the night air like a laughing cackle. It brought a warm and pleasant smile to his face.

He began to pace into the water, until he was waist deep. Then without hesitation, he dived down below the depths, swimming like a speeding torpedo into a surreal world of scattered, decaying ship wrecks covered with barnacles, along a terrain seldom seen by the human eye. One particular shipwreck caught his attention. It was an old passenger ship with the name "North Atlantic" barely visible on its hull.

He swam closer to curiously check it out, and also noticed a large gaping hole in its side as though it had been hit by a torpedo. He pondered entering the wreck, but was joined by a pair of Nereid sentries who beckoned him elsewhere, and sped in front to lead the way. Several species of fish, including a pair of sharks whizzed by him, barely taking notice.

In no time at all, he glanced downward to see the lights of a spectacular, sprawling underwater city nestled at the deepest point of the Atlantic. *"Nereida"* he thought to himself, as the two sentries took hold of his hands, and led him spiraling toward the amazing sight. Several other Mermaids and Mermen cordially greeted him with a smiling nod as he swiftly swam by them.

Suddenly, Steven heard Loraine's voice calling to him, and he looked back upward, and into a blinding light that sent his spirit quickly reeling back to the bedroom. He abruptly awoke, gasping, flailing, and spitting up water. Loraine had entered the room, and turned on the overhead light, not realizing he was asleep.

"Steven! What on earth!" Loraine exclaimed as she hurried to his aid. "You're soaking wet, and you smell like sea salt."

Steven only blinked his eyes rapidly, and tried to catch his breath as he came to his senses.

"Stay right where you are, and I'll fetch you a bath towel."

Steven had somewhat recovered by the time Loraine returned to the room, and she immediately began to dab the towel around his face and matted hair.

"I'm guessing that you physically travelled somewhere in your dreams. It's been quite some time since that happened."

"I did. I swam to the depths of the ocean, and was escorted to a beautiful underwater city by two Nereid Warriors. I think it was the kingdom of Nereida."

"Do you think Amphitrite's spirit may have been involved?"

"She wasn't there."

"What do you think the dream was trying to tell you? There obviously had to be a message in it somewhere."

"I really don't know." Steven cluelessly shrugged. "But I can tell you that swimming at those depths was one of the most calming experiences I've ever felt." He struggled to find a further explanation. "I recall seeing a shipwreck called the North Atlantic that quite intrigued me. For some reason, it was all so strangely familiar."

"Perhaps you were experiencing déjà vu from a previous lifetime." She theorized. "What happened next?"

"As we approached the city, I heard your voice, and looked back toward the surface, and into a blinding light that pulled me back a bit too quick, I suppose."

"That was my fault." She sighed. "I saw Bumpers and Midnight bolt from the room like they were fleeing a fire, and my first instinct was to turn on the light, and investigate."

Steven uncomfortably reacted to his wet bed clothes and sheets. "We won't be sleeping in that bed tonight."

"That's fine. We can sleep in the guest quarters tonight." She smiled. "But first you need to get a shower. You smell like a giant tuna."

Steven stood up, and Loraine helped him to take his wet shirt off.

"Perhaps this giant tuna could persuade you to join him for that shower." He flirted, prompting a sly grin from Loraine.

"I don't believe you'll have to twist my arm, Mr. Spencer." She replied with a giggle.

Loraine swiftly slipped out of her dress, and wrapped her arms around Steven's waist.

"We've barely had time to catch our breath or even enjoy the things we love so much about this place." She sighed.

"I know." Steven replied as he pulled her in closer. "This has been very hard on all of us. But let's just forget all of that for tonight, and enjoy the peace and quiet of this grand old house."

"I'm definitely all for that."

The couple passionately kissed before Loraine lovingly rested her head against his chest with an expression of foreboding worry.

Steven slept peacefully throughout the rest of the night without any further unexpected journeys. He was early to rise the next morning, and anxious to get to the City Diner where he was to meet with Philip. As he passed from the South Wing to the Foyer, he noticed a good bit of the staff congregated in the Sitting Room, anxiously viewing the large screen TV. Curiously, he paused his progress to see what was going on.

"Good morning, everyone!" He joyfully announced. "What major event am I missing?"

"Oh! Mr. Spencer!" Mary exclaimed. "There's been a bunch of mass shootings, explosions, and disasters that took place overnight. Several people are dead."

Steven paused to view the reports with much concern. "The Secret Society is countering our moves." He muttered.

"You think the Secret Society is actually behind all of this?" Andrea asked. "What purpose would they have?

"To flex their power." He sneered. "They know we have them in a compromising position, and they are fighting back in the lowest possible way."

"But why attacks on innocent people?" Mary further inquired.

"Because they're evil, and want to spread fear among the population." He explained. "A fearful multitude is much easier to conquer."

"This is terrible!" Mrs. Porter replied. "What on earth can we do?"

"Not be afraid, and carry on with your lives as you normally would." He calmly answered as he turned to depart, but then abruptly turned back. "And quit listening to the lying bastards on the news. They're all in on it as well." He added angrily, before finally storming from the room."

It was shortly after 7:30 when he arrived at the City Diner. Philip could already tell by the expression on his face that he had heard about the world happenings.

"I won't even ask." He stated as Steven pounced into the seat across from him.

"What will they do next?" Steven asked with frustration. "These vermin have no soul."

"They're definitely keeping us on our toes." Philip added with equal frustration.

Suzie scampered to the table with a pot of coffee, and promptly filled Steven's cup.

"How are you this morning, Mr. Spencer?"

"Much better since I saw your smiling face, Suzie." He said with a wink.

She simply shook her head with a pursed smirk in response. "Two eggs scrambled, turkey sausage, and rye toast?"

"That sounds heavenly." He answered cheerfully.

All the while, Philip was watching a car that was cruising unusually slow in front of the diner. Suddenly, the window rolled down, and he spotted the barrel of a pistol aiming straight at them. With cat like reflex, he dived across the table, sending food and coffee flying, as a bullet shattered through the window glass. It whizzed past Philip's head, and propelled into the back of a man's shoulder that had been sitting at the counter.

Chaos and panic ensued inside the diner in those split seconds. Philip glanced up, still shielding Steven with his huge frame. He just caught a glimpse of the dark green sedan as it sped away down the main street of town. A dazed Steven, looked up as Philip awkwardly tried to get back up from his position.

"Are you okay, Steven?"

"I feel like I just got blind-sided by a linebacker. What in the hell just happened?"

"I believe someone just tried to kill you, my friend."

By that time, several other patrons were rushing to the aid of the wounded man, and Steven and Philip moved in to help as well. A young girl hurried in from the street holding her cell phone up.

"I caught it all right here on my I-phone." She yelled.

Philip and Suzie urgently moved toward the girl, while a still stunned Steven followed.

"Please! Let me have a look at that." Philip requested.

He grabbed the phone, and observed intently, only looking away long enough to glance at Suzie. "Can I borrow your pen and pad? I think she may have caught a license plate."

She handed them to him, and then her and Steven followed him to the counter, where he looked at the video once again, and quickly jotted down a number.

"Hmm! This is interesting." He stated while looking up. "It appears our shooters were driving a car with government plates."

"Who in the government would want to shoot up my diner?" Suzie frantically asked.

"That bullet was intended for me." Steven replied in a low tone. "I'll assume with certainty that the Secret Society was involved."

"That assumption would be correct, Steven." Philip remarked before handing the phone back to the girl, and looking back to Suzie. "You'll have to cancel that order. I need to get Steven to a safe shelter, and get this plate info to Agent Guitierez."

"What should I tell the police?"

"Anything but the fact that Steven was the intended target. We have to keep that information confidential."

The two men conversed as they cautiously exited the diner with heightened awareness of their surroundings.

"You saved my life in there, Philip. Thank you!"

"I'm almost sorry that we removed your powers of immortality after the great battle."

"At least I still have the power of the lion beast within me."

Philip gave him a friendly pat on the back of the shoulder. "I have a feeling that beast will be needed, but be very careful to suppress it in unnecessary situations." He sighed as Steven acknowledged him with a nod.

"I never had the chance to mention this at breakfast, but in my dreams last night, I did a bit of astral traveling." Steven stated as they quickly got into Philip's F-150 truck. "I swam to the depths of the Atlantic, and saw the city of Nereida."

"That's impossible!" Philip replied. "No mortal human has ever seen it."

"Count me as the first." Steven quipped in response. "It was so real, that I actually returned to my bed soaking wet, and spitting sea water. Lori witnessed it first-hand."

Philip was amazed, and pondered the issue for a moment after starting the engine.

"I should add that I saw a shipwreck named the North Atlantic. Does it have any significance that might strike a chord with you?"

"Not particularly." Philip pondered. "There had to have been a reason for that dream. I'll have to consult with Ezekiel about this." He glanced at Steven in all seriousness. "In the meantime, you must not tell anyone else about it. The Nereids and Oceanids are a secret civilization, and we can't divulge or compromise any of theirs, or the ocean's mysteries."

"I promise Lori and I will keep this to ourselves." Steven assured.

Philip shifted into gear, and began to drive away. "We'll talk about this later. Right now, we need to get this info to Agent G."

Chapter Ten:
The Mistress of Evil

At the Sharondale mansion in Cambridge, Barclay descended the stairs into the foyer area just as four lovely young women were departing the Parlor area with Sharona. He paused to greet them with a nod as they walked by, and his attention drew nervous giggles from them. He listened as Sharona spoke to them.

"Thank you, ladies for coming here at such an early hour." She turned to acknowledge Bruno, who stood sentry by the front door. "I'll have Bruno drive you to the studio for your first photo session, and then he'll return you to your homes."

Bruno gave a confident nod to Sharona as he ushered the girls out the door.

After the door had closed, Barclay turned his attention to Sharona with a sly grin. "Who were your beautiful young guests?"

"A group of young fools who just made me at least 2 million dollars richer." She giggled, before continuing. "Would you like to have breakfast on the lanai?"

"That sounds fine to me. But first, I'd like you to enlighten me on what exactly you mean. After all, I am the family's attorney, and should be kept up to speed on all your business affairs."

"They answered a casting call for my studio, and I chose them out of a list of several others." She sighed.

"I'd say that they were very lucky if that's the case."

Sharona answered with a carefree grunt. "Those foolish little wanna be's think I intend to make them stars. I can only imagine their reaction when they realize my true purpose."

Barclay clenched his eyes shut with building annoyance. "Just what is your plans for them, Sharona?"

"By this time tomorrow morning, they will be shuffled off to unknown parts of the world. Auctioned off to the highest bidders."

"That's human trafficking!" He exclaimed.

"It's what we call business, Mr. Rutherford." Sharona coldly responded. "Surely, you don't think I make my billions off of the movie industry alone."

"These girls have families. How do you intend to answer to them when they turn up missing?"

"I thoroughly screened them, my dear Barclay." She confidently answered, as she seductively ran her finger up his neck to his chin. "These girls have all severed their family connections, and have no serious relationships. They'll simply join the list of missing souls who will soon be forgotten."

Barclay appeared quite troubled by her answer, and Sharona took careful notice.

"Does that not sit well with you, Mr. Rutherford?" She sneered.

"I'd be lying if I said it didn't. These are people, not cattle."

"Let me remind you of the agreement you made with my brother when you chose to legally represent us. The only way out of that agreement would be for me to put a bullet through that clever brain of yours. You're either along for the ride or you're not." She stated with an evil expression that made Barclay's blood turn ice cold. "Am I making myself clear, darling?"

Barclay gave an almost regretful nod in response.

"Now, I'll expect you to pleasure me with a bit of late morning delight when we finish our breakfast." She boldly stated. "Then you and Bruno can figure out a plan to kidnap Angelique Devine."

Sharona sauntered away in triumphant arrogance, once again leaving Barclay in her wake, with thought filled anxiety.

Meanwhile, Philip, Ezekiel, and Agent Guitierez had arranged a secret meeting with Steven at Lighthouse Point. Steven glanced fondly out at the ocean as he waited for the three men to make their way up the beach.

"At least we picked a pleasant backdrop to discuss otherwise unpleasant issues." Steven quipped.

"This is the safest and most secure area we could think of." Ezekiel answered.

"So, did you gentlemen find out the identity of my would be assassin?"

Agent Guitierez stepped to the forefront to answer. "He's a rogue FBI agent named Nat Mullen." He stated with certainty. "He's one of the operatives assigned to this area."

"How in the hell did all these rogue agents, politicians, and their allies regain power?" Steven expressed with frustration. "I thought we defeated and exposed them."

"We didn't go deep enough into the Justice System." Guitierez replied with equal frustration. "The media never reported it to the public, and they were all pardoned, and allowed to return to their positions."

"And of course, they fixed the election so that their man, Gerald Terrell would defeat President Chalmers." Steven further fumed, while Guitierez acknowledged with an agreeing sigh.

"Obviously, just as we had thought, the Secret Society has put out a hit on you, Steven." Philip stated with great seriousness. "It's important that you keep yourself confined to the estate until further notice."

"I can't just sit around here, and put my life on hold." He protested. "Loraine and I have tickets to go to the Goodspeed Opera House to see a musical this weekend. We also have reservations at the Gelston House."

"You're just going to have to cancel." Ezekiel boldly ordered.

"It's in East Haddam for God's sake! Half the world doesn't even know where it's at on the map."

"The FBI and CIA could find you in the farthest regions of the world." Guitierez remarked.

"I'm still going!" Steven defiantly stated. "Loraine and I haven't had a romantic getaway since before the epidemic."

The other three men exchanged weary glances.

"In that case, Tina and I will just have to go with you." Philip suggested.

"I think Meryl would enjoy a good musical. Count us in as well." Ezekiel added.

"So much for a romantic getaway." Steven muttered under his breath while turning to Guitierez with a sigh. "You and Agent Bannerjee might as well come along too."

"We could use an escape from the norm." Guitierez smiled before continuing. "I also looked into Midland Enterprises. It's owned by the infamous mobster, Angelo Costanzo. We've successfully tied him to several property scams, drug dealings, and most recently to human trafficking. But somehow, he's always been able to weasel out of every indictment."

"Sounds to me like he has a lot of insider help." Steven theorized.

Guitierez answered with a reluctant nod. "Unfortunately. But the good news is, Agent Arcovio was able to hack into the recorder of deeds office, and change the ownership back to the Branch Family Estate."

"I'd pay to see Mr. Costanzo's face when that's revealed in court tomorrow." Philip chuckled.

"I also did a little research on Sharona Van Arsdale." Guitierez continued. "She's been pegged as an accomplice to Costanzo in the human trafficking ring. It appears she gets the girls by holding fake auditions for her studio."

"And, let me guess. She's also managed to evade prosecution." Steven replied disdainfully, while Guitierez gave another weary nod.

"Her and Costanzo continually slide like an omelet on Teflon." Guitierez sarcastically added.

"On a more positive note." Ezekiel interjected. "Branchcoin continues to climb on the BCI Index, and more of our stores and distributors are switching over to it."

"On that note, I should probably get back to the bunker before Agent Bannerjee sends out a search party." Guitierez stated with raised brow. "Good day, gentlemen."

As he walked away, Philip couldn't help but be amused. "That woman has him wrapped around her finger." He then turned abruptly to Steven. "What did you find out about the North Atlantic?"

"I found out there have been several ships with that name over the years, but one small passenger line stands out." He paused. "It was torpedoed by the Germans in World War II. One hundred and seventeen people perished. Although many attempts were made, the wreckage was never found."

"That has to be our ship. If it was anywhere near Nereida, it would be at a depth that no human could endure." He turned to Ezekiel. "I can't think of any significance it may have to us or to the Nereids and Oceanids. Do you recall anything about it, brother?"

Ezekiel only shrugged cluelessly, and shook his head no, before putting his full focus on Steven. "I'll secretly be in attendance at your court date, just in case you may need me."

Steven gave him a thankful nod, and Philip then took control of the conversation once again.

"I took notice that a Judge Henderson will be presiding. From what I understand, he is an upstanding representative of justice. But my intuition tells me that I should pay him a little visit this afternoon."

"Be cautious, brother!" Ezekiel warned.

"I suppose since I'm a prisoner in the confines of this estate, I'll do a bit more research on Sharona Van Arsdale." Steven vented with frustration.

"Was there any info you turned up that you couldn't mention in front of Agent G?" Ezekiel asked.

"A bit." He answered. "I researched Sharona's family tree, and found out that Liddy Mc Pherson was briefly married to Clifford Laszlo. They had one son Charles, and you know the rest of that story."

"You mentioned that Liddy and Clifford were only briefly married. What happened there?" Philip curiously inquired.

"He died a short time afterward." Steven answered with raised brow. "Having experienced the carnage of Liddy first hand, we can surely surmise that his ending came tragically."

"I think we should take a closer look at who Clifford Laszlo actually was?" Ezekiel suggested.

"I'll check into it." Steven replied. "I'm also eager to find out how Sharona was so familiar with her grandmother. She would've died long before she was even born."

"Unless!" Philip pondered with enlightened thought. "Perhaps Liddy travelled through the portal of time to visit with her granddaughter."

"You have a valid point there, Philip." Ezekiel stated. "Her and Daniel Branch the 1st were quite familiar with the workings of that portal."

"I know of another friendlier time traveler who just might be able to help us figure that out." Steven replied with a sly grin.

Both Philip and Ezekiel answered simultaneously. "Stargazer!"

On Main Street in Lockeport, Tre Russell casually strolled along the sidewalk during a lunch break from his job at Branch Consolidated. He froze in place as he saw Deanna LeRoux walking toward him. "Deanna! Deanna LeRoux!" He called out to her.

Deanna sauntered closer without saying a word. "I don't know if you remember me, but my name is Tre Russell." He stammered.

"Uh huh! I remember you." She boldly proclaimed with a smirk. "You were the big football star who was always picking on me when I was a little kid."

"I was just being stupid." Tre pleaded.

"And, as I recall, you were very full of yourself as well." She grinned.

"I've changed quite a bit." He meekly replied. "I was away when I heard about Marcus. I'm so sorry about what happened. He was one of my best friends."

"Thank you, Tre." She sighed. "I still think about him every day." She tried to quickly change the subject. "I also heard you're somewhat of a local hero. You saved Mrs. Spencer from that intruder."

"It wasn't any more than anyone else would do." He shrugged.

"Nevertheless, I'm quite impressed."

Tre fidgeted nervously, and checked the time on his watch. "I have to get back to work right now. But maybe we could get together sometime, and maybe, you know, talk or something."

Deanna stared at him for a moment with a calculating glare, before breaking into a smile. "Can I see your cell phone for a minute?" She asked.

"Yeah! Sure!" Tre answered nervously, as he handed it to her.

She entered her name and number in his contact index, before handing the phone back to him. "Call me." She nonchalantly stated, as she breezed by to continue on her way. She walked several steps before turning with a sly grin. "I'll be home tonight."

As she turned to continue on, Tre could barely contain his exuberance. He pumped his fist victoriously. "Yes!"

In the private chamber of Judge Henderson, Philip appeared in the corner of the room while the judge poured over case files that were on his desk. "Good afternoon, your honor." He announced, causing the judge to jump back in his chair with surprise.

"Who are you, and how did you get past security?" The judge demanded.

"That's not important right now." Philip sighed as he paced forward. "I need to discuss a case with you."

The judge quickly reached for his phone. "I'm calling security to have you removed from this chamber."

"Pity that they won't find any trace of me." He chuckled as he took the receiver from his hand, and placed it back in its' cradle. "That won't shine too favorably on your sanity now, will it, Judge?"

The judge nervously settled back in his chair. "I'd have to guess by your tough appearance that Costanzo sent you here to further intimidate me."

"On the contrary!" Philip replied with mild surprise, as he gestured to the files on the judge's desk. "I'm on the side of the good guys, and if those are the deed copies to the Branchview Estate, I need to inform you that their fraudulent."

The judge suspiciously glanced down toward the opened files. "How do you know that?"

Philip answered with a sly, confident grin while taking a seat. "Go to the Public Records site on your computer. You'll see that the Deed is in fact not registered to Midland Enterprises, but is in the name of Branch Consolidated Industries with Steven Spencer as the appointed guardian of the estate."

The judge paused to give a long look at Philip before typing in the search on his computer. After a few seconds, he glanced back up. "You are right about that Mr…"

"My name is of no concern your honor." He interrupted, while handing him one of his Trident calling cards. "This should be sufficient, and will provide all the assurance of protection you'll need."

The judge looked at the card, and then glanced back up with an expression of bewilderment. "How is this card supposed to protect me?

That bastard Costanzo threatened my family. His men will be at my house tomorrow awaiting word on the verdict.”

“Is that so?” Philip smugly chuckled, before pausing in thought. “What if I had a plan to counter that threat?”

“That sounds all fine. But how can I trust you?”

Philip stood and paced a few steps. “The people who are behind that threat go far beyond Costanzo. He’s just their puppet.” He sighed. “Those same people know my calling card, and know very well what I’m capable of doing.”

The judge’s eyes widened as Philip continued to talk.

“I promise you this.” He paused with assurance. “I will be there with your family tomorrow, and no harm will be done to them. But if you choose to unjustly rule in the case, I will make sure the fraud is exposed to the bar association.” He emphasized with a quick nod. That’s all I’ll say for now. You’ll have to trust me on this.”

“But…” Before the judge could say anything further, Philip had turned, and disappeared from the room, causing the befuddled judge to quickly look around in confusion. He then glanced once again at the calling card, and let out an anxious and worrisome sigh.

At the Seagraves household, Tina was feeding the babies when Angelique strolled into the room, and plopped down into a chair. “I’m bored! Do you suppose we could go into Lockeport today, and do some shopping?”

“I’m sorry, Angelique. I can’t get someone to watch little Mikey without advanced notice.”

"Couldn't we just take him with us? I just want to get out and see the world." She mulled in response.

"Maybe tomorrow." Tina stated, while continuing to tend to the child.

"I could always go alone."

"Absolutely not!" Tina exclaimed. "You are still quite naïve to the ways of the world, and I promised Philip I'd keep an eye on you."

Angelique pouted, and pondered for a moment before responding. "Could I just go to Branchview, and visit with Loraine?"

"I suppose that wouldn't hurt." She sighed. "I'm sure Nebriana and the Woods People will watch over you along the pathway."

"Oh, thank you!" Angelique trilled as she leapt from her seat, and planted a kiss on Tina's cheek. "You're like the sister that I never had." She added before hurrying from the room.

"In more ways than you could imagine, my dear." Tina muttered sarcastically under her breath.

Meanwhile, Steven busied himself in his office study at Branchview, researching anything he could on the North Atlantic ship liner, and Clifford Laszlo. Loraine and Meryl hurried in from another portion of the household.

"We got here as quick as we could." Loraine announced. "Were you able to find anything out?"

Steven glanced up with a raised brow. "I found out plenty."

"Don't keep us in suspense. We want to hear everything." Meryl impatiently urged as both women settled into their chairs.

"Aside from being a movie mogul, Clifford Laszlo was also involved in international investments. He brokered land deals in several foreign countries as well as the U.S." Steven stated.

"With a resume like that, I have no doubt that he was a cherished member of the Secret Society." Loraine commented.

"Oh! I'm not finished yet." Steven continued. "He was also rumored to be a Nazi agent planted in this country prior to WWII, and he was based in New York City. He had been under surveillance by the CIA at the time of his death."

"Those Nazi's were a nasty lot." Meryl interrupted. "Ezekiel could tell you many stories."

Steven and Loraine exchanged a wide-eyed glance.

"So, how did he meet his demise?" Loraine impatiently asked. "I'm willing to bet Liddy had some sort of hand in it."

"This is where it really gets interesting." Steven paused with a sigh. "He was a passenger on the North Atlantic with several other suspected Nazi agents."

"That doesn't make any sense." Loraine insisted. "Why would the Germans sink a ship with their own agents aboard?"

"They didn't." He replied with a clever grin. "I had Agent Arcovio hack into the CIA archives, and we learned that the British sunk it."

"Now I'm really confused!" Loraine exclaimed.

"It appears that intelligence intercepted information that they were carrying some sort of catastrophic secret weapon that they planned to unleash on the United States."

"Did they mention what sort of weapon it may have been?" Meryl further inquired.

Steven shook his head in response, and Loraine reacted with much anxiety.

"That means that the weapon is still on board The North Atlantic.

"And in deep waters close to Nereida." Meryl added. "That could be very troublesome for them."

"We have to inform Ezekiel and Philip on this ASAP." Steven stated with urgency. "I'll also have to consult with Stargazer. Perhaps he knows some valuable information from his many time travels. He should be on his way here as we speak."

"What can I do?" Meryl offered. "I'm an Oceanid, but the Nereids are like extended family."

"Nothing for right now." Steven answered. "But I may need you to utilize your psychic powers to gather any other sort of intel that might be valuable."

Meryl got a sudden enlightened expression on her face, and exuberantly spoke up. "I think I just got something." She paused, gazing off into the corner of the room. "I see a cave. It's somewhere on the coast of Greenland." She pondered further while Steven and Loraine patiently listened. "I see a search party probing deep into the cavern. He's there!"

"Who's there, Meryl?" Steven urged her on.

"Clifford! Clifford Laszlo! I feel his energy. It's very dark and sinister."

Just then, Stargazer entered the room. "Greetings everyone!" He announced.

Meryl's concentration broke, and Steven let out a sigh of frustration. "Did you get anything else?" he asked.

She shook her head with frustration. "I'll have to ponder on it further in private."

"I hope I didn't interrupt anything important." Stargazer commented.

"We're just trying to unravel a mystery." Steven replied.

"That's a daily occurrence around here." The old Shaman chuckled, also prompting an amused smile from Steven. "Have a seat, Stargazer. We need your help on something."

Loraine stood and motioned to Meryl. "We'll go about our way, and leave you two gentlemen alone."

"I'll let you know if I get anything else." Meryl added with an assured wink.

After the women left the room, Steven gave an uncomfortable smile to a sober faced Stargazer. "How is the room over the stables working out for you?"

"It's quite nice." Stargazer replied, barely changing his expression.

"I have to ask you about Liddy McPherson and the portal. Perhaps you can help me solve a mystery."

"I'll try."

"In recent years when you traveled through the portal, did you ever encounter Liddy."

"Many times."

Steven expressed surprise by his answer, and probed further. "How is it that she travelled often to modern times, when she's been dead since the early 1940's?"

"Like me, she mastered the time continuum equation of the portal, and could choose whatever time she wanted to visit." He answered.

"So, what you're basically saying is that if Liddy wanted to visit her granddaughter in the future prior to her own death, she could do so at any time she wanted?"

Stargazer gave a confident nod. "I know she visited the future quite often in the 1990's."

Steven sunk back in his seat in pondering thought. "That would make sense. Sharona would've still been a little girl during that time period." He paused. "That might also explain how Luke Underwood was able to bring Liddy to the future as his ally."

"If this Luke you speak of was the immortal that I knew as Hades, I know for a fact that he also had knowledge of the portal, and how to manipulate it." He paused before continuing. "But in the situation with Liddy, I'm certain he had help from the man you know as Lucifer Morningstar."

"The leader of the Secret Society?"

Stargazer answered with a sober nod. "He's also known by other names such as, the father of lies, and the lord of the underworld."

"Are you saying that Morningstar is actually Satan?"

"One in the same."

Steven was totally flabbergasted. "Why didn't you ever tell me about this, Stargazer?"

He shrugged cluelessly. "You never asked."

On the two-lane road that led into town from the Branchview Estate, an SUV with Bruno driving, and Barclay Rutherford as a passenger cruised along slowly surveying the surrounding woods.

"We have to find the most accessible point of entry to the property." Barclay declared. "One where we can maneuver our heavy equipment under cover of night, without being noticed."

"On the other side of the estate, a road branches off that leads to Lighthouse Point." Bruno commented. "Hardly anyone travels that road anymore."

"Let's check it out."

"Mr. Costanzo's crew could clear at least a quarter of this land in one night." Bruno added as they continued to cruise along.

Barclay smiled. "That's right, Bruno. And a quarter of this timber should be worth a fortune on today's market."

Bruno suddenly became distracted by someone wandering along the berm of the road ahead. He slowed down to get a good long look. "I don't believe it." he stated. "Are you seeing what I see?"

"Surprise! Surprise! I do believe that was Miss Divine." Barclay replied as they passed. "I guess we can ditch our elaborate plans to kidnap her."

Angelique was naively oblivious to the two men watching her as she strolled along, as she took in the beautiful scenery around her.

Bruno immediately turned the car around, and headed back toward her.

"This'll be way too easy." He laughed. "It's like she just fell into our laps."

"There's nothing quite like unexpectedly killing two birds with one stone toss." Barclay quipped.

"Ms. Sharona should be quite surprised, and very pleased." Bruno further stated with a smirk.

In the Branchview kitchen, Andrea and Mary chatted as they strolled in to begin preparations for supper. Mrs. Porter had already gotten a head start, and was nervously scuttering about. She paused as the two women entered, and placed her hand on her forehead.

"Are you okay, Mrs. Porter?" Mary asked with concern. "You don't look too well."

"I'm alright!" She replied with a hint of annoyance in her voice. "I just haven't been myself lately." She shook her head. "I guess it's all this turmoil in the household that's getting to me."

"You should go lay down for a while, sweetie. Andrea and I can take up your chores."

Mrs. Porter waved her off. "I'll be fine, Mary. Since you two ladies are here, I'll go help Sharie get the dining room prepared." She hurried from the room, and the two women continued to talk as they worked.

"I worry about Ms. Ethel. She's getting a bit up in years to be doing this kind of work."

Andrea grinned as she brought a bag of flower from the pantry. "After all my time here, you're the first person I've heard mention her first name." She commenced to open and pour the flower into a large mixing container, while Mary added water.

"She don't want nobody calling her anything but Mrs. Porter." Mary chuckled. "Says Ethel sounds too much like an old lady's name."

"But why Mrs.?" Andrea asked. "From what I understand, she never married."

"Trust me on this, child." Mary schooled with a shaking finger. "Don't you go calling her anything else other than Mrs. Porter. That woman has more than earned her respect in this household, and she deserves to be addressed in any way she sees fit."

Andrea only initially answered with an agreeing smile as the two women continued busying themselves with their chores. "It is hard work." She commented. "Why did you ever choose to come back to it, Mary?"

"Because I love this old house, and the people in it." She answered. "Hopefully, you'll never know what it's like to not have a roof over your head, or know where your next meal is coming from." She smiled fondly. "I serve this household with a thankful heart."

Just then, Tina entered from the back entrance. "Good afternoon, ladies! Have you by chance seen Loraine? She hasn't answered any of my texts."

"Lori is having tea with Ms. Markopolous in the Sitting Room." Andrea answered.

"What about Angelique? Is she there with them?"

Mary and Andrea exchanged clueless glances. "We haven't seen her all day, Ms. Tina." Mary answered.

Tina collapsed against the kitchen counter, and Andrea quickly quit what she was doing, and rushed to her side.

"What's wrong, Tina?"

She looked upward with a sigh before answering. "I knew I should've never let her leave the house by herself."

"Lord have mercy!" Mary exclaimed as she also quit what she was doing. "Where do you suppose that child went?"

"She wanted me to take her to town to go shopping." Tina sighed. "When I told her I couldn't, she asked if she could visit Lori. That was two hours ago."

"We can say with certainty that she hasn't been here." Andrea stated.

"I hope you didn't leave little Michael and Dimitri all by themselves at the house." Mary scolded.

"No ma'am! I left them at the Carriage House with the Benson's."

Tina collapsed into a nearby chair. "Where on earth could Angelique have gone? Philip is going to be furious with me for letting her out of my sight."

"Now, just don't go worry yourself, child." Mary rushed to her side. "You just sit right there, and I'll go fetch Ms. Loraine."

Mary hurried from the room, and Andrea went down on one knee beside Tina. "She may have just wandered off into the woods."

"Or she may have been kidnapped by that horrible witch, Sharona Van Arsdale." Tina stated with dread. "I'm sure she'd love to find out how Angelique transformed into a real woman."

She smiled assuredly. "One way or the other, we'll find her."

Chapter Eleven:
Many Troubling Returns

Kenneth Laszlo diligently plucked away on the keyboard of his laptop in the dimly lit study of his London home. Morningstar casually strolled into the room unnoticed, and hidden within the shadows.

"Kenneth!" His deep voice bellowed, momentarily startling Laszlo's concentration. "I understand you're making your grand return to the United States."

"In a few days." He glanced up with an arrogant smirk. "I still have a few loose ends to tie up here." He paused from his work. "All of our players have been pardoned by the courts, and free to return to their positions in the States." He paused with a chuckle. "I have to believe it's safe for me to finally return as well.

"It's amazing how the justice system will bend to your desires when you grease a few palms." Morningstar smiled as he settled into a comfortable seat.

"Money is the universal key to open even the most difficult doors." Kenneth added with a smile. "My sister and special assistant have done quite well in keeping my interests in check during my absence."

"And what a surprise it will be for the inhabitants of Branchview when the identity of that special assistant is revealed."

Laszlo only answered with a wide-eyed expression, and yielded to Morningstar's further boastful rant.

"Victory is closer than you or any other in The Society could ever imagine" He pressed on. "With the open borders of the U.S. being overrun by immigrants from all over the world, the identity of America will change to that of a third world nation. Cultures will clash, crime will be rampant, the middle class, small business, and capitalism will totally disappear. That will enable our chosen individuals to be perpetually elected by an illiterate and needy population" He looked off with a grunt. "When we're able to institute a mandate that requires proof of a vaccine in order to purchase anything or live a normal life, we will have them all in a compromising position that they can't escape."

"Not without mentioning that making it necessary to obtain endless boosters will add to The Society's wealth, and eventually kill off a good bit of the populace."

"I'd prefer to call it population control, Mr. Laszlo." He laughed. "Less mouths to feed, and more illnesses that will be dependent on our pharmaceutical industry."

Laszlo laughed. "it's a genius plot for world domination."

"We already have the rest of the world in our pocket. We can only be triumphant if we're able to destroy and banish that blasted U.S. Constitution once and for all." He grunted indignantly. "The one that dares to grant freedom and rights to the common man."

Laszlo nodded his approval before continuing. "Would you care to join me on the trip, Mr. Morningstar? We should arrive just in time to celebrate our acquisition of the Branchview Estate."

"I'll hold off for right now, and continue to advise the Conglomerate Bank officials with the Great Reset." Morningstar answered with a raised brow. "However, I'm aware of the troubling issues in the town of Lockeport." He tapped his clasped fingers together. "I understand that Branch Consolidated has created a pocket of extreme resistance in an area that is otherwise in our control, and that Steven Spencer is still alive and well." He indignantly sighed as he shifted in his seat. "I'm not happy with that fact, and fully expect you to look into it."

"I'm quite aware of all of that, and I plan to handle it promptly." Laszlo assuredly answered.

In the town of Lockeport, FBI agents Nat Mullen and Frank Parker, along with another agent, confidently strolled into the town jewelry store. They casually glanced at the items in the glass display cases, until the owner, Mr. Garrity approached.

"Good afternoon, gentlemen! Can I help you find anything specific?"

Mullen glared at him momentarily in a very intimidating manner before he pointed to a Rolex watch in one of the displays. "I kind of have a fancy for this watch. How much does it cost?"

"That's a beauty!" Garrity smiled. "That'll cost you one tenth of a Branch Coin, or $6, 450 dollars."

Mullen turned to the other two agents. "One tenth of a Branch Coin." He repeated mockingly, before turning back to Garrity. "Do you take monopoly money as well?" All the agents laughed, as a now nervous Garrity pressed the panic button below the counter.

"I'll take it." Mullen smirked.

"What form of payment do you plan to use, mister…?"

Suddenly, Agent Parker, and the other agent pulled out small batons from under their suit jackets, and smashed through the top of the display case. Mullen promptly reached into the case, and grabbed the watch.

"I said I'd take it." He arrogantly grunted. "I didn't say I'd buy it."

Before another word could be said, Sheriff Albertson and Officer Petty stormed into the shop with their guns drawn. "Police! Put your hands up!' the sheriff warned.

With a sigh, all three men slowly raised their hands, while Garrity now aimed a sawed off shotgun at the backs of the trio. "You're making a big mistake sheriff. We're FBI." Mullen stated. "If you allow my men and I to reach into our jacket pockets, we can show proof."

"Do it slowly." The sheriff ordered. "Any sudden moves, and all three of us will blast you full of holes."

The three agents slowly reached into their inner pockets, and displayed their identification badges, while the sheriff and Petty carefully checked them out.

"They're who they say they are, sheriff." Petty shouted.

"Okay! Now, what in the hell is going on here?"

"They stole a Rolex from the display case." Garrity said before any of the agents could answer.

"Put the watch back." The sheriff further ordered, before Mullen reluctantly tossed the watch onto an unbroken display top. "Now, I want answers."

Mullen strolled to the forefront as the officers and Garrity continued aiming their guns. "You can put your guns away, sheriff."

"We'd rather not." Albertson answered.

"You do understand that as federal agents, we hold special privilege over your measly little police force."

"Not in this town you don't. I run the show here."

"You're asking for a heap of trouble, sheriff." Mullen warned with a smug chuckle. "Your town is operating as an independent sovereignty, and using alternative and unapproved forms of currency."

"We have a right to run things as we see fit according to our Constitutional Rights." Albertson stated with intent. "Now, take your fancy suits and badges, get into the car out there that our taxpaying money paid for, and get your asses out of my town."

The three slowly departed the shop, and Mullen paused for a final word. "You'll regret this, Sheriff Albertson."

"I seriously doubt that."

Without further word, the men got into their car, and sped away while the two officers and Mr. Garrity observed.

"Should we take his threat seriously, sheriff?" Petty asked.

"Let's just say that I don't think we've heard the last from Agent Mullen and his treasonous goons."

At Sharondale, Sharona confidently strode into the hall of statues with Barclay following at a distance. Bruno stood guard at a cage that housed Angelique, and was purposely set close to the statue of Mario.

"Well, well!" Sharona chuckled as she moved close to the cage. "How do you like your new surroundings, dear?"

Angelique glared at her with contempt as she gripped the steel bars. "If I ever get out of this cage, I will tear you apart with my bare hands."

Sharona glanced at Bruno with a smirk. "Feisty little vixen. Isn't she?" She ran her fingers across a deep abrasion above one of his eyes. "That must've hurt."

"She put up quite a fight." Bruno answered.

"What do you want with me, witch?"

"I want you to enlighten me on how you were able to reverse my grandmother's spell that turned you to stone so many years ago."

Angelique spit in her face, and Sharona stepped back with rising anger. Without warning, she wielded a cattle prod, and thrust it through the bars, and on to her bare arm. The shock caused Angelique to reel back against the opposite side of the narrow cage with excruciating pain.

"Now, we can either do this the easy way or the hard way, darling."

"I'm not telling you anything, bitch."

Sharona thrusted the prod at her once again. This time, striking her in the ribs, and causing her to collapse in pain as tears flowed from her eyes.

Sharona then menacingly clanked the prod against the bars. "I could keep this up all night." She glanced at Bruno, then at Barclay with an evil grin. "Isn't this entertaining fun, gentlemen?"

Barclay could not hold back his feelings any longer, and spoke up in loud protest. "I'll have no part in this inhumane torture." He narrowed his eyes with angst toward Sharona. "You are a vile and evil human being." He added as he stormed off.

Sharona raised her voice as he quickly departed. "And you are a weak and pitiful man, Barclay Rutherford." She then turned to Bruno in a huff. "I'm afraid he's going to be a problem for us."

"Do you want me to take care of that problem?"

"Not just yet, Bruno. We'll wait until my brother returns from England before we determine Mr. Rutherford's fate." She pounded the prod against the palm of her hand as she turned her attention back to Angelique. "Are you going to tell me what I want to know, or am I going to have to place this prod between your two breasts?"

Angelique was weary from the torture, and weakly spoke. "I had nothing to do with bringing myself back to life."

"So, it was the White Witch, Loraine Spencer who made you breathe again."

She shook her head in response, which further angered Sharona. She pointed the prod toward her, and sneered. "I suggest you tell me who was responsible then."

"It was the little girl. She touched me, and I came back to life." She answered with tearful frustration.

Sharona's expression turned to one of intrigue, as she stepped in closer to the cage. "What little girl?"

"Loraine Spencer's daughter, Olivia."

Sharona stepped away once again with a look of enlightenment. "There, there, that wasn't so hard now, was it dear?

Angelique only covered her face and wept, while Sharona handed off the prod to Bruno. "I want you to award our guest with a morsel of food. I'm sure she must be hungry." She began to walk away, but turned with a sinister grin. "If she gives you any further trouble, give her a double shock with that prod."

"I suppose you want me to snatch that little girl." Bruno stated. "That could prove to be a tough task since Branchview is like an impenetrable fortress."

Sharona bit her lower lip in thought before answering. "No Bruno. I have a much better idea."

As she sauntered away, the sound of her high heels clicking rhythmically against the marble floor echoed through the cavernous room. Mario's statue, which was positioned to face the cage, helplessly observed the whole unfortunate scenario as it took place. Tears noticeably flowed from his still eyes, and trickled down his cold, stone face.

At that same moment, the gods conferred with Steven and Loraine in the Sitting Room of Branchview. Tina and Meryl were in attendance as well.

"I just know that witch, Sharona Van Arsdale has poor Angelique." Tina stated with frustrating anger.

"We can't jump to any conclusions." Ezekiel sighed. "Angelique is a very naïve young woman. She may have just wandered off, and lost track of time."

"How could you have let her leave the house on her own?" Philip roared in anger toward his wife.

Steven held a calming hand toward him. "Philip! I think she feels bad enough already. Let's just stick to the task of finding her."

"Thank you, Steven." Tina gratefully acknowledged while staring darts toward her husband.

"I, for one, tend to agree with Tina." Loraine chimed in with quivering anxiety. "I think she's attempting to rescue Mario by herself, and has no idea of the danger she is facing."

Meryl raised her hands to cut in on the conversation. "Why don't I try to use my powers to locate where she might be."

"At least one of us is thinking out of the box." Steven quipped.

Meryl reached over, and took hold of Tina's hand. "The two of you have formed a special bond. Perhaps you can help me find her."

"I'll try anything to get an answer or clue." She replied.

Both women closed their eyes, and everyone remained silent as Meryl focused, weaving back and forth in her seat. After a few impatient minutes, she broke the silence, startling everyone with a raised voice. "I see a large room with several statues lining each side of it."

"The hall of statues!" Loraine exclaimed, as Steven and the gods quickly silenced her with stern looks.

Meryl refocused, and carried on in a semi trance with a perplexed expression on her face. "There's a large circle at the center of the room with what appears to be an eternal flame."

Loraine wanted to speak up again out of enthusiasm, but Steven halted her again by shaking his head.

"I see her at the far end of the room. It's very dark." Meryl gave a confusing pause. "She appears to be in some sort of a small cage."

Loraine rolled her eyes with great stress and anxiety, but nevertheless, held her tongue until she finished.

"She's very scared." She paused, and shook her head with frustration. "I'm sorry! That's all I'm getting right now."

"I just knew it!" Tina exclaimed.

"She's in danger!" Loraine added. "We can't just sit here. We must go and bring her back."

"Now wait just a minute." Ezekiel warned. "We can't just barge in without a plan. We could be putting her life in jeopardy."

"Ezekiel's right." Philip stated with agreement. "Sharona is a very evil woman, and there is no telling what she'll do to Angelique, or even to Mario's statue." He paused. "We have to remember that beneath that stone, there is a real, living man."

"Then what do you suggest we do?" Tina asked with increased frustration.

"We simply wait." Ezekiel answered with great thought.

"Are you out of your mind!" Loraine screamed as she jumped from her seat, and Ezekiel quickly moved to calm her.

"Sharona wants something in return. Otherwise, she wouldn't have gone through the trouble of kidnapping her in the first place."

"Perhaps this is a scheme to bribe Branch Consolidated into conceding to the Secret Society." Steven suggested.

"I don't think so" Philip answered with a thought filled pause. "Sharona is a very selfish individual who has aspirations beyond that of her brother. Whatever she wants, it has nothing to do with the Secret Society."

"I sense Ezekiel and Philip may be right about this." Meryl added with assurance.

"I'd bet that we'll be getting a call within the next 12 hours or so, and that she'll state her demands at that time." Ezekiel concluded. "Until then, we all need to get a good night's rest. Steven has that court date tomorrow morning, and the rest of us will have our work cut out for us as well."

Sharona sat in her Parlor at Sharondale, sipping pensively on a glass of wine. Barclay descended the stairs to the Foyer carrying a suitcase, and Sharona swiftly rose from her chair, and met him at the bottom.

"Where on earth do you think you're going?"

"I'm leaving!" He answered with a pause. "I have a court date in the morning over in Lockeport, and I don't feel like getting up in the middle of the night to drive there."

"You're staying in a hotel?" Sharona asked with a smirk.

"Yes! I would much rather stay in a lowly hotel than to spend one more moment in this torture chamber that you call a home."

"You're softer than I thought, Barclay." She grinned in a sinister manner. "I never thought you'd back away from your expected duties."

Barclay pointed angrily at her. "My duties were never meant to include the trafficking and torture of innocent women and children."

Sharona backed away sarcastically at his remarks, as he continued his angry tirade. "Oh yes! I fully understand that you plan to kill Loraine Spencer, and then traffic her young daughter and Angelique to the highest bidder."

"Oh! You're much smarter than I expected." She paced away still talking. "Loraine Spencer must die to atone for what her and the inhabitants of Branchview did to my beloved grandmother and her mother."

"You're a sick woman, Sharona."

"She turned quickly with an expression of enlightenment. "Should I perceive that you may still be in love with your precious Loraine?"

"We're finished here." Barclay angrily concluded as he stormed out the door, slamming it in his wake. Sharona only reacted to his departure with an evil, carefree laugh.

Late that evening, after most of the inhabitants of the Branchview Estate had retired for the night, Steven sat in the darkness of the Grand Corridor, and eloquently played the piano. After finishing the final notes of a Classical tune, the spirit of his father stepped from the shadows to join him.

"You sound better every time I hear you play." He said with a nod of approval.

"I've been playing this old piano quite a bit as of late." Steven replied with a sigh. "I find it's the best way to handle all the stress I'm dealing with."

Jack sat down on the piano bench next to his son. "Talking about it with your dad also helps."

"I just feel overwhelmed, dad." Steven vented with frustration. "It seems like we put out one fire, and five more ignite."

"That's the cruel reality of life, Steven."

"These people we're fighting are much bigger, and hold more influence than I could ever imagine. If I fail at all of this, I'll be letting everyone down."

"You won't fail, son." Jack answered. "You and Gerard were chosen for this task for good reason, and I have faith that you will succeed."

"He's right, Steven." Another voice chimed in as Daphne's spirit also emerged from the shadows with little Maggie close behind.

Steven subtly smiled. "I guess we're having a family reunion here."

"You should know we're always watching." She said as she ran her hand lightly across Steven's shoulder. "We just don't always make ourselves known."

Maggie joined the trio at the side of the piano, and listened with wide innocent eyes.

"These bastards from the Secret Society want to kill me." Steven further vented.

"Of course, they do." Jack agreed. "You are their greatest threat, and they fear you."

"How do I know they won't succeed?"

"None of us know for certain what will happen in the future." Jack answered with a shrug. "How could I have known that Charlotte would have a hand in my death, as well as that of your mother, and that we would eventually forgive her for it?"

"Or that I would have met my tragic fate at the bottom of the main stairway? Daphne added.

"What about me?" Maggie chimed in. "I never knew I'd be crushed by a falling statue in this very room."

"There's nothing sure in life, Steven." Jack continued. "You just get up, and live each day as though it was your last."

Steven soaked in the words of wisdom for a few long moments before speaking. "I didn't realize that you and mom had gotten the opportunity to forgive Charlotte. I thought she was forbidden from communicating with spirits in the light."

"She's still unable to visit us where we are, but we're permitted to visit her on occasion there at her home in Avalon."

"How is she?"

"Her and Manny are quite happy, and very much in love I must add." He answered with a smile.

"I suppose I'll never have to forgive Daniel or Daniel Jr. for their atrocious crimes to this family." Daphne commented, before adding. "I'm not sure that I ever could."

"I can say with certainty that no one here will ever venture to the place where those two presently dwell." Jack stated, and Daphne answered with an agreeing raise of her eyebrow, before turning to Maggie.

"Maggie had a revelation that she needs to share with you, Steven."

All eyes focused on the little girl as she seriously spoke. "I think that Lori and Olivia may be in great danger. We have to do everything we can to protect them."

"Olivia?" Steven questioned as he pondered heavily over what was said.

He then leaned forward to address the little girl directly. "Would this danger happen to involve Angelique Devine, and a women named Sharona Van Arsdale?"

Maggie answered with a sober nod of certainty, and Steven looked upward with enlightenment.

"I think I know what this might be all about." He pondered further. "Angelique is missing. Is she being held against her will by Sharona?"

Once again, Maggie gave a sober nod, and Steven continued to evaluate the situation.

"I think Sharona may know how Angelique was brought to life."

"Oh dear!" Daphne exclaimed. "That would definitely put Lori and Olivia in danger."

"Thank you for that information, Maggie." The little girl appeared quite pleased that she was able to help, and Steven stared off into the darkness of the room, still pondering the situation.

"I'll need to consult with the gods about this as soon as possible."

"With that said, I think it's probably time for us all to move on." Jack told the other spirits as he stood up. "Steven has a big day tomorrow, and desperately needs his rest"

"Wait!" Steven halted them, and they all paused to listen. "I need a little enlightenment on another issue." He stood up as well, and continued with uneasiness. "I keep having these dreams where I astral travel, and I'm actually swimming to the deepest depths of the Atlantic Ocean." He paused. "Nereid escorts have led me to the perimeters of Nereida.

Jack and Daphne exchanged quick glances.

"How can that be? Humans are not permitted, nor able to go to those extreme depths." Jack stated.

"Then why am I able to? Realistically, my human lungs would implode under such circumstances."

Jack shrugged cluelessly, searching for a logical answer. "You do have a Nereid bloodline."

Steven reacted with astonishment. "I didn't know this. Why didn't you ever tell me?"

"You never asked."

Steven rolled his eyes with frustration. "I seem to be getting that same answer from a lot of people lately. Could you please elaborate?"

"Maybe I can help." Daphne chimed in. "Ironically, both my mother and Elizabeth Branch, though not related, were transformed Nereid maidens. Perhaps my mother's genetics were passed down to you through me."

"Just what do you mean when you say they were transformed?"

"When a young Nereid maiden turns eighteen, she's permitted to walk on land for a week, and then given the choice to either remain in her human form or return to her life in Nereida." She answered.

"Kind of like selkies?"

"I suppose you could say that." She said with a sigh.

"Nevertheless, I've heard that on rare occasions, a select human with a Nereid bloodline to one of these maidens is deemed worthy to gain access back to the secret world of Nereida." She further added. "It appears that for some special reason, they chose you, and you were beckoned there through your dreams."

It was visibly apparent that Steven was still a bit perplexed by the revelation, and further questioned. "Why do you suppose they chose me?"

"Perhaps it was by grand design." Jack theorized. "I'm sure it will all be revealed in due time."

Just then, a portal of light opened at the other end of the room, and they all glanced in that direction. "Just as I thought." Jack chuckled. "Your mother is calling me back to the light."

"Tell her I said to come visit me sometime." Steven quipped.

Jack answered with a wink and a smile, then turned to Daphne. "Are you coming too, mother? There are others over there that have been waiting for you."

Daphne reacted with apprehension. "I don't know if I'm quite ready."

"It's time to do it, Miss Daphne. You can always come and go, just as I do." Maggie suggested.

Daphne glanced at Steven as though begging his input.

"Go ahead. I know for certain that grandfather is there patiently waiting for you." He gave an assuring wink."

"Be sure to tell Loraine that I finally decided to go through with it."

Steven answered with a nod as Daphne then looked to the light, and gasped with surprise and excitement. "I can see him! It really is Darren!"

Both Jack and Maggie extended their hands to her, and she hesitantly took hold of them, her eyes still firmly fixed on the light with hypnotic wonder.

"Let's go have that long awaited reunion with my father." Jack urged her on.

Without further word, the trio slowly strolled together into the light, and the portal abruptly closed, leaving Steven in darkened silence.

"Well!" He emotionally paused, and pounded out a final, subtle few notes on the piano keys. "At least one thing made me happy today." He sighed as he looked upward, and further whispered with a fond, reflective smile. "Good night, everyone."

As the rest of the world surrounding Branchview was settling into their nights slumber, evil was wide awake, and active on the north end of the estate. Under cover of night, heavy equipment and logging apparatus were intruding on the deep woods near the access road to the Lighthouse. Clint Buzzanco, a tough, rugged looking foreman barked out orders to the handful of on-site workers. "Get that machinery in place, and let's get started. We have to clear as much of this timber as we can before daybreak."

Just as the workers were ready to fire up their chain saws, deafening whispers arose from the trees around them. They all paused to cluelessly search the darkness with their eyes. Suddenly, the beams from the generated work lights, and the headlights of the vehicles captured two individuals who had emerged from the deep woods.

"What in the hell is this?" Buzzanco cussed out, as he marched to confront them with a drawn gun.

He laughed out loud as he laid eyes on Nebriana and Green Man, and the workers that converged behind him also erupted into laughter.

"I think you two got lost on your way to the costume party."

"No!" Nebriana defiantly answered, while Green Man remained stoically silent. "You are the ones that are trespassing on sacred lands, and for that you must pay."

The whispers rose from the surrounding trees like a chorus of accusers, and all the workers paused with fearful expressions.

"I don't know what your game is here, sweetheart." Buzzanco asserted with impatience. "But I'm the one holding the gun, and along with my men, I do believe you're a bit outnumbered."

"Don't count on that." Nebriana warned, which further enraged Buzzanco.

"Now you listen here, little lady." He fumed. "You, and your big dumb friend need to get the hell out of our way, or we'll plow you under, along with the rest of the underbrush."

The whispers grew ever so louder, and were joined by other sounds of unseen creatures of the night. Some of the workers, recoiled in fear, while one brash, and arrogant young man stepped to the front with Buzzanco, and eyed the attractive, and tantalizing Nebriana with lustful eyes.

"I think we should kill Big Foot here, and then all of us can take a turn at this little sweetie." He smacked with sarcasm.

Just then, practically out of nowhere, a wolf came onto the scene, and joined the duo in their stance against the workers. Countless Woods People carrying tiny lanterns, and a host of marsupial creatures also emerged from the darkness of the deep woods, with their illuminated eyes being the only proof of their presence. The wolf snarled an angry warning at the men, and Buzzanco responded by aiming his gun at it.

In a flash, before he could get a shot away, the wolf leapt high in the air, and the previously silent Green Man growled in a roar that shook the surrounding woods. The behemoth creature then extended his long bark skinned arms to grab the two men by the throat.

The other men tried to retreat, but were snagged, and pulled to the woods floor by the creeping, crawling root system and underbrush beneath their feet. The more they struggled to get free, the more entangled they became.

Fearful cries of anguish echoed throughout the enormous woods, as the gods, and the forces of nature violently attacked their enemy. After a long, few minutes, it was all finished, and a peaceful, but eerie silence once again prevailed in the sacred woods, almost as if nothing had ever happened. The only sound that remained was the nighttime symphony of the crickets, and of unseen creatures of the woods that communicated with each other in their own coded language as they retreated back into the deeper regions of their natural home.

Chapter Twelve:
The Shield of Njord

Morning arrived relentlessly fast at the grand old estate. The first light of day caught Steven and Loraine snuggled closely in their bed. Loraine was the first to stir, and squinted her eyes against the sliver of light that streamed through an opening in the window curtain. She immediately took notice of the damp sheets, and the stench of sea salt. "Oh no! Not again." She loudly whispered.

She carefully crawled from beneath the covers, as Steven began to stir from his sleep. Her eyes caught sight of a still sea soaked, dirty, and time worn satchel that was leaning against the side of a chair.

"What in the world did Steven bring back from his nighttime astral ventures?"

Steven rolled over, and wiped the sleep from his eyes just as Loraine carefully removed the large item from the satchel. It was an ancient metal shield with a large ruby colored stone implanted in the center. As the sliver of light from the window caught the ruby, it glowed like a red hot coal.

"Put it down, Lori!" Steven yelled as he leapt from the bed.

The light reflected in the ruby stone, and sent a rebounded ray of light back across the room. It shot past Steven's head like a powerful laser bullet, and exploded against the wall, blowing a hole clear through it.

Loraine dropped the shield to the floor, as Steven scampered to cover it from any further light. He then hurried to embrace his now trembling wife.

"What in God's name just happened, Steven?"

"I have no idea." He breathlessly answered as he stared in equal shock at the gaping hole in their bedroom wall. "I'm just grateful that I was able to get out of the way."

"Where did you find that shield?"

"The last memory I have of my venture was a Nereid Mermaid escorting me into the wreckage of the North Atlantic. We swam deep into the damaged hull of the ship, and she pointed toward a watertight container that was partially buried in the silt."

Loraine held him at arms length, and listened with great concern, as he attempted to recall more. "That was the absolute last thing I remember. I had no idea I retrieved what was in that container."

They both stood for a moment, still in shock, and stared at the now covered shield. "Whatever that shield is Steven, it has some sort of lethal power that is triggered by the light."

Steven sighed with anxiety as he tried to evaluate the situation in his mind. "All I know, is that we have to keep it under cover until I'm able to consult with Ezekiel and Philip."

"What about that hole in the wall?" Loraine stressfully asked. "What will we tell the others?"

"We tell them nothing right now." Steven pulled away, and paced in thought. "I'll call Tony right away, and have him put a temporary tarp over it until it can be professionally repaired."

"That shield needs to be removed from this house." Loraine ranted. "We have no clue as to the other powers it may hold."

"No, honey! We can't chance having it fall into the wrong hands." Steven anxiously continued to pace. "I have to get this court issue taken care of this morning. We'll just have to keep it under wraps until I find out more about it."

"Oh, Steven! The complications continue to accumulate. Will our lives ever return to normal again?"

Steven embraced her tightly, and kissed her on the forehead. "Believe me, I'm working very hard to make that happen, sweetheart."

In the Branchview Dining Room, Gerard made his way to the breakfast table, and was met by Sharie who immediately filled his coffee cup.

"Thank you, dear." He said as he snuck in a quick kiss to her cheek. "Have you seen Steven yet this morning?"

"Not yet." She replied, as she sat down next to him.

"I wanted to wish him luck on his court date this morning."

"That has me very concerned." She stressfully sighed. "Those scoundrels will go to any length to get their hands on this property."

"We have our best team of lawyers working on this." He took a sip from his coffee cup, and continued. "Even if they win this round, we'll continue to fight."

"I'm waiting for everyone else to come to the table. I have to wonder if anyone else heard that loud boom this morning." She stated with emphasis.

"I don't know how they couldn't." Gerard chuckled. "It shook the whole house, and practically knocked us out of bed."

"I haven't had a chance to mention it to any of the help. They were all too busy stirring about in the kitchen."

Just then, Gerard's cell phone rang, and he quickly answered. "This is Gerard." He paused to listen. "Yes, sheriff. I imagine Steven hasn't turned his cell phone on yet this morning." He paused to listen again, and his expression turned to one of great concern. "I understand. I'll get over there as soon as I can."

Sharie reacted with equal concern as he ended the call. "What was that all about?"

"I guess I'll have to put breakfast on hold." He announced as he stood and took another quick sip of coffee. "That was Sheriff Albertson. There seems to be some sort of problem on the north side of the property."

"Perhaps that had something to do with that loud boom." Sharie replied anxiously.

"I'm sure we'll find out soon enough." Gerard stated as he gave her another kiss. "I'll round up Tony, and we'll go see what this is all about."

Sharie shook her head nervously as her husband finished a final gulp of his coffee. "There never seems to be a shortage of problems around here."

Gerard only sighed, and gave an agreeing nod as he departed.

At the home of the Honorable Judge Henderson, his wife, teen aged daughter, and twelve year old son huddled in fear on the living room couch, as two thugs casually watched over them.

"I beg you!" His wife pleaded. "If things shouldn't go as planned, please take me, and leave my children out of this."

"Lady!" One of the thugs chuckled as he leaned forward. "If everything goes as planned, as I'm sure it will, my friend and I will walk out that front door, and you'll all be safe as can be." He glanced at his other accomplice with a smirk. "Isn't that right, Geno?"

"It'll be like we were never here." Geno laughed out loud.

The judge's wife cowered, not fully convinced with the answer.

Just then, an unexpected knock came upon the front door, and both men paused, shooting quick, anxious glances between them. The thug that appeared to be in charge, motioned for Geno to go answer it.

Geno slowly, and cautiously proceeded to open the door with his gun drawn, and pointed it at a calm, unwavering Philip who stood on the other side. "Who are you, and what in the hell do you want?"

With lightning quick speed, Philip gripped the surprised thug by the throat with one hand, knocked the gun from his hand with the other, and held him off his feet in a powerful grip. "I am your worst possible nightmare, punk." He sneered, while Geno gasped for air, and stared with wide eyed shock at the angry god.

In the north end of the woods at the Branchview Estate, Gerard and Tony arrived to find Sheriff Albertson waiting for them at the side of the access road with his hands firmly placed on his hips. The men emerged from the SUV, and casually strolled toward him.

"What's going on sheriff?" Gerard inquired.

"A lighthouse maintenance worker arrived to find the gate to the access road open, and decided to investigate."

Both men took notice of the damage from vehicles leading into the woods. "It looks like whoever broke the gate also cleared a clean path into the woods." Tony commented.

"You gentlemen haven't seen anything yet. Follow me." The sheriff chuckled as he motioned them along.

Gerard and Tony exchanged baffled expressions before proceeding. About fifty yards into the woods, the men came upon a patch of clearing where several abandoned pieces of heavy equipment rested with roots and underbrush practically covering them. Several crime scene investigators were scattered about, scouring the area for evidence.

"My question would be." the sheriff began. "How is it possible that a path that looks freshly cleared would lead to all of this?

Gerard gave a clueless shrug. "This equipment looks like it's been parked here for at least ten years."

"My thoughts exactly." The sheriff answered. "But if that were the case, I'm sure it would've been discovered long before now."

One of the investigators called out to the sheriff. "We found recent registrations in the glove compartments of the trucks." He trudged closer. "They're registered to Midland Enterprises in Boston."

"I shouldn't be surprised." Gerard stated. "That's the company that we're fighting in court as we speak."

"That still doesn't answer any questions for me." The sheriff stressed. "What happened to all the workers? Did they just disappear into thin air like those other guys did several weeks back?" He looked to Tony, as though searching for an answer. "You've been awfully quiet, Mr. Freeman. What's your take on all of this?"

"Well, sheriff! They do say that these woods are haunted."

Just then, a breeze blew through the woods, and the rustling leaves sounded like loud whispers that caught the attention of all three men, as well as the investigators.

"I've heard that said, and considering the cases I've handled here at the estate, I'm beginning to think it may be true." The sheriff vented with a tinge of sarcasm. "Is there any other enlightenment you can give me as to what the hell might be going on here?"

Gerard and Tony exchanged quick glances, and Gerard began with a sigh. "I think you should come by the main house around 1:30. Steven, Mr. Sphere, and Mr. Seagraves should all be back by that time. They might be able to answer some of your questions, sheriff."

"Why can't they just meet me here?" He further probed.

"I think you may want to be sitting down when you hear what they have to say." Gerard answered with a serious nod.

At the Lockeport Courthouse, Steven arrived with Ezekiel and their two attorneys. As they strode down the hallway toward the court room, Ezekiel subtly gestured toward a broad built man in a tailored suit that impatiently stood waiting near the door.

"That's your opponent, Steven. Angelo Costanzo himself."

Steven casually observed him as he continually glanced at his watch, and scowled. "He looks every bit as full of himself as I could ever imagine."

Just then, Barclay Rutherford hurried onto the scene, and began conversing with his client. "Unfortunately, I've already met that scoundrel." Steven indignantly stated.

"Obviously, it wasn't a pleasant encounter. There's smoke coming out of your ears." Ezekiel chuckled.

"That's an understatement." Steven grunted. "He's one of Lori's old flames from when she lived in England."

"I won't take that one any further." He answered as they both observed the two men in deep, serious conversation.

An officer of the court motioned all parties into the room, and directly addressed them. "Judge Henderson will meet with all of you in his chamber."

In response, both Steven and Angelo looked toward their representatives with a puzzled expression as they all followed the officer into the judicial chamber. When they entered, the judge simply glanced up from his paperwork, and motioned for all of them to have a seat.

After a few moments, he glanced up again with a sigh. "Gentlemen! After looking over the evidence, I've reached the decision to declare this a mistrial."

Angelo immediately flew into a rage as he rose from his seat. "On what grounds?"

"I would sit down if I were you, Mr. Costanzo." The judge warned, as the officer moved in closer.

He waited for him to settle back into his seat before continuing. "I have the copy of the deed that Mr. Rutherford here supplied, but interestingly enough, it doesn't match the online copies that I researched, or the physical copies that my assistants were able to find in the courthouse archives."

"They must've hacked in, and changed it." Costanzo charged while pointing an accusing finger at Steven."

"On the contrary, Mr. Costanzo." The judge shot back. "It appears that the online records were accessed by an IP address in England that interestingly traced back to Mr. Rutherford's residence."

Rutherford shot a desperate glance toward Costanzo. "That proves nothing. They are public records after all."

"True!" The judge thoughtfully replied. "But I'd have to say it was interesting that all this took place shortly after Daniel Branch III named Steven the heir of the estate, and long after the death of Daniel Branch II, who Mr. Costanzo claims transferred the property to him."

The men exchanged urgent glances as the judge continued. "I've written a recommendation to the bar association to have Mr. Rutherford's license to practice in America revoked." He turned his glance toward Costanzo. "And, you're quite lucky I haven't charged you with fraud, Mr. Costanzo."

"You're going to be sorry you screwed with me." Costanzo raged as he rose from his seat, and pointed to the judge.

"Should I record that as a threat on a presiding judge?" He shot back as he shot a glance between him and the court officer.

Costanzo, though visually steamed, smartly backed away, while the judge nodded to all in attendance. "This court is hereby dismissed."

Before departing, Costanzo shot an angry glance toward Steven. "This ain't over, Spencer."

Steven only answered with a confident grin, as everyone rose from their seats to leave. "That was all quite interesting." Ezekiel commented, as they walked away.

"Yes, indeed!" Steven added.

When everyone had left, the judge picked up Philip's calling card, and examined it closely. "Whoever you are, I surely hope you kept your promise" He muttered to himself.

Once outside of the courtroom, Steven and Ezekiel paused to watch a raging Costanzo as he lit into Rutherford.

"I would not want to be in Mr. Rutherford's shoes." Ezekiel stated.

Steven chuckled with amusement. "It couldn't have happened to a nicer guy."

Costanzo then took his phone from his pocket and urgently dialed a number.

The cell phone rang that was sitting on the passenger seat of Philip's truck, and he answered it with a chuckle. "Hello Mr. Costanzo." He held the phone away as Costanzo demanded to know who the hell he was. "Who I am is of no importance." Philip sternly answered. "Listen up! You'll find your men tied and gagged in the back seat of their car in the parking lot of the Lockeport public pier. I left my calling card on the dash. You need to put this issue with Steven Spencer to rest, and if you even think of harming the judge or his family, I will hunt you down, and kill you. That, my friend, is a promise." He promptly hung up, as Costanzo screamed out a profane laced rant on the other end. Philip grinned with amusement as he rolled down the window, and tossed the phone away.

In downtown Lockeport, Deanna LeRoux and Tre Russell were enjoying a romantic lunch at an outdoor café when they were rudely interrupted by a passing Latashia Hampton.

"Well! If it isn't Deanna LeRoux." She arrogantly announced.

Deanna narrowed her eyes in contempt. "What do you want?"

"That's not a proper way to address a fellow sister of color." She smacked back.

"You're the furthest thing from being a sister." Deanna replied.

"Just what I'd expect from someone who was raised in a White privileged household." She snarled back.

Tre stood up, and attempted to break the tension. "Ms. Hampton, I'd appreciate it if you would just leave."

Just then, a procession of black government cars breezed by on Main Street with blue and red lights flashing, and all paused to take notice until they passed.

"I wonder what that's all about." Deanna remarked.

A wicked smile broke across Latasha's face as she replied. "Oh, you'll both find out soon enough."

Without further word, she strutted away with the same arrogance she had when she first approached. "I totally detest that woman." Deanna fumed.

"I don't get a good feeling about those government cars, and how she reacted to them." Tre commented with uneasiness. "What do you suppose is going on?"

"Whatever it is, if it has any connection to her, it can't be good."

The answers to their questions would become very evident a short time later as the six cars pulled to a stop in front of the Lockeport police station with their lights still flashing. A flurry of Federal Agents flooded from the cars with their guns drawn, and surrounded the building.

Inside, Officer April Simmons sat at the reception desk, and nervously witnessed the happenings through the double glass entrance door. Detective Hank Petrala anxiously approached, and stood watching beside her desk. "What in the hell is all this?"

Before April could say anything further, Agent Mullen took a stance outside the glass doors, and mounted what looked like a rocket launcher on his shoulder.

"Run for it!" April yelled, as a smoking cannister exploded through the glass, sending a cloud of tear gas throughout the station.

The agents then donned gas masks, and stormed the building, loudly announcing themselves as Federal Agents. They herded the stumbling, and coughing police personnel from the precinct like cattle, disarming them one by one. As they all fell to their knees on the front lawn, agents surrounded them with automatic weapons aimed.

"You have no right to do this." Officer Simmons remarked. "We're all officers of the law in this town."

Mullen approached, and stepped menacingly close to her face. "We have every right, officer." He grunted. "This police precinct is hereby occupied by government agents, and we are also taking jurisdiction of this town."

"On what grounds?" Detective Petrala defiantly asked.

"All of you, and the rest of this town is being charged with treason against the United States of America."

"That's outrageous, and an outright lie." Officer Simmons charged.

Mullen only chuckled arrogantly in response, and paced in front of the personnel that now had become his prisoners. "Where is Sheriff Albertson?"

"He's out on a call." Simmons answered as she exchanged a quick glance with Petrala.

Mullen once again stepped in uncomfortably close to April. "I need you to get on your cell phone, and tell the sheriff he's needed at the station, and don't even think of trying anything stupid." He brushed the back of his hand across her cheek, and she defiantly withdrew from it, causing him to continue with a smirk. "I certainly wouldn't want to hurt that pretty face of yours."

In the meantime, Steven and Ezekiel had triumphantly returned from their court date, and were now meeting with Sheriff Albertson. The men casually sat in the Sitting Room sipping coffee, and going over the details of the court hearing, and the discovery in the Branchview woods.

"You expect me to actually believe that the woods are protected from evil by some strange supernatural power?" Albertson asked as he placed his coffee cup down on a nearby table.

"You can take it any way you want sheriff, but it's all true." Ezekiel maintained. "There are much greater things in this world that exist than we can ever imagine.

Steven gestured in agreement, and added further commentary. "You have to also consider that long before this property was Branchview, it was deemed sacred grounds by the Wangunk Indians. If you have time to stop over at the stables, I'm sure Stargazer could give you a history lesson about that."

"As interesting as that all sounds, it still doesn't explain what happened to those workers, and the two other missing men."

Just then, the sheriff's cell phone rang, and he promptly answered. Steven and Ezekiel took note of his changing expression as he listened to the voice on the other end.

"Yes, I understand." He nodded with nervous anxiety. "I'll get down there as soon as I can." He ended the call, and quickly rose from his seat to address the other two men. "That's rather odd."

"Trouble in town, sheriff?" Steven inquired.

"I'm not quite sure." He answered with a thought filled pause. "My deputy just asked me to pick up a dozen of doughnuts. That's our secret statement to signal a dangerous crisis."

"Steven and Ezekiel exchanged a quick, anxious glance, as the troubled sheriff prepared to depart.

"We'll continue this conversation later." Albertson firmly stated. "There's people who are missing out there on your property, and I can't just let this all slide like nothing ever happened."

"We understand, sheriff." Ezekiel concluded.

At that moment, Loraine swiftly entered the room, and the sheriff tipped his hat to her as he passed her on his way out. Both Steven and Ezekiel could tell from her expression that something was terribly wrong.

"What now, honey?" Steven asked with a weary sigh.

Loraine waited until the sheriff had exited the house before answering. "It's just as we had feared, Steven. That horrid woman has Angelique."

"What does she want? Money?" Steven further inquired with frustration.

Loraine folded her arms in front of her, and paced nervously. "I wish it were that simple." She paused. "She wants to know how Olivia managed to bring Angelique to life."

"That's preposterous! We don't even know the answer to that." Steven ranted.

"Precisely! That's why she's demanding that I bring Olivia to her."

"Absolutely not, Lori! That's insane!"

Ezekiel politely intervened. "I absolutely agree with Steven. We can't endanger the child in that way." He paced for a moment in thought. "Now since we know where Angelique is, we can surely come up with a plan to rescue her."

"Those are the exact words I'd hoped to hear, but Sharona firmly stated that if anyone else intervened, we'd never see Angelique again." Loraine answered with heightened anxiety.

Tony entered the room from the outer foyer, unaware that a serious conversation was taking place. Ezekiel looked his way with slight annoyance.

"What is it, Tony?"

"I apologize for interrupting, but I was hoping Steven and Loraine might explain how they came about having a gaping hole in their bedroom wall."

Steven and Loraine exchanged sheepish glances, as Ezekiel turned his full attention toward them. "I can't wait to hear this one."

"I had hoped to speak about that when Philip returned." Steven replied with a weary sigh. "It appears I somehow brought some sort of lethal weapon back from my astral travels."

Ezekiel distressfully put his hand to his head. "Yet another crisis in this household." He announced with vented frustration, before quickly pacing the length of the room. "Where in the world is that blasted brother of mine anyway?"

"I just want to know what type of weapon did the damage. The suspense is killing me." Tony sarcastically stated.

Before Steven could speak further, his cell phone rang, and he quickly answered. His expressions ran the gamut from being perplexed, to gradual rising anger as he heard the distinct British accent on the other end.

"What do you want, Barclay?" He sternly asked, as the others in the room immediately took a shared interest in the unexpected call.

"How do I know I can trust you?" He questioned again, before listening further, and then quickly glancing at the mantle clock. "Can you meet with me here at the estate in an hour?" Steven listened once again, and nodded. "I'll have the front gates opened."

Steven ended the call, and all eyes in the room were directed at him, eager for an explanation.

"Surprisingly enough, that was Barclay Rutherford." He paused with a look of disbelief. "It seems he's somehow found a conscience, and wants to help us get Angelique back safely."

Before anything else could be said, Philip marched into the room with a candid stride. "Hello everyone!"

All in attendance addressed him simultaneously with a frustrated impatience that took him completely off guard. "It's about time you got here."

While the inhabitants of Branchview dealt with an ever growing myriad of problems, trouble was also brewing in other segments of their world. At the makeshift bunker in the basement of Branch Consolidated Headquarters, Agent Guitierez stepped to the front of the room to address everyone.

"I just received word from one of my inside sources that we've been compromised." He paused to glance around the room. "It appears that we have a rat here in the basement that's been funneling information to the enemy."

Agent Gordon who was standing very close to an exit door, quietly stepped out of the room, as everyone began to suspiciously look at each other. She evaded everyone's notice except Millie, who had her eyes on her the whole time.

"Everyone will be required to surrender their cell phones, and no one leaves this bunker until we discover the leak." Guitierez ordered.

Millie waited a few minutes, before she, herself departed the room in pursuit of Gordon.

Moments later, she cautiously entered the women's restroom with her gun drawn. From one of the stalls, she could hear Agent Gordon speaking with someone on her cell phone.

"That's right, sir. They have no idea who it is, but they are aware that there is a mole in the room."

Millie leaned against a wall, and listened as Gordon ended the call. "Yes sir. I think it's a good time to move in."

Millie waited a few seconds, then kicked the door in, knocking it from the hinges.

"Agent Sandstrom!" Gordon exclaimed with surprise, as she was caught placing her phone back into her purse. "What in the hell is this all about?"

"Oh, you know very well what this is all about, Agent Gordon." She sneered. "Don't make any sudden moves, and tell me who you were talking to on that phone."

"I was checking in with my mother. She's been very ill."

"Really? Do you always refer to her as sir?" Millie chuckled as she eyed Gordon still squatted on the toilet seat, not moving a muscle. "Should I also assume that you always go to the bathroom without pulling your pants down?"

Gordon very quickly drew her gun from her purse, creating a showdown between the two women.

"Now I know how my friend David was compromised, and how the Secret Society knew where my husband was."

"I'll never understand why MI6 reactivated an old fossil like you." Gordon snickered. "If you were as good as you said you were in all those excruciatingly boring stories you told, you would've had me pegged by now."

"Oh, I am that good and more, sweetheart." Millie replied without flinching. "I'm quite curious, however. Do tell me what they offered to make you turn against your oath, and your country."

Gordon let loose with a laugh before answering. "Let's just say that it was a far superior compensation plan than Uncle Sam could ever offer."

"I happen to know for a fact that we're both ace shooters. If we both pull the trigger, neither of us will walk out of here alive." Millie stated.

"That's right, Agent Sandstrom. And, no one will ever know what happened."

"I have a better solution." Millie suggested with a wise crack grin. "Why don't we place our guns at opposite sides of the room, and fight each other. Surely, you'll have an advantage since I'm nothing but an old, washed up fossil."

"Old lady, you have no idea what you're getting yourself into." Gordon chuckled. "I grew up on the tough streets of Baltimore, and was a champion student in my Army Tae Kwon Do class."

"We shall see, sister. This old London girl is certainly no pushover."

The women tossed their guns to opposite sides of the room, and began to size each other up.

Gordon let loose with an unexpected high kick that caught Millie off guard. The sharp point of her shoe grazed her above the right eye, causing a deep cut, and sending her reeling back against the counter as blood flowed down the side of her face.

Gordon grabbed hold of the stall door that had come off the hinges, and swung it wildly at her. Millie ducked out of the way, and the wall mirror shattered into large slivers as the steel door struck against it. The door also broke one of the sink faucets, causing an explosion of water to fountain upward. Millie used the distraction to attack with a flurry of punches that stunned Gordon, and followed with a kick to her mid section.

Gordon recovered quickly, charging forward with a renewed head of steam, as she tackled Millie. The force sent both women pummeling back into the stall, where the violent struggle continued. Gordon was able to grab Millie's hair, and plunge her headlong into the toilet bowl, holding her head underwater.

"I'm going to drown you, you old bitch." She sneered, while Millie struggled.

Millie somehow managed to lift up with the strength of her legs, and forced Gordon backward with a quick thrust of her elbows. Gordon slipped on the wet tiles, falling back against the counter and the jagged shards of glass that penetrated clear through the base of her skull, and was now protruding out the front of her throat.

A surprised, and stunned Millie stumbled from the stall to see the gory results, and Gordon's now vacant eyes staring upward toward the ceiling.

She cringed at the sight, quickly looked away, and cupped her own mouth to stall the rising nausea she felt.

"I have to admit, Agent Gordon." She commented to herself, as she wearily retrieved her weapon. "You were one tough bitch."

Moments later, Millie managed to stammer back into the bunker room, dripping wet, bleeding, and visibly in pain. She collapsed to the floor as Guitierez , and several others rushed to her aid.

"Millie! What in the world happened to you?" Guitierez asked with urgency.

Millie looked up with weary eyes, and calmly answered in a way that only she could.

"I found a nasty leak in the women's restroom, and I promptly fixed it."

Sheriff Albertson returned to the Lockeport Police Station accompanied by reinforcements from the Connecticut State Police. He and Officer Norville calmly walked toward the front door, and was met halfway by Agent Mullen who strolled out holding his badge in the air.

"Officer, you and your men need to turn around, get in your cars, and leave. This is of no concern to you."

"What the hell is this all about?" Norville demanded. "This part of the state is my jurisdiction, and this town is under Sheriff Albertson."

Mullen arrogantly strolled closer. "As a Federal Officer, I outrank both of you." He paused to make his point clear. "The Sheriff is being arrested for drawing a weapon on myself and another agent. He, his officers, and the people of this town are being charged with tyranny against the United States."

"That's total insanity! I've known the sheriff, and the people of this town for years. They're among some of the most Patriotic people I know."

Mullen chuckled and moved intimidatingly closer to Norville. "Officer Norville, Patriotism ceases when people go against the rules of their government. If you and your men don't want to be held as well, I'd suggest you leave."

Norville hesitated a moment, and exchanged an anxious glance with the sheriff.

"You can do this the easy way, or the hard way." Mullen stated as he motioned toward his armed men, who began to form a line behind him.

"I'm sorry, Donnie." Norville regretfully told his friend.

"Just do as he says, Ren." The sheriff answered. "We'll make due."

With a reluctant nod, he turned, and motioned for his men to back off.

As the State Police departed, the other agents moved in, disarming, and apprehending the sheriff.

Back at Branchview, Steven and Loraine finally got around to telling the gods about what had happened to the bedroom wall. Tony also sat in, and listened as well. Much anxiety filled the room, as Philip drew a deep breath and began.

"I have no doubt that this shield that's in your possession is definitely the Shield of Njord."

"Who is this Njord?" Steven asked.

"He was also a god that lived several centuries ago in the area we now know as Scandinavia." Ezekiel answered. "He was granted that shield by the Supreme God for his own protection as well as that of his people."

Philip continued the story from there. "When he chose to return to his native planet, he hid the shield at an undisclosed location somewhere in Greenland. No mortal man could be trusted with the power that the shield possessed."

"I can certainly understand that." Loraine stated sarcastically.

"It's believed that the Nazi's somehow found it during WWII." Ezekiel continued. "Allied forces were secretly alerted to the particular ship it was being transported on, and according to our sketchy intelligence on the matter, it was supposedly sunk by British forces."

"All these years, it's been a mystery even to us, as to where that wreckage was in the Atlantic." Philip added.

"I'd have to guess that the Nereid's knew all along, and took every measure to conceal the secret from the rest of the world." Ezekiel theorized. "Perhaps they were the ones who were secretly working in concert with Allied Intelligence."

"But why would the Nereid's allow Steven to retrieve the shield?" Tony questioned. "After all, he is a mortal man."

Steven looked upward with sudden enlightenment. "I think I can explain that." He stated as all eyes moved toward him with intense curiosity. "I recently came upon the knowledge that I am in fact of Nereid ancestry."

"How can that be?" Ezekiel inquired.

"My grandmother Daphne's mother was a Nereid, and surprisingly, so was Elizabeth Branch. They departed Nereida around the same time period, and chose to live on land as humans."

Everyone, including the god's, reeled from the revelation.

"Obviously, the Nereid's must've chosen Steven to utilize that shield in our fight with the Secret Society." Philip further theorized. "They now consider him as one of their own."

"That is quite an honor to behold." Ezekiel added with assurance. "Perhaps Amphitrite knew of this all along, and simply failed to tell us."

"That alone would certainly answer several of our unanswered questions." Philip sighed.

"But it was in Loraine's possession when it activated, and blew a hole in their bedroom wall." Tony reasoned, changing the whole direction of the conversation. "If Steven was the chosen keeper of the shield, why did it become a weapon in her hands?"

Philip stood, and paced in deep thought, searching for an answer. "The shield will only activate in the hands of the first living being that holds it." He paced a bit more, then turned to Steven. "Did you ever remove that shield from its cover before or after you returned from your astral dream?"

"No, I don't believe I did." Steven answered.

Philip took a deep breath before continuing. "It seems apparent that when Loraine removed it from its' protective cover, she became the first human, presently alive to lay hands on it."

"So, I became the keeper of the shield." Loraine assumed, and Philip confirmed it with a nod.

"That shield will only work for her as long as she lives, and breathes." He answered. "Only upon her death will anyone else be able to possess it."

"Oh, dear!" She anxiously exclaimed, sinking further into her seat. "How do I manage to get myself into these predicaments?"

Mary opened the double doors to the Sitting room, peeked in, and announced with little enthusiasm. "Mr. Rutherford is here. Should I send him in?"

"Have him wait in the foyer, Mary." Steven answered. "We're almost finished here."

Steven waited for her to leave, and then spoke in a low voice. "We'll continue this conversation later."

Just then, Ezekiel received a text on his phone, and paused to read it. "It's Agent Guitierez. There seems to be a problem down at Branch Consolidated."

"What sort of problem?" Steven asked.

"He didn't say. But he needs me there immediately."

"I'll stay here with Steven and Loraine." Philip stated. "Be sure to alert me if I'm needed."

Ezekiel nodded to his brother, then swiftly departed. Steven followed to receive Barclay who was waiting in the foyer.

"Follow me." He ordered in a less than enthusiastic tone.

Rutherford followed him without saying a word.

"Make yourself comfortable Mr. Rutherford."

A normally confident Barclay, nervously took a seat as all the others still in attendance glared at him with disdain.

"Now, would you proceed to tell me how you think you can be of assistance?"

Barclay cautiously looked toward Philip. "Who's he?"

"He's a trusted associate of mine. His name is Philip Seagraves." Steven answered without taking his eyes off of Barclay, pressing him to continue.

"Sharona knows that the child has special powers, and feels that she could be a valuable asset for her, as well as the Secret Society."

"That woman is more demented than I first imagined." Loraine quipped with disgust.

"If it's also for the benefit of the Secret Society, then why are you helping us?"

"I'm a dead man walking, Mr. Spencer." He anxiously sighed. "Once Costanzo and Sharona notify Laszlo of my failures, I'll become expendable." He paused, and became very adamant. "I may have done some underhanded things in my life, but I can't condone the abuse of children, and enslavement of humans."

"So, there actually is a heart beneath all that pompous arrogance." Steven sarcastically remarked.

"Yes, there most certainly is." Barclay shot back in defense of himself.

Philip checked a text message on his phone, and squirmed uncomfortably in his seat. Steven and Loraine took notice, but nevertheless continued conversing with Barclay.

"So, what is this grand plan of yours?" Loraine sternly asked.

"I can get you and the child into the house tonight while everyone is asleep." He paused to lean into the conversation. "I have a key, and the passcode to the security system. We can free Angelique from her cage, have little Olivia turn Mario back into a human, and we can all escape out the secret back entrance.”

“Absolutely not!” Steven protested. “I won’t have my wife and child put under such danger. Especially in the middle of the night.”

“I have to agree with Steven.” Philip spoke for the first time in the conversation. “We need to come up with an alternative plan.”

“The only other option we have is that Loraine and the child go there tomorrow as Sharona had planned.” He answered with an expression of great warning. “If you do that, I can guarantee that you’ll never see the two of them ever again, nor Angelique and Mario for that matter. Sharona is setting a trap, and they’re walking right into it.”

Loraine who had been silently following the conversation, nearly jumped from her seat as she spoke. “We’ll go tonight!”

“But, Loraine….” Steven started, but was cut short by his wife.

“You and Philip seem to forget that both Olivia and I possess special powers. I’m sure I can protect myself from any danger she tries to impose on us.”

Both Philip and Steven rolled their eyes in frustration.

“I had planned on going with you tomorrow.” Philip voiced. “You’ve seemed to have forgotten that I possess special powers as well.”

Barclay followed the conversation with curious eyes, and caught sight of the trident tattoo on Philip’s forearm as he stood up.

"You're the one that Laszlo and Morningstar have been talking about. The mystery man with the trident calling card."

Philip sat back down with renewed interest. "What did they tell you about me?"

"Not much. But I do know that you have thwarted a good deal of their plans."

"I can't go tonight." Philip started with a sigh, and was interrupted by Barclay.

"I know what that message was about. There's trouble in town, isn't there?"

Philip exchanged quick glances with Steven and Loraine before setting his attention back on Barclay. "What do you know about it?"

"I know that Agent Mullen and his rogue agents plan to take control of this town, and invade Branch Consolidated Headquarters." He paused. "They know all about the resistance movement that's bunkered in their basement."

"Is that so?" Philip's glance momentarily returned to Steven and Loraine. "Perhaps that was the urgent business that Ezekiel had to take care of at the Corporation."

"Don't worry! I can handle this alone, Philip." Loraine asserted. "You've seemed to have also forgotten that I now have possession of a new secret weapon." She added with an assured wink.

Philip only answered with an expression of enlightenment.

"What kind of weapon would that be?" Barclay curiously inquired, which prompted a stern reply from Philip.

"It wouldn't be a secret if we told you. Would it now, Mr. Rutherford?"

Barclay humbly declined to respond, as Philip shifted his attention back to Loraine.

"Very well." Philip stated in an unsettled way. "Just be very careful in the way you use it."

"Now wait just a minute." Steven stirred. "I'm not trusting my wife and child to go without me."

"Very well then, Steven." Barclay quickly answered in an anxious huff. "You shall be a part of this as well."

"Before I leave, you'll need to surrender your cell phone, Mr. Rutherford." Philip ordered.

Without protest, he handed it over, while Steven pointed a finger of warning.

"And, if you even think of double crossing us, I will kill you with my bare hands."

"No need, Steven!" Loraine exclaimed, as she set a stern glare on Barclay. "If Mr. Rutherford turns on us, I'll kill him myself."

Philip and Steven exchanged wide eyed glances, while Barclay somewhat cowered.

"I'll go take care of the issues here in town." Philip stated.

"I'll go get Olivia prepared for the trip." Loraine added as she rose from her seat, never taking harsh eyes off of Barclay.

After the two departed the room, Steven looked to Barclay with a half grin.

"I guess that just leaves you and I. Can I get you a cup of coffee?"

At Branch Consolidated, Agent Mullen and his crew arrived at the closed front gates where they were met by the armed security force, as well as Agent's Guitierez and Bannerjee with their team.

Mullen confidently sauntered up to the closed gate, and Agent Guitierez confronted him from the other side. Ezekiel stood alongside him, though he remained unseen to the enemy.

"Guitierez!" Mullen announced. "You and your team have committed treason. You'll all rot in GITMO for this."

"That's funny!" Guitierez shook his head. "You pitiful individuals accuse people of being exactly what you are."

"You need to open these gates right now." Mullen ordered with rising anger. "We're in charge here."

"The way I see it, it's a standoff, Agent Mullen. And, we have you heavily outmanned, and out armed."

Mullen's agents raised their guns, and the forces on the other side of the fence did the same.

"We've declared this property sovereign from your rogue government." Guitierez confidently declared. "You have no authority on this side of the gate."

"We'll see about that, Guitierez." He grunted. "I'll be back. But this time I'll have the state police, and the National Guard with me. We'll break this gate down if we have to."

He paused to glare intimidatingly at Guitierez, but the agent remained still and unshaken. After a few moments, Mullen signaled for his men to leave.

As he walked away, he dialed a number on his cell phone. "It's time to sweep this town clean." He smirked.

Ezekiel turned to Guitierez with a nod. "You handled that quite well. You need to stay hunkered down here, while Philip and I coordinate things on the outside."

"These bastards have no idea what their getting into."

"Oh, you're so right about that Agent G."

A short distance away, Philip stormed toward the police precinct like a bull that had seen red. As he plowed open the double glass doors, Agent Frank Parker sat lethargically at the front reception desk.

"Who the hell are you?" He yelled as he jumped up from his seat.

Before he could react, Philip picked him up off his feet, and slammed him against a nearby wall.

"Where are you holding the sheriff and his officers? He sneered.

A terrified Parker motioned with his eyes. "They're all in the holding cell."

"Where is the key?"

Parker was reluctant to answer, so Philip tightened the grip on his neck. "Mullen has it!" He gasped.

"And where is Agent Mullen and the others?"

Parker pointed to his neck, pleading for him to let up on the pressure. Philip obliged, and Parker bent over breathless, before he answered. "They went to Branch Consolidated to apprehend the traitors."

Philip grunted in response. "I seriously doubt if they had much luck with that."

"Whoever you are, you're in deep trouble, mister."

"I seriously doubt that as well." Philip laughed. "Give me your handcuffs."

Parker reluctantly handed them over, and Philip promptly bound his hands.

"If you try anything stupid, I'll separate that pencil neck from your shoulders." He warned as he marched toward the door leading to the holding cell.

He pulled on the door to find it had a magnetic locking mechanism. "I hate modern day security." He mumbled, as he kicked the door in with one try.

"Mr. Seagraves!" The sheriff exclaimed with much surprise. "I don't know how you broke that door down, but I don't think you'll have the same luck with this cell."

"Don't underestimate me, sheriff." He smirked as he pointed his finger toward the lock, and the door sprung open, much to the surprise of everyone in the cell.

As the officers quickly herded into the squad room, and retrieved their confiscated weapons, Mullen and his agents were pulling into the parking lot. Philip led the handcuffed Parker out the front door, and all the officers followed with their guns drawn.

Mullen stepped from his car with a sigh, and pulled his weapon. "I'll shoot the first person that walks any further."

"Oh no, you won't!" yelled another voice, as Suzie and Rick stepped from the dark, both aiming guns directly at Mullen.

"Are you sure you two bacon and egg slingers know how to use those things?" Mullen laughed.

"If they miss, the rest of us won't." Tony quipped as he, Andrea and Eddie Benson stepped into the light aiming their pistols, and with at least a dozen armed townspeople behind them."

"Tony!" Philip chuckled. "How did you know?"

"Loraine told me where you went, so I decided to round up a few friends to come help."

"That's my boy." Philip mumbled with a smile, as he pushed Parker ahead toward Mullen, and handed off his trident calling card. "Show this to your puppet masters. I'm sure they're well aware of me by now."

Mullen reluctantly accepted the card, and glanced at it. "You're all making a terrible mistake that I promise you'll pay for."

"Save the speech, Agent Mullen." Philip stepped intimidatingly closer. "You and your agents need to leave this town immediately, and don't even think of coming back."

Mullen hesitated, and Rick stepped forward, placing the long barrel of his gun to the back of his head. "I'd do exactly as he said, sir."

Mullen holstered his gun, and pointed a finger of warning. "Oh, we'll be back, with reinforcements."

"We'll be here waiting." Philip shot back with a chuckle.

Mullen motioned with disdain toward Parker. "Get in the damn car."

Parker helplessly held his cuffed hands up, prompting Mullen to open the door for him. As the agents retreated, victory cheers rose from the Patriot crowd. Some spit on, and struck the cars with their fists as they sped away.

Ezekiel stepped onto the scene, and took a stance next to his brother. "I thought you might need me, but it looks like you have things under control."

"If we weren't convinced before, we definitely now know that the people of this town have a strong backbone." Philip commented with a grin.

The two immortals strolled away from the others, who were now all congregated in a group.

As they walked along on that pleasant early summer evening, they casually conversed.

"I do believe it's time to escalate our battle plan even further, brother." Ezekiel firmly stated.

Philip answered with a thought filled, agreeing nod. "I think it's time we bring in a few long, lost friends into the fray."

"Who did you have in mind? Charlotte Locke, or Dr. Grayson?"

Philip shook his head. "They both deserve to rest in peace." He paused in thought. "I know that Linda Sanchez would be a willing ally, and I may have to resurrect an old lover of mine that you and Metis's spoiled daughter Athena diabolically turned into a monster."

"Now Philip, you can't fully blame Athena." He countered. "You knew she harbored strong romantic feelings toward you, and out of all the places you and Medusa could choose to have sex, why did it have to be in her palace?"

"To add injury to insult, your son Perseus killed her." Philip continued with rising rage. "Then he decided to inadvertently leave the planet without any logical explanation."

"He put the poor soul out of her misery, and spared any future innocent casualties from those blasted, venomous snakes, and stone, cold stares." Ezekiel argued.

Philip came to a halt, and held his hands up in surrender. "Let's not open any old wounds that could cause a distracting hemorrhage." He sighed. "I think Medusa's weapons could help us flush out the rogue agents in the FBI and CIA."

"Then what would we do?" Ezekiel questioned. "We can't just turn her loose in modern society, and it would not be proper to kill her again."

"It was your lineage that cursed her, and took her life. So, now you can reverse what's been done." Philip reasoned. "We'll reward her by removing that curse, and letting her live her life as a normal human being."

The two men sat down on a park bench to further plot their plan.

"I see a problem brewing there." Ezekiel chuckled. "Tina certainly won't tolerate you resurrecting an old lover."

"I'll deal with it." Philip answered with a stressful sigh.

"Do you plan on bringing back any other monsters?" He sarcastically asked.

"As a matter of fact." Philip paused in deep thought. "I'm considering bringing back the Minotaur."

"Why in God's name would you want to bring back the evil beast that was created by your own rage, and ironically was killed by your own son, Theseus?" Ezekiel roared.

"I'm sure you'll agree that one of our key enemies is Minotaur Pharmaceuticals. They are the distributors of the poisonous vaccines that are proposed to slowly kill off the world's population, and make them and the Secret Society richer, and more powerful in the process."

"And…" Ezekiel urged him on.

"I say we give the bastards a taste of their own medicine." Poseidon stated with a grin. "Perhaps the old boy would come in handy should we have to go into battle."

"How could we control such a beast?"

"Simple. We also promise him a normal human life when this thing is over and done."

Ezekiel pondered the answer for a moment, before offering his own thoughts. "Perhaps he and Medusa could be a romantic match as humans. That certainly would solve any residual dilemma from the whole situation."

Philip pointed a finger, and winked at his brother. "Now you're thinking logically."

Ezekiel slowly rose to his feet. "Maybe we should go and check on Steven and Lori up in Cambridge."

"I think they'll be alright, as long as Lori uses that shield properly." Philip replied. "Besides, you and I have a lot of work to do elsewhere, brother."

In Cambridge, Barclay, Steven, Loraine, and little Olivia arrived at Sharondale under the cover of night. Loraine held tight to the shield for good measure. As they quietly made their way to the front door, Olivia pulled on her mother's arm.

"Mommy, I'm tired, and I miss London."

She went down on one knee, leaning against the shield, and holding her finger to her mouth to silence her daughter.

"I know sweetheart." She whispered. "But we have to be very quiet so that no one hears us. Would you be a big girl, and do that for us?"

She gave her mother a nod, and Loraine continued. "We'll be finished here in no time. Then you can go home to sleep, and be with your brother.

Loraine and Steven exchanged anxious glances, while Barclay opened the front door, and they all tiptoed into the large foyer. As they proceeded into the dark, cavernous hall of statues, Olivia tugged on her mother's arm once again.

"Mommy, I have to go to the bathroom." She whispered.

"Oh, good grief!" Loraine stressfully murmured. "Could you please just hold it for just a bit longer?"

"I'll try." The little girl answered, as they all set eyes on the narrow cage on the far side of the room, from where an imprisoned Angelique desperately watched.

All three adults placed their fingers to their mouths as a signal for her to be very quiet. Other than a few dim accent lights, the eternal flame at the center of the room was the only illumination against the dark. The statues all seemed to be watching them curiously as they silently passed.

"This place gives me the he-bee gee bees." Steven whispered in his wife's ear.

When they reached Angelique, Loraine carefully propped her shield against a nearby pillar. She gazed at the lock on the cage with hypnotic concentration, and after a few seconds, the door popped open, sending a loud echo throughout the room.

"You are quite talented at this magic thing." An impressed Barclay commented in a whispered tone.

Steven sternly looked toward him, gesturing to be quiet, while Angelique stepped free of the cage.

Loraine went down to one knee again, and motioned Olivia's attention toward the statue of Mario. "Sweetheart, I need you to use your magic to bring Mario back to life, just like you did with Angelique?"

Olivia nodded, and proceeded to touch the stone hand of the statue, while closing her eyes. After a few moments, a spark passed from her little hand, and ignited life into the stone. It swiftly spread up Mario's arm, and extended throughout his entire being. Within seconds, an overwhelmed Mario came to life for the first time in over a hundred years.

He paused for a moment, examining his now living body with wonder. Then with a breath of excitement, he embraced his beloved Angelique.

"We need to hurry." Barclay warned. "We can escape out the back entry way."

Steven handed off a bundle of clothes he had brought to the bare naked Mario. "Here! Put these on." He quietly ordered.

"Oh, yes! Please do!" Loraine added as she shielded her daughter from the sight.

Mario quickly put the clothes on, and Barclay nervously motioned for them all to follow.

Just then, the lights went on in the large hall. A pistol toting Sharona confidently strode into the room, dressed in her sheer night gown, accompanied by Bruno, and two other armed thugs.

"Well, well!" Sharona chuckled. "My dear Barclay. Why wasn't I invited to this little after-hours party?"

He only answered with a deep surrendering sigh, while all the others remained still, as the armed men surrounded them.

"Is she the bad lady, mommy?" Olivia asked, as Sharona sauntered closer.

"Yes, sweetheart." Loraine answered sternly. "She's the evil woman that took Angelique."

"Oh, Loraine!" Sharona mockingly exclaimed. "Spare me the drama."

Sharona's eyes widened as she laid eyes on the shield, resting against the pillar, just out of Loraine's reach. "Oh my! The Shield of Njord!"

She walked closer to examine it. "My grandfather was the last person to possess that shield. We've been searching for it for a very long time"

"We know all about that, Sharona." Steven stated, as she spun around to address all of them.

"Then surely, you know how powerful that shield is in the hands of the person that possesses it." She laughed. "And, you very foolish people hand delivered it directly to me."

"I wouldn't celebrate just yet." Loraine quipped. "The shield is only effective in my hands."

"Then I suppose I'll have to kill you, so that I can be the new owner of its' power." Sharona arrogantly remarked.

Steven's eyes glowed red at the threat made to his wife, and the beast began to rise within him.

Bruno noticed, and quickly stepped forward, jabbing the barrel of his pistol against Steven's head. "Whatever kind of beast you are, I'll shoot you before you can transform."

"No, Steven! Don't!" Loraine warned, as Olivia buried her head into the thigh of her mother.

Steven growled, then settled at her command, while Sharona looked to him with amazement. "What sort of beastly magic do you possess, Steven Spencer?"

Steven only sneered at her in response, as she proceeded to pace in front of them. "Here's the deal." She smirked. "We'll kill Mr. Spencer, and collect on his bounty." She then looked to Barclay. "We'll also kill this traitor, and surely garner the favor of my brother." She chuckled as she then set eyes on Loraine. "I'll personally kill you my dear, and take possession of that coveted shield." She then glanced toward little Olivia, who was now in tears. "And, I shall use your gifted little girl for whatever purpose I choose."

"What about us?" Angelique asked as her and Mario nervously embraced.

Sharona sauntered closer with a sarcastic grin. "I will have my little magician here turn Mario back into a statue. And, a beautiful creature such as yourself, my dear, shall fetch me a fortune in the human trafficking pipeline." She chuckled. "As usual, I win, and become even richer in the process."

"You're as sick as you are evil." Loraine remarked with disgust.

Sharona then turned to her armed guards. "Would one of you gentlemen take our little friend to the kitchen, and find her some ice cream. I wouldn't want her to witness what's about to take place."

One of her thugs stepped forward, and pulled the child away from her mother. Olivia fought against him the best she could, and bit down hard on his hand. The thug howled, and retaliated, pulling her by her hair.

"You little…"

Barclay used the distraction, and leapt toward one of the other armed men, knocking him to the floor. Bruno reacted quickly, and shot Barclay in the lower torso as the two men struggled. The beast within Steven could hold back no longer. He transformed, and with the quickness, and agility of a lion, he pounced onto the thug who was struggling with his daughter.

Loraine alertly grabbed the shield, and swung around, aiming it toward a charging Bruno. The shield came to life in her hands, blowing a gaping hole clear through him, and also taking out the other armed thug behind him.

Mario grabbed hold of Olivia's little hand, pulling her along, and away from where Steven's beast had just torn her attacker to shreds. The beast then stood, and roared ferociously at a trembling Sharona.

"Hurry! Come with us, little one!" Mario cried out.

Along with Angelique, they fled the unfolding carnage.

Sharona turned to retreat toward the center of the room, as Steven's beast let out another angry roar, and poised itself to pursue her.

Before it could, Loraine grabbed its' bulging, muscular arm, and attempted to calm its' rage. "Steven! No! Let me handle this."

Her familiar voice immediately settled the beast, and it began to transform back into Steven. But in the meantime, Sharona uncorked her witching powers, hurling a lethal ball of dark energy toward him from the palm of her hand.

Much to her surprise, Loraine lifted the shield, and blocked the destructive orb of black smoke short of its target, sending it hurling back toward her. She managed to sidestep it just in time, but after it flew past her, it struck the main valve of the natural gas pipeline that fed the eternal flame. It immediately ruptured, and the backlash of gas vapor through the line sent the flame shooting upward like a giant blowtorch. Sharona was a bit too close, and got caught within its wide spectrum.

Before she could react any further, her flimsy nightgown ignited. She screamed in terror, and flailed about as the flames quickly turned her into a moving mass of fire. As Steven and Loraine watched in shock and horror, a second explosion shook the room as the rest of the escaping gas ignited. It created a giant, rolling wall of flame that swept across the room like a fiery hurricane. The immense force from the blast caused a good bit of the structure to collapse around them.

Sharona's final agonizing screams quickly muffled to a halt amidst the fury.

Dazed from the blast, Steven and Loraine struggled to their feet as flames danced all around them. Loraine grabbed the shield with one hand, and took hold of Steven's hand with her other. She then stalled in terror.

"Steven, where is Olivia?"

He looked all around them, and yelled back with trembling worry. "I don't know. I lost sight of the others as well."

Through the thick smoke, Loraine could see a hand reaching upward from the rubble. She pointed toward it, as she winced against the intense heat.

"I think it's Barclay."

The couple hurried to his aid, and Steven frantically began digging him out. In the process, he noticed that aside from the gunshot wound, a huge shard of wood had impaled his chest, and he was bleeding out profusely.

"Come on Barclay." Steven cried. "We're going to get you out of here."

"No! No!" Barclay breathlessly panted. "Save yourselves. I'm already a dead man." He replied.

"We're not leaving you behind." Loraine defiantly stated.

Barclay anxiously glanced at her, and took hold of her hand. "I want you to know that I never stopped loving you, Loraine." He emotionally gasped as a tear rolled down his charred face.

Barclay's words caused Steven to pause in his frantic rescue effort to watch his wife's reaction. Barclay painfully, and longingly glared at Loraine before his hand went limp within hers. With one last labored breath, his eyes rolled back into a vacant death stare."

"Come on, Steven! Let's try to stand him up!" She hysterically cried.

"He's gone, Lori!" Steven sadly exclaimed.

Just then, a portion of the ceiling collapsed, barely missing them both.

"We got to get out of here, sweetheart." Steven urgently stated.

Loraine turned to glance one final time at Barclay's sad, desolate stare, before her and Steven fled away through the flames.

Outside the burning structure, Mario, Angelique, and little Olivia huddled together, in horror, as they watched the flames leap high into the night sky.

"Maybe I should go back in, and look for them." Mario remarked in broken English.

"No!" Angelique cried as she held tight to a weeping Olivia. "I lost you once, and I couldn't bear losing you again."

A terrible, ungodly groan arose from the massive old structure as a major part of it succumbed to the fire. The terrible sound took their breath away, as they continued to watch.

"Those statues!" Mario emotionally exclaimed. "They were all innocent men, just like me."

Suddenly, they spotted two figures struggling toward them in the darkness. They could hear them coughing, and wheezing from the smoke.

"It's Steven and Loraine!" Angelique yelled out. "They made it!"

"Mommy! Daddy!" Olivia cried out as she broke free from Angelique's grip, and ran toward them, and into their waiting arms.

Angelique and Mario followed, and paused short to observe the happy reunion. "How did you two ever get out?" Mario asked.

"It was truly a miracle." Loraine breathlessly answered. "The entranceway was obstructed with burning debris. The shield parted the flames, and cleared a path for us."

"What about, Barclay?" Angelique further inquired.

Steven sadly looked up, and shook his head in response, as he and Loraine continued to embrace their weeping child. Everyone paused to listen to the harrowing sound of approaching sirens in the distance.

"We better hurry, and get out of here." Steven warned, as Olivia innocently looked up at her parents.

"Can we go home now?" She asked, quivering with emotion.

"Yes, sweetheart. We can all go home now." Loraine replied.

Minutes later, as they sped away with Steven at the wheel, there was an eerie silence within the car. Steven could still see the glow from the massive blaze in his rearview mirror, even though they were now miles away. In the back seat, Mario and Angelique were huddled in silent reflection, while Olivia sat on Angelique's lap with her head resting comfortably against her breasts. Mario eyed his surroundings with an expression that bordered on both fear and amazement.

"What kind of carriage is this? He asked. "It's like nothing I've ever seen."

"It's called a BMW SUV." Steven answered as he glanced up in the rearview mirror once again. He grinned at Mario's puzzled reaction to the answer. "I'll need to get you caught up on things. Much has changed in the past century."

"Apparently." Mario stated as he leaned his head against Angelique's shoulder, and shut his eyes.

Steven also took notice of the shield, which could partially be seen in the storage area behind his passengers. He feared its power, almost as much as he savored it.

Beside him, Loraine silently stared out the side window, into the darkness. Steven reached over, and placed a sympathetic hand over hers.

"I'm sorry, Lori." He whispered.

She answered with only a brief, pain filled glance, before turning her attention back toward the window.

Chapter Thirteen:
Unexpected Allies

In the dimly lit Secret Cave, Philip and Ezekiel emerged from the shadows, accompanied by a somewhat baffled Medusa and the beastly Minotaur.

"What is this place?" The Minotaur asked with a bellowing voice, that sounded like tires on a gravel road.

"This, my friend is what we call the Secret Cave Room." Philip answered.

"Although, as of late, it's not much of a secret anymore." Ezekiel added with a tinge of sarcasm, as he motioned for them to sit down.

"I'd prefer to remain standing." The Minotaur bellowed in defiance.

Philip rolled his eyes, and turned his attention to Medusa. "And, if you'd be kind enough to keep your sunglasses on at all times, we'd certainly appreciate it. There's already enough statues of my brother and I in Greece, and elsewhere in the world."

"And, please keep those nasty snakes in check." Ezekiel winced at the hissing reptiles that squirmed atop her head. "I hate snakes."

"You told us why we're here, but why should we help?" Medusa insistently asked. "After all, it was Zeus's daughter who turned me into this hideous beast, and his son who beheaded me." She turned her tirade of complaint toward Philip. "I warned you that we shouldn't have had sex in Athena's palace, but no, you were just too horny to contain yourself."

"That bastard son of yours, Theseus killed me." The Minotaur angrily vented at Philip as well. "It was also from your wrath that I was created in the first place." He added, stepping within inches of Philip's face to make his point.

Philip drew back with an unpleasant expression, and looked to his brother. "Remind me to get him some mouth wash for that putrid breath."

The Minotaur put his hoof to his mouth, retreating back with embarrassment.

Philip then continued where he left off. "Ok, now! For starters, you're both to address us by our land names at all times." He paused, and shook his finger at Medusa. "If memory serves me correct, we both drank a bit too much wine that night, and you were just as horny as I was." He then turned to the Minotaur. "And you would have pillaged yourself across Greece and beyond if Theseus had not stopped you."

Ezekiel intervened. "Good grief! That was all centuries ago." He huffed. "It's a much different world now."

"One that creatures like us are not accustomed to." The Minotaur remarked.

"Actually, from what you've told us, humanity has not changed all that much since we last walked the earth." Medusa sarcastically added.

Philip motioned for calm. "My brother and I promise that if you both help us in this cause, we'll grant you the right to walk this earth again as normal human beings."

"You have to make me very handsome and rich as well. I must be able to attract a beautiful woman." The Minotaur groveled.

"And you must restore my beautiful hair, and enable others to gaze upon my alluring green eyes once again." Medusa demanded.

"That shall be granted to both of you." Ezekiel stated, while Medusa continued studying them both from behind her dark glasses for a long moment.

"Would it also mean that you'd finally take me as your wife, Poseidon?"

"You need to call me Philip." He aired with annoyance. "No! I cannot marry you, or have any sort of affair with you ever again." He paused for a moment before continuing. "I'm a happily married man now, and quite settled."

Medusa laughed out loud, and even The Minotaur found amusement in the revelation.

"You, happy with one woman." She joyfully chuckled. "That one's hard to believe."

"it's quite the truth!" He intently declared. "I'm very much in love with my wife, and I've changed considerably over the centuries."

Medusa turned her amusement toward Ezekiel. "What about you? You were quite the wild one as well, if memory serves me correct."

Ezekiel humbly, and rather sheepishly answered. "I'm also happily remarried to my first wife, Metis."

Both the Minotaur and Medusa laughed hysterically at that revelation.

"Hearing all of this alone is worth being brought back to life." The Minotaur snorted, while the gods exchanged frustrated glances.

"Enough!" Philip angrily exclaimed. "Are you two with us or not?"

The Minotaur placed his hoof to his chin in ponderance, and exchanged glances with the shaded Medusa. "Count me in." The Minotaur declared.

"Me, as well." Medusa added with a reluctant sigh.

At that moment, Linda Sanchez strolled in from a shadowed corner of the room. "Well! From the sound of the echoing laughter, there must be one heck of a party going on here."

"If you aren't a sight for sore eyes." Ezekiel enthusiastically declared.

"I'm happy to see you gentlemen as well." She replied with a cordial nod.

"I hope you're ready to get to work." Philip stated.

"I'm always ready to help for a good cause." She confidently answered as she eyed the two beastly beings with a perplexed expression. "Are they who I think they are?"

"Unfortunately, yes." Philip said with a sigh.

It was the pre-dawn hours before a weary Steven and Loraine returned to the Branchview Estate. Angelique and Mario followed close behind through the front door, still holding hands, as they all entered the main Foyer area. Little Olivia clung tight within her father's embrace, as he carried her in. Mary greeted them all, still dressed in her nightgown and night bonnet.

"I've been up most the night waiting for you folks to return."

"There was no need for that, Mary." Steven expressed.

"Well, I had to make sure Ms. Loraine got this message." She nodded. "Her mother is in the hospital. I guess there was some sort of accident yesterday evening."

"Oh dear!" Loraine wearily sighed. "What more could go wrong?"

"Take my car, and go." Steven urged, as he handed off his keys to Loraine. "I'll put Olivia to bed, and you can call me if I'm needed."

Mary stood back, and examined the couple with a critical eye.

"You two look like you done been through quite an ordeal."

"Oh, Mary! You don't know the half of it." Loraine responded, as Steven leaned in to kiss his wife goodbye.

After Loraine hurried back out the door, Mary and Steven turned their attention to Angelique and Mario who giggled and fussed with each other as most young lovers do.

"Could you please set these two up in a guest room, Mary? They haven't been together in over a hundred years."

"I'll do just that, Mr. Spencer." Mary eagerly replied. "I'll be sure to put a do not disturb sign on their door as well."

At an interstate truck stop on the outskirts of town, Philip and Linda walked through the front door, and immediately drew attention from the few partially awake truckers who rested at the counter, savoring their essential coffees. The couple were hard not to notice. Linda had the appearance of a movie star, and the broad-shouldered, long-haired Philip looked like a bad ass rock star.

Philip scanned the room with his intense eyes before the duo strolled back toward a near empty dining room at the rear of the building. Every eye in the place watched as they passed by.

They slid into a booth opposite Agents Guitierez and Banerjee, and they all greeted each other with a nod.

"Good to see you two again." Linda cordially stated.

"You as well." Banerjee smiled.

"Kind of a strange place for a meeting." Philip chuckled.

"It's probably the last place anyone would suspect. Especially at 5AM." Guitierez countered. "Besides, they have a killer breakfast omelet, and a bottomless cup of coffee."

"So, what's the update on things?" Philip impatiently pressed

"We've officially been compromised." Guitierez sighed. "Agent Gordon was the mole."

"Where is she now?"

"She's dead!" Guitierez paused, taking note of the surprise, wide-eyed reaction between Philip and Linda. "This has caused quite a bit of setbacks for us. All of our allied federal agents have been arrested, and are being held at an undisclosed location. Which means we no longer have inside help.”

“No doubt they’re all being grilled for information as we speak.” Philip stated. “Are there any of our people still on the inside?”

Guitierez shook his head. “We alerted as many as we could, and they’ve all gone into hiding.”

“That could be a good thing.” Philip commented before they all cautiously paused their conversing while the waitress poured their coffee.

“My brother and I do have a plan.” He resumed. “But after hearing this news, I think we’ll need to move a bit quicker.”

“Anything you’d like to share with us right now?” Guitierez asked.

“Unfortunately, you’ll just have to trust us on this. But I will say it might get a bit messy for them. This could be our only route to victory at this point.”

“How soon do you plan to move?”

“As soon as possible. Today, Linda and I will start with that lead you gave us on the human trafficking connection between Sharona Van Arsdale, Angelo Costanzo and Juan Cardones.”

“I’m eager to see that pipeline shut down permanently.” Linda firmly stated.

“Perhaps you haven’t heard today’s news.” Agent Banerjee announced. “Sharona Van Arsdale’s mansion burned to the ground during the night. They think she may have perished in the fire.”

Philip and Linda exchanged worried looks, and Philip immediately took out his cell phone.

"If you'll all excuse me, I need to check in with Ezekiel concerning this issue."

Without further word, he swiftly departed the table, leaving a somewhat baffled Guitierez and Banerjee to look toward Linda for answers.

"Is there something you'd like to fill us in on here?"

Linda drew an uncomfortable, stressful breath, and leaned into the conversation. "Steven and Loraine Spencer may have been in that house as well.

Both agents reacted with speechless surprise, and shock at the unexpected revelation.

At Lockeport General Hospital, Loraine rushed into her mother's room where she surprisingly found her sitting up in bed with an IV in her arm, and looking severely battered and bruised. Bill sat on the edge of the bed, casually holding her hand.

"Good grief, mother! You look as though you've been in a dog fight."

"More like a cat fight." Bill chuckled.

"You should talk." Millie countered, as she surveyed her daughter out of the one eye that was not swollen shut. "You look as though you've been thoroughly barbecued."

Bill conveniently interrupted as he stood, and yielded his spot to Loraine. "I was just leaving to get myself a cup of coffee, and a hot tea for Millie. Can I get you anything, Lori?"

"A cup of hot tea would be heavenly."

She politely waited until Bill had exited the room before she turned her attention back to Millie.

"Now, please do tell me what happened, mother." She urgently pressed, as she wearily pulled a chair up close to the bed.

"Oh Lori! You're shedding charred embers all over my clean bed sheets." She complained and fussed, while an impatient Lori only answered with an annoyed expression that pressed her further. "Very well!" She surrendered. "Agent Gordon and myself simply got into a bit of a tussle. Now, do tell me about your predicament, sweetheart."

"Don't sidestep me on this, mother." she sighed. "How did Agent Gordon fare through all of this?"

"Not very well, I'm afraid. Agent Gordon's dead."

Loraine was rendered speechless by her mother's reply, and leaned back in her chair, staring at the ceiling, with a multitude of questions running through her mind. Millie continued on rambling, despite her daughter's shocked silence.

"The whole ordeal reminded me of an experience I had in Budapest back in the summer of '92." She paused to reflect. "One of our allied agents went rogue, and if I hadn't acted in an alert fashion, I have no doubt she would have killed me." Millie paused to look over toward

Loraine, who was now mildly snoring with her eyes closed, and her mouth wide open.

"Well!" Millie indignantly shifted in her bed, and grunted. "The last thing I intended to do was to bore you to sleep, my dear."

Outside a doughnut shop near New Haven, Agent Mullen opened the door of his car as a gentle rain commenced to fall, and handed a coffee to Agent Parker as he crawled in.

"I hope you got me a mocha cappuccino." Parker stated.

"I got you a regular cup of coffee." Mullen grumbled. "Only women and fairies drink that other sugary crap."

Parker refrained from speaking his true thoughts, and shifted the conversation. "So, what's on the agenda today other than rain?"

"A road trip." Mullen promptly answered as he took a sip of his coffee. "We need to drive over to Cambridge, and find out what we can about that fire at the Sharondale Estate last night. But first, I need to make a few phone calls concerning our problems in Lockeport."

"You have any ideas on how we can handle that situation?" Parker further inquired.

"Oh yes! I sure do, Agent Parker." Mullen arrogantly chuckled. "Next time we visit Branch Consolidated, and the fine citizens of Lockeport, we'll have the state police and the National Guard to back us up. Those dimwitted Patriots will have no choice but to surrender."

"How do we know the state of Connecticut will go along with it? After all, it is against the Constitution."

"You need to get this straight Parker. The Constitution is no longer valid under our new system of government." He paused with seething emphasis. "Besides, I have enough powerful connections in this state that are able to override that outdated document."

After a long flight from London, Kenneth Laszlo arrived at his lavish Estate near Greenwich. As he entered the front door, he was promptly greeted by his uniformed butler.

"Welcome home Mr. Laszlo." He nodded. "I can take your luggage, and place it in your room. You have a guest waiting for you in your office."

"Thank you, Marlin." He replied with a rather curious expression. "Anyone in particular?"

"The gentleman made it very clear that he wanted to surprise you." He answered as he proceeded up the grand staircase with luggage in hand.

Moments later, Laszlo strolled into his large office, and glanced around the room. The swivel chair at his desk swung around, revealing the mystery guest, and bringing a smile to Laszlo's face.

"Grandpa Roger! It's been a long time."

A grin curled onto Roger McPherson's face when he saw Kenneth. "My boy! You're looking quite handsome and dapper."

Laszlo sauntered over, and sat down in a chair on the opposite side of the desk. "What special occasion has prompted a visit from my favorite time traveling relative?"

"Actually, I've been here for nearly a year while you were exiled in London." He answered, much to Laszlo's surprise. "Your house staff has been quite hospitable in your absence."

"And quite secretive I might add." Laszlo stated with a smirk. "I had no idea."

"I travelled here to check on Liddy. She came through the portal quite a while ago, but never returned." He paused. "When I was unable to locate her, I tried to return myself, and found that the portal had been permanently sealed."

"She was in our time quite a while ago, but she mysteriously disappeared." Laszlo said as he stood up and began pacing in thought. "We all assumed that she had returned through the portal."

"How long ago was that?"

"Almost five years." He answered with concern. "It must've been a powerful witch, wizard, or warlock to have permanently sealed that portal."

"More powerful than that." Mr. Morningstar commented as he strolled from the shadows of the room, startling both men. "I believe this man and his brother may have been behind that." He handed a Trident calling card to Roger, whose eyes immediately grew wide.

"I've seen that symbol before." Roger spoke up, while Laszlo and Morningstar listened with heightened interest and surprise. "It was on the forearm of the man who saved me from piracy in 1697." Roger paused in thought. "Blast! For some reason, I can't seem to remember all the details, but I'll never forget that tattoo."

"He obviously purged your memory" Morningstar smirked. "That man was none other than the immortal god Poseidon, and I do believe he may have been responsible for the explosion and fire at Sharondale last night."

"What fire? I wasn't made aware of this." Laszlo inquired with shocked surprise.

"I hate to be the bearer of bad news, Kenneth." Morningstar casually replied. "Your sister's estate burned to the ground last night while you were in transit. They believe she may have perished."

"I'm sorry, Kenneth." Roger solemnly added. "I only learned of it a short time ago myself from that information box that your employees call a T.V."

"I wouldn't be surprised if the gods and Steven Spencer may have had a hand in all of this." Morningstar theorized.

"If so, I believe I may know what this was all about." Laszlo sighed. "It might've had something to do with one of the last conversations I had with Sharona just a few short days ago."

Roger shifted his attention to Morningstar. "We haven't been formally introduced, sir. My name is Roger McPherson."

"I know very well who you are, Mr. McPherson." He answered as he offered his hand in a greeting. "My name is Lucifer Morningstar."

Roger laughed aloud, and turned his attention to Laszlo. "This narcissistic bastard thinks he's the devil."

"I wouldn't anger him, grandfather." He warned with a stressful sigh. "He most certainly is who he claims to be."

Roger became sober faced and speechless at the response, while Morningstar strolled closer, and took a seat next to Laszlo.

"If the immortal god Poseidon indeed exist, is it so hard to believe that I do as well?"

Roger answered with only a quick shake of his head, as Morningstar entwined his fingers, and leaned forward.

"What is it that you desire most, Mr. McPherson?"

"I only wish to gather my Liddy, and return to 1920's era Paris. It's the only place I've ever found peace and true happiness."

"Ah! Gay Paree! I've dallied there occasionally myself." Morningstar stated with a reflective pause, before leaning in closer, and lowering his voice. "Peace and happiness are only an illusion, my dear Roger." After another pause, he leaned back in his chair. "I hate to inform you of this, but Liddy is dead."

Roger stared down at the desk in front of him with remorse. "Who was responsible?"

"The same men I mentioned earlier. Steven Spencer happens to be the heir to the Branchview Estate."

"I should've guessed it was either a Branch or a Locke. Liddy travelled to this time period against my wishes in order to destroy what remained of those two blasted families." He looked away with rising anger. "How did it happen?"

"Liddy became allies with Hades, my army of demons, and the Secret Society in their attempt to take over Branch Consolidated. They went into battle against the gods Poseidon and Zeus, and the current inhabitants of Branchview." Morningstar paused to gather his thoughts. "I had also granted your wife Jenny a second chance at life, but she perished as well at the hands of The Spirit Witch, Charlotte Locke."

Roger only replied with a remorseful stare, while Morningstar leaned closer once again.

"You need to join us, and The Secret Society in our continuing battle against Steven Spencer and his allies. They must be destroyed." Morningstar grinned in a sinister manner. "Your dark magic could be a valuable asset to us, Roger.

"What's in it for me?" Roger sarcastically asked.

"I could reward you with your inner most desires."

Roger's eyes darted between Morningstar and Laszlo, before he slammed his fist on the desktop and stood in rage. "Why in the bloody hell would I ever do that?" He paced like a caged animal. "That blasted Secret Society was responsible for destroying my family. I'd rather see those elitist bastards banished from the earth." He pointed toward Morningstar with a sneer. "Besides, if you are who you say, you do not own my soul."

Morningstar also stood, and his eyes glowed red with rage as he confronted Roger, coming within inches of his face. "I beg to differ, Mr.

McPherson. You sold your soul when you decided to practice the dark arts."

"That is a blatant lie! I never forged an alliance with you or anyone else, and unlike Jenny and Liddy, I would never sell out to The Secret Society. I closed the chapter on my feud with the Branch and Locke family long ago."

Morningstar settled a bit, and backed away, surprised by Roger's resistance. "The Secret Society didn't destroy your family, Roger. It was Jonathan Locke and his descendants." He growled as his anger rose once again. "You're a fool if you dare refuse my request, for I will be forced to destroy you in a most excruciating manner. You will never return to your supposed happy life." He began marching away, but paused to point a finger of warning at Laszlo. "I would highly suggest that you talk some sense into your grandfather." He then stormed from the room, slamming the door in his angry wake.

At a business park outside of Boston, Philip and Linda began their crusade against injustice. They entered into the offices of Midland Enterprises where two of Angelo Costanzo's thugs were sitting comfortably near the receptionist's desk. The two men immediately recognized Philip from their previous encounter, and stood up, reacting with heightened anxiety.

"Look Mister, we don't want any trouble with you." Geno stated with fear in his eyes.

"Then leave." Philip responded with a chuckle, before turning to the frightened young woman at the desk. "Where is Costanzo?"

She motioned toward the back office with her eyes before fleeing the room herself. As they prepared to head back that way, the door swung open, and a mean looking, very muscular man aggressively blocked the doorway. When he laid eyes on Linda, a slight smile graced his face.

"Who are you, cupcake?"

She boldly confronted him, while Philip stood back with a smirk.

"I am the cupcake who is going to kick your ass."

Before the big man could react, she swiftly maneuvered him into a painful, submissive arm hold. She then spun around, landing a hard karate kick to his face that sent him pummeling to the floor. Philip stepped over him, pausing to approve of his partner's handiwork.

"It's quite true that the bigger they are, the harder they fall."

They proceeded to the back office where Angelo Costanzo sat calmly waiting at his desk.

"I figured you'd be paying me a visit sooner or later." He flashed the trident calling card. "I assume this is you."

Philip only answered with a quick nod as Costanzo's eyes wandered to Linda.

"Who's the hot babe?"

"That hot babe is the one who very easily disposed of your oversized goon."

Costanzo was quite impressed. "What about Geno and Delaney?"

"I'd have to say that by the way they fled the office, they must've peed themselves when they saw me."

Costanzo's bodyguard had somewhat recovered, and now stumbled into the office with his gun drawn. With lightning speed, Linda landed another kick to the side of his head, sending him down for good.

"She's one tough cookie." Costanzo commented.

Philip brandished his war knife, and plunged it down in the middle of Costanzo's desk, stunning him with fear.

"Do you know what this knife is, Mr. Costanzo?"

"A very sharp and wicked looking knife." He answered with wide eyes.

"That's the knife that I plant between myself and my enemy when I declare war."

"What do you want from me?" Costanzo asked, shivering with anxiety.

Philip calmly paced in front of the desk. "I have dealt with common criminals in the past, but I must say there is a certain type that I cannot tolerate." He paused to momentarily exchange a glance with Linda. "I have no patience with human traffickers, and pedophiles."

"Look! You're way in over your head here." Costanzo warned. "I'm just a small player. The other's you're dealing with are way bigger." He paused. "The Chinese, Russian, and South American Cartels. High ranking government officials. Not to neglect mentioning some of the world's wealthiest and most powerful people."

"I'm absolutely shaking in my shoes, Angelo." Philip sarcastically quipped, while Linda stepped to the forefront.

"We'll eventually take care of the others." She spoke with confidence. "The one we want right now is Juan Cardones."

"And, if you're smart, you'll tell us where we can find him." Philip added.

Costanzo's eyes lowered in defeat. "If I tell you, these people will kill me."

"That leaves you with quite a dilemma then, Mr. Costanzo." Philip paused. "Because, if you don't tell us, we'll kill you. So please, do not try our patience."

"He operates from the Port of Miami, but he holds his assets in an underground facility outside of Washington D.C."

"You mean his victims." Philip asserted, while Costanzo answered with a quick nod.

Philip seized a piece of paper, and a pen from the desktop, and slid it in front of him.

"I need an address of where this facility is located, and the address of where I can find Cordones himself."

"That's easy." Costanzo stated as he jotted on the paper, and handed it back to him. "The facility is on the same grounds that house the FBI and CIA, and the other address is Cordones' penthouse in Miami."

Philip looked to Linda with wide eyed surprise, before he retrieved his knife from the desk top, and holstered it.

"One more thing, Mr. Costanzo." He strolled back and leaned against the desk in an intimidating way. "You are to never go near the

Branchview Estate, nor bother Steven Spencer and his family ever again. Is that understood?"

Costanzo answered with a reluctant nod before speaking once more. "What in the hell happened in that woods?"

Philip answered with a sigh. "Your men trespassed on very sacred land, and they paid the price for it."

"Are they all dead?"

"Let's just say that the earth ingested their miserable carcasses, and we'll leave it at that."

Costanzo's eyes grew wide at the revelation, and Philip pointed a finger in warning.

"And, don't even think of alerting Cordones, or anyone else either. If you do, we will hunt you down, and kill you."

Costanzo swallowed the warning with a nervous gulp, as Philip and Linda then calmly exited the office.

At Branchview, Steven passed the time typing away on his desktop. Mrs. Porter quietly peeked in the door of his office, and he glanced up to acknowledge her.

"I'm sorry if I bothered you, Steven. I just wanted to look in to see if you needed anything."

Steven grinned. "What I'd really like is for you to sit down and visit with me, Mrs. Porter."

The elder woman fully entered, and took a seat opposite him. "Is everything ok?"

"Well." Steven began. "I'm not very happy about being confined to this house, but the others assure me that it's in my best interest."

"They're right, Steven. There's a lot of evil people who would wish to have you out of the way."

Steven gave a thoughtful nod. "You and I haven't had one of these talks for quite some time. We've certainly been through a lot together. Haven't we?" He smiled.

She gave a reflective nod before answering. "I am so proud of the wonderful man you've become, and I'm sure your adoptive parents would've been proud as well." She teared up. "No matter how old you get, I'll always think of you as that cute little boy that used to follow me all over that old farmhouse."

They both chuckled, and took an emotional pause.

"I know my parents were very sick in those last few years. Thank you for filling in, and being a parent to me. I know that had to be quite a sacrifice for you"

Mrs. Porter reached across the desk, and took hold of Steven's hand. "I wouldn't have wanted it any other way." She smiled. "I need to thank you as well for giving me a home, and a family when I had nowhere else to go."

Steven gave her weathered, frail hand a gentle squeeze. "I wouldn't have had it any other way either, Mrs. Porter. You and I will always be family."

The warm noon day sun streamed through the windows of the Grand Corridor and Ballroom, creating a calming beam of light that shined upon a daydreaming Olivia as she sat on one of the side benches. The rapid echoing footsteps preceded a frantic Loraine's arrival.

"Olivia Spencer! We have been looking all over for you, young lady."

"I'm just looking at the pictures, mommy."

Loraine sighed as she sat down on the bench next to her little daughter. "You should never wander off like that without telling us."

The little girl's stare never wavered from the portrait of Penelope on the wall in front of her. "Grandma Penelope was very pretty."

"Yes, she was." Loraine replied with a smile. "She had an identical twin named Charlotte that was just as beautiful."

"I know." The little girl acknowledged. "She was very evil, but then she turned good."

"I don't recall telling you that, but yes, it's true." Loraine answered. The sisters both had dark hair and blue eyes just like you and I."

"That's because they were twins of the Summer Moon. Just like we are." Olivia proudly proclaimed, much to her mother's surprise.

"How do you know about all of this, Olivia?"

"Maggie told me." She soberly replied.

"Ahh! Little Maggie!" Loraine snickered. "Where has she been hiding lately?"

"She's been around."

"Oh! Thank goodness you found her!" Andrea proclaimed with relief, as she arrived carrying little Dimitri, and with London and Michael tagging along as well.

"Livie!" London squealed as he rushed to hug his sister.

Michael also hurried to join the group hug as the mother's observed the heartwarming moment.

"I'm so sorry, Lori." Andrea announced. "I was tending to Dimitri for just a few short seconds, and when I turned around, Olivia was already gone."

"It's quite alright, Andrea. I should've been in the room as well."

"I've been meaning to mention this, but we have been spread a bit thin with help around here lately."

"Believe me, I've given that fact very careful thought." Loraine replied. "These children are a lot more active than they were as babies."

Both women paused to pleasantly watch the little ones as they laughed, and chased each other's shadows within the sunbeams on the tile floor.

"We simply can't hire a stranger off the street." Loraine sighed. "With all the secrets and paranormal activity going on within this house, I'm afraid that would result in further dire circumstances."

"We could always hire Angelique to help." Andrea suggested. "I don't think her and Mario will be leaving anytime soon."

"That is a very good idea." Loraine answered with an enlightened nod. "I'll definitely have to speak with her about it, but certainly not before their honeymoon has worn down."

Both women exchanged wide eyed glances, and giggled at the thought as they rounded up the energetic children, and herded them along.

In a high rise condo on Miami Beach, Juan Cordones was relaxed in an easy chair, sipping on a mid afternoon cocktail, and enjoying the spectacular view from his penthouse. He was calmly stunned when the door to his unit suddenly flew open, and Philip and Linda boldly marched in.

"The pitch fork man and the little Caribbean mermaid." Juan sarcastically quipped. "I must applaud you for being able to maneuver past my state of the art security system." He raised his cocktail toward them. "Can I fix both of you a drink."

"This is far from being a social call, Cordones." Linda firmly stated.

"Then, what special occasion would bring you two to my splendid residence?" He paused as he rose from his seat, and sauntered closer. "Hopefully, your muscular friend here isn't going to kick my ass."

"Why should I have him do something that I could easily do myself?" Linda shot back.

"Ooh!" Cordones chuckled as he retreated back a bit.

"We're here to collect your client list." Philip finally spoke in a calm manner. "We already know where your central holding facility is located."

Cordones laughed. "Then you must also realize that if you handed me over to the authorities again, I'd be back on the street, and back in business in less than an hour."

"We won't make that same mistake again." Philip replied in a cold manner.

"You have no idea of the power and wealth behind all of this." He reasoned. "If you were to kill me, someone else would rise to take my place." He lowered his voice to a near whisper. "We are unstoppable."

"Then we'll just have our hands full now. Won't we?" Philip defiantly countered.

Cordones paced daringly close. "Of course, if you were foolish enough to let me live, I'd promise that I'd find a way to destroy you, pitch fork man." He turned to Linda, pointing his finger and sneering. "I would also hunt down this mermaid, and gut her with my fishing knife."

"Oh Juan! You really shouldn't have said that." Philip sighed.

Linda challenged him with an eye to eye stare. Then with cat like reflexes, she snatched the cocktail drink that he had set on a side table, and smashed it into his face."

Cordones reeled back, and tried to unholster his gun. "You bitch! I'll kill you right now!"

Before he could draw, Linda landed a hard round house kick to his midsection that took him completely by surprise. The force from the kick drove him back, and sent him crashing through the plate glass window. His fading screams could clearly be heard as his body rapidly dropped from the top floor of the high rise.

"Oops!" Linda meekly exclaimed with wide eyed surprise. "I guess I got a bit carried away."

Philip strolled over to the window, looked over the edge with a wince, and shook his head.

"We certainly won't have to worry about him anymore."

Linda looked around, and spotted Cordones' cell phone and laptop on the countertop.

"At least we have those." She stated as she moved to collect them.

"We'll take those back, and let Guitierez and his team collect whatever they can from them." Philip added.

"I need to take a quick swim, and then we can move on to Washington to finish this job." She boldly proclaimed.

"I think we should call it a day." Philip pondered. "We'll go back to the cave, and regroup."

"What do you mean?" Linda huffed. "Why quit when we're on a roll?"

"I think it's time for my brother, and our new friends to be pressed into action." He smirked. "We'll be able to slay more giants in a lot less time."

Back at Branchview, Steven wandered into the dining room where Sharie and Mary were taking their lunch break.

"Well! How are you doing, Steven?" Sharie inquired.

"I'm going absolutely out of my mind." He answered. "I need to take a walk around the property."

Angelique and Mario also entered the room, not looking as if they had even a bit of rest.

"How are you two lovebirds doing this afternoon?" Sharie cheerfully asked.

"Absolutely marvelous!" Angelique exuberantly answered. "We barely slept, but the sex was totally awesome." She added, while Steven and the ladies reacted with slack jawed, and wide eyed, speechless surprise.

"Now Angelique, you need to be a bit more discreet when it comes to private matters." Mario scolded, showing obvious embarrassment.

"If we could've only been flies on the wall in that room." Mary murmured under her breath to Sharie, who was already struggling to maintain a straight face.

"I'm absolutely famished!" Angelique exclaimed. "Are we too late to be fed?"

Sharie cleared her throat as she rose from her seat. "I'll see what I can fix up quick in the kitchen."

"Better be a lot. That woman eats like a horse." Mary whispered.

"Mario! In the meantime, would you care to join me for a short walk down by the water?" Steven asked.

"I would love to see the ocean again, sir. It's been so long."

Steven then turned to Sharie and Mary with all seriousness, and spoke in a low tone. "Whatever you do, don't tell anyone I left this house."

"Our lips are sealed, Mr. Spencer." Mary assured.

A short time later, Steven and Mario commenced their casual stroll along the beach at Lighthouse Point.

"One thing that never changes over time is the beauty of the ocean." Mario proclaimed as he pleasantly looked out to sea.

"I fully agree with that Mario." Steven paused to enjoy the picturesque scene himself. "Tell me a little about your life before."

"I had a simple, but happy life." He fondly recalled. "I had a small shop in town, at the corner of Franklin St. and Main."

"I know exactly where that is. There's a florist shop there now."

The men proceeded to walk as they conversed.

"I had begun to receive commissions from all over the world, and people would often gather at my front window to watch me work." He smiled. "Still, I was all alone, and couldn't seem to find a woman that suited my fancy."

"So, you decided to design your perfect image of a woman." Steven assumed with a grin.

Excitement rose in Mario's voice as he continued. "It was as though the hands of God had seized control of mine, and it was He Himself that chiseled away at the stone."

"I wouldn't discount that fact at all." Steven replied, as the men settled onto an outcrop of rocks near the lighthouse. "How is it that Angelique came to breathe life?"

"It was a miracle." His eyes sparkled as he reminisced. "One evening, shortly after I had finished her, I sat marveling at her beauty. I wished in my heart that she could live and breathe" He dramatically recalled. "I couldn't help myself. I approached her with such love, and kissed her on the lips."

"And, she came to life?" Steven urged him on, fascinated by the story."

"Yes!" He smiled. "From that moment on, she was my constant companion, and no one suspected that she was indeed the beautiful statue I created." His smile turned to an angry frown. "No one except that witch, Liddy McPherson."

Steven rolled his eyes, and gave an all knowing nod. "Tell me about that."

"That woman! That witch!" He trembled with anger. "She would often frequent my shop while I worked on Angelique, and greatly admired the male statues I'd created. She noticed the remarkable resemblance between Angelique and the figure I had sculpted. She was also aware that the statue was mysteriously missing from my shop."

"And, I'm assuming she wanted to know your secret."

Mario nodded rapidly. "I tried to deny that Angelique indeed was the statue, but she knew I was lying." He clenched his eyes shut for a moment. "She persisted, and when I refused her request to bring one of the male sculptures in my shop to life, she snuck into my living space late one night, and turned both me and Angelique to stone."

"If it was at night, I would also have to assume that was the reason that your statues were naked."

Mario nodded. "She surprised us as we made love."

Steven was totally flabbergasted by his story, and pondered a long moment before speaking again.

"What date were you born, Mario?"

"June 17th. He proudly answered. "My parents often said I was a child of the summer moon, and that was how I received my artistic gifts." He could see the enlightened expression on Steven's face. "Why do you ask, Mr. Spencer?"

"I think everything is beginning to make sense." Steven answered with great ponderance. "Were you by chance a twin as well?"

"Yes, I was." He replied with curious amazement. "My sister was also quite gifted." He paused, taking note of Steven's continued deep thought. "Can you please tell me why this is so interesting to you?"

"I'm beginning to see a strange pattern, Mario. This may surprise you, but my children, my wife, and my mother were also twins of the summer moon. Like you, they also had dark hair and blue eyes."

Mario was rendered speechless by the revelation, and Steven casually glanced at his watch.

"We'll discuss this further at another time." Steven promptly stated, as he took the opportunity to change the subject. "By the way, I'd like to introduce you to my father-in law, Bill Crawford later today. He's our resident artist, and also the butler at the estate. He has a workspace in the East Wing, and it's big enough that we should be able to create an area there for you as well. At least until other arrangements can be made."

"I would truly appreciate that, sir."

"Myself, and the others will try the best we can to bring you up to speed on the modern world as well." Steven could not hold back a smile. "In the meantime, you'll need to help us instill proper etiquette, and lady like qualities in Angelique. We can't have her strolling around the estate in the nude, or discussing her sex life openly." He chuckled before adding. "You also need to tame that woman's voracious appetite if you expect her to maintain her perfect figure.

"Of course!" Mario laughed. "I'm afraid I may have failed at giving her all those necessary qualities when I created her."

Steven stood up, and patted him on the back of the shoulder. "Other than that, you created a true masterpiece, my friend."

Mario beamed with pride as he stood, and took a deep breath of the ocean air. Steven then motioned him along.

"Come on! Let's get you back to Branchview, and get you fed before that beautiful woman of yours eats everything in sight."

In the Secret Cave, the Minotaur paced impatiently while Ezekiel, Meryl, and Medusa sat calmly around the ornate granite and crystal topped round table. The Minotaur let out an angry snort, causing the snakes on Medusa's head to rear back and hiss. The sight made Ezekiel cringe uncomfortably.

"Could you please keep those nasty vipers under control?" He winced.

"How can I do that with this groveling beast stomping about the cave?" Medusa replied with frustration.

"Who are you calling a beast?" He angrily countered.

"Silence! Please! All of you!" Meryl pleaded with raised hands.

"How much longer do we have to wait for Poseidon and the Ebony Mermaid?" Minotaur complained, pointing to Ezekiel. "I know you didn't bring us back to life to spend all of our time in this blasted cave."

"Although it is quite energizing." Medusa added as she gazed upward at the large crystals that made up the ceiling and walls.

"He and Linda should be back before days end." Ezekiel reasoned. "We can't have creatures such as yourself wandering this world in plain sight."

"Who are you calling a creature?" Medusa pointed in anger. "It's not our fault that we look this way."

Ezekiel only exchanged a frustrated glance with Meryl, and buried his forehead into his hand.

"What's all the bickering about?" Philip inquired as he and Linda surprisingly appeared from the shadows of the room.

"Praise the Almighty God!" Meryl exclaimed. "I'm not sure how much more we could tolerate of these two."

"What were you able to accomplish?" Ezekiel asked in a less than enthusiastic tone. "I didn't expect you back until much later."

"A lot!" Philip expressed with emphasis. "We took care of the problem with Costanzo, and paid a visit to Cordones in Miami as well."

"You covered a lot of ground." Ezekiel grinned. "Did you hand Cordones over to Guitierez and his team?"

"Not exactly." He sheepishly answered. "Linda got a bit carried away with her temper."

"And…?" Ezekiel narrowed his eyes."

"And, he took a head first dive from the 21st floor."

Ezekiel placed his fingers to his temples, and shook his head with frustration, while Linda only responded with a hapless shrug.

"We were able to seize his computer and cell phone however, and we did hand that over to Guitierez." Philip stated.

"We also found out that they're holding and processing the human slaves in an underground facility below Washington D.C." Linda added.

"Below FBI and CIA headquarters no less." Philip further added with a sarcastic tinge.

"When are you going to use us?" Minotaur ranted, with drool propelling from his mouth. "I'm going stir crazy in this damn cave."

"Just settle down big fella." Philip ordered. "We'll be using you and Medusa quite extensively, starting tomorrow."

"Are we all going to storm Washington together?" Ezekiel inquired.

"Not exactly." Philip paused to ponder the strategy. "Minotaur and I have business to take care of at the pharmaceutical firm that bears his name."

Minotaur let out a pleasing grunt, and clapped his hooved hands together in response.

"What about the rest of us?" Medusa inquired.

"The rest of you are all going to Washington." He smiled as he motioned for all of them to gather around the table. "I'll tell you what I have planned." He suddenly paused, and looked off into a corner of the room.

"What's wrong, brother?" Ezekiel asked.

"I'm being summoned by someone in New Haven." He answered with a perplexed expression.

Meryl narrowed her eyes toward him. "It's someone from your distant past."

"Yes." Philip nodded, still appearing quite baffled. "I'm not quite sure how it could be possible, but I do sense it's rather urgent." He stood back up. "We'll go over the plans later this evening. I really need to go meet this person right now."

"Wait!" Linda exclaimed. "I'm going with you. I somehow sense that I may know this individual as well."

Philip replied with a reluctant, agreeing nod, while Minotaur also stood, ready for action. "Should I go too?"

"Absolutely not, Minotaur. We can't risk you being seen in public."

"I'm sensing a bit of danger in this." Meryl warned. "Be careful, Philip."

Chapter Fourteen:
You Reap What You Sow

In a small pub in New Haven, Officer Ren Norville of the Connecticut State Police, and Captain Benjamin Scott of the Connecticut National Guard took a seat at the far end of the uncrowded bar.

"Thanks for meeting me here, Captain Scott."

"You picked a good place." He answered. "I assume this has something to do with our orders to move on Lockeport."

Norville nodded. "We took a vote among my officers, and no one is in favor of it."

"My troops aren't eager to comply either."

The two men paused as the bartender set two drafts down in front of them. They waited until he strolled away.

"So, what should we do?" Norville asked. "These are American citizens. We can't just aggressively turn on our own people."

"I guess if we don't comply, it will be the end of our careers." Scott sighed.

"If we do, it could be the end of our country." Norville replied.

Captain Scott gave an agreeing nod, and pondered the situation. "I think I might have a solution." Norville listened attentively as he continued. "I say we march into Lockeport as though we're going to clean house."

Norville reacted with a defiant expression, but Scott calmed him with a hand gesture, and continued on. "At the moment we confront the citizens, we'll promptly join them, and then turn on the real enemy."

Norville couldn't contain his enthusiasm. "That's absolutely brilliant, Ben!"

The two men clinked their mugs, and took a swallow of their beer.

"The citizens of Lockeport are good people." Norville stated. "Have you ever been there?"

"It's funny that you asked that." Captain Scott answered. "My platoon was on the beach at Lighthouse Point when the earthquake and tsunami struck four years ago." He paused to reflect. "For some strange reason, none of us can remember how we got there, nor how we managed to survive without being swept out to sea."

Norville simply pondered the scenario for a moment before speaking. "You know, there has been some strange happenings that occurred at the Branchview Estate over the years. In fact, there has been a few unexplained incidents there recently."

Captain Scott also carefully thought out his next response. "Well, Ren!" He tipped his beer toward Norville. "If it can't be explained, then perhaps some mysteries are better left unsolved."

Norville smirked at the answer, and also tipped his mug toward Captain Scott. "I say we open up a can of whoop ass on those treasonous government bastards."

Captain Scott laughed, and chugged the last of his beer, before motioning to the bartender. "I'll buy the next round, and definitely drink to that."

A short distance away, Philip and Linda strolled along the walkway of Long Wharf Park on the New Haven waterfront. They spotted a familiar figure ahead, leaning against the railing, enjoying the view of Long Island Sound. They casually approached, and flanked him on opposite sides.

Roger's stare never wavered from the vast body of water in front of him. "Thanks for meeting with me."

"I have to admit, we were both rather surprised." Philip replied.

"You haven't aged a bit, but you've definitely lost that distinct Scottish brogue." Linda commented.

"And you're just as beautiful as I remember, Mermaid." Roger chuckled. "You've also lost that Jamaican accent that I remember all so well."

"I suppose we've all evolved a bit over the centuries." Philip stated with a grin.

"I'll cut right to the chase." Roger stressed. "I travelled here through the portal of time, and haven't been able to return to my life in 1920's Paris."

"That's because my brother and I closed that portal almost two years ago." Philip answered. "How long have you been here?"

"For at least that long. I cashed in some of the gold that Liddy had stashed in order to sustain myself, but the money didn't last long in this blasted economy."

"Money certainly doesn't go as far as it used to. Where are you staying now?" Linda asked.

"I've been staying at my grandson's estate just outside of New York for the past year."

"Who is your grandson?" Linda continued to curiously probe.

Roger drew a reluctant sigh. "Kenneth Laszlo."

Philip and Linda exchanged an alarming glance. "You do realize that he's an enemy of ours?" Philip countered.

Roger gave a slight nod. "When he returned from London today, another man named Morningstar accompanied him." He paused to chuckle. "The arrogant bastard actually thinks he's Satan." He pulled one of Philip's cards from his pocket, and held it up for him to see. "He gave me this card, and I knew it had to be you."

"Why did you summon us here?" Philip asked with rising anger.

"I need your help." Roger sighed. "This Morningstar threatened my life if I didn't lend my powers to the cause of the Secret Society."

"I'd take that threat very seriously, Mr. McPherson." Philip warned.

"I want no part of that blasted Society of fools." Roger fumed. "They've done nothing but destroy my family."

"You actually expect us to trust you after all the destruction your lineage has caused?" Linda questioned.

Roger clenched his eyes shut in a moment of anxiety before explaining. "For years, both Liddy and I cheated death by traveling through time. I fell in love with a woman in Paris, and vowed to change my life forever. I gave up the dark magic, and my centuries long feud with the Branch and Locke family." He shook his head with frustration. "I should've never left to come to this time period." He looked to both of them with pleading eyes. "Can you please just help me return to my own time?"

"First, I need you to tell us how you managed to arrive through the Branchview portal without anyone there noticing."

Roger eyed them both with a perplexed expression. "I didn't come through the portal on the Branchview estate. I arrived through the portal that's connected to it."

Both Philip and Linda reacted with shocked expressions. "There's another portal?"

"Yes!" Roger exclaimed. "The one on Deer Island."

"The island in the middle of Lake Candlewood?" Philip curiously questioned.

Roger impatiently shook his head. "The old Deer Island. I believe it's now referred to as Haddam Island State Park." He appeared confused by Philip's cluelessness. "Are you saying that you don't know about it?"

"I don't. But I certainly know someone who would."

"Stargazer?" Linda spoke up, and Philip promptly nodded.

"Perhaps we could discuss this further over dinner." Roger stated. "I am quite hungry."

"I'll have to find accommodations for you as well, Roger." Philip stressed. "We can't let you go back to Laszlo's house tonight."

Roger stubbornly shook his head. "I can go back. I can serve as a spy for you and the others."

"It's far too dangerous!" Philip seriously warned. "Morningstar is exactly who he says he is, and he will kill you."

"I'll take that chance." Roger reluctantly stated. "I owe you at least that much for saving my life in 1697."

"I could've sworn I purged your memory of that event when I left you in that bar in Antigua." Philip smirked.

"I remembered just enough to piece everything together." He laughed. "However, it did take a few centuries to figure it all out."

Philip motioned ahead on the path. "Let's walk. There's a café a short distance away where we can get a bite to eat."

A short time later, the trio sat at an outdoor table enjoying a pleasant evening meal.

"So, you found love in Paris." Linda smiled. "Tell us about that."

"Her name is Celeste DuBois." Roger announced. "I met her at an art exhibit." He paused, brimming with enthusiasm. "When I first laid eyes on her, everything evil within me melted away."

"How romantic!" She replied.

"She made me realize how much life I had missed by holding on to hate and bitterness." He looked downward with emotion. "I miss her very much."

"I'm sure she misses you as well." Linda assured.

Philip raised his glass of wine toward Roger. "I can honestly say that it takes centuries for some of us to realize the true meaning of life and love." He took a sip from his wine, then leaned into the conversation, speaking in a lower tone. "I'll need to speak with my brother and Stargazer about this portal on Deer Island. I promise I'll do everything I can to return you to Celeste."

"How long do you suppose it will take?" Roger desperately asked.

"It may take a while." Philip reluctantly answered. "As you're well aware, we have to wait for a full moon, and we must determine the approximate position in order to get you back to the precise time you left." He paused. "We also have our hands full right now trying to defeat the Secret Society."

Roger gave an understanding nod. "I'll need to somehow secure passage from here, and back to Paris as well."

"Don't worry. Just go to the water's edge, and call my name. I'll do what I can to get you on a steamer from New York." He smiled. "I believe we've done that drill before."

"In the meantime, is there anything you can tell us about what Laszlo and the Secret Society may have planned?" Linda asked.

Roger thought for a moment before answering. "Kenneth was talking to a woman on the speaker phone this afternoon. I believe her name was Latasha Hampton."

Linda and Philip exchanged an anxious glance before Roger continued.

"They were discussing something about kidnapping a woman named Deanna LeRoux." He paused. "Kenneth also mentioned that an Agent Mullen would be seizing control of Lockeport."

"How soon is this taking place?" Philip urgently asked.

"Tomorrow evening." He answered.

Linda leaned back in her chair, and took a deep breath. "It looks like we'll have to postpone our other plans in order to prevent this from happening."

"I'm sure Medusa and Minotaur will not be happy about that." Philip quipped with a sigh.

"Medusa? Minotaur?" Roger questioned as he glanced at each one of them with a smirk. "You are kidding, right?"

Philip simply responded to him with only a matter of fact expression.

Later that evening, at the estate of Kenneth Laszlo, he and Morningstar had called together members of the inner circle within the Secret Society. Morningstar paced around the long table, addressing those in attendance.

"Tomorrow evening should bring a major victory for us all." He smiled. "Our foot soldiers shall move against the resistance in Lockeport, and with the help of the State Police and the National Guard, we will capture that cesspool of a town." He grunted with indignance, then grinned once more. "We'll then seize Branch Consolidated Industries, and burn it to the ground."

"What about Steven Spencer and Gerard LeRoux?" An older gentleman asked whose appearance wreaked of extreme wealth.

At this point, Roger McPherson had returned, and was eavesdropping behind the closed door to the room.

Morningstar chuckled to himself, and continued to pace around the table. "After tomorrow night, Gerard LeRoux will no longer exist. As for Steven Spencer, I'll allow Kenneth to answer that." He motioned for Laszlo to speak.

"Aside from the tragic news of my sister's demise, there might be reason to celebrate." He paused with emphasis. "Mr. Spencer has not been seen in public for over a week now. Some of us have reason to believe he may have been at my sister's estate and perished when the explosion took place."

"Perhaps he's just hiding out at Branchview." One woman flippantly suggested.

"I agree. How can you be so sure he's dead?" The same gentleman also further inquired.

"There were several remains found in the rubble, all burned beyond recognition." He pondered for a moment. "If my assumption is correct about Mr. Spencer, Branch Consolidated is practically in our grasp."

Morningstar casually sauntered to the door, and swung it open, taking Roger completely by surprise.

"Mr. McPherson! Being that you're so interested in eavesdropping on our conversation, please come in and have a seat."

Roger sheepishly entered, and Morningstar ushered him to a chair. Laszlo drew a deep stressful breath as his eyes followed his grandfather into the room.

"Would you like to tell us where you were this evening?" He asked, as he lurked over him intimidatingly.

"I don't see where that's any of your business."

"Everything that takes place in this household is my business." He growled.

"Really now? I thought this was Kenneth's house." He countered.

"I suggest that you answer my original question." He warned with seething anger, while everyone in the room drew an anxious breath.

"Very well! I borrowed the butler's car, and drove up to New Haven to have dinner." Roger calmly answered.

"There! That wasn't so hard now, was it?" Morningstar then abruptly turned away, and proceeded to address the others in the room. "Shall we continue at the point where we were so rudely interrupted?"

"I've finished what I have to say." Laszlo replied, motioning for Morningstar to continue.

"After we've effectively seized the town of Lockeport and Branch Consolidated, our rebels will also burn Branchview to the ground with all its inhabitants in it."

The room applauded his announcement. "What's next after that?" Another dapper gentleman at the table asked.

Morningstar rubbed his hands together and chuckled as he paced. "We then unleash the new virus which will wipe out half the world's population who were unwilling to receive our original vaccinations and boosters.”

“None of us took that shot for obvious reasons. But how will we be protected from this new pandemic?” Another woman at the table asked.

Morningstar smiled. “My dear lady, we will all have the anecdote that the common person will not have access to.”

“Brilliant!” Another man at the table exuberantly groveled as he raised his glass of wine in a toast, and everyone else applauded.

Roger sat silent with wide eyed terror at what he had just heard.

As the sun set over the Atlantic, Philip entered the stables where Stargazer was tending to the horses. He glanced up, and grinned when he saw who it was.

“I haven’t seen much of you lately.”

“I’ve had quite a full schedule.” Philip chuckled. “How are you liking your new residence?”

Stargazer paused from cleaning one of the stalls, and strolled out in the walkway to meet him. He paused to give an affectionate, light pat to the side of a horse’s snout. “I can’t say that I enjoy life in this time period. But I do like my quaint apartment above the stables.” He paused to glance around the pristine barn. “And most of all, I enjoy being around these marvelous creatures.”

“Sometimes they’re better company than humans.” Philip smirked before switching the subject. “What can you tell me about Deer Island?”

"It's one of the last places that the Wangunk inhabited before the settlers drove us away for good." He sadly paused for a brief moment. "Today, it's a State Park that's heavily infested with deer ticks, poison ivy, and briar."

"Is there another time portal there that's connected to the one at Branchview?"

Stargazer answered with a sober nod. "It's where I entered this spectrum of time."

"Why didn't you tell us this?"

"Because you never asked." He answered, prompting a frustrated eye roll from Philip. "I would've thought you and Ezekiel would've known."

"Obviously, that's one secret that the Wangunk kept concealed. I wasn't even aware of Deer Island prior to this."

"How did you find out about it?" Stargazer curiously inquired.

"From another time traveler named Roger McPherson. Like you, he's trapped in this spectrum."

"Liddy's father." Stargazer answered with an enlightened nod. "They were among the very few outsiders that knew about that portal."

Philip pondered the situation for a moment, then continued. "How would you like for Ezekiel and I to temporarily open that portal, and send you back to another time?"

"Is that possible?"

"It's never been attempted, but I believe we can." He answered with a confident gesture. "What time period do you prefer to be in?"

"I'd like very much to go back to the 1960's. I thoroughly enjoyed my stay in that era."

"Didn't we all?" Philip chuckled, while Stargazer settled onto a nearby bench.

"What do you know about the other time portal at Branchview?" Philip continued. Stargazer glanced up at him with a clueless expression. "I wasn't aware that there was another portal there."

Philip strolled over toward a stall, and split his attention between the conversation, and a curious horse that had peeked over its' stall door. "It's in one of the large mirrors in the Grand Ballroom. We keep it covered during full moon cycles to prevent unexpected guests from wandering through it."

Stargazer pondered in thought for a moment. "Perhaps Daniel Branch the first succeeded at creating another portal. I do know that he and Liddy were experimenting with time travel for quite a period." He pondered a bit further. "Maybe Roger and I could return through that portal."

Philip shook his head. "Ezekiel and I have no way of controlling the coordinates. You could end up in any time spectrum other than the one that's intended. We just can't take that chance." He paused. "The Midsummer Moon should be sometime next week. That gives us enough time to finish our business, hopefully defeating the Secret Society, and then we can try to send you two back through the portal on Deer Island."

"For the sake of all of us, I pray that happens." Stargazer humbly replied.

Philip checked his watch, and sighed. "I have an important meeting over at Branchview. We'll have to talk more about this later."

"I'll be here."

Meanwhile, at Branchview, Ezekiel started the meeting of the inner circle without Philip. He stood at the head of the Dining Room table to address everyone in attendance.

"We'll go ahead and get started here. Philip had business to take care of, and should be along shortly." He stated.

"I'm already here!" Philip announced as he hurried in to join his brother.

"Philip and Linda were able to gather some reliable information late this afternoon." Ezekiel continued as Agent Guitierez straightened in his seat to listen attentively.

"That's right." Philip said. "We found out that Mullen and the Neo Nazi's are planning to seize Lockeport, and Branch Consolidated tomorrow evening."

"And supposedly, they have help from the State Police and National Guard." Linda added

"I knew Mullen wouldn't stay away for long." Guitierez voiced with frustration. "Should I call in some of my sleeper agents to help?"

"No!" Ezekiel firmly responded. "They wouldn't be able to get here in time, and besides, we have alternative plans for them that we'll cover with you later."

"Just what do you intend to do? We can't fight an army by ourselves without using our supernatural powers." Steven anxiously spoke.

"Steven's right." Loraine vented with equal stress. "As you well know, we simply can't display those powers publicly."

"You seem to forget that my brother and I have the power to erase the people's memory of anything that we might not want them to see." Philip reminded with a clever smirk.

"You also keep forgetting Lori, that you alone possess the power of an army with the Shield of Njord." Ezekiel added.

"Oh no!" Steven protested as he stood. "I refuse to put my wife in that sort of danger. What if a stray bullet got past that shield?" He shook his head. "I'd never forgive myself if I lost her that way."

Guitierez stood up with a totally baffled expression "The Shield of what?"

"I'll fill you in later, Agent G." Ezekiel sighed.

Loraine carefully pondered the situation for a moment before enthusiastically exclaiming. "I'll do it!"

"But Lori…"

"I have to do this, Steven." She interrupted. "We have to defeat these scoundrels, or they'll kill us all."

"Then I'm going too." Steven grumbled.

"We were just getting to you, Steven." Philip motioned to calm him. "Apparently, the Secret Society thinks you're already dead. We have to make them believe that's true."

"What am I supposed to do in the meantime? Just sit here in this house twiddling my thumbs, while my wife, and the townspeople take on an entire army?"

"At least until this phase of the operation is over." Ezekiel ordered.

"I'll be okay, sweetheart." Loraine lovingly assured. "I'm certain the immortals have this thoroughly planned out."

"You have to trust us on this, Steven." Philip concluded, while Ezekiel took a deep breath, and continued.

"There's more." He gestured toward Gerard and his family who were also in attendance. "It appears that Mullen and Latasha Hampton are also plotting to kidnap Deana, and kill Gerard."

"Before that happens, I'll rip that bitch in two with my bare hands." Deana angrily responded.

"Watch your temper, young lady." Sharie warned. "We all have to keep a cool head, and go along with whatever Ezekiel and Philip have planned."

Ezekiel locked fatherly eyes on Deana. "I understand you're an excellent student of the martial arts. I'll let you handle Ms. Hampton personally." He grinned.

"Now, wait just a minute." Gerard protested. "I've already lost a son, and I can't bear the thought of losing my daughter as well."

"That's exactly why I devised a fail-safe plan in which you play a major role. I'll go over that with the two of you after the meeting." Ezekiel explained.

"We'll kick some ass as a family, daddy." Deana confidently remarked, while Gerard drew a deep sigh, and gave an agreeing nod.

"With that out of the way, let's get down to the business of planning all of this out." Philip anxiously stated.

In the town of Lockeport, Pamela Priestly entered her house, carrying several bags of groceries.

"I'm home!" She yelled. "Come help me with these groceries."

She paused for an answer, but was only confronted by an eerie silence. From an adjoining room, Agent Mullen and Latasha Hampton arrogantly strolled in to greet her. Mullen held a gun with a silencer attached.

"Your family won't be replying, Mrs. Priestly." He chuckled. "They've been permanently silenced.

Pamela fell to her knees, and wept with anguish and sorrow, while Latasha triumphantly stood over her with a smirk.

"I warned you Pam, just as I did the others, not to interfere with my plans." She paced around her. "But you and your friends at Branchview had to start your own school, and you stole a good number of our impressionable minds."

"You had no right to do this to my family." Pamela countered.

"We have every right to do as we please, Mrs. Priestly." Mullen arrogantly replied. "We're the ones who are in charge." He strolled closer, and aimed his gun at her. "It's a pity that you and your family had to be used as an example."

With that said, Mullen pulled the trigger without remorse, and the bullet left the chamber with an ungodly, silencing thump.

Chapter Fifteen:
Tides Turn Amidst the Sorrow

The mellow morning sun streamed through the kitchen widows at Branchview, as Mary joyfully entered the room through the swinging door. She paused to notice Mrs. Porter sitting at the table with her head resting within her crossed arms.

"Good morning, Mrs. Porter." She glanced that way, when she uncharacteristically didn't answer. "If you're not feeling well, you should go back to bed, sweetie."

Despite no answer, Mary continued on with her morning routine, and talked as she worked.

"Andrea will be along real soon. She's tending to that youngin' of hers in the nursery." She took some dishes from an upper cabinet. "If we have to, we can get Angelique to help."

When she still didn't respond, Mary paused again, and looked that way. "Mrs. Porter?"

She strolled over to her with great concern. "Are you okay, Ethel?"

She placed her hand on the elder woman's fragile shoulder, and then realized that her body was limp and lifeless. With a sorrowful sigh, she looked upward and subtly cried out. "Oh Lordy!"

In Lockeport, Priscilla Russell was just serving up breakfast to her son Tre when the front door blasted open. Frank Parker and another FBI agent rushed in with their guns drawn. Stricken with surprise, Priscilla immediately grabbed at her heart, and fell into one of the dining room chairs. A frantic Tre's eyes darted between his mother and the agents as they roughly pulled him from his chair.

"Mom!" He cried as they placed cuffs on his hands. "Take me, but please get help for her." He pleaded.

"Should we put a bullet in the old lady?" The younger agent asked.

Frank paused for a moment, watching her struggle. "She's having a heart attack. Just let her die naturally."

Without remorse, they proceeded to muscle a struggling Tre from the house. After they departed, Priscilla stumbled to a nearby table where Tre had placed his cell phone. She picked it up, and managed to dial 911.

"I need help!" She breathlessly exclaimed. "Please hurry!"

As the household at Branchview dealt with the unexpected death of someone very dear to them, a sorrow filled Steven gathered everyone for a meeting in the main dining room. He waited for everyone to settle, and then motioned for silence as he prepared to speak.

"I'm sure that by this time you've all heard of the untimely death of our Mrs. Porter." He took time to scan the sad faces of everyone in attendance before continuing. "She died peacefully this morning doing what she enjoyed the most. Taking care of all of us." He began to emotionally choke up. "Under normal circumstances, this would put a temporary halt to our daily routines. But under present circumstances, I don't think she'd want that. She would want us to fight on, and defeat the enemy that is trying to destroy us."

Everyone nodded in reluctant agreement. Angelique then meekly stood, raising her hand, and Steven motioned for her to speak.

"Mario and I plan to join the townspeople in defending Lockeport tonight." She took time to glance at everyone in the room. "I say we all participate to honor the memory of Mrs. Porter. Who's with us on this?"

Without hesitation Bill Crawford stood first, followed by everyone else in attendance. The action brought a sentimental smile to Steven, and Loraine squeezed his hand affectionately as she stood as well.

"I wish I could be there with all of you." He whispered to her.

"You'll have your chance, Mr. Spencer." She smiled and winked.

"Just be careful. If something happened to you, I'd never forgive myself."

"Don't worry, darling. I have the gods, the shield, my white magic, and the armor of the Almighty God to protect me. That's more than enough." She confidently proclaimed.

"Yes, it sure is." He answered as he lovingly embraced her.

In the townhome of Latasha Hampton, a handcuffed Tre Russell was forcibly pushed into a room by Agent Parker and his accomplice. A few moments later, Latasha strolled into the room with a smirk on her face.

"Just make yourself comfortable, Mr. Russell." She stated in a calm voice.

"I should've known you were behind all of this." He replied.

"Relax! You're only bait for a much bigger catch." She further stated.

"What are you talking about?" Tre questioned with visible annoyance.

She sauntered within inches, and spoke in a low tone. "When your darling little Deanna finds out we have you, her and her father will obey our demands, and come rushing here. In the process, they'll fall directly into our trap."

"Are you serious? What do you hope to gain from all of this?" He further questioned.

She grunted in response, and her and the agents exchanged looks of demented amusement.

"You just don't get it. It's all about the power my handsome friend, and crushing anyone who prevents us from attaining it." She paused while she paced in front of him. "We've found that the best way of conquering a society is through their children's minds. Once we attain that, we're unstoppable."

"You are one sick bitch." Tre sneered with great disdain.

Agent Parker sucker punched Tre in the face, and the force of the blow sent him reeling backward. Dazed, he managed to keep from falling, and stood glaring back at them with anger.

"For that remark, I'll make sure you're able to witness both the moments I carve the still beating heart out your beloved Deanna, and my two friends here slit the throat of Gerard LeRoux."

Tre pointed a finger of warning at each one of them. "You left my innocent mother to die. Now you want to kill two more innocent people.

"In every war, there has to be casualties, Mr. Russell." Latasha nonchalantly replied.

"If I ever get out of this, I will hunt down all of you, and kill you with my bare hands."

Agent Parker answered him with a mocking laugh, and shook his head. "Big words from a powerless man. Too bad you won't live to make that little pipe dream a reality."

"If you take these cuffs off of me, I'll make you regret that little sucker punch." Tre taunted.

The comment prompted all three to laugh as they arrogantly departed the room, slamming the door in their wake.

In the Secret Cave, Philip arrived to find Minotaur pacing back and forth impatiently, while Medusa rested calmly in one of the throne chairs.

"You're wasting a lot of energy snorting and pacing." Philip commented.

"I'm about to go out of my mind in this blasted cave." Minotaur roared. "Why can't I go with you tonight? I could take out 50 soldiers with just one swipe of my hoof."

"I don't doubt that for one moment."

"Oh please! Take him with you. He's nearly driving me insane." Medusa distressfully moaned.

"Both of you need to rest. I guarantee that you'll get all the action you need tomorrow."

Minotaur grunted his displeasure as Philip settled into the other throne chair.

"Besides." Philip continued with a sigh. "We have Loraine Spencer as our secret weapon tonight."

"How can a measly, mortal woman be a secret weapon?" Minotaur angrily complained.

"Take that back, or I'll remove these sunglasses, and turn you into a statue." Medusa threatened.

Philip placed his hand to his head in annoyance. "Would you two please settle, and quit acting like children?"

"He instigated it." Medusa replied, which prompted a threatening stare from Philip.

"Now! If the two of you must know, Mrs. Spencer possesses a powerful shield that I'm sure the two of you are very familiar with.

"You're not talking about the shield of Njord?" Minotaur questioned with a peak of interest, and Philip answered with an assured nod.

"I thought you and the other gods buried that cursed relic years ago." Medusa stated with alarm. "How did it come into her possession?"

"It's a long story, that I'd rather not get into at this time." Philip replied. "Let's just be grateful that we have it, and our enemy doesn't." He paused with emphasis before focusing on Minotaur, and continuing. "Tomorrow morning, I'll let you run like a bull in a china shop when we invade Minotaur Pharmaceuticals."

Minotaur snarled with pleasure at the comment. "It will be just like old times."

"Only this time, you're pillaging for the good instead of the evil." Philip added.

"I like the sound of that." He snorted, as he wiped the drool from his snout, prompting an expression of disgust from Medusa.

"What does Ezekiel have planned for me?" She inquired. "All I know is that we're going to a place called Washington D.C."

"You'll be invading FBI and CIA headquarters." Philip answered. "Your powers, along with those of Ezekiel, and Lorain's shield should be more than enough to pave a path of victory for the agents who are on our side."

"Sounds like fun!" Minotaur exclaimed with excitement, while rubbing his hooves together.

"It will indeed be a glorious day of victory for us all." Philip proclaimed.

In the Branchview Foyer, Steven stood staring at the ticking grandfather clock which had come to symbolize a beating heart within the grand old house. It chimed at two o'clock, and echoed across the high ceilings in a haunting, yet comforting manner.

"You love that old clock as much as I do." A soft voice spoke, somewhat startling Steven.

He turned to see the spirit of Daphne standing behind him.

"Grandmother! I was beginning to think that you permanently moved on from this old house."

"I've been spending a lot of time with Darren in the light. But I've been secretly looking in on all of you from time to time." She paused, lovingly placing her hand to the side of his face. "She's with us now." She nodded with a smile. "Maggie and I escorted her into the light this morning."

"Is she happy?"

"You know Mrs. Porter." She chuckled. "She's happiest when she's taking care of everyone, and she's already like a mother hen to the rest of us."

The answer brought an amused smile to Steven's face, and before he could say another word, a different voice addressed him.

"Mr. Spencer!" He turned to see Angelique timidly standing there, holding a cup of coffee. "I thought you might like an afternoon cup."

"Thank you, Angelique. That was very nice of you." He accepted the cup.

"Were you talking to someone?"

Steven hesitated as his eyes searched the room for Daphne, but she was now gone. "No. I was just talking to myself. I do that sometimes."

He took a sip from his coffee, and could not hide his displeasure with its taste. Angelique immediately frowned at his reaction.

"Is there something wrong?"

"What kind of coffee is this?"

"It's called Citrus Mocha Cappuccino." I found it in the pantry."

Steven rolled his eyes with enlightenment. "That's the special blend of coffee that Sharie drinks. I only drink Chock Full o Nuts."

"I'm sorry. I can't seem to do anything right like Mrs. Porter did. I'll never be able to fill her shoes."

Steven set the coffee down on the side table, and attempted to console the visibly upset young woman."

"Listen. No one expects you to take Mrs. Porter's place. You still have much to learn, and we all realize that."

Angelique forced a smile, before Steven continued. "You are a very special young lady. Mario did a superb job creating you simply from the love he held within his heart." He smiled. "Just be patient, and before long you'll have the routine of this house mastered as well as Mrs. Porter did."

"Thank you, Mr. Spencer."

In a burst of naïve exuberance, Angelique planted a quick kiss on Steven's lips, totally taking him off guard, and by surprise.

"I'll brew you some Chock Full o' Nuts right away."

"No, no. That's okay, Angelique." A rather flabbergasted Steven answered. "It can wait. I think I'll take an afternoon stroll along the beach instead."

As the young woman hurried from the room, Daphne reappeared.

"That girl has so much to learn about life."

"And, etiquette." Steven added with a sigh.

"It was fortunate that Loraine didn't see that kiss."

Steven took a deep breath, and shook his head up and down in agreement. "Fortunate for both her and I."

At his sprawling estate on the banks of the Hudson River, Kenneth Laszlo strolled slowly along the perimeters of his scenic yard. Out of practically nowhere, Lucifer Morningstar sauntered up to his side.

"Anything on your mind you'd like to share, Kenneth?"

"Just enjoying this marvelous view, Mr. Morningstar." He smiled. "I can't help thinking that by this hour tomorrow, the town of Lockeport will be reduced to rubble, and Branch Consolidated will be in our possession. Next, we'll take the coveted Branchview Estate."

Morningstar gave an agreeing gesture, and abruptly changed the subject as they both continued walking.

"Do you plan on having a memorial for your sister?"

"That would be a waste of time." Laszlo laughed. "As you would say, there is no life beyond this one. She's dead, and that's final."

"You've learned well. It's best not to dwell on the dead." Morningstar grinned. "It detracts from the purpose that we have in this life."

"And for us, that purpose is to accumulate all the wealth and power while we can." Laszlo mused.

"So true." Morningstar enthusiastically agreed. "We are masters of our own destiny who deserve to exist in this life as gods."

Laszlo confidently strode ahead, while Morningstar remained still, watching him with an evil smirk. He chuckled to himself, and whispered under his breath.

"Delusional fool."

In the basement bunker room of Branch Consolidated, Guitierez somberly addressed his agents and staff, along with Ezekiel, Gerard, and Deanna.

"I just received word from Sheriff Albertson. They found the murdered bodies of Pamela Priestly and her family in their house this morning."

A sorrowful groan arose from those in attendance, but Deanna spoke up with a burst of anger.

"LaTasha Hampton and Agent Mullen were responsible for this. They have to be stopped."

"And they will, Miss LeRoux." Guitierez assured.

"I'm not waiting any longer." She angrily replied. "They have Tre right now as we speak. Hopefully, he's not already dead as well." She further fumed. "For me, this has become personal." She looked to her father. "Are you coming with me daddy?"

Gerard nodded, before she stormed ahead, and out of the room. He exchanged a quick glance with Ezekiel who gestured toward the door.

"Let's do this. I'll be right there with you." He assured.

"What about the tiger?"

"Unleash it if you see fit."

Without further word, the two men swiftly exited in pursuit of Deana.

At Branchview, all the inhabitants other than Steven and Mary had left to aid with the resistance in Lockeport. Steven paced nervously in the Foyer as Mary entered the room.

"Mr. Spencer! You're done going to wear out those tile floors with all that pacing back and forth."

"I just wish I could be there with them. I feel helpless."

"Now don't you worry child. God's gonna take care of them. You got to have faith."

Steven only managed a slight smile in response. "Why don't you go sit down in the dining room, and I'll fix you a cup of coffee." She suggested.

"I'm nervous enough. I better not drink any more coffee."

"Then I'll just have to fix you something else."

"What would I do without you, Mary?"

The foyer clock chimed at 7:00, and they both paused to listen until it finished.

"Go on ahead, Mary. I'll be there in a few minutes."

After she left the room, Morningstar appeared out of virtually nowhere.

"Steven Spencer! Just as a surmised. You indeed are alive."

"Who the hell are you, and how did you get into my house?"

"My name is Morningstar. Lucifer Morningstar."

Steven reacted with an enlightened smirk. He had heard the gods speak of him on several occasions, but this was the first time he had actually encountered him.

"I figured you'd make yourself known sooner or later. What do you want?"

"I want to offer you a chance to join us, Mr. Spencer. I could make the opportunity quite worth your while."

"Is that so?" Steven sarcastically encountered.

"You don't actually believe your little band of commoners can stand a chance against the Society's wealth and power?" He chuckled. "The people you aligned yourself with are nothing but lowly servants meant to be our slaves. We are by far, the more superior beings."

"We have help from the gods, and are protected by the Almighty God as well." He countered. "Our God is more powerful than you or that elitist society could ever hope to be, Satan."

Morningstar sneered with anger at his bold statement.

"Now, if you're finished with your drivel, I command you in the name of our God to leave this house. You're not welcome here."

Mary had heard the two conversing, and entered from the other room.

"Is everything okay, Mr. Spencer?"

"Mr. Morningstar was just leaving, Mary. Could you show him to the door?"

"Gladly."

Morningstar chuckled arrogantly as he turned to walk away. "I'll be seeing you soon, Steven."

"I figure that to be true." He sarcastically shot back.

At that, Morningstar strolled through the open door, and Mary quickly closed it behind him.

"Who was that man?" She shivered. "He gave me the chills."

"With good reason." Steven answered. "If you read throughout your bible, you'll find he's the main antagonist."

"You talking about the devil?"

"Yes Mary. He indeed walks among us." Steven continued to peer at the now closed door with anger.

As the evening began to set in, and a cool breeze blew in from the Atlantic, Gerard and Deanna approached a front door to a home on the side streets of Lockeport, followed closely by Ezekiel. As Gerard rang the doorbell, he looked back toward Ezekiel with concern.

"Aren't you afraid you'll be seen?"

"Everyone in this house other than Tre is of impure soul. They're unable to see me."

"I keep forgetting who you actually are." Gerard quipped in a moment of amusement.

"I'll be observing, and will step in if needed."

Both Gerard and Deana gave a subtle nod as the door opened, and Latasha suspiciously scanned the surroundings before ushering them in, concealing, and pointing a pistol from close to her side.

"You did well in coming alone."

"Where's Tre?" Deana impatiently pressed.

"Your precious Tre is in the other room with two of our agents. We're all going that way." She motioned with the pistol. "We'll have one big loving reunion before the agents take you all on your last ride."

She pushed them ahead into the room where they had Tre cuffed and gagged. Deana hurried toward him, but was halted by Agent Parker, who frisked her down, while the other agent checked Gerard.

"There'll be plenty of snuggle time for you two while pops here rides in the trunk."

"Where do you intend to take us?" Gerard inquired. "I'd like to know in advance where my final destination will be."

"You'll just have to wait and find out." Parker sarcastically answered, while Gerard could barely contain the rising beast within him.

Tre noticed Ezekiel in the room, who put his finger to his lips to silence him.

"Take Tre and Mr. LeRoux out first." Latasha ordered. "I want a few moments to beat down this snotty little bitch."

The agents pushed the two men from the room, and shut the door. Latasha placed her gun on top of a dresser, and motioned with both hands to Deana.

"Let's see if you have the moxie to back up that smart, privileged mouth of yours."

She was much taller, and had a bigger frame than Deana, but she confidently accepted her challenge.

"I was so hoping you'd say that." She chuckled as the two women squared off.

As the men reached the kitchen area, they were ordered to a halt.

"I lied." Parker arrogantly stated. "It all ends right now." He pointed his gun to Tre's head. "Mr. Russell here goes first, and then I'll personally slit your throat from ear to ear, Mr. LeRoux."

Gerard could hold the beast no longer. It rose from his core, and his eyes glowed red as the seams split on his clothes. Before either agent could react, the tiger beast grasped onto the younger agent, pitching him like a broken toy across the room. The impact of his body hitting near the ceiling of the old plaster wall, smashed his skull, and instantly snapped his neck and spine. A trail of blood splatter followed to where his body slid to the floor.

The tiger beast roared as a shocked Agent Parker and Tre stood trembling before it. Ezekiel spoke to Tre in a voice that only he could hear.

"Don't worry! He won't hurt you, Tre."

Parker raised his gun to the beast, and Tre alertly kicked the back of the agents' leg, causing his knee to buckle, and sending him to the floor in excruciating pain.

The beast roared out again, but Ezekiel spoke to it. "Back down Gerard. Let Tre handle this."

The beast calmed as Tre kicked the gun from Parkers' hand, sending it sliding across the floor. With his cuffed hands, he hit the agent as hard as he could in the side of the head, rendering him unconscious. He managed to pull the gag from his mouth, and stood over his conquest.

"That's payback for that cheap sucker punch, you son of a bitch."

Gerard had shapeshifted back to his true form, but was a bit dazed as Ezekiel approached, and stood next to him.

"I knew the boy had it in him." Ezekiel stated.

"What in the hell did I just see?" Tre questioned with wide eyes that quickly shifted to Ezekiel. "And who are you?"

"We'll explain later." Ezekiel answered with a calm sigh.

"Just get these cuffs off of me. Parker has the key in his front pocket."

Gerard had now fully recovered. He fished the key from Parkers' pocket and quickly freed Tre.

The men all paused and listened to what sounded like a violent cat fight taking place between the two women in the other room.

"We should go check out the action." Ezekiel jokingly gestured.

Tre quickly placed the cuffs on Parkers' limp hands, then retrieved the discarded gun, and pointed it at the unconscious agent.

"Don't worry about him." Gerard commented. "I don't think he's waking up any time soon."

The men swiftly made their way to the other room, where Deana had unanimously gained the upper hand in the fight. She stood over a now barely conscious, and bloodied Latasha who was slumped in a corner.

When Deana saw Tre and her father, she quickly darted across the room to embrace them. As the happy moment took place, Latasha struggled to her feet, managing to grab her pistol from the dresser top. As she stumbled forward, ambitiously aiming it at Deana's back, Ezekiel called out her name in warning.

Without a second thought, Tre raised the gun he held in his hand, and fired twice, striking Latasha in the upper torso.

She let out an ungodly shriek that made everyone cringe as she fell to her knees. She then slumped to the floor, before gasping one last desperate breath.

"That takes care of that." Ezekiel stated with an obvious sigh of sarcasm.

"We need to get Parker to the Sheriff, and help the townspeople in the standoff." Tre spoke with breathless, and nervous excitement.

"We'll take care of Parker." Gerard assured. "Right now, you need to get yourself to the hospital."

"I'm fine. I'm not injured, Mr. Le Roux."

"I didn't mean for you." Gerard answered with a grin. "There's someone there that's very anxious to see you."

"My mother is alive?" Tre inquired with surprise.

"She's had a mild heart attack. But she's doing just fine." Ezekiel further stated. "We promised her we'd get you out of this alive."

Tre shook his head with amazement, trying to make sense of everything, as he scanned the carnage in the room. Deana glanced at Latasha's body, and pointed with horror.

"What the hell is that? She transformed!"

Ezekiel cautiously approached the body to survey it.

"I thought I recognized that horrible shriek. She shapeshifted to her true form."

"She looks like some sort of reptile hybrid." Gerard observed.

"She's a Draconian. They have infiltrated the human race for centuries."

"Draconian?" Tre cried out as he shifted his attention toward Gerard, and pointed.

"What about that tiger beast?" He was totally perplexed as his eyes darted between the three others left in the room. "I don't understand all of this. Who exactly are you people?"

Deana kissed him on the cheek to calm him. "I'll explain some of the family secrets on the way to the hospital. Ezekiel will have to tell us more about that thing later." She pointed to the body with a look of disgust.

"I'm not sure I really want to know." Tre added as he glanced with horror at the hideous shell.

"Just remember what we're capable of, young man. That is, should ever decide to break my little girls' heart." Gerard firmly warned Tre, who listened with sober expression.

Both Ezekiel and Deana smirked, and reinforced his remark with a matter of fact nod.

In the Cave Room, Minotaur had finally settled, and he and Medusa now rested in the large throne chairs, staring up at the sparkling crystal ceiling above them.

"I wish I could see the crystals without these blasted sunglasses." Medusa complained.

"Just don't take those things off. A single glance could turn me into a permanent statue." He warned with a snort, before settling once again. "I will say, it is quite a beautiful sight. They sparkle like the stars in the sky"

"At least I can feel the energy from them." She smiled, before changing the subject. "Have you thought about where you'll go once the gods turn us into mortal humans?"

"I suppose I'll go back to Greece. That's the only place I've ever known as home."

"From what I understand, things are much different than what we remembered." She paused. "The world we were warned about now exist."

"I wouldn't know where to go in this country if I stayed here." Minotaur replied anxiously. "Where would I fit in?"

"Ezekiel tells me that there's a large Greek population in a place called Tarpon Springs, Florida."

"Perhaps we could go there together." Minotaur enthusiastically suggested.

"You'd definitely have to have better hygiene and manners as a human." She sarcastically quipped.

Minotaur looked away with frustration, and snorted. "You aren't so perfect yourself with your attitude, and those nasty serpents all about your head."

After a few seconds, they saw the humor in their comments, and shared a hearty laugh.

"Listen to us. We're bickering like an old married couple." She stated as they laughed some more.

"You are right, Minotaur. We should stay together. At least for a while." She added seriously.

Medusa placed her hand on top of Minotaur's hoof. "We're both venturing out into a strange world tomorrow. I wish you luck with your mission."

"And, I wish the same for you as well, my friend." A rare smile erupted across his beastly face.

As dusk settled on the seaside town, a caravan of four busses arrived, escorted by numerous State Patrol Vehicles. Following them were a platoon of National Guard Troops. All the vehicles came to a stop in the unusually empty parking lot of the Bayside Park.

Agent Mullen emerged from the lead bus first, along with one of his agents. He looked around at the seemingly abandoned town with suspicion.

"Something isn't quite right here. Where are all the people?"

"Maybe they all got smart, and left town." The other agent commented, as both Captain Scott, and Officer Norville approached.

"I certainly hope you two didn't do anything stupid, like tipping off the towns people." Mullen said with accusing eyes.

"We're just as clueless as you are." Norville answered.

Suddenly, from every corner of town, the people did emerge. An evil smile broke across Mullens' face. "Stupid fools! It will be like slaughtering innocent lambs."

Norville and Scott exchanged a fleeting sober glance in response to Mullens' remark.

Philip and Loraine led the way as they moved toward the confrontation. Loraine held tight to the shield which was still concealed in its' dark cover. She looked quite awkward in her body armor, helmet, and face shield as they marched forward.

"This apparatus and shield weighs as much as I do. I can hardly walk." She complained.

"When I tell you, go down to one knee, and remove the shield from its cover." Philip instructed while focusing straight ahead. "Don't worry, I'll protect you."

Mullen arrogantly approached the two, purposely stepping beyond a comfortable distance.

"So, the townspeople chose a muscle head, and a petite woman in clunky body armor as their leaders." He laughed, and pointed to the covered shield. "Is that supposed to be your weapon, Mrs. Spencer?

"As a matter of fact, it is, you arrogant oaf."

An angered, and much stronger Mullen pulled the covered shield from her grip. "Let's have a look at this so called weapon."

"I wouldn't remove that cover, Agent Mullen." Philip warned.

Mullen disregarded the warning, and reached inside the covering to pull out the shield. He immediately howled in painful anguish as the shield severely burned his hand. Loraine went to one knee at seeing Philip's nod, and awkwardly tried to grab hold of the dropped shield that had bounced hard against the pavement.

As she tried to steady the heavy shield within her grip, the reflection of a street lamp caught the large stone in the center of it. A laser beam shot outward from the shield, passing between Mullen and Philip, barely missing both of them. With straight line precision, and a sound likened to an approaching freight train, it beheaded the bronze statue of Nathan Hale that stood in the nearby park.

"That was a little too close for comfort." Philip sighed. "Keep that thing pointed downward."

"I'm so sorry about that." Loraine replied sheepishly.

Mullen stood stunned, still holding his hand, and looking with amazement toward Loraine and the shield. "The shield of Njord."

"How do you know about it?" Philip inquired with much surprise.

"My people have been searching for years to find it."

"Your people?" He further inquired. "The FBI and CIA knows about it?"

Before Mullen could answer, a heavy breeze blew in from the Atlantic, carrying with it a sound that could be best described as the chatter of a thousand dolphins. Everyone paused to look out to the ocean.

Within seconds, a multitude of Nereid warriors, both Mermaids and Mermen emerged from the sea, scaling the seawall in their human form. Linda Sanchez led the charge along with Hermia, the queen of the Nereids, and her Merman husband Heroditis, accompanied by their consort Damaris. All, except for Heroditis, carried the customary bows. He toted a large instrument that looked like some sort of oversized water gun. As they took their place next to the immortal and Loraine, Philip smirked, and spoke under his breath.

"You brought out the Pulse weapon."

"We've kept it concealed for all of these years." Heroditis answered.

All parties stood for a moment, sizing each other up. Officer Norville and Captain Scott stood several steps behind Mullen and his agents. Their platoons were behind them, and the hired foot soldiers of the Secret Society brought up the rear.

"What in the hell is going on here?" Norville whispered loudly to Captain Scott. "Who are all these people?"

"Just stay with the script, Ren." He answered. "Somehow, I feel like I've experienced this movie once before."

Mullen began laughing, as he shook his still hurting hand.

"The Nereids have finally made themselves known to the real world." He looked to all that stood behind him, and then back to the group that stood before him. "Do you really think you stand a chance with your archaic weapons, and that contraption you're holding in your hands?" He looked to Loraine, and mockingly pointed toward her. "This little woman has no idea of the power she holds in her hands, nor does she know how to use it."

"Like bloody hell I don't." Loraine angrily replied, as she pointed the shield toward the parked busses.

A bolt of laser energy passed from the shield, hitting the first bus, causing a chain reaction of explosions that immediately imploded all four in a ball of flames. Heroditis and Philip couldn't help but muster a smile.

"How does this land dweller know about us?" Hermia whispered to Philip, who answered with a shrug.

"That is the six million dollar question."

Mullen raised his hand, and commanded with a sneer. "Platoons come forward."

"I don't think so, Mullen." Norville said as he stepped forward, and pointed his gun toward him.

Likewise, Captain Scott's platoon and the State Police SWAT squad pointed their guns toward the agents and the foot soldiers.

"More treasonous individuals in the mix, I see." Mullen barely batted an eye.

"The only treasonous individuals here are you and your people. You'll all hang for your crimes." Captain Scott answered.

Mullen only scoffed at the comment, and turned his attention toward the newcomers. "I suppose since the Nereids were brave enough to make themselves known, then perhaps it's high time for us to reveal our true selves as well.

Everyone was somewhat puzzled by his remark. But soon, gasps arose from those in attendance as Mullen, and several others shapeshifted into eight foot tall reptile like creatures. Several of those who were behind Mullen that did not transform, quickly fled in horror when they saw other's they thought they knew, transform into their real image.

"Draconians!" Philip exclaimed.

"Not all of them." Hermia replied.

The transformed Mullen pointed, and spoke in a deep, gravel tinged voice. "And you, Philip Seagraves, are none other than the mighty Poseidon. This I know as fact."

"That's correct." He replied with a bit of surprise.

Philip calmly blinked, and his trident appeared in his grasp.

"What the…? Norville blurted out with shock.

"Don't worry." Captain Scott assured. "Just thank God that he's on our side."

"We got this." Heroditis assured in a calm, confident tone as he raised the pulse weapon.

"Tell your people to stand out of harms way, Poseidon." Hermia ordered. "This is our fight to win."

Philip motioned the townspeople to fall back to a safe distance, and then turned to Officer Norville and Captain Scott.

"Have your troops fall back to a safe distance as well."

They more than gladly obliged, and Philip turned to Loraine next. Before he could even say anything, she defiantly answered him.

"I'm not going anywhere. As long as I have this shield, I will use it to fight alongside all of you."

"Very well." He answered. "I will be sure to stand by you for protection."

"As will I." Steven proclaimed, as he surprisingly stepped onto the scene.

"Welcome to the party, Steven." Philip smirked.

"My wife's stubborn nature is rubbing off on me." He grinned. "I couldn't stay penned up in that house any longer." He raised his fist in the air. "Where we go one, we go all."

"Then you'll be the first to die, Steven Spencer." Mullen cried out in anger as he swung his reptilian arm, and caught him with a surprise blow.

Steven reeled back, but was only dazed for a moment as he transformed into the Lion Beast, and roared.

Mullen's reptilian face reflected surprise, and he immediately yelled to his troops. "Attack!"

Loraine raised the shield toward Mullen, but held back as the Lion Beast leapt onto the Draconian first.

Heroditis took a stance in front of the Nereids who had their bows aimed as well. He pulled back the trigger on his weapon, and a shock wave went forward from it, obliterating several onrushing Draconians into dust particles. Even Poseidon was awestruck by the display. The Nereids fired off arrows to repel and slow down the other onrushing giant reptiles, while lightning from the tip of Poseidon's trident, froze the bullets fired from their guns in mid air. All the while, the pulse gun quickly recharged itself with the oxygen in the air around it, and was ready for another volley.

Loraine blasted several more Draconians, and charging foot soldiers with her shield, while Philip and Linda repelled the ones who were trying to reach her from all sides. Mullen and the Lion Beast continued their violent fray, while Loraine kept a vigilant eye on the action.

The Draconian was wounded and bloodied by the struggle, but with its' great strength, managed to toss the Beast away momentarily, sending it reeling. It then set its' beady eyes on Loraine and the shield, as it let out an ungodly deafening shriek.

Loraine took careful aim, and blasted the Draconian into pieces before he could take another step. Blood, and body parts rained down on her and the others in the aftermath. The Lion Beast recovered, and roared as it quickly took station next to Loraine. She blasted several more onrushing reptiles, while the Beast easily repelled two more with blows to their vulnerable necks from its' sharp talons. When the few remaining Draconians, and foot soldiers saw that Mullen had been killed, they tried to retreat, but Heroditis showed no mercy, as he obliterated them all with a final shot from the pulse gun.

It was all over in less than five minutes, and there was a short lull of silence, while everyone was cautious that no more Draconians or foot soldiers remained. Miraculously, there were no casualties on the side of the Patriots and their allies.

Slowly, those who had sought safe shelter from the battle emerged, wandering back onto the scene to survey the carnage. Steven transformed back to his human form, and Loraine carefully set the shield down, awkwardly trying to remove her heavy flak jacket.

"Please help me get out of this blasted body armor, Steven."

Norville and Captain Scott were flabbergasted by what they had just witnessed. They both examined the pulse gun that Heroditis still held in his hands, and stayed well clear of the downward facing shield.

"What type of advanced weapons are these?" Captain Scott asked.

"They are from our world." Hermia answered. "Your civilization is not yet ready for the advanced technology. But they will be in due time."

As the towns people and the others realized that their allies were victorious, cheers arose, and several young Mermaids and Mermen rushed to embrace the humans. Damaris set her eyes on a handsome young man passing nearby. She boldly spun him around, and planted a passionate kiss on his lips that he quickly surrendered to.

"We seemed to have forged a new bond with the citizens of your world." Hermia quipped with a chuckle.

"That's quite apparent." Heroditis grinned as he draped his arm around his wife. "Should we all join the celebration?"

"I think we've had enough excitement for one night." Loraine answered as she securely placed the shield back into its pouch. "Steven and I are going home to wash the remnants of this battle from our bodies."

"What about you two?" Hermia inquired, eyeing both Philip and Linda. "It isn't often that we venture onto land for our entertainment."

"We have a big day ahead of us tomorrow." Philip answered as he held out his hands for the weapon Heroditis held. "I'll take that weapon, and hold it in a secure place for you."

"That's an excellent idea." He answered. "We wouldn't want that to fall into the wrong hands."

"Have fun, you two." Steven stated in conclusion as he snuggled Loraine close.

"We'll see you in your dreams, Steven." Hermia keenly winked as the Nereid couple strolled away arm in arm.

As Captain Scott and Officer Norville walked away, they met up with a grinning Sheriff Albertson.

"I don't understand all of this Alby." Norville shook his head. "But I sure would like to discuss it over a beer."

"I think we could all use more than one, and a few shots to boot." Captain Scott added.

"The sheriff took the lead, and gestured toward the jubilant crowd. "Gentlemen, let's do just that."

In the basement bunker at Branch Consolidated, Guitierez and Banerjee watched the events that took place in Lockeport on the surveillance cameras, along with their other agents. Even in the aftermath, they still reacted in stunned silence.

"I can't believe what we just witnessed." Banerjee commented.

"Remember all those Secret UFO files and the info on the Ancient Aliens? Guitierez questioned her.

Banerjee responded with a subtle nod.

"I do believe the lid may have just popped open on all of that." He replied, before turning to address all of those present. "I'll notify Ezekiel and the other agents guarding the front gate that the threat has been neutralized. In the meantime, I'll need all of you to focus on collecting as much intel as possible to help us succeed in tomorrow's mission."

"What exactly is the plan for tomorrow?" Banerjee asked.

"You and I are going to Washington with Ezekiel and Loraine. It's time to shift this mission into high gear."

"How? We can't take a commercial flight. The rogue agency has us on their radar."

"We're taking the private jet of Branch Consolidated Industries. We leave in an hour."

"An hour?" Banerjee sighed.

"We have to strike while the iron is hot." He paused, pulling her into the shadows, and giving her a quick kiss. "Just don't be shocked at who our other companion will be on that flight."

Banerjee laughed. "Are you kidding? After witnessing what just took place in Lockeport, there's not much else that could shock me."

At Lockeport General Hospital, the trio of Tre, Deana, and Gerard entered the room where Priscilla Russell was reclining in her bed, and watching TV. Tre rushed to her side, while Deana and Gerard stayed back, and observed the happy reunion.

"I thought for sure you were dead, mom."

"Oh! It's gonna take a lot more than that to kill this old lady." She weakly chuckled. "The doctor says I should be well enough to go home in a few days." She looked to the door, and motioned the father and daughter in. "Come on in, you two. I want to hear all about how you saved my son."

"Go on." Gerard urged his daughter along. "I'll stop by later, after I check on how things are going in Lockeport."

At Branchview, a weary Steven and Loraine entered the front door, and Mary hurried from the Sitting Room to greet them.

"Praise the Lord, you two are safe!" She proclaimed. "They said on the news that the government had seized control of Lockeport."

"What?" Steven cried with disbelief.

"Hurry! They're talking about it right now."

The three rushed into the Sitting Room to watch and listen.

"This is totally false information. We soundly defeated those treasonous invaders." An enraged Loraine declared.

"That isn't even Lockeport." Steven added while pointing to the screen. "That's footage from the riots that took place in Minnesota two years ago."

"Are you saying we actually won? The people of Lockeport were spared?" Mary inquired with excitement.

"Yes!" Steven exclaimed. "Everyone is celebrating in town."

"This is totally false propaganda." Loraine fumed as she continued watching. "It makes me even more determined to go to Washington, and finish this thing tomorrow with Ezekiel and the others."

"I'm going with you." Steven declared.

"But Ezekiel told you…"

"They know I'm alive, Lori." He interrupted. "Whatever we do from now on, we do it together."

"I'll leave you two to work this out between you." Mary stated as she began to exit the room. "This old lady is going to bed."

Loraine looked to Steven with a weary sigh. "If you insist on going, then we need to get a move on. Our flight leaves in less than an hour."

Steven rolled his eyes at the revelation. "When exactly did you plan to spring that news on me?"

"Why do you think we didn't stay, and celebrate the victory, Steven?" Loraine quipped with a clever smirk. "After all, it is supposed to be a top secret mission."

Steven drew a deep sigh, and chuckled. "I think the secret agent side of your mother is beginning to rub off on you."

Chapter Sixteen:
The Battle Rages On

In the late night hours, the private jet took off from a small airfield outside of Lockeport. On board, Ezekiel sat next to a nervous Medusa who clutched tight to her seat, and looked out the window with her shaded eyes as the jet smoothly sailed through the night sky.

"This high speed flying chariot amazes me. Is it the same sort of contraption that our ancestors etched on the ancient walls?"

"A less advanced variation." He replied. "There is so much more for you to learn about life in these modern times."

"I only hope that I can adjust."

"You'll do just fine." Ezekiel confidently assured.

Behind them, Steven and Loraine sat, clutching each other's hand. Steven had already started drifting off into sleep, but Loraine stared straight ahead in anxious thought. She winced at the restless vipers that were protruding from Medusa's head, and peeking over the top of the seat. She shut her eyes, so she wouldn't have to see them, and eventually sleep caught hold of her as well.

In the seats across the aisle, Agents Guitierez and Banerjee also sat in silent thought while observing the others.

"Is that really who I think it is?" Banerjee asked while soberly gesturing toward Medusa.

"Straight from the pages of Greek Mythology." He answered quietly under his breath.

"What's next on the agenda? Pink polka dot unicorns and dragons?" She inquired with a tinge of sarcasm.

Guitierez only answered with an amused grunt. "Get some sleep. We have a long night and day ahead of us."

Around this time, the celebration in Lockeport was beginning to wind down. Sheriff Albertson returned to the police station, and checked in on his only prisoner. Parker stood, and clutched the bars in anger.

"I need to see a doctor. I've sustained a bad concussion."

The sheriff looked closer at his heavily swollen and bruised face.

"Yeah! It sure looks like somebody beat the hell out of you." He calmly replied. "But you'll live. At least for the time being."

"They'll send others to get me. I'll be out of here by this time tomorrow, and this whole town will hang for treason."

"I don't think that's going to happen, Parker." The sheriff chuckled. "As far as I'm concerned, you can stay in that cell until you rot."

"You have no idea who you're fighting against." Parker angrily seethed.

"I know a good bit of you are big ugly lizards. I'm surprised you didn't shape shift into one, and break out of here."

"What in the hell are you talking about?" Parker cluelessly asked. "Are you drunk?"

"I've had a few celebratory drinks. But, I'm still of sound mind, and certainly not on duty."

"What are you celebrating? How are you and the others still here?"

"I take that no one filled you in on what took place tonight. We soundly defeated the Draconians and their foot soldiers. Albertson replied. "Mullen is dead."

"That can't be."

"Well! I'm happy to say it's true." The sheriff smiled. "Things didn't turn out quite the way all of you planned."

Albertson began to stroll away, but Parker desperately beckoned him back. "Wait! What is all this talk about Draconians and giant lizards?"

The sheriff approached him again with curiosity. "You really don't know? Do you?

"Look! I'll admit that I took bribes to go along with the Secret Society's agenda. But I'm sure as hell not a lizard."

"In that case, you're lower than a lizard. You not only sold your soul, but you also betrayed your country." The sheriff nodded. "I'll get you some ice to put on that swollen face. But just don't fall asleep, Parker. If you do have a concussion, you just might not wake up."

Parker reacted with a worried expression, while the sheriff walked away with a victorious smirk.

After arriving in Washington D.C. in the early morning hours, and dropping the others at a safe house, Agents Guitierez and Banerjee now waited patiently on the top level of a parking garage. After a few moments, a dark colored SUV pulled to a stop in front of their vehicle. They both shielded their eyes from the bright headlights as two rugged looking men emerged, toting semi- automatic rifles.

"Let's just hope we haven't been set up." Banerjee stated as she kept her hand gun concealed between the seat and the door."

The men strolled to each side of the car, and motioned for them to put their windows down. Guitierez cautiously displayed his badge, before the two men motioned them out, and proceeded to frisk them down, confiscating the agent's weapons.

"You'll need to leave those weapons in your car." One of the men ordered while the other placed the guns on the front seat.

They then motioned them toward the SUV.

"Walk to the back passenger window, and the Senator will speak to you from inside."

Both agents strolled over as the window slid down, and a dignified looking man in his mid 60's peered out at them.

"This better be good, Agent Guitierez. I don't particularly enjoy being called upon for late night meetings." He stated.

"Believe me. This is very important, Senator Moxley."

His eyes darted between the two agents before speaking again. "I thought everyone in the bureau had gone rogue."

"There's still quite a few of us that remain Patriots, and are working undercover behind the scenes." Guitierez answered.

"That's comforting to know." Moxley replied as he gestured toward his bodyguards. "I apologize for the informal greeting. One can never be too safe in these times."

"We certainly agree." Banerjee replied as she eyed the pair of grim faced, armed men that stood sentry to the meeting.

"We were told that you're one of the few remaining politicians who are still loyal to the Constitution." Guitierez continued.

"There's a group of us." Moxley further replied. "We often meet together in private." He paused, shaking his head. "I can boast that I personally have turned down more bribes, and thrown more corporate lobbyist out of my office than you could ever imagine. I've also had countless threats against myself and my family." He motioned once again toward his guards. "That explains the private security."

"We understand, Senator." Banerjee replied.

"What is it that you want me to do?" He asked.

"We need you to notify everyone in your group on a secure, private device." Guitierez stressed. "Tell them to stay as far away as possible from their jobs at the Capital tomorrow."

The Senator eyed them both with suspicion. "Just what exactly do you have planned?"

"We're bringing down the entire criminal cartel." Guitierez proclaimed.

The Senator couldn't help but chuckle. "That's a pretty ambitious, and damn near impossible task."

"Trust me on this, Senator." Guitierez grinned. "We most certainly have the means to make it happen."

Later, just prior to dawn, Philip, Linda Sanchez, and Minotaur arrived in separate cars at the Minotaur Pharmaceutical Plant just outside of Secaucus, New Jersey.

"It's showtime." Philip announced to Minotaur. "Are you ready?"

"I'm more than ready to get out of this blasted chariot." He snorted. "It certainly wasn't built for a beast of my size."

"What do you want me to do, Philip?" Linda asked as she leaned into the driver side window.

"You stay out here, and keep an eye on any possible trouble." He answered. "As soon as I get my hands on that evidence, I'll need you to drive it directly back to our FBI allies in Lockeport."

"What about me?" Minotaur anxiously asked.

"Just follow my lead." Philip instructed. "I'll get that evidence, and then we'll obliterate this place from the face of the earth."

Minotaur tapped his hooves together with joy. "I can hardly wait."

Later that morning, at the safe house outside of Washington, Steven, Loraine, Ezekiel, and Medusa, along with two agents watched the television news which was showing footage of a large, raging fire. Guitierez and Banerjee entered the house, and immediately joined them.

"My brother succeeded with his mission." Ezekiel announced as he gestured toward the TV.

A smile broke across Guitierez' face as he watched. "I'd say that mission appears to be a blazing success."

A chorus of laughs erupted from all in attendance.

"I only hope he was able to obtain what he went there to get." Banerjee seriously added.

"I have no doubts." Ezekiel replied. "Philip will text me when the next phase of his mission is over."

Guitierez anxiously glanced at everyone present. "Is everyone ready to make this happen?"

"I can't say this enough." Steven answered as he put his hand out, palm down, as everyone else piled their hands on top. "Where we go one, we go all."

"Amen!" Ezekiel concluded.

"Let's finish this thing." Loraine sternly added.

After destroying Minotaur Pharmaceuticals manufacturing facilities, Linda Sanchez headed back to Lockeport, while Philip and the real Minotaur drove to the company's headquarters a short distance outside of New York City. Onlookers stared and pointed with disbelief as the beast casually strolled through the front doors of the opulent building with Philip. A man in a suit approached with exuberance.

"Wow! That's some great outfit. Is this some sort of new promotion?"

The Minotaur growled in response, and drool flew from its' mouth, dowsing the man in the face. The man wiped away the slime with disgust, and moved away with fear. Two armed guards wearing business suits surrounded them with their guns drawn.

"Down on your knees! Hands Up! Now!" One of them ordered.

With one quick swing of its' sharp hoof, the Minotaur slit one of the men's throat. The other quickly surrendered, and ran in terror. Everyone nearby stampeded toward the exit of the building or hid wherever they could, while the two continued on.

The Minotaur paused his progression to look at the humongous statue of his likeness that stood prominently in the center of the lobby. He sneered at it with anger.

"How dare these deplorables use my likeness to reap great profits." He growled.

"We have other business to tend to. Don't let that be a distraction." Philip answered, while urging him on.

A few moments later the door to the CEO's office flew open with such force that it blew off the hinges, landing several feet into the room. Inside, sitting cool and unrattled behind his ornate desk, George Winklebauer III glanced up at the two intruders, then to the door that laid on the floor between them.

"You could've just knocked, and walked in." He chuckled as he calmly stood, and strolled around the desk to confront Philip and the beast.

"This is far from being a social call, Mr. Winklebauer." Philip stated.

"I know." He said with a smirk. "I'm guessing you two had something to do with the explosion and fire."

The Minotaur only grunted in response, and Winklebauer moved closer to examine him with great interest.

"This specimen is amazing!" He proclaimed to Philip. "Did you create him through some sort of genetic engineering?"

"No. You're looking at the real deal." Philip answered as he handed him one of his calling cards.

Winklebauer glanced at the card, and chortled as he handed it back. "There's no need for introductions, I know who you are pitch fork man. You've made quite an impression in hindering our objectives as of late."

"Then I must obviously be doing a good job."

Winklebauer strolled back behind his desk, and sat down once again, studying both his guests as they moved in closer. "You're actually foolish enough to think you can defeat us, Mr. Seagraves?" He grinned. "That little stunt you pulled this morning will only temporarily slow our process. We have facilities in several other countries that are very friendly to our cause."

"And, what exactly is that cause, Mr. Winklebauer?"

"Extreme wealth, and power over the masses." He stated, sitting forward with a sinister smile. "I'm sure that you've already figured out that the vaccines we offer to the people are the actual virus itself."

"Among other various poisons as well, that will surely induce other illnesses and eventual death." Philip sneered, prompting an arrogant nod, and point of the finger from Winklebauer.

"And of course, those illnesses will need meds, which will further our profits, and the deaths and sterility from the side effects will help reduce world population." He further asserted.

"These are people you're speaking of, not lab rats."

Winklebauer shrugged off the comment. "These lowly individuals are only a commodity, Mr. Seagraves. Once we totally displace humans with robots, the only purpose they'll serve is for genetic experimentation.

"I'm guessing that the chosen elites will be spared from this atrocity."

"We'll be as gods in this universe." He declared boastfully.

"Can I just kill him now, and get it over with?" Minotaur impatiently pleaded, as Philip calmly raised his hand to settle the beast.

"I think instead of that, Mr. Winklebauer more than deserves a little taste of his own medicine." Philip stated with an assured wink, as he pulled a syringe from the inside pocket of his sport jacket.

Winklebauer's confident expression faded to one of panic as Philip filled the syringe with a large dose of the vaccine he had confiscated from the lab.

"You can't give me a dose that big. It will kill me." He nervously stated as he rose from his seat.

"Really?" Philip smirked "In that case, I'll fill it to the max."

He then gestured to Minotaur, who threw Winklebauer back down in his chair, and pinned him down while Philip jabbed the large syringe into his bicep.

Within seconds, Winklebauer went into convulsions, foaming at the mouth. His eyes bulged until blood leaked from the sides, and boils broke out all over his body. He shrieked loud enough to shatter all the breakables within the office.

"There it is." Philip proclaimed as both he and the Minotaur winced from the high pitched shriek. "The death cry of a Draconian."

With one final gasp, Winklebauer went limp in his chair, transforming to his true form.

"I thought my appearance was repulsive, but I must say that he is one ugly bastard." Minotaur remarked.

A few minutes later, the duo had made their way back to a now empty lobby. They could see through the plate glass entrance doors that the building was surrounded by police.

"How can I escape?" Minotaur inquired. "You can become invisible, but I can't."

Philip calmly pondered the situation for a quick moment. "Are you ready to become a man, Minotaur?"

He looked at Philip with surprise, then glanced at the looming statue. "Let me do one thing first." He smirked.

He walked over to the base of the statue, and with one lunging grunt, he toppled the huge monument with his immense strength. As it creaked from its foundation, it collapsed, taking a large part of the balcony with it, and crashed loudly to the floor. The whole building shook in its' wake, and shattered all the windows.

"Damn! That felt good!" Minotaur proclaimed.

Philip wasted no time in stepping forward and placing his hand atop the beast's head.

"From this day forward, for the rest of your mortal life, you will live as a human man. You'll now be known by the name Constantine Gianakos."

Within seconds, the beast transformed to a handsome young man. He stood stunned for a moment, examining his body carefully before looking at Philip.

"Thank you, Poseidon." He beamed with excitement. "What do you want me to do now?"

"Exit the building with your hands raised over your head. Be sure to speak in your English accent, and tell the authorities you only escaped the building after the beast toppled the statue." He gave an assured pat to his shoulder. "Speak nothing beyond that. I'll be waiting at the car for you."

Constantine gave a nervous nod, and proceeded to hurry from the building. Philip took a deep breath, and whispered to himself as he pointed upward. "Another victory."

Meanwhile in Washington, the SUV driven by Ezekiel approached the check in gate to FBI headquarters. The vehicles carrying Agents Guitierez, Banerjee, and the others followed from a distance, staying in contact via Bluetooth. Loraine was in the passenger seat already sporting her bullet proof vest, while Steven and Medusa rode in the back seats. Medusa wore a large knit cap to conceal the snakes from being seen.

"Remember, don't lower those sunglasses until I give the signal." Ezekiel instructed Medusa.

"Are you sure all of the innocents are out of harm's way?" A worried Loraine inquired.

"Agent G assured me that all were alerted ahead of time. Whoever remains here are presumed to be allied with the enemy." Ezekiel answered. "We're in a war here, Lori."

The car pulled to a stop at the gate, and two stern faced guards came out of the guardhouse to greet them. While one approached the driver side window, the other walked around the perimeter of the vehicle, checking the undercarriage with a mirror attached to a long pole.

Ezekiel lowered his window, and handed over the fake ID that Guitierez had prepared for him. The guard went back inside to check things out on his computer, and the other guard soon joined him. They stood inside the guardhouse for a few moments, conversing between themselves, and looking out toward the car. The one guard made a call on his cell phone, before glancing out towards them once again.

"Something's not right." Ezekiel stated.

"Do you think someone may have tipped them off?" Steven asked.

"We'll soon find out." He answered as he looked in his rearview mirror toward Medusa. "I want you to casually open your window, then watch me in the rear view mirror. If I give you a slight nod, I want you to lower the glasses, and stare directly at them."

The two guards exited the gatehouse, and approached the car cautiously before drawing their weapons.

"We'll need you all to step out of the vehicle very slowly." One of the guards ordered.

Ezekiel glanced up in the mirror, signaling to Medusa. She lowered her glasses, and with one hardened stare, the guards were turned to stone.

Without further delay, Ezekiel stepped on the gas, and crashed through the gate arm, tearing it from its moorings.

"Okay, Agent G. You're clear to enter." He spoke through the Bluetooth. "I think these bastards must've been onto us."

"Copy." Guitierez' voice answered through the SUV's system. "Pull over and wait for us."

"You'll catch up." He replied with a smirk, as he glanced in the mirror at Steven. "Get the shield out of the back for Loraine." His glance shifted to Medusa. "Get ready to release those snakes."

Several seconds later, a convoy of cars carrying the allied agents followed Guitierez as they breezed past the stone statues of the two guards at the checkpoint.

As Ezekiel drove closer to the headquarters, it was apparent they were being ambushed. Rogue agents lined the front of the building behind their cars ready to fire on them.

"Get ready, Lori. When I tell you, aim the shield out your window, and blast the hell out of them." Ezekiel ordered.

"What about the snakes?" Medusa inquired.

"Let them loose at the same time."

Without warning, he slammed on the brakes, sending the SUV into a sideways slide.

"Do it now!" He yelled.

The aimed shield struck its' mark, exploding a row of government vehicles, and eliminating several agents in the process. Medusa ordered the snakes to attack, and they quickly slithered forward from her head toward their targets. Several other snakes morphed from the existing ones, all in pursuit of those they sensed as evil.

Many of the rogue agents managed to get shots off from their semi automatic weapons, riddling the SUV, as all the occupants except for Ezekiel ducked for shelter, and Loraine huddled behind the large impenetrable shield.

Screams emerged from the rogue agents as the venomous snakes relentlessly attacked. Meanwhile, the allied agents arrived, pulling to a screeching halt behind the SUV.

Ezekiel then marched toward the entrance, sending lethal bolts of lightning from his fingertips, while Loraine followed, blasting away with her shield. Medusa and Steven quickly exited the vehicle, and followed them. As rogue agents emerged from the sides, Medusa lowered her glasses, and turned them to stone with her cold stare, while the allied agents picked off the others.

One rogue who made it through the fury, tried to grab hold of Loraine. Steven immediately shape shifted into the lion beast, and with one swift pounce, he proceeded to tear the villain to pieces. He then set sights on the building, and roared as the others marched ahead.

Loraine blasted the front entrance with the shield, sending debris flying, and several more rogues to their death. Medusa caught up, and huddled behind the shield with Loraine, as they entered to a flurry of bullets that Ezekiel repelled in his progress.

A rogue popped up from behind an overturned desk in the lobby, brandishing a rocket launcher that was aimed directly at the ravaging lion beast. Medusa alertly lowered her glasses, instantly turning him to stone.

"Good shot, Medusa. I never saw that one coming." Loraine remarked, as she blasted more rogues off the balcony with the shield. The snakes infested the building, inflicting their venomous bites on every enemy rogue in their path. The Lion Beast picked off others with his quickness and immense strength.

Agent G. and Banerjee led their team from behind, picking off any that might have remained. The rogues never had a chance in the fight, and soon the resistance in the lobby was eliminated. More screams could be heard from throughout the other portions of the building as the snakes progressed further into it.

"I'm certainly glad those slithering reptiles are on our side." Ezekiel winced.

"We have to make our way to the computer room, and then the underground tunnels." Guitierez commanded, as he and his agents took the lead.

Once they moved to the interior of the building, Banerjee led a group of agents toward the computer room, while Guitierez and the others entered a secure area in the basement where a large steel door led to the underground tunnels.

The snakes had handily disposed of any resistance that may have been guarding the room.

"Do you have the code to get in that door?" Ezekiel asked.

"Only a chosen few have access." Guitierez answered, as he turned his glance toward Loraine.

"Blast the damn thing off its hinges."

She proceeded, while the others took refuge from the flying debris of the immense blast that left a gaping hole in the wall.

Severed electric wires sparked in the aftermath, and everyone coughed from the smoke and dust that it stirred up. Several snakes slithered ahead into the tunnels to pick off any resistance they might encounter.

As the Patriots cautiously entered the tunnel, everyone marveled at the seemingly unending path that lied ahead. It was eerily quiet except for the hum of the overhead lighting.

"I've often heard stories that these tunnels extend for miles below the city." Guitierez stated.

"It almost reminds me of a more modern version of the tunnels beneath Lockeport." Ezekiel commented.

"Magnify that by at least five times." Guitierez further quipped.

The Lion Beast stayed very close to Loraine as they cautiously led the way with the shield. Medusa stayed close behind them with Guitirez, Ezekiel, and the other agents. Sporadic, terrifying screams echoed through the tunnels as the vipers systematically disposed of any evil beings in their path.

"Where in the world do these side hatchway doors lead to? Other tunnels?" Loraine asked.

"That's a good question, Lori." Guitierez replied as he climbed onto the side wall ledge, and muscled the circular valve on one of the doors. "Stand back! Hopefully this doesn't lead into the sewage lines."

With a groan, he turned the valve, and the door popped open. As he pulled on it, a guard surprised him on the other end with his weapon pointed within inches of his head. The lion beast alertly leaped between them, and disposed of the guard with one mighty swipe of his talons, sending the rogue agent tumbling over the railing of the cat walk.

As they all carefully entered onto the cat walk, and peeked downward into the immense room below, they all gasped at the sight. The room was packed with a sea of humanity, mostly women and children who all looked upward with fear in their eyes.

"Oh, mi Dios!" Guitierez exclaimed, blessing himself with the sign of the cross. "This indeed is where they house their trafficking operation."

Across town, the loyal military descended on the Capital and the Pentagon. They marched in, arresting the entire rogue, treasonous Congress, Senate, and military hierarchy, along with their staff.

At the Progressive News Network headquarters in New York, personnel rushed to get ready on set as a director hurried into the room in a panic. He turned cluelessly to an executive that stood nearby.

"I was in the lunchroom. What in the hell is going on?"

"The military just invaded the Capital Building and the Pentagon."

"Do you think the Patriots actually made that move?" He further questioned.

"I don't know. But we need to spin the story that way to the public. We have to make it look like a violent coup."

"I'll have the archives bring up old day time footage of the riots." He assured. "The stupid viewers will never know the difference."

The executive smirked. "Get right on it."

Simultaneously, at an undisclosed military bunker near Cape Canaveral Florida, officers of the Space Force were viewing satellites in outer space on the big screens in front of them. A voice over an intercom spoke dramatically.

"Targets are locked, ready on three, two, one. Fire!"

One of the men pressed a red button, and in a split second, all the satellites targeted were struck by a precision laser beam, and decimated. Cheers arose throughout the room as the intercom voice proclaimed, "Mission accomplished."

Back at the Progressive News studios, they were ready to go live with a report when all power was lost.

"What in the hell just happened?" The executive yelled.

"We lost our damn feed." The director answered.

"Get the engineer to bring it back up. We can't let the other networks get ahead of us on this."

"All the other Networks are dead as well." Another employee stated. "Even the internet's down. It's a total communication blackout."

"Those bastard Patriots must've taken out our satellites."

In another studio near Tampa, a switch was flicked, and the Patriot News Source came to life through the satellite feed created jointly by Branch Consolidated and the Space Force. In an instant, the whole world was connected by the new separate internet and wireless feed, totally replacing the one that had existed.

One of the smiling anchors announced in the opening with much exuberance. "Welcome to the Patriot News Source, your only source for true news, minus the propaganda."

Steven, now transformed back to his human form, and Loraine strolled away from the site of their victory with their arms draped around each other. Loraine wearily carried the now covered shield in one hand, it's weight almost pulling her toward that side.

"Are you sure I can't carry that for you?"

"I don't want this thing to leave my side until I know that it's in a safe place." Loraine replied.

"I was so proud of the way you handled yourself." Steven beamed. "You're every bit the bad assed woman that your mother is."

"Don't tell her that." She laughed.

Ezekiel and a much different looking Medusa minus the snakes and sun glasses, waited for them to catch up. Steven and Loraine marveled at the beautiful head of dark brunette hair and sparkling green eyes that she now sported.

"I can't believe she's actually the same person." Loraine proclaimed. "She looks absolutely gorgeous."

Medusa smiled with exuberant delight when she heard her compliment, as did Ezekiel.

"I'd like to introduce you both to Anastasia Kontos." Ezekiel announced.

"He even gave me a new name." She added with excitement.

"And a lovely one at that." Steven stated with a grin, before turning his glance to Ezekiel. "You did a fine job in transforming this young lady into a true Greek goddess."

His comment drew hearty laughter between all of them.

"I just got word from Agent G. that all the other missions were a success as well." Ezekiel continued.

"We actually brought down the Secret Society?" Loraine asked with a breath of exhilaration.

"Let's just say we thoroughly crippled their mission." Ezekiel answered with a hint of caution. "We still have to thoroughly finish the job." He concluded with a brief sigh. "Shall we all go somewhere comfy, and bring ourselves up to date on the true news of the day as it happens?"

"Absolutely!" Steven enthusiastically replied as he patted him on the shoulder.

Ezekiel glanced down at the shield that Loraine was toting, and motioned to it.

"Philip and I can return that to the Nereids. They'll bury it at a depth where no human will ever find it." He paused with another longer sigh. "At least in this lifetime."

"You know what?" Steven paused his progress. "I think instead, Loraine and I will return it together." He pulled her in closer. "I think it's time for me to show my wife the world that my ancestors descended from."

Puzzled expressions turned to enlightened smiles.

"I think I'll borrow an expression I've often heard, and say that I'll drink to that." Anastasia quipped, prompting further chuckles from the joyful lot as they continued on.

In his large mansion outside of New York City, Kenneth Laszlo panicked and worried as he tried to keep up with his interest in the Stock Exchange. He and Morningstar watched the events on the theater sized screen as they took place on the lone surviving cable channel of the Patriots News Source Network.

"Can't you pull our money out any quicker?" Morningstar grumbled.

"Blast it!" Laszlo answered with frustration. "The damn phone lines are jammed with everyone else trying to liquidate."

"The market has crashed almost 9,000 points in the past three hours. This will bankrupt us all." Morningstar complained as he nervously paced. "Can't you do something to shut down the market?"

"We just have to ride this out. The military has converged, and are overseeing things on Wall Street."

"Call a meeting for this evening. We need to get the main General Committee together." Morningstar ordered.

"That's impossible!" Laszlo exclaimed. "Our people from other parts of the country can't possibly get here that quick."

"Then we'll just have to proceed without them. This is urgent!"

"I'll get right on it." Laszlo sighed.

Morningstar stormed from the room, and entered the Main Foyer just as Roger McPherson hurried down the stairs.

"Where in the hell do you think you're going?"

Roger slowed his pace, and bravely confronted Morningstar. "I'm not your servant. What makes you think I need to inform you on my itinerary?"

"Have you forgotten what I'm capable of?" He countered in a threatening tone, that somewhat sobered Roger a bit.

"Very well! I'm going out to meet a friend for dinner." He paused. "Is there any other personal information that you feel the need to know?"

"You're going out to dinner at the very same time that your grandsons' interests are collapsing?"

"My grandsons' business is no concern of mine." He sternly replied.

Morningstar reluctantly stepped aside, allowing Roger to pass.

"Good day, Mr. Morningstar." He concluded with a sneer as he departed.

Laszlo entered just as Roger walked out the door, and he took note of his mentor who appeared to be in pondering thought. "Is everything okay?"

"Do you know who your grandfather is meeting with?"

"I don't have any idea, and I could equally care less." He replied. "I have other more pressing issues to worry about." He firmly stated, before rushing up the stairs.

The corporate jet carrying Agents Guitierez and Banerjee, as well as the others, left Washington in the late afternoon. The jet would make a brief stop in New York to leave the agents off to complete their mission, while Steven and Loraine would accompany Ezekiel and Anastasia back to Lockeport.

"We'll be meeting up with Millie and a group of our agents to take down Laszlo and the General Committee of The Secret Society. It's now time to cut off the head of the snake." Guitierez announced.

"Please just make sure my mother returns to us safely." A worried Loraine pleaded.

Guitierez answered with an assuring smile. "Like you, your mother is a very tough woman. I'm sure she's been through a lot worse than this."

"I'd have to say that Laszlo should be the one to worry." Steven laughed. "I would not want Millie Sandstrom on my bad side."

"Shouldn't I go with you?" Ezekiel inquired.

Guitierez shook his head no. "You've done your fair share, Ezekiel. Besides, I know you have important business to tend to." He concluded with a clever wink.

After completing their mission, Philip and Constantine were on their way back to Lockeport as well. Constantine was quiet as he stared out the passenger window of the car as it traveled along the freeway.

"This modern world is so much different than what I'm accustomed to. I only hope I can adjust to it." Constantine stated with concern.

"You and Medusa will be in good hands with Father Antonopoulos. He's a good man."

"Will Medusa be transformed as well when we return to the cave?"

"I'm certain that my brother has already taken care of that task." He assured, before glancing at his wrist watch. "We'll have to take a little side trip before we go back. I have to meet someone in New Haven."

"Will we eat? I'm very hungry."

"As a matter of fact, the restaurant we are going to has very good food. You can order anything from the menu that you'd like. But eat like a gentleman, you no longer have hooves." Philip smirked.

Constantine clapped his hands with excitement, garnering an awkward glance from Philip.

"And, please refrain from doing that."

"Of course!" Constantine replied with obvious embarrassment.

A short time later, the duo entered the eating establishment, and approached a booth where Roger McPherson anxiously waited. They slid into the bench seat opposite of him, as Roger's eyes nervously darted between the two men.

"Who's he?" He asked with anxiety in his voice.

"Constantine Gianakos." Philip calmly replied. "He's a trusted associate of mine."

"I heard about everything on the Patriot news." Roger stated. "I'm happy for them." He nodded, then paused a moment before shifting the subject. "Is everything set for Saturday night?"

"So far, so good." Philip answered. "I'll need you to be on the island at 9:00 PM sharp. There will be a row boat waiting on the south shore of the river, and whatever you do, make sure you dress appropriately, and bring bug spray. That place is infested with ticks and mosquitos."

"I can't wait to go back." Roger expressed with excitement in his voice.

Philip sighed. "You do know that things get rather rough there in Paris after the 1920's?"

Roger lowered his eyes, and answered with a slight nod. "I read about the Great Depression, The Nazi's and World War II." He grunted indignantly. "How ironic that the same people you're fighting today were responsible for all of that as well."

"As much as I regret doing so, I'll have to erase your memory of everything before I send you back. We can't have you affecting even the slightest bit of history."

"I understand." He replied, as a waiter stopped by the table to leave menus and pour water.

"We'll send you back first at exactly 10:03 PM. When you arrive in 1920, go to the water and call for me. I'll be able to secure safe passage to get you back to Paris."

Both men took note as Constantine voraciously eyed the menu with consuming interest, before continuing their conversation.

"What time will you be sending Stargazer back?"

"He'll be going back to 1967 at 11:36 PM precisely. Ezekiel and I will then close that portal forever. There's no way that either of you will ever be able to travel back."

"Where's that waiter?" Constantine interrupted. "I know what I want."

"I'm very thankful for all this, Philip." Roger continued.

Philip replied with an assured nod, and an impatient Constantine interrupted once more.

"Can we please eat now. I'm starving!"

"Yes, Constantine." Philip smiled. "We can eat now."

Unnoticed by any of the men, Lucifer Morningstar sat with his back to them in another booth, listening to every word of their conversation. An evil, all knowing grin graced his face before he promptly disappeared into thin air.

Back at Branchview, Steven and Loraine were ready to turn in early for the night. They had one task remaining that they had to complete while they slept. Steven embraced his wife in his arms.

"Are you ready to do this, sweetheart?"

Loraine answered with a nervous nod. "Just tell me what I have to do."

"Take the shield, and hold onto it tightly." He waited for her to retrieve it, then led her toward the bed, where they both crawled on top of it, and huddled closely. "Now take my hand, close your eyes, and we'll drift off into sleep."

"They both exhaled, and snuggled closer. Loraine held the shield close to her side. Within a very short time, they both fell into a very deep sleep.

In the Secret Cave, Ezekiel and Anastasia waited patiently for the arrival of Philip and Constantine. Meryl and Linda were also present for the meeting.

Meryl paced nervously. "I can't shake this strange feeling of foreboding. I certainly hope everything is alright with those two."

"I'm quite certain they'll be along shortly, darling." Ezekiel replied with little concern before turning to Linda. "Will you be staying the night? You have quite a long swim ahead of you."

"I really should be getting back to the Caribbean."

"You could always join us on the flight to Florida tomorrow. Tarpon Springs is right on the Gulf of Mexico."

"Thank you, Ezekiel. But I could really use the solitude of a long solo swim to clear my head."

Philip and Constantine arrived at that time as they all conversed. Meryl drew a sigh of relief when she saw them. Constantine and Anastasia's eyes immediately locked on each other.

"Minotaur?" She questioned. "Is it really you?"

"Medusa!" He breathlessly exclaimed. "You're so beautiful!"

"I think we have a winner." Philip commented under his breath as he took a place next to his brother.

"May I present to you Anastasia Kontos." Ezekiel gestured to Constantine.

"Anastasia! This is Constantine Gianakos." Philip announced.

Neither seemed to acknowledge the brothers. Instead, they touched each other's face and hair, never taking their eyes off of each other."

"I think we've all simply disappeared from the room." Meryl quipped.

"They are quite lost in each other." Linda added.

Ezekiel cleared his throat to get their attention. "You need to quit pawing at each other like two horny school kids."

"Ezekiel's right." Philip sternly agreed. "You'll be spending time in an Orthodox sanctuary, and you'll be expected to remain celibate."

"You're not exactly a prime candidate to speak on the subject of celibacy." Anastasia balked.

"Please!" Philip warned her. "Let's not even go there, young lady."

Both woman as well as Ezekiel flashed a wide-eyed glance his way. Constantine then stepped forward to address the gods.

"Perhaps this father Antonopoulos could join her and I in marriage."

The brothers glanced at each other with surprise, and Ezekiel spoke first.

"That would all depend on if Anastasia agrees to it."

Anastasia immediately took hold of Constantine's hand, and spoke with certain clarity. "That's exactly what I would want."

"Then I'd have to say that you two most definitely have our blessing." Philip stated. "You will still have to remain celibate however, until after the holy union takes place."

"Then the good Father must join us as soon as we arrive in Tarpon Springs." Constantine proclaimed. "I'm barely able to control myself in the presence of her beauty."

"Oh Heavens! I feel the same way toward him." Anastasia purred as she clung to his side.

Linda and Meryl could hardly hide their amusement as they watched the infatuated couple.

"I would love to be a little mouse in the room when those two unleash their passions on each other." Meryl mused.

"Oh yes!" Linda sighed. "I'll be thinking of that scenario all the way back to the Caribbean."

"Very well!" Ezekiel then concluded. "Being that we must keep you two apart until the marriage, Meryl and I will have to take Anastasia to Branchview for the night."

"But darling, I have to escort Linda to the water." Meryl countered, prompting Philip to intervene.

"You stay here with lover boy." He smirked. "I'll escort the future bride to Branchview. I have to stop by the stables to see Stargazer anyway.

"Just don't linger too long. I'm sure that Tina is waiting patiently for you to get back home." Ezekiel lectured.

"Absolutely!" Philip answered as they all turned their attention back to the two lovebirds conversing.

"I won't be able to rest until I see your beautiful face again." Constantine further proclaimed as he pulled her into his embrace.

"Me neither!" Anastasia breathlessly sighed as she melted in his arms.

"Oh boy!" Philip exclaimed. "We've certainly outdone ourselves this time. Haven't we?"

"Yes, we have." Ezekiel agreed.

At that very moment, members of the General Committee of the Secret Society clamored about in the Ballroom of Kenneth Laszlo's mansion. Laszlo stood before them behind a podium, adjusting his blue tooth microphone. A restless Lucifer Morningstar paced behind him like a wild animal, ready to release his rage.

"Ladies and gentlemen of the General Committee. I welcome you all into my home." Laszlo announced. "As you all know, this has not been a good day for the elites. It appears that we've been outmaneuvered in the United States for the time being." He gazed out over those in attendance. "But the good news is that the rest of the world is still within our grasps."

"It's all your fault that this happened." An angry man yelled. "You were supposed to kill Steven Spencer and Gerard LeRoux."

"Yes indeed!" A grim faced woman chimed in. "With all your wealth, and power you should have easily been able to get the job done."

The room erupted in dissention, and Morningstar could not hold his rage any longer. He erupted, and pointed to everyone in attendance.

"You bloated, egotistical fools! You're the ones to blame." He charged. "How dare you come into this house and blame us for your miseries. We're not your hand servants."

"If you're as high and mighty as you often claim, then why couldn't you prevent all of this?" An older man in the crowd indignantly countered, which caused Morningstar momentarily to pause, and clench his eyes shut.

Without warning, he pointed to the man, sending a bolt of lightning from his fingertip that immediately reduced him to a hulk of sizzling flesh. The crowd gasped in horror as his body crumpled to the floor. Even Laszlo flinched at the sight.

Morningstar settled, and peered out over the terrified, and quieted audience.

"Would anyone else like to speak out of arrogance?" He asked to the hushed multitude who only exchanged fleeting glances toward each other.

He responded to them with an evil laugh that shook the room before shaking his head with disgust.

"You, pitiful lot!" He grunted. "Perhaps it is time for me to take matters into my own hands."

At that, Morningstar stormed from the room, leaving a tense silence in his wake

Laszlo motioned for calm in the room before continuing what he had to say.

"The authorities will be coming for all of us very soon." He stated. "I have two charter busses outside that will be taking us to a private airstrip where a 737 is waiting to whisk us off to secure sanctuary."

"Where can we go?" A man asked. "The arms of justice have a long stretch."

"My contacts in Switzerland have agreed to grant us immunity from extradition." Laszlo answered. "Since that's where we all have a good bit of our wealth parked, we should be able to live comfortably for the time being."

"What about our possessions here?" A woman inquired.

"They'll no doubt be confiscated by the authorities." He answered. "It's your choice. Either stay here and go to prison, or come with us, and regroup." He reasoned. "As I mentioned before, if we can garner the rest of the world, the despicable Patriots will most certainly be overpowered the next time. We've been defeated before, but we always come back stronger."

"What about the rest of us that couldn't be here?" Another man questioned.

"Well, unfortunately for them, they'll just have to find their own way out. At this point, it's every man and woman for themselves." He concluded. "Now, I need to ask you all to please begin exiting the room, and proceed directly to the busses. Time is definitely of the essence."

While the multitude was filing out of the mansion, Roger had returned, and was struggling through the crowd to get in the house. He approached Laszlo and Morningstar who were now overseeing the exodus from the Main Foyer.

"Why are those busses here? Where is everyone going?" He questioned.

"We're all leaving this blasted country before we're arrested for treason." Laszlo replied as he prepared to join them. "Are you coming with us, grandfather?"

"Hell no!" Roger firmly exclaimed. "I want no part of any of you."

"Very well." Laszlo answered in a regretful tone. "Feel free to remain until the authorities evict you from the estate."

With that, he casually joined the others who were filing out toward the busses. Morningstar remained, holding a stern, angry glare on Roger. Laszlo paused his progress, and gestured toward him.

"What about you?"

Without answering, Morningstar joined him, still holding his intimidating stare on Roger as he passed.

A short distance away, Guitierez and his crew readied themselves to converge on the estate. His phone rang, and he quickly answered, and listened. He ended the call quickly, then turned promptly to address the others.

"Damn!" He exclaimed. "Laszlo and his inner circle are on the move. They just loaded up two busses."

"They can't get very far." Banerjee replied. "Where do you think they might be going?"

"I think I may have an idea." Millie answered as she stepped to the front. "There's a large private airfield near the estate. My hunch is that they have a jet there waiting."

"That's a mighty wild guess, Millie." Guitierez remarked. "What if you're wrong about that?"

"Agent Guitierez, I have been in this line of work since before you were a twinkle in your daddy's eyes." She smirked. "When I have a hunch about something, I'm usually correct."

"Okay." He deeply sighed. "If we move now, we might be able to head them off in time."

Aboard one of the busses, Laszlo and Morningstar sat next to each other in pondering thought.

"I know you're mulling over something." Laszlo remarked. "Tell me what it is."

"I'll accompany all of you to Switzerland as you wish, but I plan to return as soon as possible."

"Whatever for? There's nothing here for us."

"I don't take defeat lightly, Mr. Laszlo." He seethed. "I will get my revenge, and destroy them all. I will defeat this country single handedly."

"What do you intend to do?"

"I can't disclose that." Morningstar angrily quipped as the busses pulled to a stop on the airstrip near the waiting 737. "For now, let's just get on that damn plane."

By the time Philip had returned to his home, Tina was already in her night gown, and sitting on their enclosed porch that overlooked the Atlantic. He approached her from behind, and kissed her affectionately on the cheek.

"The sunsets colors were beautiful tonight." She smiled. Dimitri stayed up, and waited as long as he could.

Philip snuggled next to her on the swing, and looked out over the water, lit by a half moon. The lighthouse beacon also revolved across its surface like a melodramatic search light in the dark.

"I've missed far too many sunsets, and sunrises with you" He replied. "I'm truly sorry for that."

Tina only answered with a sad, but forgiving expression, as she stared at him with dreamy eyes. "I understand you had quite a productive day."

He answered with a short nod. "Very tiring as well." He looked off into the darkness with a thought filled sigh. His eyes welled with penned up emotion.

"Sometimes I wish I wasn't who I am." He lamented. "I just wish for once that I could have more time to be a good husband and father."

"You're far too hard on yourself, sweetheart." Tina stated with an affectionate kiss to his cheek. "That little boy in the other room thinks you are the most important man in the world, and so do I." She stroked the hair from his face. "When this is all over, we should get away to someplace special."

"We'll do just that. Maybe next week." He assured. "Ezekiel and I just have one remaining task, and then hopefully we'll be done with the Secret Society. At least for a while."

"Would you like to go into town tomorrow?" She asked. "I hear they're going to begin the 4th of July celebrations a few days early because of the victory."

Philip answered with an intent nod. "I don't care where we go. I just want to be with you."

They lovingly embraced, and kissed.

By the time Guitierez and his agents arrived at the airstrip, the 737 was already taxiing for takeoff. Millie rode shotgun with him and Agent Banerjee in the lead car, and they all watched with despair as the jet turned at the farthest end of the runway, picking up speed for the takeoff.

"Damn it! We missed him again! Guitierez complained as he angrily slapped the steering wheel with the palm of his hand.

Millie quickly retrieved a missile launcher that she had on the ready in the seat next to her, and kicked her door open.

"Oh no, Laszlo!" Millie exclaimed with a determined tone. "You're not getting away this time."

She mounted the weapon on her shoulder, and braced herself against the car. She then waited until the jet raced by, before she pulled the trigger. With a loud whoosh, the missile fired, hitting directly in the APU duct of the tail section just as the jet lifted from the ground. It immediately exploded into a huge ball of flame that slammed back onto the tarmac with a thunderous, clamoring rumble that shook the ground violently.

Guitierez and Banerjee sat in silent shock as they watched the twisted hulk of burning metal near the end of the airstrip. They eventually glanced with disbelief toward Millie, who was still hypnotically staring at the results of her feat.

"I guess that takes care of that." She stated with a carefree shrug.

Suddenly, a grotesque figure emerged from the flames. It paused momentarily to stare at the convoy of agents with eyes that glowed like red lasers in the dark. It roared loudly with the ferocity of an angry beast, before running off, full speed into the nearby woods.

"What in the hell was that thing?" Banerjee inquired in a trembling voice. "There's no way any human could've ever survived that inferno."
Guitierez sunk back into his seat, knowing exactly what it was. He let out a long, anxious breath before answering.

"That indeed was the devil, and I do believe he's quite pissed."

Chapter Seventeen:
The Beginning of The End

A gentle, steady rain fell on that following morning. There was a noticeably peaceful atmosphere at the Branchview Estate that hadn't existed for quite some time. It was as if the heaviness had lifted, and the rain was washing away the residue that was left behind.

Steven and Loraine awoke in their bed from a deep and peaceful night sleep, embracing each other lovingly. Loraine smiled without even opening her eyes.

"What a wonderful experience that was." Loraine softly remarked as she snuggled closer to him. "I almost wish it didn't have to end."

"You did well for someone who didn't know how to swim." Steven said as he kissed her on the forehead. "Although you did nearly have a collision with that whale." He joked.

"My big, strong husband pulled me out of the way just in time." She giggled while tickling his ribs.

Steven leaned back contently, staring at the ceiling with pondering thought. "I'm so glad that the Nereids now have possession of that shield."

Loraine glanced up toward the ceiling as well. "It was so beautiful down there. Can we go back again sometime?"

"From now on, you and I will have many more pleasant adventures together." He proclaimed.

"Is that a promise, Mr. Spencer?"

"Yes, it is. I will never take one moment for granted that we're able to spend together."

"Oh, Steven…" They emotionally kissed.

The tender moment was interrupted by a tapping on the bedroom door, and they both looked that way with a disappointed sigh.

"That was nice while it lasted." He commented before calling out. "Come in!"

They pulled the covers over themselves as the door slowly opened, and Angelique peeked in.

"I'm sorry to bother you two, but I wanted to let you know that they delivered Mrs. Porter's headstone a short time ago. The groundskeepers are placing it as we speak."

"Thank you, Angelique." Steven's eyes glazed over with emotion. "I'll be dressed shortly, and I'll walk over to the cemetery to check on it."

She gave a simple sympathetic smile before departing.

He crawled from beneath the covers, and sat on the edge of the bed in sad reflection. Loraine placed a comforting hand on his shoulder.

"I know." She nodded. "With all the distractions, none of us have had time to mourn her loss."

Steven didn't have to answer. His somber expression spoke volumes.

"Would you like me to go with you?"

He turned, giving her a quick kiss. "It's raining." He slowly shook his head. "We'll schedule a remembrance service sometime in the next few days."

At the City Diner, Suzie was serving up food to an early breakfast crowd when Meryl entered, and motioned for her attention.

"Meryl! She joyfully greeted her. "Can I get you a cup of coffee?"

She shook her head. "I just need to talk to you for a moment." She nervously glanced around before continuing. "Have you had any dreams or visions that involve Ezekiel and I?"

She gave a hesitant sigh before answering. "As a matter of fact, I have. I've had visions that concern all of us that are very difficult to understand."

Meryl anxiously rolled her eyes. "I was afraid that was the case. They no doubt are the same ones I'm having.

"Why don't we have a seat here at the end of the counter, and we can talk about it?" She motioned toward the other waitress. "I can have Trudi keep an eye on my tables."

"I can't." Meryl answered with a trembling voice. "Ezekiel and I are catching a flight to Florida in a half an hour. Perhaps we can sort it all out when I return in a few days."

Suzie gave an understanding nod, and a warm smile. "I'll be here for you."

The two women took each other's hand in assurance, and Meryl slowly let go with a sad, worried expression. "I'll see you soon."

Suzie watched anxiously, and with concern as she exited the diner, opened her umbrella, and hurried off in the morning rain.

The rain had finally eased a bit by the time Steven made his way to the family cemetery. He had previously placed a stone bench in front of Mrs. Porter's grave site for when he would visit it. Much to his surprise, there was someone already sitting there when he arrived. The person had their back to him, and sat under a large umbrella. As he approached, he could see that it was Joey Arcovio.

"May I join you?" He politely asked.

Joey only answered by scooting over to give him room. Steven quietly sat down, and admired the newly placed head stone that had her name, date of birth, and death at the top, and the words "Our Mrs. Porter" written in cursive below it. Tears welled in his eyes.

"They did a beautiful job on the stone." He stated.

"I miss her so much already." Joey replied sadly.

"I know. We all do."

"I feel so lost. I don't have anyone to confide in now." Joey expressed with frustration, which caused Steven to immediately counter. "You have us." He paused. "You'll always be a part of this family. Never forget that."

She looked at him with a mix of surprise and doubt. "Do you really mean it?"

He gave her an assured nod, and draped his arm around her. "We were all brought together for a reason, Joey." He concluded. "We all need each other."

"That means a lot." She softly said as the sun suddenly found its way through the thick clouds.

Steven looked up and squinted against the brightness. "Look at that." He emotionally grinned. "I think that's Mrs. Porter's way of telling us that she's happy."

Joey answered with an agreeing smile, and leaned her head securely against his shoulder.

As the private jet soared through the sky to its destination, Meryl fondly watched Anastasia and Constantine while they leaned lovingly close to each other in the adjacent seats.

"They are so much in love. They remind me of you and I, Ezekiel." Her remark prompted a pleasing glance, and she affectionately took hold of his hand. "Remember all those times you would meet me on the shores of the Aegean Sea, and we would simply sit for hours in each other's embrace?"

"How could I forget?" He patted her hand with assurance. "It's hard to believe that was centuries ago. It seems like only yesterday." They snuggled closer, before he continued. "Father Antonopoulos secured a Bed and Breakfast for us in a place just south of Tarpon Springs called Palm Harbor. We'll only have a few days there, but at least we'll be together, and you'll be able to refresh yourself in the warm waters of The Gulf."

"That sounds nice." She paused in pondering thought. "Perhaps when you and Philip have finished with your business, we could also spend some time together on The Isle of Rhodes. I do miss being there so very much."

"I'd like to check in on some of my holdings in Crete as well." He replied with a wink. "We'll definitely make that happen." He concluded, as they snuggled ever closer.

The rainy morning turned into a beautiful day on the Connecticut shore. The citizens of Lockeport had put together an impromptu celebration day, aside from the upcoming 4th of July weekend. All the shops proudly flew their American flags, and held major sales that drew in customers eager to find great deals. The fiat money had become virtually worthless, and prices were slashed to reflect the ever growing value of the new Branchcoin. The only products being sold by the merchants in town were those made by Patriot backed companies that were aligned with Branch Consolidated.

In the nearby waterside park where a confrontation had taken place only a few days earlier, a small carnival had also opened a couple days prior than originally planned. A large bounce house for the kids had also been set up on the far end of the parking lot. There were smiling faces, and happy events taking place everywhere.

All along Main Street, proud owners of classic cars parked their vehicles in a row for everyone to view. Steven eyed them all with the excitement of a child. As he wandered along, Loraine quietly approached from behind, and slipped her hand into his.

"Sweetheart!" He exclaimed with surprise, as he looked around. "Where are the twins?"

"Oh, they're with the other kids, having an absolute jolly time at the carnival bounce house." She could see the concern in his face, and answered his next question before he could answer. "Not to worry. They're under the capable guardianship of Philip and Tina."

"Those two are actually here?" Steven chuckled.

"I know. I was surprised as well that Philip actually took a much deserved day off." She smiled. "That's the happiest I've seen Tina in quite some time."

Steven's attention was quickly diverted to the sight of a 1963 T-bird convertible roadster. He dragged Loraine along as he moved in to get a closer look at the dark blue beauty that shined like a diamond in the noon day sun.

"That is quite a beautiful car." Loraine commented as Steven let loose of her hand, and examined every detail.

An older man who had been sitting in a fold up beach chair near the back of the vehicle, stood up, and approached them. "My grandfather purchased this car when it was brand new. It's been in my family ever since." He proudly proclaimed.

"How come I've never seen you drive this car before, Mr. Finch?" Steven quizzed.

"I only take it out occasionally." He answered. "This is the first time in awhile that I've brought it into town."

"It looks like you just drove it off the showroom floor."

"I've been a good caretaker." He sighed. "Unfortunately, my son and his children don't have the same appreciation for it."

"I don't understand why anyone wouldn't love this car. It's an artistic masterpiece." Steven stated as he viewed the pristine interior.

"I've been thinking about selling it, Mr. Spencer."

Steven looked up with surprise, then glanced at Loraine with a mother may I expression on his face.

"Don't look at me, Steven." She responded with a half smirk, quickly detaching herself from the conversation.

"How much are you asking for it, Mr. Finch?"

The older man pondered in thought before answering. "I'm really not sure what it's worth under our new monetary system."

"Would a quarter of a BranchCoin be a fair price?"

The offer nearly made him faint, and it took a few moments for him to regain his composure. "According to my calculations, that's equivalent to about seventy one thousand dollars."

"That sounds about right." Steven answered in an agreeing tone of voice.

Finch immediately extended his hand to Steven, while holding up the keys in his other hand. "You have yourself a car, Mr. Spencer." He grinned as the two men sealed the deal with a firm handshake.

Later, shortly after sundown, Steven and Loraine joined a festive party taking place on the open lanai of the Mermaid Inn. As a special promotion, all the women in attendance were given paper mermaid tails, and a tierra to wear on their head. Everyone danced joyfully to the lively, upbeat music being played by the DJ. The loving couple settled at a table a comfortable distance from the dance floor, where they could talk, but still absorb as much of the positive energy as they could.

"Oh Steven! This has been the most wonderful day." Loraine declared.

"Are you sure you're okay with me buying that car?" He questioned.

"As long as it makes you happy, and as long as our daughter doesn't turn it into a beautiful woman." They both laughed before she continued. "Besides, I fully expect you to let me drive it on occasion."

"Oh, really?" He smirked in response.

The music caught Loraine's attention, and she began moving to the beat.

"I love this song." She took hold of Steven's hand. "Let's dance!"

They strutted onto the floor, and blended in with the other revelers. Just to the right of Steven, the Mermaid Damaris happily danced with the young man that she had chosen as her special beau. Steven chuckled when he took notice of her paper tail that slapped about as she moved her hips.

"I think the real tail compliments you far better." He commented.

"Sometimes a girl just has to improvise." She winked as the couple sashayed away.

The DJ lowered the music for a transition, and spoke into the PA as a slow song began. "This is a special request for Steven and Loraine Spencer."

The couple looked at each other with surprise, and Steven then caught a glimpse of a grinning Philip standing on the side with Tina. He raised his glass in tribute, and Steven acknowledged with a grateful nod, as he pulled his wife in close.

"I wish this positive energy could last forever." She smiled, while looking dreamily into his eyes.

"Unfortunately, there's always negative energies that are trying to gain the upper hand." He replied. "That's an unpleasant reality."

"I suppose it's up to us to keep those energies balanced."

Steven twirled her around, nearly taking her breath away, before pulling her back in close. "Not tonight, Mrs. Spencer."

With that, he reeled her in for a long, passionate kiss, just as the first fireworks exploded into the night sky above the bay. Hoots, cheers, and applause erupted from those in attendance, but nothing disturbed the special moment, as the two lovers hypnotically swayed in their romantic embrace.

Chapter Eighteen:
The Devils Revenge

A magical night eventually gave way to the arrival of another morning. The sun peeked through the shades of the bedroom window, casting long shuttered shadows across the white linens on Steven and Loraine's bed, where the loving couple rested comfortably in each other's embrace. Loraine slowly opened her eyes, and squinted against the brightness. Steven followed suit soon afterwards. He smiled, and hugged her tighter as she buried her head into his chest.

Just then, the door to the room swung open, and Olivia and London joyfully rushed in, jumping onto the bed with their waking parents.

"That peaceful moment was quite nice while it lasted." Loraine remarked as she pulled the sheets up to securely conceal both of them.

"Can we get under the covers too?" London asked.

"Oh, dear!" She stammered. "I don't think that would be a good idea, sweetheart."

Steven simply cleared his throat, while Olivia looked toward her brother with sober seriousness. "Mommy and Daddy are naked."

The couple exchanged a quick, wide eyed glance.

"I think our daughter is going to grow up to be a real pistol." He stated with a smirk, which prompted giggles from both children.

Angelique sashayed through the door next, and reacted with embarrassment in realizing she had intruded on a private moment.

"I'm so sorry." She expressed. "I heard the children giggling, and had no idea you two were still in bed."

"That's okay, Angelique." Steven motioned to her. "Come on in, and join the party."

The young woman timidly entered in further. "There's a gentleman in the Main Foyer that wants to see you, Mr. Branch."

"That's funny. I wasn't expecting anyone."

"He said his name is Alton Sinclair." She explained. "He brought his entire family with him."

The couple looked at each other with speechless surprise, before Steven turned to address her once again.

"Thank you, Angelique." His thoughts raced. "Make them feel at home, and we'll be along as soon as we can get ourselves ready.

"Yes sir!" She acknowledged before swiftly exiting the room.

"Wow!" Steven exclaimed. "I certainly wasn't expecting that."

In different quarters, across the estate, Philip and Tina were also waking in each other's embrace.

"Good morning, beautiful." He stated, prompting a pleasing smile from his wife.

"I wish you didn't have to go away again." Tina stated sadly.

"I'll be back by late tonight." He gazed out the window at the ocean. "I want you to take Dimitri over to Branchview this evening, and then you and I will leave for our journey first thing in the morning."

"Where are we going?" She asked with excitement.

"It's a surprise." He stated with a clever grin as they snuggled closer.

"I like surprises." She giggled happily while Philip planted a kiss on her forehead.

Back at Branchview, Steven and Loraine made their way to the Sitting Room to meet with their unexpected guests. They all greeted each other in a joyous manner before settling into their chairs to converse.

"I have to say. This is somewhat of a surprise. Especially at this hour of the morning." Steven expressed.

"I wish we would've known you were coming." Loraine added. "We would've been better prepared.

"There wasn't much time for us to even give it a thought." Alton sighed. "We had to flee Canada by cover of night in my private jet."

"We had to leave everything behind." Audrey distressfully explained.

"I don't understand." Loraine shrugged. "I knew there were problems in your country, but what caused you to have to flee?"

"When the Socialist authorities saw what was happening in the U.S., they decided to clamp down, and arrest anyone who appeared to be a serious threat to their agenda." He paused. "We got a tip that they were ready to move on us."

"They would've sent us all to a re-education camp somewhere in northern Saskatchewan." Heather stated with anxiety.

"Needless to say, they've no doubt confiscated all of our personal assets by now." Alton explained further.

"All we have is what we brought with us." A traumatized Daniel Jr. finally spoke up.

"At least you're all here, and safe." Steven assured with a smile toward a now teenaged Daniel. "You grew up since the last time I saw you, young man."

"I'm fifteen now." He answered.

"It seemed like only yesterday that you were a little kid playing with his toy truck in this very room." He shook his head with disbelief.

"I remember that, uncle Steve." He grinned.

"You all must be very hungry." Loraine interrupted. "Please join us for breakfast in the Dining Room, and we can talk some more."

"It's not like we have anywhere else to go, Loraine." Alton answered with great anxiety.

"There's always room here for family." Steven sympathetically stated. "We can all get caught up on things, and discuss what steps we can take next."

Alton gave a grateful pat to Steven's back, as the two men took the lead in leaving the room.

As the rest all stood to depart as well, Audrey paused to glance around with sentiment, and tear filled eyes. "I never thought it would feel so good to be back in this old house with the rest of you."

Loraine draped a consoling arm around her as they strolled away, following the others as they made their way toward the Dining Room.

Later that day, Roger McPherson was strapping up his hiking boots in the now deserted mansion of Kenneth Laszlo. He wanted to get an early start on his journey to Deer Island. He stood, and took a deep, exhilarating breath.

"By tomorrow night, I'll once again see the lights of Paris, and be reunited with the woman I love." He exuberantly stated to no one else but himself.

At that, he took one final glance around the room, and grunted. *"Good riddance!"*

As he swung the front door open to triumphantly exit, he was unexpectedly met by the grim, and terrifying presence of Lucifer Morningstar.

"Going somewhere, Roger?" He sneered sarcastically.

Steven Spencer sat pensively in the Branchview Garden as the evening sun made its way to the western horizon. Two doves landed on the railing within inches of him, and serenaded him with comforting coo's. They quickly flew off, as someone approached from the main house.

"There's a man in deep, contemplative thought." Alton pleasantly commented as he took a seat nearby.

"This is the first time in months that I've had a moment to slow down, and catch my breath." Steven chuckled.

"We all still have a bit of a fight ahead of us." Alton replied. "I was lucky enough to transfer a majority of my liquid assets to Branch Coin before Canada confiscated everything else."

Steven leaned into the conversation with great concern. "We'll make sure you have a prominent spot at Branch Consolidated, and we'll do whatever we can to get you all re-settled. In the meantime, you can stay here at Branchview for as long as you want."

"I appreciate that, Steven. You're a good friend."

"We'll talk more about our future plans over breakfast in the morning." Steven smiled. "I have some great ideas to pitch your way."

"I look forward to hearing them." Alton looked at him with a slight grin. "Maybe we can cruise down to the diner in that sweet roadster of yours."

"Most definitely!"

"I think I'll retire early." Alton sighed. "It's been a very long day."

"Have Lori and Audrey returned from New Haven yet?"

Alton shook his head. "They probably stopped somewhere to eat. Send those two on a shopping spree, and time becomes irrelevant."

The two men shared a laugh. "What about Daniel Jr. and Heather?"

"I'm sure Daniel's either exploring the woods, or hanging out at Lighthouse Point, and Heather is probably off catching up on the local gossip with Andrea."

Steven responded with an agreeing smile as Alton stood to depart. "I'll see you first thing in the morning, Steven."

"Sleep well, my friend." Steven leaned back in his chair, and sentimentally basked in the glow of the now setting sun.

On Deer Island, dusk had settled in, and the moon was just rising as Philip made his way through the thick overgrowth, and entered the large clearing where the Portal was located. He stood near the central point where a large, round rock marked the spot, and searched the tree line and brush surrounding him.

"Where is everyone?" He questioned only to himself. *"It's quite unusual for my brother to be late for this sort of thing."*

In the eerie silence, he suddenly heard rustling in the bush, and much to his dismay, Lucifer Morningstar approached with what looked like a laundry bag slung over his shoulder. He boldly joined Philip at the center, and set the bag down between them.

"So, this is where the other mysterious Portal is located." He glanced around "Quite remote, if I should say so myself."

Philip angrily glanced down at the bag, and then back up to Morningstar. "Should I ask how you were able to find it?"

Morningstar grunted sarcastically. "If you haven't guessed already, Mr. McPherson won't be joining us this evening."

"What did you do, Satan? He was an innocent man who only wanted to right all the wrongs he had committed in his life."

"The same way you did, Poseidon." He laughed. "I will say that I had to torture him severely in order for him to reveal this location."

Philip clenched his eyes in disgust. "I suppose you did the same to Stargazer."

"Oh, no! Not yet anyway." His eyes quickly darted to the dark brush that surrounded them. "I'm certain he's lurking somewhere in the overgrowth in his wolf disguise, but I'll definitely catch up with him later, just as I will all the others."

"What do you hope to accomplish by killing innocent people."

"Satisfaction." He began to pace, sporting an evil smirk before continuing. "The elimination of my opponents, and ultimate power."

"You are sick and demented, Satan."

"On the contrary, Poseidon. I am brilliant. I am the king of this world, and I will not be further hindered in my mission by those of the likes of you." He arrogantly grunted before pointing to the bag on the ground. "Aren't you even curious about what I have in that bag?"

"Why should I be?"

Morningstar reached into the bag, and much to Philip's horror, he pulled out the severed heads of Ezekiel and Meryl.

A traumatized Philip reacted with visible shock. "What in the hell have you done, Satan? Don't you understand that we are one hundred times more powerful in spirit? You have gone against all the rules."

"I no longer follow the rules that your God set down. I make my own rules."

"You will suffer the wrath of the true God for doing this."

Morningstar laughed off his statement. "So be it. But I'm far from being finished." He reached back into the bag, and retrieved another severed head. "I have one more, and this one should really strike home."

He held up the mannequin head of Philip's beloved Tina by the locks of her hair. As a grief stricken Philip collapsed to his knees. Morningstar recklessly tossed the now fiberglass head to the ground in front of him. Her marble blue eyes now vacantly stared upward.

"You bastard! She never harmed anyone." Philip cried.

"She was created from evil intent. It was only appropriate that she be destroyed by evil."

"Where is my son? What have you done with him?"

"Regretfully, he was not at your residence when I came calling. If he was, then his head would've been there alongside his mothers."

Philip looked up, and sneered with tear filled eyes. "I will petition the Almighty God to allow me to strike your final death blow before His Son binds you, and tosses your miserable carcass in the lake of eternal fire."

"How noble of a statement." Morningstar mocked.

"Why don't you just kill me now, so I can come back to haunt your every move?" Philip tauntingly begged.

"Not yet, Poseidon." He turned away with a sadistic smile as a sword materialized in his hand. "I'll let you live, so that you can witness me destroying everything and anything that you care about." He glanced off in momentary thought. "Or not!" At that, he swung back around with the swiftness of a feline and lopped off Philip's head with one mighty stroke. It rolled to a rest right alongside Tina's.

"Goodbye, Poseidon." He mockingly laughed.

He turned to the dark brush surrounding him. "Come out, Stargazer. You can't escape me."

Thick clouds suddenly obstructed the moons glow, making it totally dark. Thunder rolled in the distance, warning of a pending storm. Morningstar looked up, and all around him.

"Come down, Son of God. Let's finish this right now." He arrogantly pleaded.

"Soon Satan!" A deep voice roared from the thick, turbulent clouds. "You'll not know the hour, nor minute. I will come as a thief in the night."

"I've been hearing that for centuries, Almighty God. No one believes it anymore, and neither do I."

"Do not mock me, Satan. Your mouth dribbles with senseless blasphemy.

"I destroyed your Son many years ago, and I will do it again. His army of angels, and pitiful spirits are no match for me and my army of demons." He replied maniacally. "I also have additional armies of clones, robots, and Draconians as my allies. I am invincible!"

"You will all suffer my vengeance, with no mercy granted."

Morningstar laughed, and further mocked. "I'll be waiting for the Prince of Peace with sharpened sword."

"Be careful what you wish for, Prince of Darkness." The voice concluded with a stern, angry tone.

There was an eerie silence in the wake of the voice's departure, and not even a leaf stirred in the trees. For a brief moment, Morningstar even displayed an anxious expression that quickly turned to a smirk. He took a moment to revel in his accomplishment as he took one final glance toward the severed heads.

"My tirade has only begun. I will destroy all that is good in this world." He proudly proclaimed aloud to himself. His bellowing voice echoed across the dark desolation of Deer Island.

A mild rain began to fall, and quickly escalated to a soaking rain, which in turn, ushered in an intense lightning storm. Morningstar laughed maniacally as he stared upwards into the full fury of the storm.

Chapter Nineteen:
Paradise Lost

The intense storm lasted throughout the night, affecting the entire region along the Connecticut coast. It curtailed just before dawn, and as the sun rose over the now calm Atlantic, the world surrounding Branchview was waking up to a crisp, beautiful July 4th morning.

With the victorious events of the previous week, this Independence Day was far more special in meaning than it had been in quite some time.

The town of Lockeport was stirring to life a bit early in anticipation of the days' events. An American flag flew proudly in front of every business along Main Street, and nearly every residence along its side streets, and adjoining neighborhoods.

The rains from the previous night, along with the salt air from the ocean, thoroughly cleansed the air. Steven Spencer filled his lungs with a deep breath of the refreshing oxygen as he returned from his morning walk, and prepared to enter his Branchview residence. He turned momentarily to admire the flag that flew gallantly from the flagpole in the courtyard.

He had mostly a sleepless night between the fury of the storm, and the racing thoughts that were going through his mind. He and Gerard, along with the Branch Consolidated affiliates were about to become key players in the recovery of the country from the ravages of the Secret

Society. Though he was happy in their victory, he knew that a large task awaited them in the coming months.

Neither he, nor anyone else at Branchview could've ever imagined the terrible events that had taken place the night before on Deer Island. Only Suzie McVea had any sort of inkling of the horror that was taking place behind the otherwise serene scenario.

As she hustled around the City Diner, waiting on her first customers of the day, her head pounded as she anxiously thought of the terrifying visions she had seen in her dreams. Not even she understood exactly what they meant.

Loraine and Angelique had awakened early to make sure all the children of the household were fed. They were all gathered in the Dining Room when Steven cheerfully breezed in, and greeted everyone.

Almost simultaneously, Alton Sinclair entered from the kitchen, clutching a fresh cup of coffee.

"Good morning, Alton!" Steven chimed as he looked up from hugging his children.

Alton responded with a nod and lift of his coffee cup. "I'm glad you're up early. Are you ready to go for breakfast at the City Diner. You and I have a lot of business to discuss." Steven stated.

"Are we taking that sweet roadster like you promised?" Alton quipped.

"Most certainly. It's a perfect morning for a cruise." Steven answered.

"Oh Steven! Can't business wait? It's Independence Day, for crying out loud." Loraine complained.

Steven quickly calmed his wife with a kiss. "We'll be back way before noon, and then we can go anywhere you and the kids want to go."

"Okay!" Loraine kissed him on the cheek. "Just make sure you're back here no later than 10:30."

"Yes, ma'am!" He smirked.

Alton chuckled at the exchange as he set his coffee cup on the table, and departed with Steven. He paused on his way to make a parting request to Loraine.

"Be sure to tell Audrey where I am. She's still a bit stressed over having to flee our home in Canada."

She responded with an assured smile. Angelique rose from her seat as well. "I need to gather up some breakfast for Mario. He's been up since the crack of dawn working on another project in his studio."

"Hopefully, it's not a statue of another beautiful woman." Loraine teased.

"I certainly wouldn't allow that to happen." She grinned, before swiftly exiting to the kitchen.

Meanwhile, a weary Stargazer had returned from witnessing the horrifying events on Deer Island. He checked on the horses before heading to his quarters where he splashed cold water on his face. He looked in the mirror at his now young face. Something he now considered a parting gift from his murdered friend, Poseidon.

"I must warn Nebriana, and everyone at Branchview. Satan vowed to destroy us all." He muttered to himself.

With little time to waste, he patted his wet face with a hand towel, and hurried off. Before leaving the barn, he took time to open all the horse's stalls, and also left the barn door open so they could escape the coming wrath of Satan.

Steven and Alton exchanged a bit of small talk on their pleasant cruise into town. "This baby rides like a dream." Alton commented.

"State of the art for its' time period." Steven answered with a pleasurable smile.

"It's a shame they can't build a simple car without all that damn computer garbage. I miss doing routine maintenance on my own vehicle."

"Funny you should mention that." Steven chuckled. "I've been working on that very idea with some of my investment partners. When all the major car companies financially drive themselves off of a cliff, I think that may be a niche for a small startup company."

Alton simply answered with an enlightened, thought filled glance.

A wolf leaped and ran through the thick woods of the Branchview Estate. When it reached the clearing, it transformed to the likeness of Stargazer. He stood in the center, and anxiously called out to Nebriana and Green Man.

Nebriana appeared first, and was surprised to see Stargazer as she remembered him several centuries before.

"Stargazer! You're so young!" She exclaimed.

"I've no time to explain." He answered breathlessly as Green Man lumbered into the clearing as well. "You two must flee the estate immediately, and send the Woods People underground to their safe place."

"Whatever for? I don't understand." Green Man cluelessly answered.

"Satan has killed the gods, and he intends to destroy this estate as well as the world surrounding it."

"But this is forbidden by the decree in the Book of Life." Nebriana protested.

"He's totally disregarded all the rules." Stargazer impatiently stated. "He's gone completely insane, and prematurely hastened the end of days."

Nebriana and Green Man exchanged anxious glances. "Please! There's no time to waste. He's on his way, if he hasn't arrived already." He pleaded with them.

"Will you come with us?" Green Man asked.

"I'm sorry. I need to warn Steven Spencer and the others at Branchview." He emotionally answered. "Hopefully, I'll see you again. Perhaps in another dimension."

Without further word, Stargazer shape shifted into the gray wolf, and scurried away in leaps and bounds through the surrounding thick brush.

At the City Diner, Steven and Alton were talking business while enjoying a hearty breakfast.

"So, this mention of numerous business opportunities. I'd like to hear more about it, Steven."

"It'll be limitless." He looked up with a smile. "Every large corporation that left the United States, and conspired with the Secret Society will be banished from ever doing business here again. We've gathered a group of patriotic investors willing to contribute to the startup of new domestic businesses to supply jobs and make the economy strong once again."

Alton took a deep breath, and leaned back in his seat, marveled by the possibilities.

"It'll be just as it was when the American economy was hitting on all cylinders."

"I proposed a plan to our allies in government to keep any one industry from growing too big. Never again will large monopolies take over the politics of this country."

"That's a clever proposal." Alton agreed. "I'd like to be a part of all this."

"And, you will." Steven smirked. "Gerard and I plan to make you our right hand man. Choose whatever niche you'd like, and we'll help you run with it."

Alton was speechless with surprise, and stuttered out a reply. "This is overwhelming news. I'm not sure what to say."

"Hopefully, you'll say yes." Steven reached across the table, offering a handshake that Alton readily accepted.

"Absolutely!" He proclaimed.

"My niche will be the entertainment industry which needs a total rebuild." Steven continued. "We need to put out movies, music, and programs that the majority of the people want, instead of only that which caters to special interest groups."

"I'm all for that." Alton replied.

"The music and broadcasting industry have psychologically been driving people insane for at least the last 35 years. They play the same songs over and over until their creative minds are programmed like zombies. It's time to give the people something new and creative." He announced with enthusiasm.

"Sounds good to me. When do we start?"

"This week." Steven answered, followed by a noticeable pause. "But for now, I'm ready to enjoy this 4th of July weekend."

Stargazer frantically banged the lions head knocker at the Branchview Mansion. He tried the door, and was surprised to find it open. He stepped into the foyer, and rang the spirit bell.

Mary rushed into the foyer at the same time Loraine entered from the South Wing.

"Lord have mercy!" Mary yelled. "I can only move so fast."

Loraine did not recognize the young image of Stargazer that stood before them.

"I demand that you tell us who you are, and what you're doing in this house, young man."

"It's me, Stargazer." He breathlessly replied.

"But you're so young."

Stargazer rolled his eyes. "Poseidon granted me youth before he….before he died."

"Poseidon is dead?"

"They all are. Satan killed them."

"Satan?"

"Lucifer Morningstar." He's coming here to kill the rest of us."

"Oh Lord!" Mary cried. "Steven was right."

Stargazer anxiously glanced between the two women. "Where is Steven?"

"He went into town with his friend, Alton Sinclair. I believe they're at the City Diner."

"I must warn him before it's too late."

"I can simply call him on his cell phone."

"Please do that. In the meantime, the rest of you need to leave here immediately, and get as far away as possible.

Loraine and Mary were flabbergasted, and anxiously exchanged glances. Just then, a loud horn blast sounded with such force that it shook the entire household.

"It has begun." Stargazer announced. "I must hurry before the second sounding." He hurried away, leaving the front door wide open.

"What was that deafening noise?" Loraine desperately asked.

"The sound of Gabriel's horn." Mary raised one hand to the air, closing her eyes. "It's the end of days."

Just then, Deana and Angelique rushed into the foyer in a panic. "The children! They're gone!" Deana cried.

"We were just getting the kids ready for the day when we heard that loud noise, and then they all just disappeared right before our eyes." A frantic Angelique explained.

A visibly distraught Loraine, anxiously put her hand to her head, as she retrieved her cell phone. "I must call Steven right away."

In the Deep Woods, Nebriana and Green Man were taking Stargazers' warnings very seriously. They met once again in the clearing, and prepared to embark on their journey to a safer place.

"The Woods People are all in their hidden place." Green Man announced.

"The last of the Forest Faires have also flown off to nearby woods and forests." Nebriana replied. "We must go as well. Time is definitely not on our side."

"But I can't move as fast as you can fly."

Nebriana took hold of his large branch like hand. "I will keep pace with you, my dear friend. I will not leave you behind to perish alone.

She could see the emotion in his green leafy face, and she fought hard not to show her own fear. "Come on! If we can just make it to the other side of the Old Post Road, we should be safe."

Panic and mayhem erupted at the City Diner, and in downtown Lockeport as desperate people called out for their children who had simply disappeared.

Rick Worth emerged from the kitchen, and moved close to Suzy who was observing the scene with shock and horror.

"Suzy! What's happening?"

"I don't know, Rick. But somehow, I think it has something to do with those terrible dreams and visions I've been having."

Steven and Alton remained in their seats quite befuddled by what was taken place. The loud noise around them prevented Steven from hearing the calls from Loraine on his cell phone.

"I don't understand what's going on, Steven."

"I somehow think it may have something to do with that deafening horn that we heard. I'm surprised it didn't shatter the windows."

Steven retrieved his cell phone, and saw the missed calls, and desperate text message for him to return to home.

"Something's definitely wrong, Alton. We have to get back to Branchview ASAP."

The two men entered the street where panic stricken people milled about, trying to make sense of the children's disappearance. On one side of the street, a sober faced Lucifer Morningstar watched as the two men hurried along the sidewalk, and his expression turned to a determined smirk.

An old man slowly drove down the busy Main Street. Morningstar took notice, and pointed his finger toward him. Inside, the old man suddenly clutched at his chest, and lost all control of the car. It slammed into the vehicle in front of it, then jumped the curb, racing down the sidewalk, and sending people scattering from its' path.

Steven and Alton turned to see it heading right toward them. Just before hurrying out of the way, Steven turned as if he had seen something that no one else could see. A little girl stood there in the path of the oncoming car, and spoke to him.

"Daddy, please come home."

All confusion at the statement was quickly set aside, as instinct kicked in, and Steven leaped to push the child to safety.

The car squarely struck Steven with violent impact, sending him air born. In those few moments afterward, everything was in slow motion. His life flashed through his mind like a fast forward movie. Then he landed hard onto the pavement. He felt a sudden surge of intense pain throughout his body at that very instance, then it all dissolved to darkness, and silence. The red eyes of the Lion Beast within him lit dimly for a moment, then faded into a blank stare.

Two separate light orbs peacefully emerged from his being, and slowly drifted upward, side by side.

As Alton rushed to his side, a horrified crowd also gathered. Someone desperately cried out. "Call 911!"

Stargazer pushed his way through the crowd, and knelt next to Alton. Alton sorrowfully looked at him, and shook his head. "It's too late. He's gone."

Stargazer took a deep breath before speaking. "How did this happen?"

"I can't explain it!" A shocked, and grief filled Alton exclaimed. "We were out of the way. Then Steven turned as though he saw something, and then just leaped in the path of the car."

While the two men were conversing, gasps arose from the surrounding crowd. When they looked back down, Steven's body was gone.

"Where did he go?" A confused Alton asked.

Stargazer thought for a moment, before taking on an enlightened expression. "The trumpet blast."

"What?" A befuddled Alton further asked.

Stargazer then glanced into the crowd of onlookers, and immediately saw Morningstar staring at him with an arrogant smirk. The Prince of Darkness raised his hand, pointing toward him menacingly.

Stargazer stood, and ran as fast as he could, shape shifting into the wolf, and sending already hysterical people hurrying to get out of its' way. Morningstar laughed out loud as he transformed into a puff of black smoke that quickly dispersed.

The two orbs continued drifting far out over the Atlantic, where one suddenly split off, and rapidly ascended upward. The other orb simply tumbled slowly to the waters below. It bobbed along the surface for a few moments, before being plucked and pulled under, as though being devoured by a large fish.

Back at Branchview, Loraine impatiently paced as the last carload of inhabitants prepared to leave. Sharie, Millie, and Bill were the last ones to depart the house. Millie and Bill paused to plead with Loraine to go.

"Please sweetheart, come with us, and save yourself."

"No mother. I'm not going anywhere without Steven, and nothing you can say will sway my decision."

Millie and Bill exchanged concerned looks and disappointing sighs, before Millie embraced her daughter lovingly. "I love you sweet daughter. I always have."

"I know. I love you too, mother."

A nervous Mary stood nearby clutching onto her bible. "I'm not going either." She maintained.

Sharie turned with shock. "But, gramma…."

"No buts child! I'm staying put with Ms. Lori for as long as it takes. God will protect us."

A reluctant Sharie went to say more, but couldn't find the words. Instead, she embraced Mary tightly. "I love you, gramma."

"I love you too, child. Now go! While you still have time."

Mary and Loraine escorted them to the waiting car, and watched as it quickly drove away. Loraine sniffed the air, and heard a sound like an approaching hurricane. She turned in horror to see the smoke, and the reddish glow in the skies toward Lighthouse Point.

"Hurry! Get inside Mary! She ordered, while herding her back into the house.

"What is it, Ms. Lori?"

"I believe the woods are on fire."

On the Branchview Pathway, Satan marched toward the main house. He laughed as his arms spread out wide, igniting the surrounding woods in his wake. The horses stormed from the barn, and joined the other terrified creatures of the woods as they tried to outpace the encroaching fire.

Loraine no sooner closed the door before there was a desperate knock.

"Steven!" She cried, nearly hyperventilating.

She swung the door open only to find an anxious Stargazer standing there. Her heart sunk.

"There's no time to waste." He announced. "Satan has set the woods ablaze, and he's heading up the pathway now." He looked at the trajectory of the sun in the sky, then quickly glanced toward the open door of the South Wing. "The portal in the Grand Corridor. It's our only escape."

"I can't go anywhere without Steven."

"Steven's dead!" He shouted, as he firmly took hold of her fragile shoulders. "Satan killed him."

"How?" Loraine emotionally collapsed into his arms.

"I'll explain everything later. We have to go now."

Mary sat down in the large Foyer chair, clutching her bible ever tighter.

"I'm not going back through that portal. I'll meet that devil face to face." She maintained. "You two save yourselves.

Stargazer took Loraine by the hand, and quickly led the way into the Grand Corridor Ballroom. The late morning sun was shining directly in the mirror, but there was little time to waste before the portal would once again close.

"Go ahead of me, Loraine."

She set out to go, but heard the whimpers of a very scared Bumpers who was hunkered under the piano bench.

"I can't go without Bumpers." She hurried and scooped the little dog into the safety of her embrace, then carefully stepped through the mirror to the other side. The suns' trajectory was quickly waning from the mirror when Stargazer heard the meows of Midnight, the black cat. He looked down, then toward the mirror.

"Follow me, little one."

He transformed into the wolf, and leapt through the mirror. Midnight jumped through as well, barely making it as the sunlight passed, and the portal closed.

The wolf bowled Loraine over as it pounced onto the other side. The cat swiftly retreated into the surrounding brush. When Stargazer transformed once again, he and Loraine sat on the ground, somewhat dazed. Loraine still held tight to a shivering and scared Bumpers, as they desperately eyed their surroundings.

"It looks like the clearing in the Branchview woods." Loraine declared.

"I think you're right, Lori. But there's no telling what year we ended up landing in."

Nothing more was said as they both exchanged expressions of uncertain anxiety.

Meanwhile, the front door of Branchview burst open, and Satan entered in his true form.

"Where is she, old woman? Where's Loraine Spencer?"

"I'm not telling you." Mary's voice quivered.

"Very well. You'll regret that decision." He warned as he moved closer.

Mary held her bible up, and bravely spoke. "I rebuke thee Satan in the name of the Lord."

Satan spread his wings, and growled angrily, just as the Foyer clock chimed at 11:00.

"The 11th hour. How appropriate!" He laughed, once again setting his sight on a stoic, yet fearful Mary.

A second trumpet sound then bellowed out, shaking the foundation of the great house. Satan recoiled at the sound, and the bible fell to the floor as Mary was raptured up.

Satan shook his fist in the air. "I curse you Almighty God."

A flash of lightning lit the Foyer, and the ensuing thunder crash was deafening. A voice from the heavens roared down. "At the third trumpet blast, the Prince of Peace will have arrived, and you will deeply regret your deeds, Satan."

"Bring it on!" He roared back before laughing maniacally. He raised his hands, and then quickly lowered them toward the floor. "My grand finale will take place now." He growled.

In the town of Lockeport, all the chosen of God had been taken up. In the City Diner, a discarded spatula on top of a hot grill, and a shattered cup of coffee on the floor behind the counter, were signs that Suzy and Rick had been raptured. On the streets, those who were left behind, wandered aimlessly, trying to make sense of what had occurred.

Satan exited the Branchview house, and lifted his arms in the air, Bellowing an angry scream toward the heavens. "I will destroy this world of Branchview, and everything in its perimeters."

The earth began to shake, and those not taken up tried to run for their lives. They cried out to God, but it was too late. They tried to escape in vain, as the earth opened, and began swallowing the entire town of Lockeport, and everything in it.

At Branchview, the Great House began to crumble, and sink into the ground with a mournful groan. The entire estate, and everything around it folded upon itself, and the ground proceeded to swallow it. As it sunk, the Atlantic Ocean rushed in, and covered it entirely, extinguishing the fires that Satan had started.

Within minutes, The Branchview Estate, Lighthouse Point, The Deep Woods, and the entire town of Lockeport were all totally gone, as though they had never existed. Only an eerie silence prevailed in the wake.

When the waters receded once again, the towns of Saybrook and Fenwick unfolded as though they had been stuffed away in a large invisible box. Within minutes, they took shape as though they had been there all along. People carried on with their business as usual. No signs of any of the former landmarks remained.

Out in the distant depths of the Atlantic, far from all the drama, a lone Mermaid raced through the waters, clutching an orb of light in her hands. She suddenly switched direction, and began swimming upward toward the surface with sheer determination, as though headed to an intended destination. When she hit the surface, there was an explosion of light, and everything turned white, and silent.

Twenty:
The Parallel World

It was a hazy summer day on the Long Island Sound, 10 miles off the coast of New Haven. A small 32' recreational boat bobbed wildly on the 2-3 ft. waves as several other vessels cruised nearby. A group of teenagers were in one of those boats, and a girl sunning on its deck took notice.

"Hey! We need to check that boat out over there." She stood and shielded her eyes from the sun. "Something isn't right. It's not anchored, and seems to be stalled out."

The curious teens shifted to low power, and slowly pulled even with the seemingly abandoned vessel.

"Hey! There's some guy passed out in there." One of the boys urgently yelled.

Another boy turned to the girl. "Get on the marine radio, and notify the Coast Guard about this boat."

As she hurried into the cabin, the two boys tied a rope to the floundering craft, and leapt onboard to check on the unconscious man. His dark hair was long, and tossed wildly about his head, and he sported a frazzled, unkempt beard. He was tanned to a dark bronze tint, but also showed the crimson signs of severe sun exposure. His once fine clothes were quite dirty and tattered.

"Who do you think he is?" One of the boys asked.

"I don't know." The other answered as he stressfully looked up. "But he must be dehydrated. Hurry up, and get him some water out of our cooler."

Hours later, and now clean and shaven, Steven Spencer opened his eyes slightly, and through a blur, he could see a man leaning over him that appeared to be in his mid-fifties. He had a kind face with deeply serious, and concerning eyes that were magnified through wire framed spectacles.

"Welcome back." Dr. Harvey Newhouse announced, while a nurse patted his face with a moist cool cloth.

"Where am I?" Steven asked with a deeply perplexed expression, as he tried to focus on his surroundings.

"You're in Yale New Haven Hospital, Dr. Spencer. You've obviously been through quite an ordeal."

"I know. I was struck by a car in downtown Lockeport." He stated, while the doctor and nurse exchanged an awkward glance.

"Where is this place you call Lockeport?" The doctor asked after a long pause.

"It's a town not far from here." He answered a bit more clearly. "It's near where the Connecticut River empties into the Sound." He smiled with a burst of exuberance as he continued. "There's a large Estate there called Branchview that sits atop the cliffs near Lighthouse Point. Surely you know where it's at."

The doctor pondered his answer, and studied Steven's face carefully before he spoke again. "I've never heard of any of those places, although I do know that Saybrook, and Fenwick are towns near there." He paused once more. "I don't recall any cliffs being in that area either."

Steven tried to sit up in bed, and reacted with confused frustration. "I've never heard of any of those places you mentioned, and I don't understand why you addressed me as Dr. Spencer." He breathed hard. "This is preposterous! Could someone please just notify my wife, Lori?"

"Where would this Lori be?" Dr. Newhouse asked.

"She's at Branchview. I can give you her cell phone number."

"Steven." The doctor sighed. "It appears you may be suffering from some sort of amnesia."

"Amnesia!" He exclaimed. "What in God's name are you talking about?"

The doctor nodded to the nurse, and she quickly exited the room. He forced a smile, but still eyed Steven with great concern.

"You've been missing for five years, Steven." He struggled emotionally. "You went out on your boat in the Sound one morning, and you were never seen again. That is, until a group of teens found you earlier today. He paused to take note of Steven's shocked expression. "It was believed that your boat had sunk, and you had perished."

"All of this is impossible! I don't even own a boat."

Dr. Newhouse seemed to ignore Steven's comment, and continued. "You were found passed out, and seriously dehydrated on that very boat about ten miles out in the Sound." He paused.

"Okay! What else do you know about me?" Steven curiously inquired.

"You were an internationally known expert in the field of paranormal psychology. You were well liked in the community, and you and I were colleagues, and very good friends." The doctor recanted with great difficulty. "Don't you remember anything about that?"

"I'm sorry, doctor!" Steven shook his head. "I've never seen you before in my life, and I'm a writer. Certainly not a doctor."

The doctor reacted with a sigh of frustration, then reached for a pen and paper that was on the table near the bed. He promptly handed it to Steven.

"Jot your wife's number down, and I'll try to give her a call."

Steven quickly wrote it down, and handed it back to him.

"Get some rest, and I'll stop back to see you later." He sadly smiled as he patted Steven's shoulder. "It's good to have you back with us again, even if you can't remember."

After the doctor departed, Steven stared anxiously toward the ceiling.

"God in heaven." He murmured. "Please help me."

He took a deep breath before closing his eyes, and drifting off into a deep sleep.

Later, when Steven opened his eyes once again, the sun was streaming through the blinds in the room. He laid still, hopelessly wishing that his predicament had simply been a bad dream. But there he was, still in the same hospital room.

The door opened, and a different nurse breezed in, and swiftly moved toward the window to open the blinds. The full blunt of the morning sun streamed in, causing Steven to squint his eyes against it.

"Good morning, Dr. Spencer."

"Good morning." He mumbled. "Could you tell me what time it is?"

"It's ten minutes after eight." She sauntered over, glancing briefly at his chart. "According to this, you've slept for over twelve hours."

Dr. Newhouse strolled in through the open door at that moment. "And, the good news is that we're releasing you from this place as soon as the nurse gets you unhooked from all those tubes."

"I'm all for that." Steven smiled. "Did you call my wife?"

"I tried to call the number several times, but it was out of service." He paced closer, as Steven pulled himself up in the bed.

"I don't understand what's going on, doctor." He wearily replied, while the nurse set about removing the tubes from his arm.

"Enough with this doctor stuff. Call me Harvey." He grinned, as he laid a stack of clothes at the foot of the bed. "I brought you some clothes, and I'm taking you out to reintroduce you to New Haven."

"Has it changed all that much?" Steven asked with a tinge of humor in his voice.

"We'll just have to see. Maybe something will trigger a memory, and reset your brain."

"I do remember that I love coffee, and I could sure use a cup right now."

Harvey laughed. "That's the Steven I remember. I'll take you to a place that you and I used to frequent quite often."

Steven didn't reply, but only eyed Harvey rather warily as the nurse continued to work on getting him ready for release.

Later, Steven and Harvey sat in a booth in a retro style restaurant amidst the clanging of dishes and silverware, and the loud buzz of conversation. A hungry Steven heartily devoured his breakfast, while Harvey casually observed. Steven paused to raise his coffee cup toward him as a signal of approval.

"I can see why we used to come here so often. It's just the type of place I like." He glanced around at his surroundings. "It makes me think of a place called the City Diner."

"Was that in Lockeport?" Harvey asked.

Steven reluctantly nodded, fearing Harvey may be taking mental notes for his evaluation.

Just then, Steven heard a distinct British accent that he knew all too well. He turned quickly to see the beautiful brunette as she entered with a little boy and girl that he did not recognize. He nearly leaped from his seat with excitement.

"Lori!" He yelled out enthusiastically.

Everyone in the restaurant stopped what they were doing to watch the scenario. Harvey observed as well with the eye of a seasoned therapist.

Loraine froze for a moment, not really knowing what to say, but then motioned to the two young children to stay put before she slowly sauntered over.

"No one's called me that name in years." She said, curiously staring at Steven. "Do you and I know each other?"

Steven's heart sank when he realized she didn't recognize him. He thought quickly to come up with a clever answer.

"We met quite some time ago."

"It would've had to been in England." She shrugged cluelessly. "This is the first time I've ever visited the States."

"Perhaps it was." Steven sheepishly answered, trying hard to hide his hurt. He gestured toward the two waiting children. "Are those your children?"

"Yes, they're my twins." She proudly answered.

"They're just as beautiful as their mother." Steven commented with a forced smile.

"I'm sorry that I can't remember you." She stated with slight embarrassment.

His heart sunk even further when another familiar face entered the restaurant, and swiftly approached, interrupting their exchange.

"Don't tell me you found someone here you know, darling." The dashing man stated as he held out a greeting hand to Steven. "I'm Barclay Rutherford." He energetically gripped his hand as he glanced to a somewhat baffled Loraine to beg an introduction.

"Barclay, this is….um." She turned to Steven. "I'm sorry sir, I failed to get your name."

"Steven. Steven Spencer."

Barclay looked to his wife for further information that she could not give.

"How is it that you initiated a conversation with this handsome chap?" Barclay inquired, while giving Steven a clever wink that hid a tinge of jealousy.

Steven quickly spoke up, saving Loraine from the awkward moment.

"Loraine and I met briefly several years ago in England." He smiled. "Even though she doesn't remember me, I must say that I could never easily forget a beautiful face like hers."

"I certainly can't fault you on that." Barclay proudly proclaimed, as he gave his wife a quick kiss, and took possession of her hand. "We simply stopped for a bite to eat. We're on our way to Newport to see the Gilded Age Mansions."

"I've been there several times. I'm sure you'll all enjoy it." Steven forced a smile.

There was an obvious awkward silence that momentarily fell between them, and Barclay chose to conclude.

I hope you'll excuse us, but we are a bit rushed, and very hungry, Mr. Spencer.

"I understand." He answered in a rather embarrassed fashion.

"However, it was a pleasure making your acquaintance." Barclay cordially added with a nod.

"Likewise." Steven politely replied. "I hope you enjoy your visit here in the States."

As the couple walked away, Steven turned back toward his table, and profoundly mumbled to himself. "*The parallel world. It really does exist.*"

Harvey, hearing what he said, looked toward him with heightened interest. "What did you just say?"

"Oh nothing, Harvey." He nervously brushed off the question. "Nothing at all."

Steven watched as a hostess ushered the family to their table. Loraine also turned for one final curious glance that totally broke his heart. He sat back down, placing his fist to his mouth as though to hold back the rush of emotions that threatened to flow out.

"Could we please just get out of here?" He pleaded with frustration. "I just need to go somewhere quiet."

Harvey gave an understanding nod. "I can take you down by the waterfront."

"That would be perfect." Steven impatiently replied.

A short time later, Steven and Harvey casually leaned against the railing along the Long Wharf walkway, staring out at the Long Island Sound.

"Harvey, could I just have a few moments alone?"

Harvey gave a subtle nod. "Take all the time you need, Steven. I'll be sitting on that bench over there when you're ready to go." He gave a parting pat to the back of his shoulder as he strolled away.

Steven continued staring out to the Sound as if desperately looking for something in the deep waters. When Harvey was out of earshot, he whispered out loud to himself.

"*Poseidon*! *If you can hear me, I desperately need your help.*"

Steven waited for the Mermaid chatter that usually preceded his arrival, but it never came. The only sounds he could hear were from the vehicles on nearby I-95, and the calls of the seagulls as they sailed above the Long Wharf, searching for a discarded French fry or some other portion of food.

After several moments with no reply, he became frustrated, and slowly strolled over to where Harvey sat patiently waiting. He quietly settled down next to him, and exhaled, still staring out at the water.

"You always did have a fascination for the ocean." Harvey stated.

Steven only continued to stare longingly out to sea. "If you don't mind me asking. Who was that woman back at the restaurant, Steven?"

"I know it sounds crazy, but she was my wife. At least in the lifetime I remember." He wiped an escaping tear away, and continued. "Her and I had two beautiful children, and I loved them all very much."

"I don't think you're crazy at all." Harvey stated with obvious sympathy.

Steven didn't respond. But instead, waited for him to continue.

"If you'd like, I can take you over to Saybrook. Perhaps you can show me where you think this Branchview Estate might have been."

"Not today, Harvey." Steven answered in a defeated tone of voice. "I've already had too many disappointments for one day."

A short, awkward silence fell between the two men before Harvey spoke again.

"You know, over the years, I've had several patients who claimed to have visited another identical world, where their identical selves had a much different role. I've always believed there might be some sort of validity to that claim."

Steven opted to remain quiet, and continued to listen intently.

"I heard you mumble something about a parallel world when we were back at the restaurant. Do you think that's where you were all this time?"

Steven glanced at him with a raised brow. "Harvey, if I told you everything I knew, you'd probably lock me in a mental hospital, and throw away the key.

Both men shared a hearty laugh, before sitting several moments in silent, reflective thought.

"It may surprise you to hear that before you disappeared five years ago, you and I were working out a theory on this so-called parallel world."

Steven looked at him with wide eyed surprise. "You and I must've been quite close as colleagues to be working on such a socially disputed project."

"You were my best friend, Steven." Harvey took a deep breath before continuing the conversation. "Considering all that you just told me, I think it may be a good time for you to meet another colleague of mine. She specializes in cases like yours, and I think she can help in ways that I can't."

"So, you're basically giving up on me." Steven responded with a grunt.

"Not by a longshot. I'm simply leaving you in more capable hands."

"Do I know this other doctor?"

"She was even closer to you than I was." Harvey smiled. "Are you ready to go see her?"

Steven sighed. "It's not like I have anything better to do."

After a short drive across town, they arrived at a quaint shingle style home in a residential area. As they got out of the car, Steven admired the beautiful landscaping, and stone paver walkway that led to a grand front porch. It surprised him to see his 1963 Thunderbird parked in the driveway alongside an SUV. He felt it best not to mention anything about it to Harvey.

"What a beautiful home she has." He announced instead, as his eyes wandered to the Captains Watch that stood prominently above the roof line. "I love that Captains Watch. I could sure spend a lot of time up there writing."

Harvey gave an all knowing nod, and couldn't help but smile as the two men continued on to the front door.

Steven was rather baffled when Harvey opened the door, and ushered him in.

"Shouldn't we have knocked first?"

"She's expecting us. She said for us to come in and get comfortable."

"That wouldn't be hard to do." Steven commented as he marveled at the meticulous design of the interior when they entered. With a smile, he took note of the several figurines that adorned the shelves, and surface tops. "She must like Mermaids."

"Yeah." Harvey simply replied, holding back an exuberant smile. He then glanced down at his wrist watch "I really should be leaving you now, Steven."

"Why aren't you staying?"

"You're a doctor of psychiatry. Surely, you know the importance of one on one consultation." He grinned while presenting his hand. "Good luck, Steven." The two men exchanged a firm, but cordial handshake. "I'll check in on you later today."

"Thank you, Harvey. For everything."

With that, Harvey departed, leaving Steven feeling very alone in the large, but comforting house. He strolled around the room, glancing at the artwork, accent pieces, and furniture that all seemed oddly familiar to him. The silence was deafening, with only the loud ticking of a grandfather clock interrupting it. It kept time like a giant heartbeat within the body of the household.

His eyes caught site of a small music box topped with a ballerina figurine that sat prominently on a shelf. He gently picked it up, and winded it before carefully setting it back down. As he listened and watched the figurine slowly rotate, a fond smile appeared on his face.

"*It actually plays Stardust.*" He whispered to himself.

He strolled over to the cherry wood dining table, and ran his hand over the smooth surface of its top. He then settled into one of the ornate, antique wood chairs that surrounded it.

He was briefly startled when a black cat with golden eyes, gracefully jumped onto the table, and began purring loudly.

"Well! Hello there, sweetheart." He stroked the cats' silky fur, and gave it a chin rub with his finger. "Aren't you a pretty girl?"

"That's Samantha!" An unexpected, but very familiar voice announced.

Steven glanced up, not realizing someone had entered the room. His heart jumped, and he gasped with surprise when he saw the red haired beauty that stood there in conservative business attire. The only other woman besides Loraine that he had ever truly loved. With a welcoming smile, she approached with her hand outstretched in a greeting.

"Hello Steven. I'm Dr…"

"…Amy Seagraves." Steven quickly interrupted, completing her introduction as he stood to accept her hand.

"Well!" She seemed both surprised and impressed. "You are partially right. My name is Amy, but where you came up with a name like Seagraves is beyond me." She chuckled.

"You just have a remarkable resemblance to someone I used to know." He meekly replied.

They both settled into chairs, and Amy placed her large embroidered hand bag on the table, pulling out a legal note pad and pen. Steven took notice of the Mermaid stitched on the side of the bag.

"You like Mermaids."

She reacted with a pursed smile. "Yes, for some strange reason, I've had a fondness for them ever since I was a child."

She then pulled a bottled water from an outer pocket of her bag, and Steven couldn't help but muster a sentimental grin.

"Amy, could we please just cut to the chase here? Can you explain where I am, and what became of the life I knew?"

Amy could see the desperation in Steven's eyes. She placed her pen down, and stared off into the corner, searching for the proper words to say. She then leaned closer, and locked her intense blue eyes on him. "I don't know where you were these past five years, or what you experienced, but I promise that I'll try to help you find an answer."

"I think I may have died, and somehow woke up in this world. Nothing seems to make sense." He vented with frustration.

Amy listened with great concern, and once again, carefully measured her next words.

"Do you recognize anything special about this house, Steven?"

"It does have a few flashes of familiarity, but I can't imagine the reasoning for it." He quickly glanced around him. "After all, it is your house."

"What if I told you that it was once your house as well?" She hesitantly countered.

Steven gazed at her with a perplexed expression, as she continued.

"I should really say, it was our house." Her hypnotic gaze never wavered. "This may be a bit of a shock as well, but my full name is Amy Spencer. I'm your wife, Steven." She sighed as he listened with amazement. "We once had a very wonderful life here, and I loved you so, so much." She took hold of his hand. "I still do." She loudly whispered, clenching her eyes with great emotion. "I never gave up hope that you would someday return to me. I knew that no one else could ever take your place."

Steven's eyes misted over, and his heart beat raced out of control as he remembered his many encounters with Amphitrite. "I think you always did love me." He smiled through the tenseness of the moment.

Amy's eyes glazed over with tears as well. "Oh yes!" She profoundly exclaimed as she looked away in pondering thought. "I have loved you since the first time I laid eyes on you in the dining hall at Brown University."

Steven looked down at the table as though being blindsided with sudden enlightenment. "And, you bumped into me in the lunch line, causing me to dump my food on the floor."

Amy placed her hand to her mouth, as though to hold back a rush of joyful, mischievous enthusiasm. "I had to get your attention somehow, Steven Spencer."

Steven laughed, and gently squeezed her hand. "You succeeded long before that incident."

"Oh Steven!" She replied, trying her best to hold her composure. "You really do remember?"

He answered with an assured nod, and Amy exhaled deeply, trying to lighten the moment. "I brewed a pot of your favorite coffee. Would you like a cup?"

"Is it Chock Full o' Nuts?" He grinned.

She cheerfully nodded, and Steven leaned in, kissing her gently on the lips. The gesture nearly took her breath away, and she hurried to recover while she nervously thought out her next words.

"I can't begin to explain how much I've missed that."

Steven leaned in once more for a much longer kiss that left Amy somewhat dazed once again, but she managed to continue on.

"I know it's hard for you to remember, but you and I also have a beautiful daughter." She paused to gauge his reaction, which was one of profound surprise. "Her name is Danielle. She's nine years old now." She nodded intently. "She has my blue eyes, and your beautiful brown hair." She paused once again as she began to weep. "She missed her daddy so much, and is so excited about seeing you again." Tears trickled down both sides of Amy's delicate face, and Steven lovingly wiped them away.

"Where is she now?"

"She's waiting patiently in the other room." She gripped his hand ever tighter, and flashed a warm, loving smile. She was so overcome with emotion that she struggled to ask her next question.

"Are you ready to reacquaint yourself with your family, Dr. Spencer?"

Steven anxiously exhaled. "Yes, I'd like that very much."

As Amy led him into an adjacent room, the little girl stood slowly, then ran to joyfully embrace him.

"Daddy! It's really you."

Steven was surprised to see that the little girl before him was the last person he saw when his life ended in Lockeport. He embraced her tightly in that tender moment.

"Yes, honey. It really is me, and I'm home to stay."

He then turned to stare into Amy's deep blue eyes that always reminded him of a clear day on the ocean. In that instance, all the negative memories of his many battles with the Secret Society, as well as the painful loss of his Branchview family, and a lifetime he had cherished so dearly, completely dissolved away as though it had never existed. Steven suddenly understood everything. His death in one life had enabled that exiled, and lost twin flame to find a way back to its' rightful place within the Parallel World.

Twenty-One:
The Librarian of Life

In another dimension and time exists a grand old oceanside residence. One that rivals the great mansions of the Gilded Age. Within its' massive Library, a stunningly beautiful librarian with raven black hair, steel blue eyes, and wearing black Victorian attire, worked far past the midnight hour at her desk. In front of her was a very old, and rather large opened book. A black cat also rested quite contently on the desktop as well.

The night was peaceful, with only the distant echoing, rhythmic sound of the waves as they gently rolled onto the nearby shoreline. An occasional hoot from a night owl could also be heard somewhere in a tree outside the open window. She paused from her reading only long enough to savor the pleasant sea breeze that wafted into the room, carrying with it the crisp scent of salt air.

She briefly turned her attention to the slumbering cat, and lightly ran her hand across the soft, velvet fur on its' back. The cat stirred slightly, opening its' glazed, golden eyes just enough to acknowledge her loving touch. She then continued on, attentively following the sentences with her long, red painted fingernail until the final word on the final page was read.

With an emotional sigh, she gazed with deep thought to the vast regions of the room. And in her mind, she recited the words she was thinking.

"For the good souls of earth who have fought valiantly against the agents of darkness that seek only to destroy that which is of the light, take heed. For the day of your victory and redemption is nigh. You shall not be forsaken. The treacherous beings that have pillaged and ravaged your world for far too long will be destroyed by Divine providence. They shall be crushed beneath the ashes of their own ruin. Never to return. But for you dear souls, I assure you that a new dimension and time awaits. One that far exceeds anything your mortal minds could ever imagine. A place where only peace, love, and happiness reigns supreme. I've read every word of all of your life stories. I've felt your joy, as well as your pain. And, I'll certainly be among the first to greet you upon your arrival in this wonderful new dimension.

She then drew a deep breath, as if to hold back the emotional feelings that threatened to spill out. She carefully closed the thick, fragile book, and took time to run her delicate fingers across its' ornate, and time worn cover. The title which was written in elaborate, raised cursive, simply read BRANCHVIEW. She subtly smiled to herself in a reflective moment, nodding assuredly as she gracefully rose from her chair, and turned off the desk lamp.

The sound of her high heels clicked across the ornate tile flooring, and hauntingly echoed throughout the large, cavernous room as she carried the heavy book to its' special place among the other countless volumes of literature assembled there. She gave the book binding a gentle pat with her hand, then sauntered toward the door, where she turned off the remaining ceiling lights. There, she paused once again, and sentimentally glanced to all corners of the dark room, as though searching out the spirits that may have been lurking there.

"*Goodnight, everyone. Sweet dreams.*" She softly whispered before departing.

Author Bio

Brian was born and raised in Erie Pennsylvania and has been involved in some capacity of writing since a very young age. After graduating from Penn State University, he lived several years in North Carolina and then Florida, where he presently resides. His accomplishments cover a wide spectrum from writing Psychology Textbooks, several essays on Metaphysics, articles on health and fitness, songwriting, and screenplays.

In 2017, he retired from FedEx after 21 years of service and began a new career as a script doctor for the movie industry. He is also very active in Historic Preservation, causes that support our Military Veterans, a fan of Classic Rock Music, and is an avid fitness enthusiast.

Branchview Series

- The Unexpected Journey
- The Epic Showdown
- The Portal of Time
- The Fall of the Secret Society

Additional Books

- Stories from the Hidden World